WARRIOR'S DELIGHT

Cochise lay on a high ledge and peered at the two columns of bluecoat soldiers below. The movements of *Pindah* soldiers are predictable as mules, decided the new Apache chief. What kind of warriors behave in this manner? The stupidity of his foe confounded him. Perhaps they are trying to trick me, he thought. But he knew no Apache leader could turn away from such a stirring challenge, such a tempting target.

Meanwhile, below, the U.S. captain in command of the dusty bluecoated column tried to stay alert for signs of the Apache. But it was hard to keep himself or his men from sliding into stupefied weariness, so sure were they all that this hunt, like all the hunts before it, would be fruitless. Once again the Indians surely had split up and vanished as if into thin air. Once again the finest fighting force in the U.S. Army would return to post with unfired weapons and wounded pride.

Before the day was done, both Apache warrior and U.S. soldier would learn a lesson about each other that they would never forget. . . .

DEVIL DANCE

DEVIL DANCE

Frank Burleson

A SIGNET BOOK

Published by the Penguin Group
Penguin Books USA Inc., 375 Hudson Street,
New York, New York 10014, U.S.A.
Penguin Books Ltd, 27 Wrights Lane,
London W8 5TZ, England
Penguin Books Australia Ltd, Ringwood,
Victoria, Australia
Penguin Books Canada Ltd, 10 Alcorn Avenue,
Toronto, Ontario, Canada M4V 3B2
Penguin Books (N.Z.) Ltd, 182–190 Wairau Road,
Auckland 10, New Zealand

Penguin Books Ltd, Registered Offices:
Harmondsworth, Middlesex, England

First published by Signet, an imprint of Dutton Signet, a division
of Penguin Books USA Inc.

First Printing, February, 1997
10 9 8 7 6 5 4 3 2 1

To Lizzie

1

Wickiups were demolished, the campsite flattened, possessions loaded onto mules and packhorses. The Chiricahua Apaches were departing for another range, where locust pods, wild potatoes, and onions could be harvested.

Warriors, wives, and children fidgeted uneasily, waiting for aging Chief Miguel Narbona to climb onto his horse. He managed to place his foot in the stirrup, then struggled to grab the horn of his stolen U.S. Army saddle, but could not pick himself up off the ground.

The People felt embarrassed for their once-great chief humbled by age. Sick all summer, he trembled, arms and legs emaciated, then his frail body went slack. He dropped to the ground, stirred, wheezed faintly. No one moved or said a word. Chief Miguel Narbona had led them for more than fifty turbulent harvests, was the greatest Chiricahua warrior who ever lived, but had grown feeble, pathetic.

Some turned away, unable to bear the grotesque spectacle. Others stared with disbelief that such a fate could befall a warrior who had been indomitable in battle, his mighty arm slaying many enemies.

Then all eyes turned to the warrior who had been designated by Chief Miguel Narbona as his successor—Cochise, son of Pisago Cabezon. Forty-two years old, Cochise wore a white breechclout, deerskin shirt, moccasin boots, and a red bandanna around his straight, shoulder-length black hair. He appeared taller than his five feet ten inches, due to erect posture, and not a muscle twitched on his face as he gazed at magnificence laid low. Finally, unable to bear the dishonor longer, he reached toward Miguel Narbona. "I will help you," he said gently.

"No," croaked Chief Miguel Narbona.

"We have a long ride today." Cochise spoke cheerfully as he raised the chief to the saddle.

"Let me be!"

"But it is time to leave."

"I am staying," replied the chief of the Chiricahuas.

No one said a word, the destruction of Miguel Narbona too painful to bear; some closed their eyes. According to the wisdom of the People, when a warrior became decrepit, he was left behind. Cochise dutifully lowered to the ground the great fighting chief.

Cochise was a veteran of countless battles himself, but nothing compared to the wars of Miguel Narbona. Now the old hero lay crippled, and Cochise prayed for guidance. The People believed all events contained spiritual dimensions, and accordingly, the new chief received a silent message from the Mountain Spirits.

He opened Miguel Narbona's saddlebags and withdrew his *Izze-kloth* Killer of Enemies Bandolier, which a warrior wore into battle. Constructed of buckskin strips woven into four strands and attached to a buckskin pouch filled with sacred pollen, it was decorated with talismans and amulets, worn across the chest from left shoulder to right hip, providing protection from enemy arrows and bullets. Cochise dropped the bandolier over Miguel Narbona's head and was adjusting it when the old chief asked in a weak, cracked voice, "What are you doing?"

"Preparing you for battle, sir."

"My battles are over," whispered the dying old man. "You take it, Cochise."

"I could not—"

"This is my last order to you. Do as I say."

Cochise, overcome with grief, found himself unable to move or even think. Then Dostehseh, wife of Cochise, stepped forward, carrying a gourd of water. She was daughter of Chief Mangas Coloradas of the Mimbrenos, and understood well the requirements of somber circumstances. Nearly as tall as Cochise, full-bodied, the mother of Naiche and Taza, she knelt beside Miguel Narbona, placed the water before him, and pressed a kiss against his forehead. Then she arose, took Cochise's hand, and walked with him toward his horse.

Then other women advanced, bearing jerked meat, acorn bread, and mescal root candy, which they lay before Chief Miguel Narbona. He sat cross-legged, shoulders hunched, head hanging low, ashamed that a warrior could no longer mount his steed.

Cochise gave his mentor one last, lingering look, then turned abruptly and climbed into the saddle. Pulling his reins to the right, he headed toward the potato-gathering ground. The others followed Cochise into the wilderness, leaving an ailing old chief surrounded by gifts and prizes. From that day onward, the lives of relatives and friends would depend upon the clarity of Cochise's judgment, the wisdom of his spirit.

Cochise had inherited tremendous challenges, for the Jicarilla and Mescalero People, to the east of the Chiricahuas, had been overrun by the *Pindah-lickoyee* White Eyes, while the Mimbreno homeland currently was under invasion. The Chiricahuas were the next Western tribe, and soon would face the dreaded onslaught of the bluecoat army, while the *Nakai-yes* Mexicans were pressing from the South. Am I strong enough for the greatest challenge of all? wondered Cochise.

He turned in his saddle for one last glance at the gallant old chief, who receded into the desert that had made him, and then was gone.

It was autumn of 1857 in the eastern lands, and the United States of America wallowed in the worst economic panic since 1837. Its financial institutions shaken by overspeculation in railroads and land, its once-humming factories closed due to lack of demand, the country was rent by widespread civic unrest, tens of thousands out of work.

The New Bedford whaling fleet lay at anchor because of diminished demand for whale oil. Tobacco growers could not sell their harvest except at half the usual price. Cotton had dropped from sixteen cents a pound to nine cents, while the largest crop in history was being harvested south of the Mason-Dixon line. In New York City raucous crowds demonstrated in front of City Hall, where Mayor Fernando Wood had told an audience, "Multitudes labor without income while surrounded by thousands living in selfishness and splendor, who have income without labor!"

These were among the dispiriting items read by Nathanial Barrington in the *Tribune* as he sat in the din-

ing room of the Saint Nicholas Hotel, nine blocks uptown from City Hall. It was two in the afternoon,
bustling waiters serving local businessmen, tourists,
and salesmen.

Attired in a dark blue suit, over six feet tall, Nathanial was on the beefy side, thirty-four years old,
with blue eyes and blond hair marked with one single
silver streak. To look at him, one might see a banker,
broker, or lawyer, except for his tanned features and
callused hands. No one would imagine that the gentleman sitting by the window had spent most of his life
in the Army, and lived for a spell among the Mimbreno Apaches.

Appearances notwithstanding, Nathanial Barrington had been an apprentice warrior known as Sunny
Bear, and once had eaten the heart of a bear, not to
mention roast mule and prairie dog stew. Nathanial
reveled in his secret life, for he fit neatly into no
group, a lone warrior against the world.

As an officer in New Mexico Territory, he'd been
shot during the Chandler Campaign of '56, and the
Apaches nursed him back to life because he'd saved
the life of Jocita, wife of Chief Juh of the Nednai clan.
After ten months with the People, he'd sworn never to
make war on them again, so he'd returned to Fort
Marcy, resigned his commission, and headed back to
his hometown of New York, after twelve years faithful service to the flag.

Clean shaven, with a faint scar on his right cheek,
he could find no mention of New Mexico Territory in
the *Tribune*, although one article featured the T'ai
P'ing Rebellion in China, and another reported on the
efforts of Emperor Alexander II of Russia to emanci-
pate the serfs. Nathanial wondered about old Apache

friends such as Chief Mangas Coloradas, Victorio, Nana the medicine man, and Geronimo of the Bedonko tribe.

Returning to the *Tribune*, Nathanial read the latest dispatch from Kansas Territory, where proslavery and antislavery adherents had been killing each other in undeclared guerrilla war for over three years. Two territorial governments had been established, antislavery in Topeka and proslavery in Lecompton, while the Democratic administration of President James Buchanan tended to favor the Lecompton government, because the solid slave-owning South was the backbone of the Democratic Party. According to the *Tribune*, the Lecompton government was drafting a constitution permitting slavery, and would submit it to Congress without allowing the citizens of Kansas to vote. The big question was whether the Buchanan administration would dare defy the majority of Kansans who opposed slavery, or defy the South. Slavery was the most burning issue in America, newspapers fanned the flames continually, and Nathanial saw his nation drifting closer to civil war, like a raft at Niagara Falls.

Sometimes Nathanial broke into cold sweats and occasionally had the urge to rip the Saint Nicholas dining room apart. He was a man of strange passions and hopeless dreams, who had felt happiest when living among Apaches, but returned to civilization for the sake of his White Eyes wife, Clarissa, and their baby daughter, Natalie.

Nathanial and Clarissa were descended from affluent old New York families, and the Panic had not touched them. They enjoyed income without labor, but Nathanial nearly had died for his country on several occasions, and unlimited possibilities carried its own hazards.

Nathanial wanted to become an Indian agent in New Mexico Territory, working for peace among Apaches and Americans, but couldn't leave New York City because Clarissa was preparing for her first public concert. She had studied piano most of her life, and an impresario named Martin Thorndyke had offered to sponsor the event at the Apollo Rooms. Now Nathanial seldom saw his wife, while their daughter was cared for by their Mexican maid. Nathanial wouldn't stand in the way of Clarissa's music, but preferred the active outdoors life to the Saint Nicholas Hotel.

Carriages, wagons, and scarlet-and-white omnibuses rolled along Broadway, while sidewalks were crowded with newsboys, elegant lady shoppers, lawyers, beggars, pickpockets, and stockbrokers. Sometimes Nathanial imagined Apache raiders riding down the famed thoroughfare, yipping and yelling, driving a herd of stolen cattle. He considered his months with the Apaches the pinnacle of his life, and twice had gone on raids, wearing his Killer of Enemies Bandolier. He even had fallen in love with Jocita, but preferred not to think of her now that he was back with Clarissa.

She entered the dining room, and Nathanial felt relieved to see her at last. His wife was twelve years younger than he, also blond, but several shades lighter, and slim, of medium height, with an open-faced freshness and aura of self-assurance. Nathanial studied Clarissa as a connoisseur considers a painting by Rembrandt, as she searched for her wayward husband. She wore a white silk blouse and plum-colored skirt shaped by crinoline, providing the illusion of enormous hips and tiny waist.

Finally, he waved, and with a harried smile, she crossed the dining room. Nathanial couldn't help noticing the many masculine eyes that escorted her.

"Sorry I'm late," she said, sitting opposite him.

They didn't kiss because both disapproved of ostentatious affection. "I thought you weren't coming," he replied.

"I'm sorry," she said softly.

"How're the rehearsals coming?"

She closed her eyes. "Oh, Nathanial, I'm so afraid."

He considered her a sensitive artist, although she'd survived two years on the frontier and once had shot a wanted criminal in self-defense. He loved her honest schoolgirl face, the sweetness of her nature, and the passions that lurked beneath her prim society-woman exterior. "What are you afraid of—hitting the wrong note?"

"Yes, because many musicians will be in attendance, plus the press. I don't want to embarrass my teachers, my family, and you, my dear." She placed her hand on his.

"What're you doing this afternoon?"

"I have to pick out a dress for the concert."

He glanced around, then lowered his voice "Let's go upstairs."

"I don't have time, but I'll be home early."

"That's what you said yesterday. Do you know how much I need you, Clarissa?"

Calmly, she sipped water from a carved crystal goblet as she evaluated her mate. He had gained considerable poundage since returning to New York, his face puffy due to excessive alcoholic beverages, fine red traceries on his cheeks. She considered him a paradox—the disciplined West Point officer, survivor of numerous battles and skirmishes, weak in his resistance to food, drink, and other flesh pleasures. A whiff of the cavalry charge enveloped him, the only man she'd ever truly loved. "Just a while longer," she said.

"I'll be patient," he replied, trying to sound pleasant, but failing. "I can't help wondering if you've changed your mind about returning to New Mexico Territory."

"Of course not."

"I suppose it's satisfying to have folks say you're a genius."

"On the contrary, how can I possibly attain everybody's expectations? That's why I need your love and encouragement."

"But you have them, Clarissa. Am I not your most enthusiastic admirer? In fact, I want to be the only member of your audience, but that's just selfishness, and I must share you with the public."

The setting sun cast red and orange streaks against the sky as Cochise led the Chiricahua People north to the potato-gathering ground. Feeling bereft, he prayed he could hold the coalition together, for there were many factions, the most prominent led by Elias and Esquiline. Yet Miguel Narbona had favored Cochise above them, and often Cochise wondered why. Although he had been an outstanding sub-chief, so were Elias and Esquiline, plus Chepillo, Aguirre, and Parte. What did Miguel Narbona see in me?

Beside him rode his wife, Dostehseh, and she too was capable of leadership, for as daughter of Chief

Mangas Coloradas, she had seen governance from an early age. Cochise glanced at her, a strongly built, sharp-featured woman with eyes fixed on the horizon, straight black hair trailing down her shoulders. She had offered Cochise wise counsel, and sometimes he credited his rise to her. *If I have doubts, perhaps I should step aside,* thought Cochise.

"You are troubled, my husband," said Dostehseh.

"I fear dissension without the steadying hand of Miguel Narbona," he admitted.

"Your worst enemy is yourself, Cochise."

"But I can't help wondering—"

She interrupted him. "This is not the time to wonder. You must use what you have learned and lead the People to great purposes."

He reflected a few moments, then said, "With you at my side, I can lead as well as anyone, I suppose."

"You are better than the others because more is required than a strong arm and fighting spirit. You have been selected because you are a better thinker than they."

Cochise decided not to mention certain doubts, because he didn't want to demoralize her. A chief was supposed to be strong, regardless of how he felt.

The warrior known as Coyuntura, Cochise's younger brother, called, "Someone is coming!"

The languid atmosphere transformed into high danger as warriors and women checked weapons. Too often the People had been surprised by enemy soldiers, and only four months ago the Mimbreno Subchief Cuchillo Negro had been killed by bluecoat soldiers in the Valley of Dead Sheep.

"It is Yrinco," said Coyuntura, who was tall like

Cochise, only thinner, with a solid, squarish jaw and prominent cheekbones.

Cochise stood in his stirrups, shaded his eyes with the palm of his hand, and detected a rider heading toward him. Evidently, due to the rider's leisurely pace, there was no trouble, and Cochise breathed a sigh of relief. Yrinco was returning from a scouting mission, for the People deployed scouts and spies across the homeland, reporting unusual events. Like a dutiful wife, Dostehseh slowed her horse and dropped back from the head of the formation, as Elias and Esquiline, the two leading Chiricahua sub-chiefs, advanced.

Yrinco, a short, squat warrior with a scar on his shoulder, came abreast of the leaders. "Where is Chief Miguel Narbona?" he asked as he scanned the assembly.

"We have left him behind," said Cochise.

Yrinco appeared taken aback, and indeed lost his train of thought. His eyes misted, then he cleared his throat and said, "The *Nakai-yes* Mexicanos have a ranch straight ahead. I counted eight men, one woman, and two children. They have many fine horses."

"Not for long," said Esquiline.

Cochise was offended at Esquiline's presumption, because he, Cochise, was supposed to make the decision. Yrinco continued his report. "They are about one day away. The nearest bluecoat army post is Fort Buchanan."

Cochise realized that Chief Miguel Narbona would not hesitate to accept such a bounty. "Esquiline is right," he said. "Those horses will be ours."

* * *

Horses and carriages rumbled on busy Broadway as Nathanial entered Pfaff's, a tavern popular with writers and journalists, five steps down from the pavement, near Prince Street. Filled with cigar, cigarette, and pipe smoke, it was here that Nathanial spent his evenings since Clarissa had become embroiled in preparations for her concert. And sitting alone in the corner, reading the *Herald*, was one of Nathanial's favorite drinking companions, the poet Fitz-Greene Halleck.

"Mind if I sit down?" asked Nathanial.

"By all means," said Fitz, sixty-seven years old, with a bright, bubbly manner and wavy gray hair, immaculately attired in a brown check suit, white shirt, and yellow cravat. "The waiter has stepped outside for a breath of fresh air, and perhaps someone garotted him." Like most New Yorkers, Fitz was fatalistic about crime.

"On the frontier," explained Nathanial, "most everybody carries guns, and garrotting is unheard of."

Fitz smiled. "Nathanial, you can't imagine how you fascinate me. There you were, living with Indians, outlaws, and renegades at the edge of the world. What a life you've led, while all I've ever done was sit in a room and scratch paper."

"Why don't you go West, Fitz? Can you imagine what it's like to breathe real fresh air, without the stench of chimneys or garbage lying in the gutters?"

"But it is the very stench and degradation of New York that keeps people like me alive," replied Fitz. "On the other hand, I wouldn't mind living with bloodthirsty savages for a while, provided they wouldn't massacre me. The Apaches are a warrior race fighting hopelessly but courageously in defense of the land bequeathed them by their gods. How sad, tragic, and beautiful."

"Why not write the true story of the Apaches?" suggested Nathanial. "Hell, look at the success of James Fenimore Cooper with the Mohicans. He's dead, and his books still are selling."

Fitz shook his head sadly. "It would require a Homer or Pindar to do justice to the Apaches, not a mere versifier such as I. But I've always been curious, Nathanial. Did you ever . . . ah . . . dally with one of their ladies?"

"Now Fitz—a gentleman never discusses such matters."

"On the contrary, dalliances are the main topic of conversation among gentlemen."

"The most eloquent experiences of my life were spent sitting in silence with my Apache friends, drinking tulapai and smoking the pipe."

"Is tulapai some sort of coffee?"

"No, it's more like whiskey, and produces extravagant hallucinations."

Fitz smiled. "Next time you go West, you must send me some."

An empty wicker jug of tulapai stood beside Chief Miguel Narbona as he lay on the blanket, his rheumy eyes focused on swirling constellations overhead, across which rode White Painted Woman, goddess of the universe, on a white horse with reins of diamonds. Weakening, delirious, the aging chief knew his hour was at hand.

"Come to me, White Painted Woman," he whispered hoarsely. "Do not make me wait long."

She appeared in no hurry to carry him away, so he lay gasping, his consciousness fading, his mind spinning with images of great battles in which he had contended when he'd been strong, hardy, a tornado of destruction, while now he lacked strength to sip sacred tulapai.

He struggled to arise, to no avail. The People believed they went to another world after death, where they joined departed family and friends, and existed more or less as in the homeland, but with no White Eyes or Mexicanos to disturb them. What a relief to get away from those devils, thought Chief Miguel Narbona.

His neck and shoulders ached fiercely whenever he moved, his stomach blazed with hunger, and worst of all, he had the most terrible headache of his life. It will be over soon, he told himself. He tried to wave to White Painted Woman, but his hand wouldn't lift off the blanket.

A gust of wind blew over him, then he heard a faint growl. Sometime later, there was a snarl. Miguel Narbona smiled. White Painted Woman has sent her servants to help me.

The coyotes emerged from the chaparral, licking their chops, glancing at each other through slitted eyes, then advanced ceremoniously. Chief Miguel Narbona could not defend himself, nor did he want to. "Eat my flesh," he whispered. "Let me make you strong."

Their leader advanced, lowered his head, and gazed directly into the eyes of Chief Miguel Narbona. "What are your last words?" he seemed to be saying.

"When I was a young warrior," rasped Miguel Narbona, "I performed great deeds."

The coyote opened his dripping jaws, then closed them around the flaccid throat spread before him. Chief Miguel Narbona finally rode alongside White Painted Woman, showered by stars, headed toward canyons of plentiful game, where no enemies would molest the People again.

2

The southwestern section of New Mexico Territory was called Arizona, an Indian word meaning *little spring*. Many considered the barren terrain unsuitable for cattle ranching, but indigenous strains of grama grass were available, though not as plentiful as on the Great Plains.

Stubbornness was required to raise cattle in such a land, but the rewards were sufficient for Raphael Fonseca, who had built a small cabin for his wife and two sons. His herd had multiplied to nearly five hundred, while his corral contained more than forty horses. He hope to become a wealthy caudillo someday.

Thirty-eight years old, with a long chin, wide mustache, and eyes that turned down at the corners, he slept peacefully in the hour before dawn, his wife, Cecilia, at his side, their two sons down the hall. He was becoming a successful man, God had been kind, and soon he'd pay off his bank loan. Life was good for Raphael Fonseca, and he had much to be proud of.

The ranch basked in the moonlight, his weary vaqueros slumbered in the bunkhouse, but José, the cook, opened his eyes in the tiny shed that served as his quarters. The first one up every day, he dressed quickly, then scratched his neck as he made his way to the main house to begin breakfast. The vaqueros wouldn't work without their bacon and beans, washed down with thick black coffee.

A ragged line of mountains sprawled across the horizon, stars twinkling merrily above. It seemed like any other night, with nothing to fear, as José reached the back door of the hacienda. He spotted movement in the corner of his right eye, but before he could turn, his jugular was sliced precisely. He toppled to the ground, as Coyuntura raised his gore-stained knife in the air. The thickets and clumps of cactus came alive as warriors rushed forward silently, armed with bows, arrows, clubs, and lances. The first glow of dawn appeared on the horizon as one contingent headed for the bunkhouse, the other toward the main hacienda. They smashed open doors, dived through windows, and the ranch was taken by surprise. In the darkness Fonseca hastily removed the rifle above the bed, thumbed back the hammer, and was slammed in the head with a war club. As he fell to the floor, the last sound he heard was the scream of his wife.

The warriors quickly overwhelmed all resistance, but there was no time to lose. They ransacked both buildings, saddled fresh horses, and their last act was to torch the buildings. Flames licked up walls and out windows, burning furniture, fabrics, and wood trim, but adobe doesn't burn; it just holds heat like a giant oven.

Singing victory songs, the People herded horses out of the corral, then headed for the open land. The roof of the barn collapsed in a mighty explosion, throwing a shower of sparks at the sky.

* * *

As victorious Apaches rode toward their camp, singing of glory, an audience of sophisticated music lovers gathered at the Apollo Rooms on Broadway at Canal Street in New York City. The featured performer was Clarissa Rowland-Barrington, and due to the economic power of the Barringtons and Rowlands, whose enterprises advertised in all newspapers, a variety of motley fellows known as music critics were in attendance, among them Reginald van Zweinan of the *Sun*, best man at Clarissa's wedding, who was disposed to write a glowing review even if she played the piano with her nose.

The Apollo Rooms had been the site of the first Philharmonic Orchestra concert in 1842, but the Philharmonic had since moved to the new Academy of Music on 14th Street, and the Apollo now was available for magic shows, the popular Ethiopian minstrelsy, plays, and legitimate musical programs such as Clarissa's.

The Steinway piano and stool stood together on the empty stage, a stark white curtain in the background. Clarissa's parents sat in the front row, beaming with satisfaction, while toward the back of the hall, between Fitz-Greene Halleck and Reginald van Zweinan, rested the performing artist's husband, wreathed by alcohol fumes.

Promptly at eight o'clock, the featured artist stepped onto the stage, receiving enthusiastic applause that did not impress her, since she knew practically everyone in attendance had been coerced into coming by her parents. Attired in a maroon dress with fashionable leg-of-mutton sleeves, she advanced toward the piano, sat on the stool, and looked at the sheets of music.

Her first selection was Mozart's *Fantasia* Sonata, and without further ado, she proceeded to finger the keys. The concert hall fell silent, except for clear notes wafting into the heavy auditorium air. Clarissa loved Mozart's sweetness, beauty, and the orderliness of whatever madness had driven him to write countless symphonies, sonatas, operas, and other works of genius, while carrying on love affairs, intrigues, and spending faster than he earned. Clarissa believed that she had penetrated the very soul of Mozart, understanding precisely what he had been aiming for.

Loyal to Mozart's spirit, Clarissa's fingers rippled over the keys, unaware that the audience was transfixed by what they considered her unique interpretation of the great master. In the back row Nathanial studied the patrons carefully, noticing that no one slept or crocheted during Clarissa's performance.

Nathanial had listened many times to his wife's piano playing and considered her a musician of exceptional talent, her feminine fire enlivening even the most placid themes. Who is this woman I married, he wondered. She is so superior; I wonder why she stays with me.

"She has Olympian grandeur," whispered Fitz, immaculately attired in a black suit, white shirt, and black tie.

"Not a bad line," replied the walruslike Reginald, writing in his notebook. "It shall appear in my review tomorrow."

"Without payment to its creator, I'm sure," noted Fitz.

"Sssshhhh," said the lady sitting in front of them, a gray-haired dowager wearing a diamond necklace. Not another sound could be heard from the audience except an occasional cough, for ventilation was not an advantage of the Apollo Rooms.

Finally, Clarissa hit the sonata's last chord, closed her eyes, and paused, fingers arched over the keys as she savored the moment of completion. She was utterly lost in the chambers of her mind, dreaming of herself as Mozart's wife, when the wave of applause washed over her. Aroused from her dream, she stood, faced her audience, and curtsied. Flowers rained upon her, gentlemen pounded their hands, while ladies tapped daintily. A huzzah went up from the throat of Reginald van Zweinan, for no one was more loyal than he, and it appeared the roof might split as Clarissa took her second bow.

She had won their hearts as with the vaqueros and bullwhackers in Sante Fe and every other audience before whom she'd performed. I must never doubt myself again, she advised herself, but how can an artist not doubt, for the truth of art is elusive, and there are no absolute standards, save those of the heart.

She waited for the applause to diminish, then sat behind the piano once more and began Mozart's Fifth Sonata in G Major. Meanwhile, the stout impresario, Thorndyke, stood at the rear of the audience, stroking his black beard. Thirty-five, a Yankee from New Hampshire, he was searching for a special talent that he could promote, utilizing the publicity techniques demonstrated by Phineas T. Barnum during the successful tour of Jenny Lind, who'd taken America by storm during 1850-52. Thorndyke had failed in numerous business ventures, but his facile explanations had managed to raise the cost of Clarissa's concert, mostly from her relatives. She's quite beautiful in an understated way, he calculated, and she has a news-worthy background, plus she certainly knows the piano. Perhaps she's just what I need.

Clarissa's final selection was "The Ship on Fire," a popular song by Henry Russell, full of rising crescendos, diving arpeggios, and crashing octaves. Accompanying herself, she sang in her clear, delicate voice of the sinking of the ship, the lowering of the boats, and a gentleman surrendering his seat to a young lady.

The song was mawkish and bombastic, when it wasn't overflowing with sentimentality and bathos. But the audience abandoned their New York cynicism, perhaps due to the dramatic talent of Clarissa Rowland-Barrington, or possibly because they lived in a heroic age. Everyone was captivated, including Clarissa's husband, as the rescue ship arrived, and Clarissa sang the final refrain:

> *Cold, cold was the night as they drifted away*
> *and mistily dawned o'er the pathway the day.*

There was silence, then the hall filled with applause like cannonades. Clarissa stood and held out her arms, realizing that the hope she'd nurtured since early childhood finally had come true as she was showered with garlands of flowers.

There comes a time when a performer must leave the stage, regardless of how wonderful the praise, so Clarissa blew them all a kiss, then turned and walked gracefully to the wings, where, alone in the darkness, shrouded by curtains and props, she closed her eyes and relished the moment. Her name was shouted, her vanity expanded like a balloon, and tears of ecstasy came to her eyes. For the first time, she felt utterly brilliant. But it's only my family and friends, she reminded herself wryly. Total strangers would never respond this way, except it hadn't been much different in Sante Fe.

Confused, wondering what it meant, she opened the door to her dressing room and was surprised to see Thorndyke seated before her mirror. "I foresee a program of concerts beginning at the Academy of Music," he declared, "and then on to Philadelphia, Baltimore, Charleston, Atlanta, and perhaps to New Orleans, up the Mississippi to St. Louis, then back east. Why, I had no idea you were so exceptional!"

Her proud husband arrived, gave his wife a firm kiss on her laughing lips, and declared, "Best I've ever heard you."

Her parents arrived next, followed by other relatives, friends, and Reginald van Zweinan. "New York has crowned a new queen tonight!" the newspaperman cried excitedly. "That will be my headline. What can I say, when I have heard perfection? And that will be my opening line."

Nathanial felt himself pushed to the side by well-wishers, while Thorndyke babbled about an international tour. Leaning against the wall, Nathanial gazed at his wife glowing in the effulgence of gaslight. He realized there was a side to Clarissa he didn't know, and in fact great ability resided within her, while he was an ordinary fellow, an ex-soldier of no special accomplishments, something of a bore. I wonder why she remains with me? he asked himself.

On the morning after the concert, Clarissa and Nathanial breakfasted together in their rooms at the Saint Nicholas Hotel. She wore a red silk robe, her long blond hair gathered behind her head with a matching red silk ribbon, and she continued to bask in the glow of her performance.

Clarissa never had known anything like the adulation of a sophisticated New York audience, not to mention the incredible offer of Thorndyke, who was organizing a new concert at the most prestigious venue in the city, the Academy of Music itself. Clarissa had received excellent reviews from bought-and-paid-for music critics, and several interesting articles had been written, emphasizing her experiences on the frontier. She recalled taking her first bow, as flowers fell like colored snowballs upon her, the penultimate moment of her life.

Meanwhile, on the other side of the table, Nathanial sat morosely. My wife has become a celebrity and doesn't need me in the least, he mulled. "Are you going to accept Thorndyke's offer?"

"I haven't made up my mind," she replied. "What do you think?"

"We couldn't leave for New Mexico Territory as soon as we'd planned, but I don't have a job yet, so I guess it won't matter."

She placed her hand on his wrist. "Are you sure you won't mind, Nathanial?"

"Of course not," he lied. "This might be a convenient time for me to visit my father, because perhaps he can help me find a position with the Bureau of Indian Affairs." She's barely listening, he suspected.

"I've got to get dressed because I have an appointment with Mister Thorndyke."

She pecked his cheek, and he caught a last glimpse of her glorious rump encased in red silk as she departed their dining room. He gazed into the grounds

of coffee at the bottom of his cup, as if to divine the
future. He feared Clarissa would leave him for her
wonderful musical career.

Nathanial had killed Apache Indians with his bare
hands, but there was something fragile at the core of
his existence, for he believed he was fundamentally
worthless, an intellectual midget not worthy of a great
woman's love. He made his way to the whiskey cabinet, poured himself two fingers of Kentucky bourbon,
knocked the potion back, and it hit him like a Broadway omnibus. Then he collapsed onto the nearest
chair, where he stared for a long time out the window
at the clear blue sky.

The sky was cloudy in New Mexico Territory, and
the stink of charred wood and adobe permeated the
air, as a detachment of dragoons advanced closer to
the ruined hacienda. A flock of buzzards scattered,
squawking disapproval at the interruption of their
feast, black wings defacing the late afternoon sun.

Captain Beauregard Hargreaves of South Carolina,
Nathanial's former West Point roommate, rode at the
head of the detachment, his nose covered with the orange bandanna of the dragoon service. Perched on his
head was a wide-brimmed vaquero hat, and he wore a
brown rawhide jacket over his blue Army shirt, plus
vaquero boots with spurs. He looked more like a brig-
and than an Army officer as he advanced onto the
scene of the atrocity.

It wasn't the first one he'd seen, nor would it be the
last. He halted his horse in front of the main house,
climbed down from the saddle, and looked around
grimly. Semi-eaten decomposing corpses could be
seen and smelled, horses and cattle gone. Apaches

had struck again, apparently within the past forty-eight hours.

Beau had been on the frontier since arriving for the Mexican War. Not very tall, with a deep chest and curly black hair peeking beneath his vaquero hat, he took out his notebook and wrote notes. "Sergeant Barlowe, please organize a burial detail."

The men grumbled as they climbed down from their saddles, because they'd joined the dragoons to fight Apaches, but spent most of their time digging, cleaning, constructing buildings, and riding about the landscape, searching for but seldom seeing the enemy.

Beau felt their frustration, because it was much like his own. He believed the federal government should send more soldiers and systematically clear the land of Apaches, but the federal government was mired in the Kansas controversy, economic collapse, and numerous other pressing issues, while New Mexico Territory was far from their minds, because New Mexicans couldn't vote.

Beau sat on the ground and surveyed the ranch as sounds of shoveling and cursing came to his ears. He could imagine the barn and main hacienda before the Apaches had struck, a bucolic rural scene, despoiled and bloodied by craven savages.

Beau hated Apaches and believed their wicked deeds far outweighed their charming qualities. His old pal Nathanial Barrington had lived among them and come to respect their so-called holy lifeway, but Beau thought Nathanial tended to romanticize Indians.

Beau watched his men drag corpses toward the big hole, and two apparently were children. He thought of Beth and Beau II back at Fort Buchanan, with his wife, Rebecca. Goddamned Apache bastards, he thought.

The soldiers lowered corpses into the hole as an eerie moan arose within the ruined hacienda. The dragoons reached for their weapons as Sergeant Barlowe advanced to investigate. "I thought we got 'em all," he said gruffly.

Sergeant Barlowe also was a Mexican War veteran, and he'd remained in the Army perhaps out of patriotism, laziness, or loneliness. With a graying mustache and a lean whiplash build, he entered the charred building, followed by four dragoons. A whimper issued from a pile of rubble in the corner of a bedroom, where part of the roof had caved in.

The men lifted away charred timbers and gradually exposed fingers covered with blood and ashes. Sergeant Barlowe leaned out the window and shouted to Captain Hargreaves, "There's a survivor."

They carried the near-dead victim outside and laid him on the ground. No doctor traveled with the detachment, but the men cleaned Raphael Fonseca off, bound his wounds, and set his broken bones. Lacking a wagon, they threw away supplies and tied him head down over a packhorse.

The gray-haired sergeant trudged toward the detachment commander, didn't bother to salute, and said, "I know what yer a-gonna say afore you open yer mouth, sir. You want me to take five men and return to Fort Buchanan with this wounded civilian. You'll take the rest and pursue the Apaches."

Beau smiled. "Sometimes I think you know me better than I know myself, Sergeant Barlowe."

Sergeant Barlowe shouted orders, the men mounted up, and the detachment split apart. One small contin-

gent retraced their trail to Fort Buchanan, while the
larger one moved out at a trot, following tracks left by
the Apache marauders. If we maintain this pace, figured Beau, we should catch up with the fiends tomorrow.

That night, Cochise slept deeply, arms entwined
with Dostehseh, as if they were halves of the same
four-legged creature. His first raid as chief had been
successful, and great riches had come to the People,
thanks to Cochise and his plans. A dance would be
held to celebrate, once they arrived at their destina-
tion.

The People slept happily when hoofbeats came
faintly from the distance, and a guard shouted, "A
rider!"

In an instant warriors and their women were awake,
reaching for their weapons. A defensive line deployed
with no orders from Cochise, for the men had been
trained as warriors from an early age. The hoofbeats
came closer, and one of the guards shouted, "It is Posito."

Posito had been guarding the backtrail, and it was
clear that someone was following them, otherwise he
would not ride at such a pace. His horse galloped
closer, and Posito leapt off the animal's bare back before it could stop.

Posito was short, wiry, with angry eyes and a vivid
scar on the side of his face. He came to a halt before
Cochise and said, "About fifteen bluecoats are following us, but they have stopped for the night."

A decision needed to be made, and Cochise wondered what Chief Miguel Narbona would do. The
answer came in an instant. He would attack, but now

White Eyes had rifles that they could fire more
quickly and accurately than old muskets. Yet at close
range, not many bluecoat soldiers could stop Apaches.

"I think we should trap them," said Cochise. "Who
is with me?"

All the warriors raised their hands, but some had to
stay behind, to guard horses, cattle, and women, and
there was no point in sending too many warriors to
manage a small task.

Cochise selected thirty warriors; they gathered
weapons, and their wives saddled horses. Then the
warriors mounted, bows slung across their backs,
Killer of Enemies Bandoliers strung across their
chests. Cochise led them toward the bluecoat pursuers, to teach a lesson in diplomacy. *This is our
land, and how dare you follow our trail, hoping to
harm us?*

No one could say exactly when the Apache wars
had begun, but perhaps a Spanish conquistador had
shot an Apache for sport, or an Apache had taken a
mule from the herd belonging to the legendary Her-
nan Cortes. The United States formally accepted responsibility for Apaches during the Mexican War, and
Captain Beauregard Hargreaves had been fighting
them ever since.

Now he rode at the head of his detachment; it was
morning, and he was following tracks of Apache marauders. He was aware of the old military adage, *don't
split your forces in enemy territory*, but the rules were
different in New Mexico, where mobility, not numbers, was the key to success.

Beau bounced up and down in his saddle as his
horse trotted over the mesa, surrounded by mountains

standing like castles of forgotten empires, turgid prisons, or needles thrusting into the clouds, as rays of purple and orange decorated the sky. He could see literally hundreds of miles, but preferred to scan nearby greasewood bushes and prickly pear cactus, for the Apaches's favorite trick was the carefully sprung ambush. He'd dispatched scouts to the front, rear, and flanks of his small unit. The worst mistake an officer could make was to get caught by surprise.

Beau recalled his old West Point roommate, Nathanial Barrington, taken by surprise in the Embudo Mountains in '54, nearly killed. Nathanial also had been ambushed near the Santa Rita Copper Mines in '51. Beau missed Nathanial, who'd resigned his commission and gone back East, after having his fill of the Apache wars.

Beau felt guilty about his old West Point roommate, because once Beau had planked Nathanial's wife, Clarissa, during the year everyone thought Nathanial had been killed in action, but instead had been living with Apaches. Beau hoped Clarissa never would tell Nathanial of this escapade, otherwise a shooting might well ensue, and Beau might have to kill his chum in self-defense. Beau didn't realize that a woman like Clarissa never would admit such a forbidden act, and in fact nearly had convinced herself that it never happened.

A cautious officer, Beau decided to check his old Walker Colt pistol once more, because dust could jam moving parts. He blew out the barrel, spun the chambers, and thumbed back the hammer. He preferred the Walker to the new Colt .36 Navy model because the Walker was heavier and therefore more useful as a club in close fighting at which Apaches excelled. I wonder if they know we're following them? he asked himself as he aimed at a clump of cholla cactus.

Cochise lay on a high ledge and peered at two columns of bluecoat soldiers below, following the trail of stolen horses. The movements of *Pindah* soldiers are predictable as mules, decided the newly crowned sovereign. What kind of warriors behave in this manner? The stupidity of his foe confounded him. Perhaps they are trying to trick me, but Miguel Narbona would not turn away from such a column.

Cochise descended the mountain and joined warriors waiting for him beside a winding arroyo. Without a word, he climbed onto his horse, then rode toward the spot where the ambush would take place, his warriors following past mesquite trees and cholla cactus. At midafternoon they staked their horses in a canyon, left one of their number on guard, and then advanced to the trail, where they dug shallow holes, covered themselves with dirt, twigs, and leaves, and lay down with their weapons, breathing through reeds.

When finished, the land appeared a barren wasteland, not a soul in sight.

The dragoons continued their dusty march, following the trail of Apache rustlers through a region where the white man seldom visited. They struggled to stay awake, boredom hanging on their eyelashes like lead weights.

Military expeditions into Arizona usually were uneventful, so the dragoons expected no difficulties beyond running out of water. They were confident the enemy would split into several units, then meet later

at a prearranged spot, eluding all pursuers, but they
had not reckoned on the desire of a new Chiricahua
chief to prove himself.

Cochise lay beneath a thin film of dirt, waiting for
bluecoat soldiers to walk into the snare. His bow in
his right hand, he was as motionless as a rock.

The possibility of peace with the White Eyes simply didn't occur to Cochise. How dare they threaten
the Chiricahua People? he asked himself. We are not
Jicarillas, Mescaleros, or Mimbrenos, and we are not
surrendering one inch of this homeland.

On the trail the White Eyes scout approached,
slouching in his saddle, and Cochise identified him as
a Papago, a tribe the Apaches had fought since the old
time. It would provide great satisfaction to kill him,
but Cochise was hunting bigger game. Pass on,
thought Cochise darkly. We will deal with you later.

Moolik the Papago rode through the Apache ambush, unaware anything was amiss. He had told lies to
obtain his job, and the Americanos assumed he was a
skilled tracker because he was an Indian, but not all
Indians are the same.

In point of fact, Moolik had been a mediocre hunter
and warrior, and that's why he'd sought employment
with the White Eyes. He carried a new Sharps breech-
loading rifle and also possessed the latest model Colt
revolver with plenty of ammunition. Ordinary Papagos only dreamed of such possessions, and no longer
need Moolik roam the wilderness in the hope of
creeping up on a deer, for now he ate with the Army,
the food appearing magically in wagons continually
arriving from the east.

Moolik hoped someday to visit the eastern lands, where multitudes of Americanos lived in towering magical villages, but usually he spent his pay on whiskey. Dreaming about exotic foreign places, drooping in his saddle, slack-jawed and lazy, the Papago rode blithely through the Apache ambuscade.

At the head of the formation, Captain Hargreaves was alert and poised, his bloodshot eyes searching every notch and gully for signs of Apaches. The way he saw it, the safety of his men, not to mention his own skin, was his responsibility.

He turned and looked at them, not the usual crabby lot of soldiers, but seasoned veterans who had volunteered for special scout duty, hoping for faster promotions or to prove they were the meanest sons-of-bitches on the range. But they too were cautious, hands near their revolvers. Death could come swiftly, and all a dragoon could do was pull his trigger as quickly as possible.

Beau had been in the Army so long, he knew no other life. Duty, honor, and country had become part of him, just as profit and loss are second nature to businessmen. He had been caught in the grandeur of the Mexican War, had fought at Palo Alto and Resaca de Palma, stormed the battlements of Monterrey, and been wounded at Buena Vista. Raised in the traditions of Southern chivalry, he considered the Army a noble calling reserved for men of honor.

Yet Beau was not well paid by common standards, because many Americans considered their professional Army a wasteful extravagance with too many Southern officers, a possible subversive force that might undermine democracy. They didn't understand the sacrifice and hardship endured not just by the men, but also their wives.

Beau thought of Rebecca in their half-completed adobe hut at Fort Buchanan, trying to raise their children. He felt another twinge of guilt, due to his moment of weakness with Clarissa Barrington, but Rebecca had been at Fort Union, and he in Albuquerque, seeking to comfort a grieving widow, when something happened.

Plagued with remorse, he tried to uphold whatever shred of honor he still retained as he led his men on the stolen livestock trail. Like the dragoons in the ranks, he doubted they'd catch Apaches, but occasionally the Army had surprised marauding Apaches, delivering heavy blows.

Beau felt the urge to check his Walker Colt again, to make sure it was ready to fire. It was a sunny day with scattered puffy white clouds and brightly colored red and yellow birds flitting among the cactus, but that didn't mean Apaches might not be in the vicinity.

In years to come, Beau would wonder what force or influence had caused him to draw his Colt at that moment, spin the chambers, and make sure all save one were loaded. Then he aimed at a yellow bird sitting among sagebrush when it seemed an earthquake struck Arizona.

A terrible shriek pierced the air, then Apaches burst into the open, drawing back arrows. One aimed at Beau, who pulled his trigger. The shot went wild, but the Apache was so surprised he jerked his bow two inches to the side. The arrow flew harmlessly past Beau's shoulder as he thumbed back the hammer and fired again.

This time the shot found its target, the Apache fell backward, and Beau glanced about excitedly, realizing he was surrounded, taken by surprise. "Rapid fire!" he ordered.

Shots echoed off distant canyons as Beau and his men triggered quickly. Then an Apache tore Sergeant Barlowe out of the saddle and beat his brains in with a club. This was not a battle of generals sitting in secluded headquarters, moving pieces on the chessboard, but bashing, stabbing, and shooting at close range.

Beau fired at an Apache coming at him with a lance. The Walker Colt barked disapproval, the Apache shaken by the force of the blow, and before Beau could ready himself for another shot, a new Apache leapt at him, war club in hand. Beau grabbed the Apache's arm, drew back his heavy Colt, and smacked him in the face, sending him to the ground.

Beau's horse raised its front hooves high in the air, hoping to punch an Apache to oblivion, but one warrior snuck up behind Beau, tackled, and tore him out of the saddle. Beau landed on his back, the wind knocked out of him, but that didn't stop him from grabbing his assailant's throat with one hand as he prepared to club him with the Colt.

The Apache caught Beau's arm in his fist, they locked together in the embrace of death, and rolled over the ground, gnashing their teeth, head-butting, kneeing, and doing anything necessary, fair or foul, to prevent his skull from being caved in. At that moment another Apache rushed Beau from behind to smash his head with a war club, but Beau managed to knee his first opponent's groin, then turn in time to backhand the second Apache with his Colt. The Apache was tossed to the side, then Beau fired again, striking an onrushing warrior in the throat.

The Apache dropped as Beau fired his fifth shot into another Apache charging with lance in hand. The bullet landed center chest as the desert reverberated with shots, experienced dragoons offering a heavy barrage, forcing the Apaches back. When one dragoon ran out of ammunition, the next covered him as he re-loaded. No one panicked, tried to desert, or pretended to be dead. Except for the initial seconds of the ambush, they had been good soldiers.

The ambush ground was covered with dead soldiers, Apaches, and horses as the attackers fled. Two dragoons chased the remaining horses while the other soldiers widened their defense perimeter. They didn't know whether the Apaches would try again, so they searched for the best cover, their commanding officer taking his position behind a dead horse.

Beau's heart beat so quickly, he thought his chest would burst. In all his battles and skirmishes, this had been his closest call. His hand trembled as he loaded the Colt, then noticed he was bleeding from his left shoulder, face, and his right thigh, plus it felt as if his nose had been broken.

"Here comes the Papago!" shouted one of the men.

Beau turned toward the trail, where Moolik was riding at full gallop, having heard shots, then waiting until certain the White Eyes had won. Moolik feared the Apaches would catch him and yearned for the safety of the bluecoat Army as he crouched low in his saddle, speeding over the desert.

An arrow flashed barely perceptibly, then pierced Moolik's left side. He screamed, his horse bucked him into the air, and Moolik landed on the ground about

three hundred yards from the dragoons, who could see
the Papago struggle to his feet. Apaches with knives,
war clubs, and lances burst from the foliage, then dispatched the traitor. Finally, they turned toward the soldiers and hurled Spanish insults in which the soldiers
were compared to pigs, donkeys, and sons of whores.

Corporal Dennison beckoned to the Apaches with
his pistol. "C'mon, you bastards! We're ready!"

The Apaches retreated into the wilderness, and the
dragoons waited to make sure they were gone. Then
Beau said, "Let's get out of here!"

They loaded their dead and wounded onto horses,
then mounted and headed back to Fort Buchanan,
while glancing warily behind them, hoping the
Apaches wouldn't follow.

When the People were certain the White Eyes
wouldn't return, they emerged to retrieve their dead.
No one felt the defeat more keenly than Cochise, for
this was his second raid as war chief. Still, there was
booty to be had. Cochise found a soldier who had feet
about the same size as he, so he sat beside him, pulled
off the man's boots, and tried them on. They appeared
to fit, and looked rather elegant, Cochise thought.

His brother, Coyuntura, peeled a shirt off the back
of another dead soldier, when a folded piece of paper
fell to the ground. He looked at strange symbols, having no idea what they meant:

Dear Mother,
   *I pologize fore not writin, but am in a new de-
tachment and don't got much time. I think of you
offen and . . .*

Coyuntura tossed the letter, and the wind caught it in its invisible net, carrying it high in the sky. Then Coyuntura put on the shirt, admiring orange stripes on the sleeves. He gave out a victorious yell, although they had captured no horses or weapons and lost eleven of their number. The steady fire of the pistols had been too much for the bravest of the Chiricahuas. Somehow, the White Eyes had been ready for them.

Coyuntura searched the pockets of another dead soldier and found a small black book with tiny letters. He opened the book and gazed at:

Then the Lord will make thy plagues wonderful, and the plagues of thy seed, even great plagues, and of long continuance, and sore sicknesses, and of long continuance.

Coyuntura gazed at the symbols, wondering what they portended, for he knew instinctively they were religious. He decided to keep the leather-bound tome, so dropped it into the leather bag suspended from his waist. Then he found what he was looking for, a black pouch of tobacco. Coyuntura opened the pouch and took a hefty sniff. As he was dropping the pouch into his bag, he heard a moan beneath him. The eyes of the bluecoat soldier fluttered; evidently he was still alive. Perhaps the soldier could be nursed back to health, even living to old age, but the People had rancor for the white race despoiling their sacred homeland. Without hesitation, Coyuntura slit his throat.

3

Nathanial rode a train to Washington, D.C. and checked into the Emory Hotel, a resting place popular among Army and Navy officers, with a house of ill fame across the street. Then he hailed a coach, directing the driver to an address in Georgetown, a sedate neighborhood of farms and cottages, where his father resided.

Nathanial hadn't seen the old soldier since the summer, after Nathanial had returned from New Mexico Territory. They had spoken little, because relations were awkward in the family, his father having abandoned his mother during Nathanial's childhood for another woman, a beautiful octoroon thirty-odd years his junior. His father and the octoroon had parted recently, and now the colonel resided with his aging Negro maid.

The coach stopped, and Nathanial bounded toward the brick mansion, then rapped on the front door, which presently was opened by Mattie, the stooped, unkempt maid. Nathanial kissed her damp forehead, for she was practically a member of the family, then she led him into the parlor, which was dusty, smelling of old curtains and decaying wood.

"I'll get your father," she said. "He'll be real happy to see you."

I'll bet, thought Nathanial, as he sat on a red velvet chair. Oil portraits of distinguished Barringtons hung on the wall, barely visible in dim light emitted by dirty windows. He'd never seen his father's parlor so untidy, with old coffee cups, dirty glasses, a pile of newspapers next to his father's chair, a dirty plate on the fireplace mantel.

Nathanial felt as if his world were cracking apart, with his wife ignoring him, and his father sinking into squalor. Nathanial received another blow when the colonel emerged from the corridor, leaning on a cane, hunched over, pale and wizened. Nathanial blinked, his mind reverberating with images of the stalwart Army officer who had so dominated his youth.

"My boy," said the old colonel, hugging him. "About time you came to see me."

His father, once a handsome man, had metamorphosed into a scrawny old buzzard with a double chin, thinning gray hair atop his head, and a medium-long gray beard. Nathanial tried to be cheerful. "There's been much to do in New York, and Clarissa has become a great success—have you heard?"

"A success at what?" The old man scowled.

"Piano."

"I didn't know she played the piano."

Nathanial felt chilled, because his father had heard Clarissa play during the round of parties and celebrations that had attended their wedding. He's losing his mind, realized the worried son.

"Let me get you a drink," said the colonel. "I can't ask Mattie, because she doesn't walk so well these days."

"Why don't you hire a second maid?"

His father turned and looked at him suspiciously. "I don't like strangers."

The colonel filled two glasses with whiskey, handed one to Nathanial, and raised the other shakily in the air. "To your mother—did you know that the Whigs intend to nominate her for president, and her running mate will be Henry Clay?"

Nathanial tried not to frown, but realized in addition to losing his memory, his father also had misplaced reality. "She'll get my vote," replied Nathanial.

His father raised his finger in the air. "The Democrats will try to assassinate her, so you'd better hurry home and protect her."

"Don't worry—Otis will protect her." Nathanial referred to a Negro servant who worked in his mother's home.

His father seemed to relax. "Suppose you're right," he agreed. "But I don't want her alone. Since you have no obligations of your own, you should move from your hotel into your mother's home."

"Apparently, you've forgotten that I'm married."

"When did that happen?"

"You were there—don't you remember?"

The old man blinked in confusion. "Oh yes," he said, "of course."

"Have you seen a doctor lately?"

"I'm as good as ever, except for the pain in my back, and I can still whup you, boy. Of course, the Buchanan administration is out to get me, because I know their dirty game. Did you know that General Scott offered me the post of inspector general, but the Buchanan administration overruled him?"

Spittle rolled down the corner of the old man's

mouth, his left hand shook, and Nathanial realized his father was ready for the asylum, but the old soldier would resist the move. "Father, I'd like to take you to a doctor."

"I wouldn't let one near me because they're in the pay of the government."

"To be honest, you're making rather strange remarks."

"The man who sees clearest is considered insane." Then the colonel's face became tender. "My dear son, I never should have left your mother, for I have ruined her life, along with yours and your brother Jeffrey's. Perhaps I'd be better off dead. What use am I to anyone?"

"You must let me hire another maid, to take care of you and Mattie, Father. And you must permit a doctor to look at you."

"Never." The old colonel laughed nervously. "I've just been joking. The Democrats don't care about me in the least. I'm just an old war horse whose best days are gone, a figment of my own imagination." He raised his hand to his forehead and sighed, "I become fatigued, lose my train of thought. Perhaps you'd better come tomorrow, after I'm rested."

The old man took Nathanial's arm and urged him toward the door. Nathanial never successfully had defied his father, who pushed him outside. Nathanial stood on the stoop as the door slammed in his face. I'll go back to New York and ask Mother, he decided. She'll know what to do.

Nathanial caught the first train north, left his luggage at the Saint Nicholas Hotel, noted his wife was not home, kissed his seven-month-old baby daughter, then rode a coach to his mother's home on Washington Square.

Amalia Barrington lived in a three-story brick building in a row of similar homes on the northern border of the square. He knocked on the door, which presently was opened by Belinda, his mother's Negro maid.

"Has she gone to bed?"

"Yes, but I'm sure she'll see you, sir."

Nathanial and Belinda behaved formally although once, in a train chugging through South Carolina, they'd nearly committed the forbidden act. Nathanial waited in the parlor as Belinda climbed the stairs to his mother's room. Nathanial gazed at the painting of himself in his West Point uniform, confident and strong, but now couldn't manage his own household.

Belinda descended the stairs. "She'll see you now, sir."

Nathanial passed Belinda on the narrow space, but they didn't tarry or flirt, for Belinda had married Otis. Nathanial knocked on the door to his mother's sitting room, she bade him enter, and he found her in a black quilted robe, for old people are troubled by chills, a bony gray-haired queen with deep-set eyes and a mouth that once had been pretty, but now was thin-lipped, surrounded by crevices.

He kissed her cool cheek, which reminded him of parchment. "I'm afraid I have bad news, and thought I should ask your advice."

"Your father has gone mad?" she asked.

Nathanial was stunned. "How did you know?"

"I know *everything*."

"He belongs in an asylum, and his maid is nearly as dotty as he."

She thought a few moments, and in the golden glow of gaslight, he imagined the eager, serious girl she must have been. Then she said, "I suppose we'll have to bring him here. We will depart for Washington on the first train tomorrow."

"What if he refuses to come?"

"He wouldn't dare," she replied.

A shiver passed up Nathanial's spine, for despite the many battles he'd fought, the only person who made him feel stark terror was the woman who had given him life.

Nathanial returned to the Saint Nicholas Hotel and discovered his wife had not yet returned home. He poured a glass of whiskey and sat in the living room, imagining himself gray, gaunt, unable to remember what he'd had for breakfast, worrying about enemy spies.

The door opened, and his wife appeared, her face flushed with happiness, wearing a purple shawl that established the splendor of her golden hair. The joy on her face vanished when she saw her husband. "Oh—you're back early," she said awkwardly.

He smiled falsely as he arose from the chair. "What an unpleasant surprise, to see your husband. Where have you been?"

"With Mister Thorndyke and a theater manager from Philadelphia. We were discussing my concert there."

"What a thrill it must be to perform for total strangers," he said sarcastically.

"More fun than drinking alone, I assure you."

"How can you assure me, when you have never experienced the rare pleasure of drinking alone?"

"By the same token, you have never performed, so you don't know what you're talking about, as usual."

"I can't help thinking that applause has turned your head."

"I can't help thinking you're jealous."

There are some remarks to which an officer does not respond, especially when they ring true. "I'll sleep on the sofa tonight," he said icily. "I wouldn't want to disturb the rest of a great artist."

"You may sleep on the floor if you like, or in the bathtub. I suspect you've had a fight with your father and have decided to take it out on me."

"I didn't fight with him at all. He's only gone mad, and my mother and I are bringing him back to New York tomorrow."

She appeared contrite. "I'm sorry. I didn't know. I'll go with you . . . to help."

"We wouldn't want to distract you from your brilliant career. After all, what is a mere old man compared to a piano?"

"Now you're being rude, Nathanial. It's not fair."

"You have abandoned your family for a life on the stage, like a cheap actress."

"You have conveniently forgotten that you abandoned me for almost a year while you lived among the Apaches, having a grand time, while I was alone with your daughter, believing you had died."

She failed to enumerate certain romantic interludes with Beau Hargreaves and another gentleman during the gloomy period when she'd believed her husband had been killed in action. She feared her husband would kill someone if he discovered the truth and nearly had convinced herself that the incidents never occurred.

Her defiance made him angry, for she was smaller and younger than he. "Far be it from me to prevent you from pursuing your tawdry goals," he said. "I have a busy day tomorrow, so I bid you good night." He proceeded to remove his clothes.

She made her way to the bedroom, where she closed the door, took out a handkerchief, and cried. She had worked, studied, and sacrificed all her life, tried to be decent, and had not committed very many sins, except for those lapses after Nathanial had been reported killed in action. Now that she needed his support, he behaved like a spoiled child. She felt betrayed and undermined by his pettiness.

She took a bath, a luxury she never failed to appreciate, since New Mexico Territory had lacked running water, and a common, ordinary bath required half a day of preparations with a wood stove. Then she looked in on Natalie, and on her way to her bedroom passed her husband on the sofa, reclining like a lumbering ox. Just because he's worthless, without a notion of what to do with his life, it doesn't mean I have to be the same, she lectured herself. Secure in her talent and the adulation of her many admirers, she crawled into bed alone.

At Fort Buchanan, far off in New Mexico Territory, Rebecca Hargreaves helped her Mexican maid prepare breakfast when there was a frantic knock on the door. Her first instinct was Apaches were attacking, so she took down the shotgun from the wall, made sure it was loaded, and opened the door cautiously.

Private Sullivan stood there, unable to restrain his excitement. "The cap'n has returned, ma'am!"

After replacing the shotgun, Rebecca ran to the middle of the scraggly parade ground. She wore a simple gray homespun dress, no cosmetics graced her careworn features, and a few strands of dark blond hair fell over one eye. Impatiently, she drew them out of the way as a detachment of dragoons could be seen about one thousand yards in the distance.

Other wives gathered on the parade ground, hoping and praying their man hadn't been killed, or lost a leg, or been mutilated by savages. "Some are wounded," said Mrs. Caroline Barlowe, wife of Sergeant Barlowe.

Rebecca bit her lip as she perceived men with bandages, a few head down over saddles. She feared Beau among the casualties, but then spotted his black beard and tan vaquero hat, gold shoulder straps on his tunic. "Thank you, Jesus," she whispered.

The women moved en masse to the orderly room, and they were as tanned as the soldiers, yet maintained their grace and femininity. Then the door opened, and Major Enoch Steen emerged, fifty-five years old, wearing a salt-and-pepper mustache, a Kentuckian cited for gallantry in the Mexican War.

Fort Buchanan had no main gate, so the arriving dragoons rode among the outbuildings, heading for the orderly room. Rebecca saw the bandage on her husband's leg, his riding posture not as it should be; evidently he and his men had fought the Apaches, although in other parts of the nation gentle souls bewailed the plight of the poor misunderstood Indian.

Beau pulled his horse to a halt in front of the orderly room, and a soldier helped him from his saddle; he limped to his wife and embraced her, giving thanks to the God who had delivered him safely home. Then he shuffled toward Major Steen, saluted, and delivered his report.

"You'd better have that leg looked at, Captain," said Major Steen. "I'll speak with you later."

Accompanied by his wife, Beau headed for the shack that was their hospital, while Major Steen returned to his office, sat at his desk, and reflected that for the sake of safety, he required at least five hundred more dragoons, but taxpayers wouldn't tolerate additional military expenditures. No one knew precisely how many Apaches were in the vicinity, but three thousand warriors seemed a reasonable guess to Major Steen. What will I do if they ever converge on Fort Buchanan? he thought.

Raphael Fonseca, sole survivor of the Apache raid, opened his eyes and wondered if he were in heaven, except heaven was said to be glorious, with angels in white robes and gold halos, whereas he lay on a cot in a dismal adobe hut, with a fierce headache, numerous scars, his body covered with blisters. Can it be that I'm alive? he asked himself.

A miracle apparently had occurred, but then he recalled the last pathetic cry of his wife. Tears filled his eyes as he thought of Cecilia and his angelic children murdered by Apaches. His dreams of a lifetime, not to mention what small amount of wealth he possessed, gone forever.

Fonseca had worked twelve years as a vaquero, learning the cattle business and saving every penny, instead of throwing wealth on prostitutes and mescal at the nearest cantina. A religious man, he'd met his wife at church in Tucson, but now wanted to die; the pain unbearable, his body had been scorched by flames, his head felt broken into a million fragments.

Worst was the memory of his wife and children, their beautiful lives snuffed out by Apaches.

Covered with bandages, listening to moans and sighs of other wounded men, he seethed with rage. If I live, I will pay the Apaches back, he swore.

Cochise knew his warriors doubted him, and indeed he doubted himself as he led them past the Dos Cabezas Mountains. They had won many horses and cattle in the first raid, but the price of the ambush had been too high. He anticipated challenges to his leadership and contemplated stepping aside, to let Esquiline or Elias take command. Cochise was willing to make any concession to keep the Chiricahuas together.

The new chief had promised assistance to widows and children of those who'd perished, but had not apologized for his failure, for he had not expected bluecoat soldiers to be prepared for an ambush. Did they see us? he wondered. He recalled the bluecoat war chief who nearly had shot him. Who has ambushed whom? wondered Cochise.

That night they camped alongside a stream. A horse was butchered, but no victory dance held, and the wailing of widows and orphans could be heard. Cochise ate little and felt as if he had failed the People. In the future he would not consider bluecoat soldiers easy prey.

He sat with his wife and sons, Taza and Naiche, the former fourteen harvests old, the latter only two. Dostehseh placed her hand on her husband's knee. "There will be other battles," she said. "Even the greatest chiefs have failed on occasion."

"But not so soon," he replied, "and not so ignominiously."

"The medicine men sing of the glory of heroes, but never their defeats."

Cochise pondered her words as he gnawed his chunk of meat. After the meal, as the People prepared for bed, Esquiline and Elias approached Cochise, who was laying his robe upon the bare ground. "We wish to council with you," said Esquiline.

Cochise stood and peered first into Esquiline's eyes, and then Elias's. "I know what you are going to say, my brothers. You want to take your clans and part company from me."

The two sub-chiefs appeared surprised by Cochise's response. They glanced at each other, then Elias said, "That is so."

"It is easy to crack a twig in two," replied Cochise. "But hold a handful of twigs, and no one can break them. So it is with the People. We are stronger together."

Esquiline lowered his eyes. "I did not want to mention my reason, but since you have disagreed, I will tell the truth. I have lost confidence in your leadership."

Cochise maintained his outward calm. "Even chiefs such as Miguel Narbona and Mangas Coloradas have suffered defeats."

There was silence at the mention of two such noble names, then Esquiline said, "You are right, but Miguel Narbona is no longer available to counsel you. We require a new war chief."

Cochise smiled. "You?"

Esquiline nodded solemnly. "You would be surprised at how many warriors would follow me."

Cochise turned to Elias. "Would you follow him?"

"Yes."

"But I thought you wanted to be chief, Elias."

"I have given my support to Esquiline."

"How many horses did he offer you?"

Elias's eyes flashed with anger. "How dare you in-sult me, just because you were the favorite of Miguel Narbona."

"It is difficult to imagine that you would support anybody if you were not paid, Elias."

Elias's lips quivered with rage as a crowd formed around the three war chiefs. Each had his supporters and detractors, and this moment had been building since the failure of the attack on the bluecoat soldiers. "You speak with arrogance," shouted Elias, "though warriors have died due to your lack of ability."

"It is true that warriors have been lost," replied Cochise. "But if you were in charge, what would you have done differently?"

"I . . ." Elias's voice trailed off.

Cochise followed his advantage. "You did not dis-agree when I planned the attack." He turned to Esquiline. "Nor did you."

"I thought I would give you a chance," replied Es-quiline, "because I respected the will of Miguel Narbona. I now see that Miguel Narbona had become old, and his judgment evidently failed him."

"If you thought the bluecoat soldiers had seen us, why did you not give the signal of danger?"

"I did not want to interfere with your plans."

"Liar," said Cochise in a conversational voice.

Warriors looked at each other, and mothers shep-herded their small children away from the gathering.

"How dare you call me a liar?" asked Esquiline, touching his hand to the hilt of his knife.

"That is what you are, unless you are also a demon,

because only a demon would permit his warrior brothers to be killed."

Esquiline took a step backward and smiled. "First you call me a liar, then a fiend. Do you have any other words for me, son of Pisago Cabezon?"

"What about *jealous*?"

Esquiline drew his knife, but before the point cleared his scabbard, a foot rose out of nowhere and whacked his nose. Esquiline went reeling backward, as Elias, war club in hand, leapt toward Cochise, but a fist slammed into Elias's mouth, staggering him. As he was trying to figure out what valley he was in, another fist collided with his ear, and it was like being struck with the trunk of a tree. Elias's eyes closed as he fell to the ground.

Cochise said nonchalantly, "If any warriors desire to go, I shall not stop them." Then Cochise turned his back and strolled toward his smiling wife and sons.

No one departed the leadership of Cochise that day.

Nathanial and his mother rode a train to Washington, D.C., then a coach to Georgetown, where they stopped at the patriarch's home. They climbed the stoop, she pounded her fist on the door, and sometime later it was opened by Mattie. The maid took one look at Nathanial, then his mother. "Oh-oh," she said, stepping out of the way.

Mrs. Barrington strolled jauntily into her husband's home. "Where is the great beast?"

"In his office, ma'am."

"I can't wait to see what work he does there."

Nathanial wondered how his mother knew where to go, since presumably she'd never visited her husband's Georgetown home, or had she? They climbed to the second floor, made their way down a corridor lined with moldering newspapers, and Amalia pounded on a door. "It's me!" she said.

A fit of coughing and other sounds of distress erupted on the other side of the door.

Nathanial frowned. "You shouldn't surprise him this way."

"Too bad," declared the deserted wife and mother.

Shuffling footsteps could be heard on the far side of the door, and then the gray-bearded colonel stood before them, food stains on his old Army tunic, a mournful expression in his rheumy eyes. "What are you doing here?" he asked meekly.

"You're coming home with me," she told him in her no-nonsense voice.

"Like hell I am," he replied.

She placed her hands on her hips and narrowed one eye. "You're filthy, half mad, can't take care of yourself, and ought to be ashamed, but shame isn't a word in your vocabulary. Follow me."

"I'll never follow you anywhere," he insisted. "You're the worst tyrant I've ever known. Has the President sent you?"

"What makes you think Ten Cent Jimmy Buchanan cares about your miserable disreputable life? You're a fool, you always have been a fool, and you always will be a fool."

She grabbed the front of his military tunic and dragged him out of the office. Nathanial was alarmed to see his mother bullying his father, but was afraid to open his mouth. The retired colonel tripped over his feet as he descended the stairs, but his wife held him erect. In the parlor Mattie was waiting, an anxious expression on her face. "You can't treat the massa this way," she said in a shaky voice.

"He is returning to his home in New York City," replied Mrs. Barrington. "You might as well come along unless you have another job."

The wronged wife pushed her husband into a chair, where he dropped with a dazed expression, sputtering and blubbering, the old soldier unable to defend himself. "You can't treat an officer in this manner," he protested.

"I'll treat you any way I like," she replied, then bent at the waist, gazed into his eyes, and said, "You never dreamed that one day I would be stronger than you, did you? You should thank whatever God you pray to that I don't give you a thrashing for deserting your family. You wanted romance with an exotic woman? Well, my fine Lothario, where is she now that you are old and ugly?"

"I have always believed the President offered her a job in the diplomatic service."

"Is it the President's fault that you haven't had a bath? Nathanial, find a trunk and pack his things—no, never mind, we'll buy new clothes in New York. And that goes for you too, Mattie."

"But my maps," pleaded the old soldier. "How can I plot strategy without my maps."

Nathanial cleared his throat. "Mother, a soldier needs his maps."

"What if the British attack?" asked the old colonel.

"All right, pack his maps and uniforms, because I know how men love maps and uniforms. But hurry, because I want to go home first thing in the morning."

She rampaged through the house like a conquering general as the old colonel suffered his worst defeat.

During his stay in Washington, D.C., Nathanial found time to visit the Interior Department, in his continuing hope of securing a position with the Bureau of Indian Affairs. Attired in a neatly tailored dark brown suit, he felt naked without his Army uniform and weaponry.

The Department of the Interior was located in the new Patent Office building on North G Street, not far from the White House. No one questioned Nathanial's credentials as he made his way through the building, because he appeared a lawyer or secretary to a cabinet officer, possibly even a congressman. Finally, he came to a door marked

BUREAU OF INDIAN AFFAIRS

He opened the door to an office filled with clerks. One of them looked up and said without smiling, "May I help you, sir?"

"I'd like to speak with Commissioner Denver if he's available."

"Sorry, but he's in Nebraska, negotiating a treaty with the Pawnees."

"Who'd he leave in charge."

"That would be Mister Mix, sir—The chief clerk."

"Please tell him a visitor is here."

"Your name?"

"Nathanial Barrington."

"Whom do you represent?"

Nathanial had to lie, otherwise he wouldn't get beyond the clerk. "I'm Senator Seward's new assistant."

"One moment, please."

The clerk walked off, while Nathanial examined rows of scriveners who never had seen an Indian in their lives, yet formulated policy that affected thousands. Finally, the clerk returned. "He'll see you now, sir."

Trying to appear as all-knowing as any government official, Nathanial pushed the door that had been left ajar. Seated behind the desk was an official in his forties, with graying hair and spectacles hanging on his small nose. He smiled as he arose, and was neatly attired in a conservative gray suit, bearing a resemblance to an owl. Shaking Nathanial's hand, he said, "What can I do for Senator Seward today?"

"Actually," said Nathanial affably, "I'm not Senator Seward's assistant, but a former Army officer recently returned from New Mexico Territory. I speak fluent Apache and Spanish and was wondering if a position might be available as Indian agent."

"How did you learn to speak Apache?"

"I lived among the Mimbreno clan for nearly a year. They accepted me because I'd done a favor for one of them."

There was silence as Mix studied the large, well-dressed gentleman. Unknown to the world, it was Mix who managed the day-to-day affairs of the Indian bureau, because commissioners were politically appointed and constantly changing, sometimes serving no more than a year or two. Despite his unassuming appearance, he knew more about Indians than any other man in Washington. "Have you met the present Indian agent, Doctor Michael Steck?"

"No, but I've seen him at a distance. The Apaches consider him a liar, while the Army thinks he's inept."

"Sounds like he could use an assistant, but I doubt we can give you the salary you require."

"You don't have to pay me anything. Just give a chance to save the Apaches from the Army."

Mix leaned back in his chair, weighing the decision. According to his information, Apaches were the most warlike of all Indian tribes, even worse than Comanches. "How soon can you report for duty in New Mexico Territory?" he asked.

"About two months, I'd say."

Mix smiled. "We'll take a chance with you, Barrington—perhaps a man with your unique qualifications and background can be helpful. I'll write a letter of introduction to Doctor Steck right now. It's a cauldron of hell you're stepping into, but good luck."

Nathanial returned to New York and rushed to the Saint Nicholas Hotel, eager to see his beloved wife, but found no one home, not even Rosita and Natalie.

Nathanial wanted to tell Clarissa he'd been awarded an important government position, although assistant Indian agents often were illiterate, their jobs lowly and of little consequence. He unpacked his bags, took a shot of whiskey, then another, and finally set out in search of his family.

His first stop was the office of his wife's manager, who conducted manipulations out of a building at Broadway and 12th Street, not far from Union Square and the Academy of Music. Nathanial climbed to the top floor, knocked on the door marked MARTIN THORNDYKE, but no one suggested he enter, so he turned the knob and pushed.

A gentleman with a long, thin nose sat at a desk. "I don't recall inviting you in," he said indignantly.

"I'm looking for my wife, Clarissa Barrington."

"You mean Clarissa *Rowland* Barrington. But we never reveal the location of our artists, sir."

"I'm her husband!"

"We make no exceptions."

"Where's Thorndyke?"

The man scowled. "It's *Mister* Thorndyke."

"You'd better tell me where my wife is, or I'll tear this office apart."

"If you don't leave at once, I shall call the police."

Nathanial moved to the side of the desk, tipped it over, and contracts, letters, checks, and the inkwell went flying into the air. The clerk shot to his feet, his face white as snow, but he wasn't accustomed to the manners of New Mexico Territory. Next, Nathanial knocked over a cabinet, threw a potted plant against the wall, then grabbed the front of the clerk's shirt, put him up against the wall, and said, "Well?"

"She's rehearsing at the Academy of Music," confessed the terrified man.

Clarissa sat on the gaslit stage, precisely fingering Frédéric Chopin's Ballade No. 1 in G Minor to an audience consisting of Thorndyke and a sprinkling of theater managers, plus her maid and daughter. The stage had been cleared, with the piano placed in its center. The big concert was tomorrow night, the house nearly sold out, thanks to articles by Reginald van Zweinan and other bought members of the press.

Clarissa didn't reflect upon crass business arrangements, as her fingers danced over the keys. She was lost in her world of glissading notes and cascading chords, never imagining disaster about to befall.

Dressed in a simple dress of vermillion wool, she wore no jewelry or cosmetics, her golden hair tied into a bun, accentuating her long neck. She bent over the piano and examined the keys carefully, as her delicate fingers caromed about, landing in the proper place at the critical juncture, the result of fifteen years intensive practice.

Her concentration sharp like the edge of a razor, in the most moving and nuanced section of the ballade, a commotion broke out backstage. "See here," said someone testily, "you can't walk in here like that."

"Out of my way!" declared an all-too-familiar voice.

Clarissa's fingers froze on the piano, a lump grew in her throat, and there were sounds of struggle. Clarissa had spent enough time in Santa Fe to know a punch in the mouth when she heard one, not to mention the singular noise made as a body hit the floor. She arose from the piano as her husband appeared red-faced in the wings.

Thorndyke shot to his feet. "What are you doing!" he screamed.

Nathanial leapt from the stage and, moving amazingly swiftly for a man his size, drew closer to Thorndyke. "You're lucky I don't throw you out the window."

"Nathanial," said Clarissa crossly, "please leave Mr. Thorndyke alone."

Nathanial turned to his wife. "Why is it so difficult to see you? Do I need a ticket or an introduction from that bloated pig to whom the world refers as Thorndyke?"

Clarissa became temperamental and even poisonous when her music was interrupted. Stamping her foot angrily, she said, "How dare you make a scene in the middle of my rehearsal!"

"I happen to be your husband, and I have important news."

"I am not interested in your news. You are behaving disgracefully!"

Perhaps Nathanial Barrington had been a soldier too long, but he looked for something to destroy, and then a wail went up on the far side of the orchestra. It was his daughter, awakened from her soothing musical slumber. Nathanial caught a glimpse of himself as an ill-mannered buffoon. He wanted to apologize, but false pride wouldn't let him. "I'll speak with you later," he said ominously, then headed for the door, after stepping over the unconscious form of the stage worker whom he'd knocked cold upon his arrival.

Broadway featured taverns on every block, and Nathanial entered the first he found, pushed his way to the bar, and ordered a glass of whiskey. When it arrived, he knocked it back with one smooth motion, then asked for another, which he carried to a table against the wall, sat heavily, and looked at his skinned knuckles.

He realized that lawsuits might be in the offing, not to mention a night in jail. It pained him to recall the expression of distaste on Clarissa's pretty face, but at least she knew he was not to be trifled with. Nathanial felt like buying an axe and demolishing every piano in New York.

The frontier Army had taught him to present a moving target at all times, so he finished his second drink, then meandered downtown on Broadway, stopping at more taverns, oyster cellars, and saloons. The afternoon became muddled, and he held inarticulate conversations with inebriated strangers, finally arriving at the Saint Nicholas Hotel at ten o'clock that evening. Bleary-eyed and weak about the knees, he opened the door of his suite, expecting to find Clarissa in tears, but the rooms were vacant, her clothing and that of his daughter and maid gone, a note atop the bed.

I've returned to my family.

Nathanial sat heavily, realizing his tirade had gone too far, but his wife's cool rejection had unhinged his mind, and he felt lost without the order of the Army. Moreover, his father was insane, and Mother had disapproved of everything he did from the day he was born. But worst of all, Clarissa didn't love him anymore. Alone in his bedroom, where no one could see him, he permitted his eyes to well with tears.

The Chiricahuas camped in broken country west of the Dos Cabezas Mountains, where women cured meat for the upcoming season of Ghost Face, when snow covered the land. Their refuge was a region of impossible-to-scale cliffs, box canyons, and trails that led nowhere. The *Pindah-lickoyee* and the *Nakai-yes* never had been there, and many peaks were available for observing the approach of enemies.

Cochise's hold on the Chiricahuas had tightened since his defeat of Elias and Esquiline, although those two war chiefs never would forgive him. He'd have to watch his back constantly, but at least his wisdom had provided food for Ghost Face, and after the snow melted, he would inaugurate new campaigns.

One morning word was received that a large number of riders approached from the south. Fearing a disgruntled warrior had betrayed their hideout, Cochise sent scouts to determine more closely the character of the visitors. When the scouts returned, Cochise was relieved to learn he would be host not to bluecoat soldiers, but Chief Mangas Coloradas and the Mimbreno People.

Cochise's heart gladdened, for Chief Mangas Coloradas was his father-in-law, and Cochise had become war brothers with Victorio, the chosen heir of Mangas Coloradas. There were many connections of friendship and blood between the Chiricahuas and Mimbrenos.

As the visitors drew closer, they sat not like stalwart warriors and women of the People, but slouched on their horses, their skins an unhealthy hue, and Cochise feared they were diseased. The Mimbrenos rode among the wickiups, and even their horses appeared sickly, their great heads passing barely above the ground. Finally, the procession came to a halt before the wickiup of Cochise, where the Mimbrenos dismounted. Mangas Coloradas and Victorio appeared twenty years older, skin hanging loosely on their faces, as they stepped forward. Cochise silently embraced Mangas Coloradas, then Victorio, and waited for them to speak.

Mangas Coloradas's voice was faint. "The bluecoat soldiers have invaded our homeland and inflicted many casualties, among them my war brother Cuchillo Negro, for whom I carry a heavy heart. We moved to the land of the *Nakai-yes* and sought to make peace with Colonel Garcia at Janos. He said to me, 'Let your people camp near us, and we will give you food and drink, so you do not need to make war.' I agreed, and the Mexicans were true to their word; they gave us plentiful food and drink, but then we became ill and realized they had poisoned us. So we have left the *Nakai-yes* and wish to live among you until we are well."

"You are welcome," said Cochise, "and one day we shall repay Janos for its crime."

An unsteady figure stepped forward with the help of a knobby wooden cane. Cochise recognized Nana, a notable medicine man of the Mimbrenos, who possessed the power of geese, the power of endurance, but it appeared his gift had been drowned in the poisoned wells of Janos. Nana's eyes were half closed, his lips tinged blue, as he leaned heavily on his cane. "We need the devil dance," he intoned.

Cochise bowed solemnly to the request, for the mountain spirits had ordained the devil dance to drive away evil, and the People believed evil the cause of all illness.

"We shall commence preparations at once," replied Cochise.

Nathanial doubted anyone would find him at the Atlas Hotel on Duane Street. Not frequented by traveling musicians and thespians, it wouldn't contain Clarissa's new friends, and neither was the Atlas visited by the foremost classes, for it was not especially luxurious. Nathanial rented a room facing the back alley, with office buildings and other hotels opposite, the air redolent with cooking odors from a restaurant below.

On the morning after the incident at the Academy of Music, Nathanial sat on his bed, pondering his prospects while smoking a succession of cigars and taking regular sips from a bottle. He reread the letter from Charles Mix, which directed him to proceed without delay to New Mexico Territory, but he could throw it out the window, and no one would give a damn.

Nathanial had come to the turning point of his life. He had to *do* something. Pacing back and forth, hands clasped behind his back, puffing his cigar, he decided to analyze the facts as coldly and objectively as possible.

He didn't want employment with one of his uncles, because buying and selling stocks and bonds at a desk until he keeled over did not appeal to his romantic vision. He found New York hideous, with buildings that blocked the sky, traffic barely moving, widespread crime, armies of prostitutes, the stink of smoke, garbage and offal, and a police force mired in corruption and scandal. He especially disapproved of the New York obsession with fashion and felt like a monkey whenever he put on one of his suits.

With a smile he remembered when he'd worn a breechclout and moccasin boots, a red bandanna around his head, and saw himself riding with Mangas Coloradas, Victorio, Juh, Nana, Geronimo, Chatto, Loco, and all the other Mimbreno Apaches, beneath the hot summer sun, with incredible vistas around them.

I was raised in New York, he thought, but I never felt more myself than when I rode with the Mimbrenos. Am I supposed to follow Clarissa from concert hall to concert hall, carrying her bags?

In his mind, Clarissa had abandoned him for her glorious musical career. But what kind of woman would desire the acclaim of the mob, and what do newspaper reviews have to do with music? Nathanial had graduated from the West Point Military Academy, fought in the Mexican War, and like many Americans, he believed the West was the future of the nation. Even Horace Greeley had said so, while New York was filth and false elegance. The frontier is where I belong, and I've got a job at Fort Thorn, so what am I waiting for? he asked himself.

Nathanial found his mother and father sitting to tea in the parlor when he arrived at their home on Washington Square. The colonel had been shaved, bathed, and dressed in clean clothes, appearing almost normal, were it not for the warped gleam in his eyes. His mother wore a yellow dress with navy blue bodice, golden earrings, and a ruby necklace. Nathanial couldn't remember the last time he'd seen her so happy. What is this love that makes imbeciles of us all? he wondered.

He sat with them as Belinda brought another cup and a selection of pastries, and after exchanging pleasantries, Nathanial said, "I'm afraid I have bad news."

"You have misbehaved in public," replied his mother. "But your father and I are used to that, aren't we dear?"

"Certainly," replied the colonel on cue.

Nathanial was amazed at their reconciliation. "I lost my temper, and I apologize if it blackened the family name yet again, but you needn't worry about my discourteous behavior anymore, because I've decided to return to New Mexico Territory, and I'm leaving as soon as I put my affairs in order."

"What about Clarissa?" asked his mother.

"If she wants to go West with me, that would make me very happy."

"But Nathanial, she has eight concerts scheduled. Do you expect her to give them up for you?"

"Perhaps she should have told me of this overweening aspiration before we married."

"She was so young—she hardly knew her own mind."

His father cleared his throat. "It's always important to know your own mind," he said gravely.

Who'd know better than you? thought Nathanial. "I'm going to West Point tomorrow, to say good-bye to Jeffrey."

"And Natalie?"

"She will stay with her mother."

His father leaned forward, as if he wanted to say something portentous. "Don't ever disappoint the Army," he told his son solemnly.

After the interview Nathanial headed for his tailor, for he couldn't wear old Army uniforms at Fort Thorn, and needed rugged civilian apparel. He felt relieved to have a plan of escape and couldn't wait to return to New Mexico Territory, where a man could feel like a king, instead of another ant on the New York hill.

He looked forward to sitting at a campfire with his warrior friends, and especially wanted to see Nana the medicine man, who had taught him the power of geese. This is America, he thought, and I can live anywhere I want. If Clarissa doesn't like it, she can go to hell.

He crossed Broadway and spotted a well-dressed, dark-skinned woman, probably Spanish or Italian, and she looked oddly familiar, like a certain Apache warrior woman, wife of sub-chief Juh, with whom Nathanial had enjoyed a brief hour of passion at the

Santa Rita Copper Mines. It had been during the summer of '51, and the woman on the Broadway sidewalk somewhat resembled her.

Nathanial had tried to put Jocita out of his mind, but now that he was virtually single, he couldn't help thinking about her and her light-haired son, who had no idea his father was a White Eyes, while Juh pretended the boy was his. Quite simply, Jocita had been the most erotic female Nathanial had ever known, with her long, sinewy legs, muscular body, and eyes that never failed to hypnotize him. *I wonder what she's doing these days,* thought Nathanial, as he approached the tailor shop. *Perhaps Juh has got himself killed, and she's free to marry again. And what about my half-breed Apache son? I'll bet he's real big by now.*

Fast Rider, six harvests old, limped along a trail near the encampment, fighting weakness and dizziness that threatened to overwhelm him. Arsenic coursed through his veins, eating his organs, but the Mimbrenos struggled to move about in an effort to work the evil out of their bodies.

Fast Rider had been told all his life that he was outstanding and believed it totally, his strange hair considered a mark of special recognition from the Mountain Spirits. In addition, his Uncle Geronimo had given him the power of the bat, which enables a warrior to be an expert horseman. Once when his friends were in danger, Fast Rider had stolen a horse and ridden a great distance for help. That's how he'd won his name.

Like every boy of the People, Fast Rider received regular lessons in bow and arrow, fighting hand to hand, hunting, and participating in feats of physical endurance, such as swimming in ice water or running up mountains. But now Fast Rider was skinny, his stomach full of red-hot coals. He would hate Mexicanos until the day he died, which he considered imminent. Sometimes it hurt so much, he wanted to cry. He felt humiliated that his family had to beg the Chiricahuas for charity. When I am a warrior, he thought, I would rather die than beg.

His legs trembled with weakness, then his knees gave out. He went crashing to the ground, but managed to hold his hands out, to prevent his nose from being broken. His head spun, his breath came in gasps, and sparks flew across his eyeballs. I should have stayed with Mother, but a warrior should not want his mother at all times.

A silver glow arose out of the ground before him, and Fast Rider narrowed his eyes at brightness streaming into his skull. The figure of an old man in white breechclout and moccasin boots appeared, a white bandanna around his head. Fast Rider was astounded to recognize old Miguel Narbona, the dead chief of the Chiricahuas. The boy became terrified as the ghost of Miguel Narbona approached, a terrible scar visible on his throat, raising his hand benevolently. "The Mimbreno People will be saved by the devil dance," he intoned. "The power of the People is greater than the power of poison. Go and tell this to the others."

Fast Rider bowed his head. "But I fear I will die, Chief Miguel Narbona."

"Your time has not yet come. Do not be afraid."

Tears streaming down his face, the boy struggled to his feet. "Don't go, Chief Miguel Narbona." Fast

Rider stumbled forward in an effort to touch the ghost, but was overcome by the power of the vision, and collapsed onto the ground, where he lay still as death.

Jocita, mother of Fast Rider, had been following him, despite her own poison-sickness, for she'd never let the boy out of her sight. She'd seen him on his knees, talking with someone, in the grip of a mighty vision.

Stooped, bent, with deep lines in her face, although she was only thirty-one harvests old, she kneeled beside him and rolled him onto his back. His breath came softly, there was foam on his lips, and she feared he was going to die. "Nana!" she screamed. "Geronimo!"

At the campsite the two medicine men heard their names. Tottering, they made their way to Jocita's voice. Nana, a full-blooded Mimbreno, was fifty-two, skilled in the medicinal arts, while Geronimo, thirty, of the Bedonko clan, was considered a rising medicine man of great potential.

They found mother and child in a small clearing. Geronimo chanted healing prayers, while Nana sprinkled the boy with sacred pollen. Then Nana rubbed the boy's limbs, while Geronimo wet the boy's pale lips with water. After an interval Fast Rider opened his eyes.

"Chief Miguel Narbona spoke to me," the boy said innocently.

"What did he say?" asked Nana gently.

"The devil dance will save us, for the power of the People is greater than the power of poison."

They helped the boy to the campsite as the

prophecy spread among the People. The Mimbrenos drew new hope from the words, while the Chiricahuas dedicated themselves more diligently to preparations for the devil dance.

No one was more pleased than Cochise, who went off by himself to pray. "Thank you for your words, my beloved chief," he whispered in the darkness of the cave. "Now I know you are with us, but why did you speak to a child instead of me, your chosen heir?"

No answer came, forcing Cochise to meditate upon his question. Who is this magical child, and what is his destiny? Will he be the one to save the People from the bluecoat army, not I?

Everyone congratulated Juh for the vision of his son, and Juh accepted their compliments manfully, although he knew Fast Rider was not his flesh and blood.

Juh was chief of the Nednai, a tribe that once had lived in the Sierra Madre Mountains of Sonora, but now traveled with the larger Mimbreno group, where he had become a sub-chief. A fierce fighter covered with scarred slabs of muscle, he was respected nearly as much as Victorio, and could become overall chief of the Mimbrenos if anything happened to Mangas Coloradas and Victorio.

But even a chief of the Nednai needed sons, so he'd left the barren Jocita for Ish-keh, his second wife. Then Jocita secretly had become pregnant by Sunny Bear, and Juh had to pretend the boy was his, otherwise they'd consider him unworthy of leadership.

Juh couldn't understand why Jocita had produced a son with Sunny Bear, but not him. It seemed as if the Mountain Spirits had played a cruel joke on Juh, espe-

cially since he'd loved Jocita more than Ish-keh.
Sometimes he wanted to kill Jocita for her treachery.

Juh tended to bury personal worries in obsessive
hatred, so his thoughts turned to Janos, where Mexicanos had poisoned him. It gave him pleasure to know
that the People would utterly demolish the town after
the devil dance had worked its cure. We shall have revenge, he told himself, as he lay in his wickiup,
breathing laboriously. Like many other residents of
New Mexico Territory, Juh found it easier to hate than
love.

4

Clarissa's Academy of Music concert was sold out, for wealthy New Yorkers in search of new thrills were eager to see the much-publicized female virtuoso who'd gone West, rubbed elbows with gamblers, cattle rustlers, and wild Indians, and played the piano with such panache. No one admitted they might be deceived by their own enthusiasm, for false hopes and joyful pretension were indispensable in New York society.

In the course of the concert Clarissa gave her audience Haydn, Beethoven, and Scarlatti, to whom they responded appreciatively. They especially enjoyed the medley of popular songs and clapped hands heartily following her rendition of "Old Folks at Home," by Stephen Collins Foster.

As Clarissa's fingers raced lightly over the keys, she recalled when she was a child, dreaming of becoming a concert pianist wearing gorgeous gowns. How many people's dreams come true? she asked herself, as her fingers pressed an emphatic chord.

How dare Nathanial interfere with my art? she demanded, as she lightly touched a high C. Who does he think he is? Dissatisfaction concerning Nathanial gave a particular edge to her performance, as if she wanted to prove she was more than merely his dutiful little wife. What has he ever done? she mused. His only talent is violence, but what talent is that?

Following her final selection, she rose from the piano, advanced to the footlights, and bowed to the audience, their cheers and shouts trembling the rafters of the hall. Flowers rained upon the stage, and one bounced off her coiffure as she blew them all a kiss. So huge was the reception that she played one encore judiciously selected for such an eventuality.

While taking her last bow, she scanned the jubilant crowd, glad her husband was absent and therefore unable to embarrass her. She'd never realized he was such a boor, and it troubled her to know she remembered him during her greatest triumph. She gazed at smiling faces, saw love and admiration, and thought perhaps she wasn't the awkward and inexperienced woman she sometimes suspected herself to be.

I always knew that greatness resided within me, she thought. Now it has been confirmed, and nothing will stop me from performing again, certainly not my ill-mannered husband. If he ever bothers me again, I'll have him arrested.

The white paddle wheeler steamship plowed up the mighty Hudson, and Nathanial stood at the rail, wrapped in a high-collared black wool topcoat extending to his calves, plus a black knitted sailor cap. He felt as if he were on the funeral barge of his marriage, surrounded by the Jersey Palisades and the towering Hudson Highlands.

It was late October, the leaves red and gold, the air

filled with the sweet odor of crumbling decay. *The Hudson valley is magnificent*, he realized, *but I love the raw beauty of the frontier, where a man can make himself anew, without regard for whether his wife has left him, or if his father is a madman.*

The steamer stopped at West Point; Nathanial and a few visitors debarked on the pier, then climbed the steps to the plain on which the great institution was situated. Nathanial remembered the day he'd first arrived, filled with optimism and fear, then walked across the parade field on which he'd marched under the watchful eyes of Army officers. Standing in the ranks with classmates, he'd dreamed of becoming a general one day, but instead had resigned his commission after a brief, undistinguished military career. *What made me think I was destined for high command?* he asked himself. *In truth, I am a useless man, but I dare not communicate my doubts to Jeffrey, because I don't want to undermine his confidence and permit him to contemplate that he might carry the disease of insanity.*

Nathanial sucked in his stomach, squared his shoulders, and pulled his chin back, as he marched into the administration building. He identified himself to the first clerk he saw as Captain Nathanial Barrington of the 1st Dragoons, neglecting to mention he'd resigned his commission, then inquired as to the whereabouts of his brother. The clerk examined a roster, then said, "Mathematics class."

Nathanial retreated down the corridor, emerged outside, and was on his way to the academic building, when a voice called out, "Is it Nathanial Barrington I see?"

A diminutive gentleman about Nathanial's age, wearing a closely clipped black mustache, gray civil-

ian topcoat, white shirt, and red cravat stood before
him. Nathanial tried to remember his name.

"George McClellan," said the former underclass-
man of Nathanial's, holding out his hand. "Don't you
remember me?"

"But you weren't wearing a mustache in those
days, and you've gained weight, I see."

"So have you," said George Brinton McClellan, son
of a Philadelphia lawyer.

Both men examined each other, estimating the
wreckage that only time can provide. Nathanial had
heard about McClellan, for the younger man had been
considered one of the most promising junior officers
in the Army, an aide to General Scott during the Mex
ican War, and Secretary of War Jefferson Davis's
choice to report on the Crimean War.

"What're you doing these days?" asked Nathanial.

"I'm vice president and chief engineer for the Illinois Central Railroad, and my office is in Chicago,
but I've come to New York for a business meeting,
because the failure of the economy has undermined
the strength of the company. In fact, I may be unem
ployed soon. Are you still in the Army?"

"I resigned my commission a few months ago and
have just secured a position as assistant Indian agent
in New Mexico Territory." Nathanial felt embar
rassed, for assistant Indian agent was many steps
down from vice president and chief engineer of a rail
road.

"Sounds like an interesting job," said McClellan,
apparently trying to be polite.

Nathanial decided to change the subject. "I fol
lowed the Crimean War in the newspapers and won
dered what really happened at the charge of the Light

Brigade. Since you were in the region at the time, what have you heard?"

"I didn't actually view the charge," explained McClellan, "but it was led by Lord Cardigan, who had bought his commission and had no real battle experience, while his commanding officer was Lord Lucan, who also had bought his commission and was equally inept. Add to that poor communications and inadequate intelligence concerning the Russians, and that's what caused six hundred men to be killed, according to what I've heard. At least in the American Army, an officer must earn his rank, not buy it like a bolt of cloth at a Broadway store."

Their conversation was interrupted by the whistle of the paddle wheeler returning to New York City. "Got to be going," said McClellan. "If you're ever in Chicago, you must look me up."

They shook hands, then McClellan ran toward the landing, leaving Nathanial staring at him in awe. Nathanial wondered why George McClellan was vice president and chief engineer for a railroad and had been selected for special European duty by then Secretary of War Jefferson Davis, while he, Nathanial Barrington, never had been selected for anything.

He continued to the academic building, where he sat on the front steps and contemplated what he perceived as his many inadequacies. I've failed at my career, two marriages, and everything else except apprentice warrior among the Mimbrenos. How odd.

Cadets spilled out of the academic building, and Nathanial arose, looking for his brother. Faces rushed past, animated with exuberance, dedication, purpose, mischief, and confusion, as had been his. He spotted a curly-haired blond lad, with broad shoulders and a slim waist, carrying books, chatting with friends. Nathanial angled toward him and said, "Hello, brother."

Jeffrey stopped. "Nathanial—what are you doing here?"

"I came to say good-bye."

"Where are you going?"

"West."

"But you just arrived!"

"Do you think we could have dinner together, and I'll explain everything."

"I'll ask my commanding officer."

Jeffrey ran off, and Nathanial vowed not to plague his brother with his lugubrious musings. After a while, Jeffrey returned and said, "I must be back by eight."

They walked toward the front gate, glancing at each other out of the corners of their eyes, for this could be their last meeting in many years, if not forever.

"Why are you going away?" asked Jeffrey.

"I've found a job as assistant Indian agent in New Mexico Territory, and Clarissa and I have become estranged. She's become a concert pianist and evidently feels imprisoned by marriage."

"But you're reasonable people. Surely you can settle your differences."

"If I remain in New York, I might well strangle the bitch. You should see how she treats me, like one of her servants. Have you ever been in love, little brother?"

"How can I be in love when I've spent nearly three years where there are no women?"

They passed through the gate and continued to the town of Highland Falls, which consisted of small homes and farms, the most notable structure a tavern known as Benny Haven's, a mecca for thirsty travelers and cadets who dared sneak away from West Point discipline.

It was a small, rough-hewn cabin with a bar and fourteen tables, military accoutrements hanging from nails banged into the walls. Only a few civilians were present when Nathanial and Jeffrey arrived.

"How're you getting along?" asked Nathanial after they were seated.

"I've been thinking about leaving West Point," replied Jeffrey.

"For what?"

"I don't know, exactly."

The waiter brought whiskey for Nathanial and lager for Jeffrey. The brothers clicked glasses, and Jeffrey studied his brother, who took a few gulps of refreshment. Jeffrey had admired his older brother at a distance all his life, Nathanial appearing almost mythic, because he'd fought in the Mexican War, slept with countless women, and lived with the Apaches. Jeffrey believed he'd never be a man like his brother.

After reflection Nathanial said, "I suggest you remain where you are, since you feel no powerful attraction to another profession. You'll receive a sound engineering education, learn self-discipline, and you're not being a wastrel. Besides, if the nation keeps on the way it's going, we'll all be in uniform anyway. It's better to be an officer, because officers don't scrub pots and pans and clean latrines. You're a Barrington, after all, and speaking of Barringtons, it may interest you to know that your father has gone insane."

Jeffrey nearly dropped his fork. "My God—is he in an asylum?"

"He's living with Mother on Washington Square, and she's pretending they're a happily married couple. When you return home for Christmas, just act as though Mother and Father never separated, and all's wonderful."

"Sometimes it's embarrassing to have such a family," said Jeffrey sheepishly.

"Every family has at least one lunatic, so I wouldn't worry about it if I were you. If you never betray a fellow soldier, you have nothing to fear."

They discussed West Point, family matters, and the Army; soon it was eight o'clock. The brothers hugged good-bye on the plain, then Jeffrey returned to the castellated barracks in which he resided, and Nathanial caught the last steamship to New York City.

Next morning, Jeffrey sneaked into the mammoth West Point kitchen, where he observed an exhausted man surrounded by huge pots and greasy black frying pans, scrubbing away in a deep sink. While studying this singular individual, who was drenched with sweat and soapy water, his color deep green, with an utterly miserable expression on his face, Jeffrey became more clearly aware of the superior benefits of becoming an officer. And thus Cadet Barrington determined to remain at West Point, manipulated by his older brother yet again.

At Fort Buchanan Major Enoch Steen stood at his map, wondering what town or ranch would be the next target of the Apaches. There was a knock at the door. "Come in," he called.

The door opened on Raphael Fonseca, the rancher who'd been found nearly dead in the Sonoita Valley, then nursed back to health at Fort Buchanan. "Good afternoon, Senor Fonseca," said Major Steen. "So good to see you up and around."

"The doctor says I am well enough to travel," said Fonseca weakly. "My brother lives in Mesilla, but I have no money, horse, or anything except my life and these clothes given me by the Army. I was wondering if I could borrow from the Army, so I can travel to my brother's home."

"There is regular traffic between Fort Buchanan and Fort Thorn, which is near Mesilla," replied Major Steen. "Next time we make the trip, we'd be happy to take you along."

"Gracias."

Fonseca shuffled out of the office, a huge purple scar on his sunken left cheek, but a more painful one on his heart. The loss of his wife and children still devastated him, and he could not believe a decent God would permit such crimes.

A detachment of dragoons approached from the other direction, but Fonseca barely noticed them, so lost was he in fantasies of retribution. He saw himself hacking Apaches with a hatchet, their arms and heads flying through the air, a river of blood beneath his feet. For only blood could compensate for the murder of his family. As the dragoons rode past, guidon flag fluttering in the breeze, Fonseca plotted his future.

When well, he thought, I shall seek out Apaches and kill as many as I can. And I won't stop until one of them kills me. For I died on the night my family was murdered, and I was spared to become their avenging angel. *Death to the Apache* shall be my creed from this day on.

* * *

Due to preparations for the devil dance, Cochise had not found time to smoke with his warrior brother Victorio. Finally, he stopped all tasks, collected pipe, tobacco, bow and arrows, and headed for the wickiup where Victorio and his family lay, recovering from poison. He called Victorio's name and said, "Come smoke with me."

There was a groan, then finally Victorio's head appeared. "I am too sick," he said.

"Soon the devil dance will cure you. Give me your arm."

Cochise helped Victorio into the wilderness, and some distance from camp, lowered him onto a carpet of needles in a grove of bristlecone pines. Cochise gathered twigs, made a small fire, added larger branches, and finally sat opposite Victorio. From a leather pouch Cochise took a hefty pinch of tobacco, placed it on an oak leaf, rolled it into a fat cigarette, and passed it to Victorio.

The smoking mixture consisted of wild tobacco and Americano tobacco mixed with herbs, leaves and roots sprinkled with mescal juice by Nana the Medicine Man. Cochise and Victorio puffed alternately and soon felt relaxed, even mildly euphoric. "How have you been faring since Miguel Narbona passed on?" asked Victorio.

"Whenever I have doubts," replied Cochise, "I ask what Chief Miguel Narbona would do."

"You have gained power, while I have suffered setbacks. A bluecoat soldier shot me not long ago." Victorio laboriously lowered his breechclout and showed a red scar on his groin. "And now I am poisoned. But we must develop plans, because the bluecoat Army is headed this way."

"That will be their mistake," replied Cochise, "because the People shall not run away. Here in the Chiricahua Mountains we will make our stand."

As they sat and smoked, planning great deeds, it appeared as if Miguel Narbona and Cuchillo Negro were standing in the bright blue sky above them, offering blessings.

Nathanial walked down Broadway, passing theaters, restaurants, and high-priced merchandise emporiums. Approaching from the opposite direction, amid stylish shoppers, were about a dozen little girls, ragged and filthy, making raucous remarks and gestures, skipping along. Good ladies clutched their purses, while gentlemen placed hands on their wallets.

One of the scandals of New York was roving bands of derelict girls who engaged in theft, prostitution, and occasionally murder, according to newspaper reports. Nathanial examined them closely as they passed, for he'd never seen such a spectacle. They looked like ragged imps, but were mostly Irish children from the poorest classes, their parents too busy working or getting drunk to care for them, and according to the *Tribune*, many had been born out of wedlock.

One of the scrawny, dirty-faced urchins, who had curly red hair, looked at Nathanial and made a face. "What're you lookin' at, mister?"

"Everything," he replied.

"Well, keep yer dirty eyes to yerself!"

If she were a man, Nathanial would have punched her through a store window. But what does one do with poor, neglected little girls? he wondered. Take her home and give her a bath? He reached into his pocket and pulled out a handful of coins, picked out a five-dollar piece, and flipped it to her. "Have a bowl of soup on me."

Suddenly, the girls were all over him, and one smacked his hands upward. Coins went flying into the air, and the little girls jumped gleefully, or crawled along the gutter, retrieving them. They reminded Nathanial of vultures at the carcass of a deer.

He joined other pedestrians crossing the street to escape from the hoydens. Then a policeman blew a whistle, and the girls scattered like Apaches. Nathanial couldn't help admiring the saucy little wretches. They are the Indians of New York, he realized.

He didn't feel like talking with a policeman, so continued on his journey to Delmonico's and a meeting with his adopted brother, Tobey. Delmonico's was at 25 Broadway, with white tablecloths and wood-paneled walls displaying oil paintings of hunting scenes. The headwaiter ushered Nathanial to a table near the middle of the dining room, where Tobey rose to his feet, a frown on his face. "You're late again, Nathanial."

"I was accosted by a band of child criminals, and I'm afraid they took my money. I hope you have enough for both of us."

"I always carry assets with me," said Tobey, a note of reproach in his voice.

Nathanial made allowances for Tobey, who had been a street urchin himself, rescued by Nathanial, or who had been rescued by him, one afternoon seven years before when Nathanial had passed out cold due to excessive whiskey consumption on a sidewalk near Printing House Square.

"I always carry money too," replied Nathanial, "and it's not my fault I was robbed."

"Why is it you're always in trouble, while most people lead perfectly tranquil lives?"

"You talk as if I'm to blame for everything."

"You are."

Nathanial studied Tobey, who looked like a gentleman of the upper classes, because he was trying desperately to escape his childhood in Five Points, the most dangerous neighborhood in Calcutta-on-the-Hudson. "The reason I wanted to see you was to say good-bye," said Nathanial. "I'm leaving for the frontier in a few days."

Tobey appeared shocked, as the waiter appeared with his notepad. Nathanial ordered baked halibut, because such delicacies were nonexistent in New Mexico Territory, while Tobey asked for roast chicken. The waiter departed, then Tobey leaned across the table and said, "What about Clarissa's concert tour?"

"Clarissa has left me, and I've landed a job with the Bureau of Indian Affairs in New Mexico Territory. Besides, I need the fragrance of greasewood in the morning, with mountains and vistas where a man can spread out his mind. For example, if we were sitting in a saloon in Santa Fe right now, I could pull out my pistol and shoot a bullet through the ceiling. But such an act would be unthinkable at Delmonico's."

Tobey appeared confused. "Why would anyone want to shoot a hole into the ceiling?"

"Sometimes it makes a man feel better."

"But that's stupid."

"Just because someone disagrees with you, that doesn't make him stupid."

"What's intelligent about shooting a bullet into the ceiling?"

"Haven't you ever felt the need to do something outrageous?"

"Whatever for?"

Nathanial realized a vast gulf lay between Tobey and himself. "I suppose you're right," he conceded in the hope of dodging the issue. "Have you been home lately?"

"I've been studying." Tobey lived in a hotel for students near the new Columbia College uptown at 49th and Fifth Avenue.

"Did you know that Father is back?"

"Of course—I visit my parents more than you."

"While I'm gone, you'll have to watch over them."

"Have you ever stopped to consider that *you* have an obligation to your parents?"

"Sounds like you're not pleased with me, little brother."

"You're a completely selfish man."

"Have you ever been in love?"

"Do you know how much reading I must do?" replied Tobey. "Sometimes I feel as if I'm going blind. And what does love have to do with anything?"

"It is the inspiration for life," declared Nathanial.

"You've become bored with Clarissa, and it's time for more adventures on the frontier—is that it? And as for little Natalie, she'll have to get along on her own."

"You've become an acerbic, self-righteous son-of-a-bitch. I can't wait to see when you're forty."

"At the rate you're going, you won't be alive when I'm forty."

"I'm sure that'll make you very happy."

Tobey leaned forward. "Do you know what happened when everybody thought you were dead? Your mother nearly died, and probably it drove your father mad. Thanks to you, Jeffrey is at West Point, anxious to follow your scandalous footsteps, and he'll probably be the first killed when he arrives on the frontier, because he's not nearly as much of a bully as you. You're driven by an abnormal need to be admired, and I shouldn't talk to you this way, but don't you appreciate all your parents have done for you?"

"Do you know what Apaches do when their people get old? They leave them behind to die in peace, and I think it's far more humane than letting them become feebleminded. Hell, I don't want to live unless I can care for myself. Have you ever stopped to think you might be killed walking the streets of this city someday?"

"Have you ever stopped to think you might be a fraud?"

Before Nathanial could respond, the meal was served. But he had lost his appetite. "You don't understand how bitter and angry you are," replied Nathanial. "If you don't put love in your heart, you'll be a dried-out old fig."

"Who'm I supposed to love—you?"

"Yes, and everyone else. That's what it says in the Bible."

"Even the Devil quotes scriptures, they say."

Nathanial decided to stop debating a law student. Neither man spoke for the rest of the meal, which they consumed hurriedly. Declining dessert, they departed the restaurant, and on the sidewalk, shook hands, wishing each other well perfunctorily, then parted and never looked back, hearts brimming with mutual disapproval.

* * *

Cochise sat in front of his wickiup, observing members of the masked dancer society making costumes, headdresses, and magic wands for the devil dance. Meanwhile, musicians practiced in a far-off canyon where no one could hear, and all Chiricahuas purified themselves through fasting, abstinence, and prayer. The more they gave themselves to the devil dance, the more likely the exorcism would be effective.

Coyuntura approached Cochise. "I have seen something amazing," he said. "The Mimbrenos have a piece of lightning-blasted wood this big." Coyuntura held his arms in a circle.

Cochise was impressed, because lightning-blasted wood was sacred to the People, and Cochise never had seen a chunk that large. "Show me."

Coyuntura led Cochise into the wilderness, passing clumps of fernbush and tomatillo. They came to a clearing where the sick Mimbrenos lay in a large circle, eyes closed, around a jagged chunk of lightning-blasted wood on a gray-and-red striped blanket.

Cochise gazed at the magic substance. Somehow it had remained intact, though scorched and ripped, whereas most lightning-blasted wood shattered into splinters. That meant the wood was stronger than the mighty thunder spirits and worthy of veneration. Cochise dropped to a cross-legged position and bowed to the wood, then closed his eyes and proceeded to meditate.

His face felt warm, time passed effortlessly, and before dusk, Nana rose slowly to his feet, the signal the devotion had come to an end. Nana stretched jerkily, then bent down to place the wood in its holy deerskin bag. Since Nana was so weak, he was assisted by

Geronimo, the warrior-medicine man of the Bedonko clan, and Mangas Coloradas himself. Cochise joined them and said, "May I touch it?"

Nana held the bag open. Cochise placed his hand on the sacred wood, which felt like a lump of warm coal, and something in his elbow twitched, a sign that power had been awarded. Cochise felt as if it were raining, although the sun shone. "Where did you get it?"

"It was given us by Sunny Bear."

Cochise didn't recognize the name. "Who is Sunny Bear?"

Nana struggled to throw the bag over his shoulder. "Sunny Bear was a bluecoat war chief who lived among us for a time, but then went back to his people."

Cochise appeared astonished. "But . . . why . . . how?"

"There was a battle, he was fighting against us, but then he saved the life of Jocita. Soon thereafter he was wounded, so we healed him and taught him our ways. After that he had many visions and killed a bear that surprised him alone in the mountains. Another day he was struck by lightning, and it left a white streak in his hair, here." Nana pointed to his head.

Cochise was astounded by this information. "Where is Sunny Bear now?"

"He has returned to the eastern lands. Or perhaps his luck has run out, and he is dead. Or maybe he will be back one day. It is hard to know about a warrior such as Sunny Bear.

Nathanial entered a small shop on Bleecker Street. Colorful dolls adorned the walls, hung from the ceiling, and were displayed in glass cases. The dollmaker was in his forties, with a graying blond beard, a small nose, eyeglasses, and eager little eyes. "How old is the child?" he asked pleasantly in a German accent.

"Almost one."

"Boy or girl?"

"Girl."

"A one-year-old girl vill vant a good friend like Fritz." The dollmaker plucked from the ceiling a rag boy doll in blue polka dot shorts.

Nathanial stared at the dollmaker's creation, whose painted face smiled back at him. "All the children love Fritz," said the dollmaker.

Nathanial tucked Fritz under his arm and prepared for the ordeal of parting with his daughter, as if a piece of his flesh was breaking away. As he strolled uptown, he cautioned himself not to lose his temper at Clarissa, but neither could he fall at her feet and beg forgiveness. I must be calm, he told himself—like General Zachary Taylor at Palo Alto.

There were taverns aplenty on his route, and Nathanial stopped at 8th Street for his first snort, setting wrapped Fritz on the bar. His second and third refills came at a cellar tavern on 15th, and by the time he hit Gramercy Park, he was mellow, philosophical, and expecting to create a spectacle before his wife and in-laws.

I'll be gone in a few days, so it won't matter, he told himself as he hit the rapper. He remembered how happy he'd been when first he'd courted Clarissa, and how furious he felt toward her now.

The door opened, and a middle-aged, kind-faced Irish maid appeared. "Hello, Captain Barrington," she said cheerily. "Right this way, sir."

She led him across the parlor, where Nathanial had sat many times with his prospective in-laws, anxious to get their daughter into bed. Finally, he'd succeeded, they had a child together, and now it had come to farewell. They arrived at a door on the second floor, the Irish maid knocked, then retreated diplomatically.

The door was opened by Rosita, the Mexican maid. "So you have come at last," she said crossly.

Nathanial did not feel obligated to make explanations, but could not look her in the eye as he headed toward the rug where little Natalie sat with a wooden rattle, gazing blankly at the great man come to visit. He lifted her into the air and kissed her pudgy cheek. Natalie hugged her huge father, who always smelled of whiskey and tobacco. A smile came over her toothless face as their cheeks touched. She looked at him in amazement, for he seemed so mighty, even stronger than Mother.

"I'm going away," Nathanial told his child. "Goodbye, my little princess. Fritz will take care of you while I'm gone."

He pulled off the wrapping, held out Fritz, and the child made gurgle sounds as she reached for the bright-colored fellow. How can I leave my child? Nathanial asked himself. But if I remain in New York, I'm liable to murder her mother or blow my brains out.

The atmosphere felt oppressive, so he kissed his child on the head, squeezed her shoulder, and headed for the door, Rosita at his heels. "I want to talk with you," she said.

Oh no, thought Nathanial.

She folded her arms and said, "This is a very bad thing you are doing."

"My wife doesn't want to be married anymore, and I don't feel like remaining in New York. If you want to return to New Mexico, I'll pay your expenses."

"Perhaps you can desert your daughter, senor. But I cannot."

"Her mother has caused this little tragedy, not me."

"You are a very clever talker."

"It's better than strangling Clarissa."

Rosita narrowed an eye. "Is it that bad?"

"Afraid so."

She nodded sagely. "Then you had better go while there is time."

"If you need anything, get in touch with my mother. And thank you for being so good to my daughter."

He hugged Rosita, then turned abruptly and descended the stairs three at a time, causing much noise and the trembling of beams in the house.

"Good day, sir," said the Irish maid, bowing at the door.

Nathanial tried to smile, but tears rolled down his cheeks as he reached the sidewalk. Nearly blinded by sorrow, he headed west on 21st Street, as the maid observed his passage, then closed the door and returned to the parlor.

"Is he gone?" asked a voice from the library.

"Yes."

The door opened, then Herbert and Myra Rowland appeared, followed by Clarissa. "Thank God," said Myra, a stout, bespectacled warship of a woman.

"What did he say?" asked Clarissa of the maid.

"He is leaving for the frontier, ma'am."

Clarissa felt relieved that the impediment had been removed, yet felt plagued by the failure of her marriage. Should I run after him? she asked herself. But fame beckoned. If he can't accompany me into my new future, it's better that he goes away.

"Clarissa, I do believe you're crying," said her mother.

"It's nothing," replied Clarissa, brushing the tear with a knuckle.

"Your mother and I tried to warn you," said her father, a portly banker in a dark green suit. "It's not surprising that he's left you."

"He's very proud," explained Clarissa.

"I think he's ignorant," replied her mother. "Giving up everything for frontier living." She tapped her head. "If you ask me, I think he's got the same illness as his father.

Clarissa said impulsively, "I'm tired of talking about him, thinking about him, and being afraid of him. If you don't mind, I've got work to do."

Before practicing the piano, Clarissa decided to look in on Natalie, who was having an incomprehensible baby conversation with a gaudy, grinning doll. Clarissa knelt beside Natalie, who glanced at her, then returned to her new companion. Rosita sat on the sofa, crying. Clarissa wanted to join her, but felt relief at jettisoning her domineering husband. She kissed her child, then returned to the piano, where she poured her anger and misery into Bach's *Italian* Concerto.

Nathanial worked his way downtown, making regular stops for liquid refreshment. When he reached Union Square, his gait was unsteady and night was dropping like a black cloud over Manhattan Island. He passed the bronze equestrian statue of George Washington at the southern end of the square, threw

him a salute, crossed 14th Street, and nearly was
trampled by an omnibus.

Offices were letting out, the sidewalks crowded
with pedestrians, and Nathanial felt as if his heart still
were in Gramercy Park. I thought Clarissa and I were
star-crossed lovers, but love is just the glorified excuse to fornicate like hound dogs.

His first love, Layne Satterfield, had left him. So
had his first wife, the former Maria Dolores Carbajal,
who resided in Santa Fe with two of his other children, Zachary and Carmen. And now his second wife
was continuing the tradition. They all loved me madly
at first, but changed once they knew me better. What
disgusting creature lurks within me?

Finally, he came to Pfaff's, filled with familiar
faces but no friends that time of day. All the tables
were taken, so he joined the crowd at the bar, ordered
a mug of beer, and sipped it among the others, hoping
someone would jostle him, so he'd have an opportunity for a fight. But he knew punches would solve
nothing, and indeed produce worse results, for the
person he blamed most was himself. There's something foul about me, he decided.

Nathanial needed fresh air, so he staggered outside,
managed to remain upright, and teetered toward
Washington Square Park, where he collapsed onto a
bench and sat in the darkness, gazing at the home in
which he'd been raised. Lights shone in the windows,
and he could imagine his parents sipping tea together.
The world seemed off-kilter to Nathanial, as if he
were slipping into the void.

I sure wish Nana the *di-yin* medicine man were
here, he thought. A smile came to Nathanial's lips as
he remembered happy times among the People. A

warrior must plunge onward and not worry about unworthy considerations. He lit a cigar as he recalled raiding with Victorio, Nana, Geronimo, and the other warriors. What a thrill it had been, a sensation of raw power. That is my world, and an Apache woman never would leave her husband for a piano. I must get out of this stinking hell called New York City, he thought, and I'll buy what I need on the trail.

He crossed the park, a new spring in his step. Continuing downtown on Mercer Street, he passed a row of whorehouses, where gentlemen entered or departed, with the occasional covey of street prostitutes chatting in the shadows.

Everything in New York is for sale, thought Nathanial. Like that damned wife of mine. Who the hell does she think she is? Why, she was nothing when I met her, and I made a woman out of her.

Nathanial wanted to fall down and howl his guts out, but he'd land in the Bloomingdale Asylum. When I return to New Mexico, he decided, the first thing I'll do is buy a horse, ride onto the desert a ways, and scream at the top of my lungs. He turned the corner onto Grand Street, deserted except for an old drunk heading toward Broadway on the far sidewalk. Nathanial looked at him and thought, that'll be me if I'm not careful.

Nathanial blinked, wondering if he were dreaming. A pack of goblins emerged suddenly from shadows beneath shop windows closed for the night, then leapt upon the man, who hollered at the top of his lungs, "Halp!"

A lead pipe connected with the drunkard's skull, he dropped to his knees, but far ahead at Broadway a group of pedestrians appeared, among them a policeman. "Halt—you little thieves!" he yelled, then blew his whistle.

The goblins scattered, some diving into the murky shadows that had spawned them, other, fleeing west on the opposite sidewalk, and one cut into the middle of the street, heading toward Nathanial, who held himself motionless in a doorway. As the imp drew closer, Nathanial realized it was the red-haired female street urchin he'd seen earlier, a crazed expression in her eyes as she clutched her victim's wallet. She ran frantically on thin legs, then glanced back to see whether the copper was gaining on her, and when she came abreast of Nathanial, he reached down and snatched her out of the night, then held the squirming struggling child and examined her at closer range.

She was filthy, ragged, smelly, and she tried to bite his hand. "Settle down," he told her calmly.

Her eyes filled with crocodile tears. "Please don't turn me over to the coppers, mister."

She spoke with a faint Irish brogue, and he guessed she was around nine years old. He realized that fate had dealt him a creature even worse off than himself. Meanwhile, the copper blew his whistle and ran toward the downed citizen, and other coppers in the vicinity whistled that they were on the way. The other thieves had disappeared.

Nathanial slipped into the alley, holding the child like a sack of flour. He ran the alley's length, crossed a street, hopped a fence, and landed behind a store closed for the night. Then he set her down next to a barrel filled with trash, and they regarded each other in the dim light. "We'll wait here," he said, releasing her.

She glanced about for avenues of escape. "What you gonna do wi' me?" she asked nervously.

"A few weeks in the Tombs might be appropriate." He referred to the city prison on Centre Street.

She attempted to run, but he grabbed her wrist. Then she made more crocodile tears. "Please don't send me to the Tombs, sir," she begged. "They'll put me with the bad girls, and one of 'em might kill me."

"Perhaps it's what you need, to cure you of your wicked ways."

"I'll never do it again, sir. Here—take the money for yourself."

She held out the wallet, her hands trembled, and he realized she was a frightened child who didn't get many square meals. "We'll give it to the police," he replied, snatching it out of her hands. "Where do you live?"

She looked at him defiantly. "Five Points."

"Where are your parents?"

"My maw's in jail, and I never knew my paw."

Poor, pathetic little thing, thought Nathanial. She might be cute if she weren't so damned dirty. "When's the last time you had a good meal?"

She placed her grimy little fists on her hips. "Well, I was gonna have one afore you come along."

"I'd take you to a restaurant, but you're a disgrace. You can come to my hotel and have a bath, but I don't have children's clothes."

She narrowed an eye. "You ain't one of them fancy fellers what likes little girls, are you?"

"I love little girls, but not the way you think. Besides, who would touch you, you're so grimy. I certainly wouldn't force you to come with me."

She smiled and wagged her hips from side to side. "Will you buy me a pretty dress?"

"Anything you want."

She seemed prepared to accompany him, then hesitated. "I'm not sure I trust you."

"I don't trust you either. But as I said, it's up to you."

"I'm not as bad as you think," she said in a surly voice.

"You're probably worse. Have you ever killed anybody, with your pipe?"

"I never stay long enough to find out."

He realized she was not inherently evil, but fought to survive like the gutter rat that she was. "I'm going home," he said wearily. "It's been a terrible day."

"Why don't you leave the wallet wi' me?"

"Because it's not yours."

"That old drunk can afford it."

"I will feed and clothe you, but I will not assist your life of crime. Wouldn't you like to be a nice girl, instead of the filthy little criminal that you are?"

"If somebody ever called me nice, I'd be insulted," she snarled. "And I ain't afraid of you, neither."

"Well, I sure as hell am afraid of you, because you're liable to walk up behind me some night and hit me with a lead pipe. Are you coming or not?"

"You won't call the coppers?"

"You belong in the Tombs, but I'm not the man who'll put you there. Well?"

"Lemme think about it."

He tipped his hat, then headed for Broadway. She stood in the dark alley, scowling at his receding figure. Hungry, alone, she shivered as cool autumn air sliced through holes and tears in her clothing. She had no family, prospects, school, or church, and feared one day she'd be sent to the Tombs.

She wanted to believe the big gentleman. He seemed softhearted and obviously wealthy. She was confident of her ability to fight, scream, or run like the wind should he get fresh. Besides, *I got nothin' to live fer anyways,* she thought. With a shrug she ran after him. "Hey, mister—wait fer me!"

Thus did Nathanial Barrington place a new burden upon himself, but she was one of God's neediest children, and Christ had admonished all Christians to *Feed my sheep*. He held out his hand. "Who are you?"

She placed her small, birdlike palm in his and said, "They calls me Gertie, but I hate that name."

"Who would you like to be?"

She pinched her lips together, then looked up, as if pondering the question. "Gloria."

"Then Gloria it is, and we'll forget old Gertie." He took her hand, towering over her as they walked side by side down Broadway, denizens of the night observing the ragged child and her well-dressed companion. "I am Nathanial Barrington."

"Can I have anything to eat I want?"

"And as much as you want. If you stay with me, I'll send you to school. Wouldn't you like to know things, like why trees grow, and why dogs bark?"

"I know why dogs bark—when they're hungry."

"And when you're crawling through the back window of a house that doesn't belong to you, I imagine."

"Once I stoled a big jool." Her eyes danced delightedly.

"What did you do with it?"

"Sold it to a feller in Chatham Square."

"Who probably robbed you more than you robbed that house. From now on you won't have to steal. And we're going on a little trip."

"Where?"

"New Mexico Territory."

"Is that near New Rochelle."

"It's on the frontier. You've heard of the frontier, I assume."

"It's where the Injuns are."

"It'll take about a month to get there, but I think you can manage it."

She stopped suddenly, tears in her eyes. "This ain't happenin'. It must be a dream." She pinched her arms. "Why are you helpin' me? I ain't nothin' to you."

The drink swirled in his mind. "I want you to show me the innocence I once had, although I doubt you have any left."

"Don't you have a wife?"

"I've had two official wives, and a few others. It's awfully complicated."

Out of the night approached a copper in his leather hat, club tucked beneath his arm. "What've we got here?" he asked suspiciously.

"My friend found something," replied Nathanial, holding out the wallet.

The copper accepted it. "What're you doing with this child, mister?"

"I'm going to feed and clothe her, and if she's agreeable, I'm going to adopt her. Unless you want to take her home with you."

"Oh, hell no. I've got five of my own."

Nathanial and Gloria continued to the Atlas Hotel and found a crew of traveling salesmen drunk in the lobby. Holding Gloria's hand, Nathanial escorted her to the desk. "I wonder if you could do me a favor," he said to the clerk. "Could you scare up a fairly decent dress and a pair of shoes for this child?"

The desk clerk wrinkled his nose in distaste. "Surely, you're not taking that to your room, sir."

"She also needs a hot meal, with ice cream and cake for desert." Nathanial dropped fifty dollars onto the counter. "Think you can manage it?"

"I can manage anything, sir," replied the clerk as he scooped up the wealth.

Gloria glanced about, bedazzled by her surroundings, for she'd peered into fancy hotel lobbies, but never had been inside. Nathanial lifted her as though she were a feather and carried her up the stairs to his room. He lit a gaslight, then led her to the bathroom and turned on the water. "Gertie can be as dirty as she likes," he told her, "but not my dear Gloria."

He closed the door, and she waited to see what he'd do, but he was puttering in another part of the suite. She knew he carried a gun because she'd felt it in his belt, and indeed had been tempted to steal it. In the mirror she stared at her dirty face and snarled hair, noting that he owned a fine brush and comb. She expected to be thrown out after he sobered up, but the sooner she bathed, the sooner she'd eat. Humming an Irish jig, she stood in front of the mirror, took a washcloth and soap, then scrubbed years of dirt and grime from her face, replacing them with angry red blotches. Often she'd wished she could be clean and well-dressed like rich children she saw on Broadway, and she didn't enjoy striking people over their heads with lead pipes, but a wild force within her had wanted to live.

Gertie knew what her mother had done for a living,

and if the truth be told, Gertie had engaged in certain disgraceful acts herself, for child prostitution was common in New York City. She believed that no matter how hard she scrubbed, the stain of wickedness would remain.

As her face emerged, she decided she was sort of lovely, and after viewing herself from a variety of angles, thought she might pass for a rich kid, as long as she didn't open her mouth, for she knew she was uneducated, unlike the strange Nathanial Barrington, who spoke like a prince. *What does he want with me?* she wondered. He had something up his sleeve, she was certain, because everybody, in her experience, had something up his sleeve, usually a knife or gun. *You'd better make the best of it, Gertie old girl,* she told herself. *And if that drunkard throws me out in the morning, at least I'll be clean fer onc't in me life.*

She undressed, slid into the bathtub, closed her eyes, and lay in the water, letting it unclog her pores. Many times she'd been bitten by rats as she slept with an empty belly in Five Points cellars, but she'd known no other life. She'd always been hungry, and sometimes her gums bled. There was something furtive about her, as if searching for her main chance.

He knocked on the door, and she stiffened in the tub. *Here it comes,* she thought.

"Are you still there?" he asked.

"Well—where'd you think I was?"

"I thought perhaps you'd floated down the drain. It may interest you to know, Miss Gloria, that supper is served."

She bounded out of the tub. "What'll I wear?"

"The desk clerk has found you a robe. Open the door, and I'll give it to you."

He's gonna grab me—I know it, she calculated, so she took down the razor from the shelf above the sink, extended the gleaming blade, and cracked the door, prepared to chop off the first hand that came for her.

Instead, a yellow flannel robe was suspended before her eyes. She snatched it out of his hands, returned the razor to the shelf, and put on the robe. Then she brushed her wet hair, wrapped a towel around it, and emerged from the bathroom, resembling an Arabian princess.

A table had been spread in the middle of the sitting room, covered with platters of roast chicken, broiled steaks, sliced ham, a variety of vegetables, a loaf of bread, and a pitcher of milk. Meanwhile, he sat on the sofa, coat off, suspenders showing, tie hanging loose, reading a newspaper.

"Don't you look sweet," he said. "Well, help yourself."

Gloria stared at the food, unable to move, then a sob escaped her lips.

"What's wrong?" he asked, dropping the newspaper, for the moods of females never failed to amaze him.

Angrily, she wiped the tears away. "Why're you doin' this?" she asked. "I ain't nothin' to you!"

"You'd better eat before it gets cold. We have a lot to do tomorrow."

She approached the table and never had she seen so much food. What the hell, she thought. I got nothin' to lose. She sat and filled her plate with helpings of everything.

Nathanial took the chair opposite her, marveling at the intensity of her appetite, and she didn't slow herself with knives, forks, and spoons. He knew she feared him, because he'd noticed the razor missing from the shelf when he'd opened the door. What dark secrets does this poor child harbor? he wondered. "Have you ever fired a gun?" he asked.

"Nawp," she replied, mouth full of food.

"I'm going to buy you your own little gun. And I'll teach you to use it, so you don't have to be afraid of anybody."

"Mister, I know you want somethin' from me. Maybe you'd better tell me what it is."

"I want you to be good for a change."

She raised a skeptical eyebrow. "What's in it fer you?"

"The honor of assisting your redemption. This may be the only chance you'll get, so you'd better make the most of it."

"In the mornin', you'll look at me and say, 'What do I need this kid fer?'"

His eyes glowed in the gaslight. "But I do need you, because you're going to be my friend. And you won't run away, because you need a friend as well. Let me remind you that despite my many shortcomings, I'm better than Five Points."

She didn't interrupt her eating during his confession and thought the biscuits better than anything she'd ever tasted. "Long as you keep yer hands off'n me," she told him, "we'll git along jest fine."

5

→

Night swept across America like a curtain covering a stage, as lamps were extinguished from east to west. Pitch black in some regions, the sun was setting in other lands, such as remote New Mexico Territory.

On a mountaintop deep in the Chiricahua homeland a fire blazed into the twilight, sending flickering shadows of wickiups against fir, aspen, and juniper trees. It was the night of the devil dance, and Chiricahua warriors carried sick Mimbrenos from their wickiups to the fire, while musicians sat with pottery drums, beating and singing softly.

The Chiricahua singers told of the People's devotion to the Lifegiver, White Painted Woman, and the Mountain Spirits, then chanted sagas of heroism, such as Killer of Enemies removing monsters from the homeland, making it fit for the People. Finally, they called upon the Lifegiver to heal their Mimbreno brothers and sisters, so they could more effectively defend themselves from encroaching enemies.

Among the poisoned lay Victorio, and with every throb of pain he hated the Mexicanos more. When I recover, we shall visit a holocaust against them, he swore.

Chiricahua women passed among the sick, carrying jugs of tulapai, letting them drink. Made from the fermented dried root of the mescal plant, spiced with holy herbs and leaves, tulapai was considered strong medicine for body and spirit. Cochise's wife, Dostehseh, approached Victorio, kneeled beside him, and held the jug to his lips. He took a few swigs, then had to stop, as fiery liquid burned down his throat.

Dostehseh passed on, Victorio closed his eyes, and on the other side of the fire, Jocita lay beside Fast Rider, holding his hand, praying fervently. The sun sank toward ragged precipices on the horizon, and she had the feeling the Mountain Spirits were looking down at her, some with compassion, others with accusation in their eyes.

Sometimes she thought the wrath of the gods had been unleashed due to her immoral behavior with Sunny Bear, but that betrayal had produced a beautiful child, who had demonstrated magical powers from an early age. And Sunny Bear had been no weasel, but a notable *Pindah* war chief who had seen many visions and been admired by Mangas Coloradas, gallant Victorio, Nana the Medicine Man, and even Juh and Geronimo, the two most ferocious warriors in camp. It was not as if Jocita and Juh had been living together in the same wickiup.

Not far away, Mangas Coloradas lay, thirst slaked by tulapai. Now he too hurtled across the vast reaches of space, wondering if his demise had occurred. The suffering of the Mimbrenos is my fault because I trusted the Mexicanos. But I never will trust them again, and if I recover, I will lead the combined Chiricahuas and Mimbrenos against Janos. Justice will be done, if the Mountain Spirits so favor us.

Chanting and singing continued, rhythmic sounds exerting a hypnotic effect on the People, augmented by copious draughts of tulapai. Close to midnight, seven balls of fire could be seen rolling down the mountain. They seemed to be dancing, spinning about, and making light paintings against the starry sky, but then, drawing closer, became torches in the hands of ceremonial Gahn dancers.

They wore tall headdresses of painted yucca lathe crests, decorated with beads and sacred stones, looking like the spreading tails of peacocks. Behind their black cloth masks, they were warriors especially selected for the honor of not just impersonating, but *becoming* the Mountain Spirits. Many regulations attended their ministry, and illness or even insanity could result if they violated the purity of the practice. They formed a straight skirmish line and swept toward the fire, then danced backward, repeating the ritual again and again in series of sacred pulsations intended to evoke the deeper energies of the universe.

The musicians sang and beat drums louder, more tulapai was consumed, and selected warriors threw logs onto the bonfire, spilling heat and light across the campsite, while high in the sky, bats circled and darted as if they too were part of the devil dance.

Then a new dancer rushed into their midst, swinging above his head a carved block of wood attached to a rope, producing a roaring sound. He was Posito, impersonating the devil, wearing horns on his head, a breechclout, and moccasin boots. Cavorting and somersaulting, he screeched incantations, whipping the air with his rhombus. The evil one caused all illness, but he was a shy deity, and suddenly turned, ran back to the mountain, and disappeared.

The Gahn dancers coaxed him back with stylized hand and arm gestures, because his presence was necessary for the healing. Meanwhile, the singers pleaded the case of their Mimbreno friends and begged the devil to forgive them.

Coyuntura, brother of Cochise, was leader of the Gahn dancers. As a mark of high office, he carried a triple medicine cross adorned with eagle feathers. He offered the medicine cross to other dancers, then withdrew as they reached. He repeated the same ceremony with the singers, who begged for the healing device.

The devil became interested in the medicine cross and drifted closer to the fire, resembling a huge dancing tarantula. Coyuntura encouraged more onlookers to join the dance and help the Gahn impersonators enchant the devil. The newcomers formed a giant six-spoked wheel and gamboled in a circle that continued throughout the night.

Finally, the devil returned to the fire, accepted the healing wand, and whirled among the sick Mimbrenos, touching them, drawing their disease into the holy implement, then raising it to the heavens and making a hissing sound, dispelling the illness to the four directions.

The devil was followed by Coyuntura, who dropped handfuls of sacred pollen upon sick Mimbrenos. Musicians sang loudly and beat drums with such energy that some of their fingers bled. More Apaches joined the dance, adding their power to the exorcism. Small boys wiggled in a circle at one end of the fire, and little girls at another, with the most beautiful maidens forming a five-pointed star and performing their own special medicine dance, carrying wands eight feet long, each with a cross at the end.

Coyuntura approached Nana, a fellow medicine man stricken with illness. Kneeling beside him, Coyuntura placed dots of pollen on his forehead, cheeks, mouth, and torso. "Soon you will be well, my brother," he murmured.

Nana barely heard him, for he had burst through the membrane between the land of warriors and the realm of gods, as essence of tulapai saturated his brain. He thought he had gone to the happy hunting ground, but could see no deer or antelope, only spirals of fire swirling in the night sky. I ask not for life or good fortune, he prayed. I ask only that you save the little ones, for they are the future of the People.

Out of the vortex of night and fire came a voice. "I will save you for the sake of your holiness, but you must never drink and eat foreign food again, otherwise you shall surely die."

It will be as you say, thought Nana, as the Gahn dancers spun in a circle around him, and gorgeous maidens continued their plaintive song.

And so the evil emancipated by the devil dance was released into the atmosphere, where it merged with other prayers, songs, dances, and incantations of the nation known as America. All events influence other events, according to the wisdom of the People, and the hateful vapors floated into every corner of the land, from the barns of Missouri, where horses sniffed the air nervously, to the Great Plains, where buffalo stirred in their slumber.

Snakes, elk, and cougars felt the emanations of the devil dance, aware that strong medicine was loose in the land. It even invaded the wharves of San Francisco, where ships filled with the jewels and silks of the Orient lay at anchor, and it dropped down the chimneys of shuttered homes in New England, where descendants of Pilgrims slept in their feathered beds.

Great mountains were strewn across America, but nothing could stop the putrid effusions of the devil dance. It even made its way into the dreams of countless citizens, and next day they'd awaken ill at ease, vaguely aware of having been somewhere extraordinary, but not certain where. The devil dance of the People even sent its stirring vibrations into the halls of the mighty and powerful, exerting its power on the important decisions of the day.

President James Buchanan was sixty-six years old, a lifelong bachelor, and a former senator, secretary of state, and ambassador to England and Russia. Known popularly as the Sage of Wheatfield by his friends, Ten Cent Jimmy by his enemies, and Old Buck by those in between, when he needed advice, naturally he turned to his cabinet. And the cabinet member he most trusted was Howell Cobb, forty-one, secretary of the treasury, ex-speaker of the House, former Georgia lawyer.

One morning President Buchanan and Secretary Cobb sat in the Oval Office, discussing the downwardly spiraling situation in Kansas. "If you were me," said Old Buck, "what in hell would you do?"

Howell Cobb was a hulking farmer's son, with a double chin that made his face appear enormous. "No respectable Northern politician," he began, "not even Senator Seward, is ready to secede from the Union, but I swear to you that many influential Southerners such as Jefferson Davis, William Yancy, and Robert Barnwell Rhett will lead their states out if the Lecompton government is abandoned by this administration."

"But the majority of Kansans oppose Lecompton," protested Old Buck.

Secretary Cobb leaned forward, adopting his most sincere tone. "Northern extremists may give speeches, but Southerners are ready to fight. Mister President, have you ever considered what will be required to subdue the South if it secedes, and how many lives will be lost? But if we maintain the integrity of the party, the furor over Lecompton will end. Because nobody really cares about Kansas. It's just a pawn in the abolitionist game."

Old Buck tended to agree because he believed the strident demands of abolitionists were the main source of dissension. "But what about Senator Douglas?"

The President referred to Stephen Douglas of Illinois, leader of "Young America," the radical wing of the Democratic party. One of Young America's main principles was "Popular Sovereignty," the right of a territory to decide by vote whether or not it wanted slavery, the very privilege the Lecompton government wished to ignore.

"Senator Douglas is up for re-election next year," replied Cobb. "If he dares defy this administration, we shall destroy him."

The most beautiful woman in Washington, D.C., was said to be the former Adele Cutts, grand niece of Dolley Madison, but not even such an exquisite creature was immune from the baleful efflorescence of the devil dance. Back in 1856, when she was twenty-one, everyone wondered what lucky gentleman would win this extraordinary raven-tressed belle, but when the time came to choose, Washington was aghast. Miss Adele Cutts had accepted the proposal of none other than Senator Stephen Douglas of Illinois, known popularly as the "Little Giant."

Not only was Senator Douglas short, stout, and twenty-two years her senior, he also had become a disheveled drunkard following the untimely death of his first wife, the former Martha Reid of North Carolina, in January of 1853.

To forget her, the Little Giant had sailed to Europe, where he roamed like a heartbroken vagabond from London to Paris, Copenhagen, Athens, Odessa, and St. Petersburg, where he had met Tsar Nicholas, who told him that America and Russia were the only two "legitimate nations" in the world, and all the rest were "mongrels." Finally, the Little Giant decided he could not escape from himself, so he returned to America, resumed duties in the Senate, and then had been introduced to the vivacious Adele Cutts by a mutual friend, Senator Jesse Bright of Indiana, during the holiday season of '55. Adele and Stephen Douglas were married on November 20, 1856.

Why did she accept his proposal? This was the question asked by one and all, but none could deny that Senator Douglas was a brilliant, powerful, and wealthy senator, unlike unformed fellows her age, and perhaps she wanted to move into the White House, where her grand aunt had resided.

With Adele at his side, the Little Giant was able to stop drinking. She brought her impeccable taste to bear on his wardrobe, and since their marriage, he'd been clean, well-barbered, with no bits of food or soup stains on his lapels, a paragon of courteous behavior. He lost the Democratic nomination for Presi-

dent in '56, but astute politicians saw him as a strong
contender in '60.

To look at Adele Douglas, one might imagine her
husband would desire to spend a considerable portion
of his nights in her proximity, but she frequently slept
alone, her husband pacing the floor in another part of
their mansion in a prosperous Washington neighborhood known as Minnesota Row.

Senator Douglas couldn't rest because like many
Americans he fretted over the Kansas debacle, which
his own legislation had unwittingly produced. But,
still, he believed in Popular Sovereignty and blamed
the Pierce and Buchanan administrations for the turmoil, due to their toadying to the South.

One night Adele put on her blue satin robe and
went to her husband, carrying a whale-oil lamp
through the darkened corridors of their mansion. She
found him in his study, pacing in front of the desk. He
had the stern face of a judge (which he had been), the
chest and torso of a wrestler or professional boxer,
and comically short legs, but no one ever laughed at
Steven Douglas of Illinois. "What's wrong?" she
asked.

"I think I'm going to take on the administration,"
he told her.

Her eyes glittered in the gaslight. "I'm confident
that you can defeat Ten Cent Jimmy Buchanan, because Americans admire a man of principle. But even
you must sleep, Stephen."

Somehow the mess in Kansas didn't seem so bad,
with the former Adele Cutts to warm his bones. He
extinguished the light in the office, then followed her
down the corridor to their bedroom. Later, after ex-
hausting themselves, they slept peacefully, an odd but

happily married couple who had chosen to challenge
the bachelor President of the United States, the Democratic party, and the solid South. It all boiled down to
a simple proposition for Stephen Douglas of Illinois.
Why shouldn't the citizens of a territory be permitted
to vote slavery up or down?

6

Dr. Michael Steck, U.S. government agent to the Apaches, sat in his office at Fort Thorn, reading reports of Indian marauding throughout New Mexico Territory and Northern Mexico. Thirty-nine years old, of Pennsylvania Dutch heritage, he held little authority, practically no funds, and was forced to compete with the Army, whose method of dealing with Apaches was unrelenting warfare.

Dr. Steck believed peace could be achieved if Apaches became farmers, but his efforts were frustrated by lack of shovels, hoes, seeds, and wheelbarrows. The government preferred to spend tax dollars on new breech-loading rifles, crates of ammunition, and forts, which tended to produce dramatic, albeit bloody, results, unlike the slow painstaking work of diplomacy.

Later that day, Dr. Steck strolled through the Mescalero reservation alongside Fort Thorn, observing resentment on the faces of the warriors, who blamed him for their plight. He knew that young men slipped away at night to augment their meager food supply, and perhaps kill a farmer or rancher in the

process. Sometimes Dr. Steck felt like returning to
Pennsylvania, but he'd migrated to New Mexico
Territory for the sake of his wife's health, which had
improved considerably since their arrival.

New settlers were pouring into New Mexico Territory, their towns moving farther west where the most
warlike Apache bands roved free. High-speed mail
delivery was planned between San Francisco and the
Mississippi River, the proposed route passing through
the sacred hunting grounds of Mimbreno and Chiricahua Apaches. They never would never tolerate such
incursions, and the Army naturally would fight back,
massacring large numbers of Indians.

Dr. Steck decided that in the spring he would visit
the western Apache tribes, in an effort to hold off war.
*Perhaps a treaty can be made in advance, without the
interference of the Army,* thought Dr. Steck, as he
gazed at a gathering of drunken Mescalero Apaches in
front of a tipi, because the Mescaleros built tipis like
plains Indians, unlike the wickiups of western
Apaches. *What good am I really doing these people,*
he wondered, *and who cares?*

He wanted a new reservation out of the path of the
stagecoach route and towns that would follow its
wake, such as north of the Gila River, otherwise the
wheel of the Apache wars would continue spinning.
After returning to his office, he wrote the Commissioner of Indian Affairs in Washington, outlining his
relocation ideas. But there was so much hatred in
New Mexico Territory, sometimes he felt helpless before it. Apacheria had been peaceful since the Bonneville campaign of the previous summer, but he
wondered how much longer it would last.

* * *

Not far from Dr. Steck's office, a stagecoach rumbled north on the trail to Mesilla, escorted by a detachment of dragoons. Inside sat two Army officers, two lawyers, a salesman, and a pale bearded man with burning eyes, Raphael Fonseca, on the way to the home of his brother, Reinaldo.

Fonseca looked out the window at a scattering of tipis near Fort Thorn, and rage overcame him at the mere sight of Apaches. The murder of his family and own near-death had driven Fonseca partially mad. He trembled uncontrollably and felt an urge to tear Apaches limb from limb, to swing their babies through the air and dash their little heads, as had happened to his children. Fonseca did not view Apaches as people defending ancestral rights, but as criminals. He felt contemptuous toward Americanos who attempted to make peace with such animals.

One of the Army officers placed his hand on Fonseca's arm. "Are you all right?"

"I'm fine," grumbled Fonseca.

Everyone appeared concerned about him, and they all offered their sympathies, but nothing would satisfy except the extirpation of Apaches. He ground his teeth angrily as the coach arrived in Mesilla, only a few miles from Fort Thorn. Fonseca looked out the window at adobe homes, the faces of the townspeople, dogs, children, but nothing moved him; he was dead inside. All he wanted was to kill Apaches.

The stagecoach stopped in front of the general store, and Fonseca's brother Reinaldo was waiting. They embraced as luggage was thrown to the ground.

"My poor little Raphael," said Reinaldo.

Fonseca picked up his carpetbag. "This is all I have left of my family, ranch, everything I ever worked for, thanks to the Apaches."

Reinaldo took the carpetbag, then led his limping brother home. "You will have to sleep with Angelito," he said, referring to his oldest son.

"I am grateful you have taken me in."

They arrived at Reinaldo's small adobe home, for Reinaldo was a peasant who worked in a store. His wife, Maria, waited with their two small children, and there was much hugging, kissing, and commiseration.

When he was alone, Fonseca reflected bitterly that he'd struggled to rise above poverty, but had been thrown back by the Apaches. Unpacking, he removed a tattered rag of cloth, stiff and stained with dried blood. It had been part of his wife's nightgown, and he held it against his face, weeping uncontrollably. Then, at the bottom of the carpetbag, he found his wife's scorched rosary beads.

Fonseca held the crucifix in the air and looked at Jesus nailed to the cross. You could not save yourself, he pondered, so how could you save Cecilia and the boys? Now we see the results of loving enemies. I spit on your religion, and I'll show you what I think of your holy Gospel.

Raphael carried the rosary outside, opened the door to the outhouse, and dropped it into the hole. From this day onward, thought Fonseca, I shall look to the devil for justice.

Brigadier General John Garland ended his leave during the fall of '57, resuming duties as commander of the 9th Department, headquartered in Santa Fe. His first official act was to confer with the officer who'd commanded during his absence, Colonel Benjamin Louis Eulalie de Bonneville.

Both were battle-scarred old war dogs, General Garland having served in the War of 1812, the Seminole War, and the Mexican War, while Colonel Bonneville had graduated from West Point in 1815 and fought Indians in many venues since, in addition to leading the Sixth Infantry Regiment in the hottest battles of the Mexican War.

Colonel Bonneville's most recent achievement had been his Gila campaign of the summer, when he had surprised Mimbreno Apaches in the Mogollon Mountains and avenged the murder of Henry Linn Dodge, Indian agent to the Navajos. Thanks to this success, a certain insouciance accompanied Colonel Bonneville as he entered General Garland's office, saluted, and reported for duty.

General Garland was a tall, florid-faced officer who resembled the seasoned old fighter that he was, while Colonel Bonneville was short, rotund, puckish-looking, and could be mistaken for a casket salesman.

In fact, Colonel Bonneville was a famous American, while General Garland was barely known to the public at all. Colonel Bonneville had been the subject of a popular book called *The Adventures of Captain Bonneville, U.S.A.*, by Washington Irving, which told of Bonneville's explorations of the northern Rockies and Great Basin during 1832-35, an epic of high adventure, low comedy, survival against the odds, and encounters with strange, elusive beings known as Indians. Although General Garland outranked Colonel Bonneville, each man examined the other through lenses of mutual respect, the shared hardship of war, and protocols governing military behavior.

"Congratulations on your Gila expedition," said General Garland, opening the interview.

"I'm more convinced than ever that we can subdue the Apaches," replied Colonel Bonneville.

General Garland made a crusty smile because he appreciated a confident officer. "If I had not returned to duty, what would you do next?"

"According to my spies and scouts," explained Colonel Bonneville, "the Mimbrenos have fled to Mexico. If we coordinate campaigns with the Mexican Army and deny the Apaches their traditional hideouts in Sonora and Chihuahua, we can squeeze them into a diminished range, where systematically we can bring them to heel."

It was not a new idea, and indeed General Garland had considered such a plan himself. "The main obstacle is the Mexican government," he replied. "They don't cooperate with the American Army because it opens them to domestic political criticism that they're our lackeys."

Colonel Bonneville glanced both ways, to make sure no junior officer was taking notes, then said, "My Gila expedition was successful because before it began I made an unofficial visit to my opposite number in Janos, Colonel Alejandro Jimenez, who drove the Apaches north into my hands."

"Perhaps I should have another unofficial talk with Colonel Jimenez."

"He's been replaced by Colonel Gabriel Garcia, a much younger man. May I make a suggestion, sir?" asked Colonel Bonneville politely, for he would not antagonize a superior officer.

General Garland appreciated the deference in

Colonel Bonneville's voice. "I'm most interested in what you have to say, Colonel."

"If you traveled to Mexico, you would attract widespread attention as I did last year. Instead, I'd send a capable officer unobtrusively to act as liaison. He should be an experienced Apache fighter, fluent in Spanish, and set high standards in all matters."

General Garland smiled. "I have a notion you've already selected this officer."

"I was most impressed by his abilities during the Gila expedition. He is Captain Beauregard Hargreaves of the First Dragoons."

"Oh yes—Hargreaves—a fine officer. But isn't he married? He won't be able to take his wife to Mexico."

"The duties of the service come first," replied Colonel Bonneville. "His wife is the daughter of Major Harding, and I'm sure she'll understand."

"You're going where?" asked Rebecca Hargreaves two days later, standing in her kitchen at Fort Buchanan with her sleeves rolled up, disjointing a chicken while her maid filled the firebox with wood.

Her husband, attired in regulation blue tunic with polished brass buttons, stood with vaquero hat in hand. "I'm being transferred to temporary duty in Janos, and you can't come with me."

She stared at him, her hands bloody, an expression of annoyance of her face. "I thought we were going home for Christmas. Why don't they send one of the single officers?"

"General Garland doesn't explain his reasoning to a mere junior officer such as myself."

She washed her hands in a basin, looked at herself in the mirror, and blew back a strand of blond hair that had fallen across one eye. Then she turned to her husband. "What about me and the children?"

"You're going to Santa Fe."

Rebecca's spirits improved instantly, because at least she'd be out of Fort Buchanan. "What will you do in Mexico?"

"Coordinate operations with the Mexican Army, but nobody's supposed to know, so don't say anything."

She embraced her husband, placing her cheek on his chest. "But we'll be apart so long. Will it be dangerous?"

"I doubt it," replied Beau, "because I'll be in Janos most of the time, and the Apaches would never dare attack such a large town, with its own Army garrison."

The acrid fumes of the devil dance continued to blow across the fields and hamlets of America, from Key West to Dakota Territory, from southern California's rockbound coast to the pine forests of Maine, dissipating the illness of the Mimbreno Apaches, who had become stronger, more clear-minded, stomach pains subsided. All proclaimed the success of the devil dance, the dancers and musicians were rewarded with horses, and soon Mimbrenos were seen walking around the Chiricahua campsite as in the old time.

One day Chief Mangas Coloradas rode off by himself, and when he found an isolated canyon, he dismounted, cut his arm with his knife, and said to the sky, "At the end of Ghost Face, when mountain passes are clear, I will make big war on Janos and wipe it off the face of the earth. This I swear before the Mountain

Spirits and the Lifegiver, and if I fail, may I fall before the gates of that wicked town!"

As autumn fell on the northeast, Nathanial and his adopted niece rode west by railway car, passing forests ablaze with color. Nathanial read books and magazines to pass time, while Gloria stared out the window at miles of uninhabited wilderness.

Never had she realized America was so huge, and how long the journey would require, but she was stylishly attired, with a trunk of pretty new dresses on the rack above the seats. A gaily costumed clown doll sat on her lap, and in the clown's back, beneath his clothes, was a buttoned flap that would conceal the gun Nathanial had promised to give her.

Gloria had filled out since being adopted, but still was on the slim side, with flaming red hair and big brown eyes. She still feared she'd wake up in a Five Points cellar, but somehow continued to live as a princess, with servants available to do her bidding, and her adopted uncle providing anything she required.

Sometimes the former Gertie missed the old days, because there was nothing quite like lifting a drunkard's wallet, after first bopping him on the head. Crime had required skill, cunning, and careful planning, whereas now she had nothing to do, no one to play with, and spent nearly all her time with the morose Nathanial Barrington, who had yet to say no to the offer of an alcoholic beverage.

She turned from the scenery and looked at her benefactor, who carried a cigar in one hand and a book in his lap, reading avidly. That he was unhappy there could be no doubt, and he'd told her his last wife had thrown him out. Yet she sensed he was a good man, and he tried to teach her proper manners, plus the niceties of the English language. With her new clothes and diction, she hoped no one would guess the vile acts she'd committed.

She poked her sharp elbow into his stomach. "What're you reading?"

He blinked his eyes, as if awakened from a dream. Then he turned to her. "You wouldn't understand."

"I ain't as dumb as you think," she replied, her sensitive feelings scratched.

"I'm *not* as dumb as you think," he said. "Gloria, you must stop using the word *ain't*."

"I keep forgettin'."

"Then you must try harder. And please stop leaving the letter *g* off words. It's forgetting."

She pronounced the word properly, to please him, and he smiled in recognition. "That's a good girl," he said, kissing her forehead. "You keep it up, you can be as dignified and proper as I."

"But yer a drunk," protested Gloria.

"But my English is impeccable, and that's all that counts. If you want to know what I'm reading, it's a book that's very popular these days, called *The Impending Crisis* by William Helper Morris."

"What's it about?" she asked.

"Slavery."

"If slavery's so bad, why don't the niggers fight back?"

"The word is *Negro*, because only the lowest people say *nigger*."

"Well, why don't the *Negroes* fight back?"

Nathanial was amazed by how quickly she cut to the core of an issue. She had no pretense, her mind unclouded by theories and ideologies, but probably not for long. "They have fought back a number of times," he explained, "such as a rebellion led by the *Negro* Nat Turner in 1831. But every time slaves revolted, they were defeated and killed. It's not easy to wage war if you don't have anything to fight with. However, the Negroes of Haiti, which is an island off the coast of Florida, revolted in 1794 and won their freedom. But they've been fighting among themselves ever since, and the argument has been that Negroes really can't govern themselves."

"I used to know a *Negro* in Five Points," she replied. "He played the banjo real well and was an excellent thief."

Excellent was a new word that she'd learned, which she dropped into conversations whether it applied or not, although this time it was on the mark. Nathanial frowned. "I don't want you admiring thieves. You should admire great people, like Zachary Taylor."

"What did he do?" she asked skeptically.

"He practically won the Mexican War on his own, and then became president of the United States. It may interest you to know that I served under the gentleman and knew him rather well. Theft may be a time-honored profession in colorful Five Points, but not nearly as honorable as becoming president of the United States."

"If you're so smart, why ain't . . . aren't you president of the United States?"

"Because I have led an extremely erratic life, and if you don't know what *erratic* means, it's sort of like your former existence, but with money."

She smiled delightedly, because there was something funny about him, perhaps his professorial manner of expressing himself, or his low opinion of past deeds, justifiable though that might be. "You can't be so bad," she said. "I never saw you kill nobody, or nothing like that."

"That's because this area of America is fairly civilized, but when we cross the Mississippi, perhaps I'll give you a personal demonstration."

He interrupted his explication on mayhem to lecture on grammatical rules concerning triple negatives in the same sentence, for he constantly worked on her young mind, molding, teaching, and attempting to elevate her above Five Points values. She had become his pretty little toy and his traveling companion whom he was manufacturing into a debutante, so he wouldn't have to worry, while returning home drunk some night, about a lead pipe cracking his cranium.

Or perhaps he simply loved her feisty street urchin nature, or her rapid mind. After ten more years of intensive instruction, she might become a useful citizen, he hoped.

Clarissa departed on her concert tour without finding time to see her lawyer, so legally she still was married to Nathanial Barrington. She barely thought of her husband, she was so busy, and suspected he may have filed papers against her.

Following three successful much-publicized performances in Philadelphia, her next stop was Baltimore, where she was met at the train station by the theater manager, who escorted her, Thorndyke, and Thorndyke's secretary, a young woman named Saddlebrook, to the City Hotel.

Thanks to advance publicity that trumpeted her as the new Jenny Lind, a parade of local dignitaries passed through her suite of rooms, including members of the city council, local artists, fools, and pretenders, not to mention the gentlemen of the press.

Clarissa accepted their praise and good wishes with a mechanical smile. Whereas compliments once flattered her, now they seemed false, vapid, and pointless, she had become so accustomed to them, recognizing that her well-wishers barely knew her and had been hoodwinked by the press. She dined with Thorndyke and his secretary, with whom he shared the same bedroom, but Clarissa tried to keep an open mind, now that she was part of the theatrical world.

She expected more outstanding reviews in Baltimore, for Thorndyke was skilled at negotiating with the fourth estate. Sometimes it was cash on the barrelhead, a case of whiskey, a dozen free tickets, a woman, or a man, depending on the taste of the journalist in question. Clarissa never had seen humbug at close range, and it sickened her, but she tried to focus on the music.

Thorndyke had said that several wealthy gentlemen had followed her from New York to Philadelphia and now to Baltimore, and Clarissa thought that curious and even frightening. Achievement in art interested her most, and therefore she was especially respectful, when in the dining room of her hotel she was introduced to William Gilmore Simms, Charleston's leading poet, visiting friends in Baltimore. He was fifty-one years old, wearing an odd diamond-shaped beard minus mustache, a solid-looking, jovial fellow with a boyish air.

Simms sat in the audience when she performed at the Front Street Theater the next night, and his very presence inspired her to bang the chords with special verve, because she wanted to demonstrate that she was not just the creation of Thorndyke. Her program included selections from Brahms, Beethoven, and Mozart, and then she sang a selection of minstrel songs, which evoked peals of laughter and flurries of applause.

Certain phrases always produced the identical result, no matter where she performed, and she had become calculating in the pursuit of audience reaction, but it removed spontaneity from her work, so she felt no special thrill when she took her bows at the end of the performance. Simms led the applause from the front row, his face glowing with satisfaction. On an impulse Clarissa lifted a bright red rose from the stage, kissed its soft petals, and tossed it into Simms's lap. Then she bowed to him, the audience roaring its approval.

She encountered the usual confusion when she returned to her dressing room, compliments rang in her ear, her hand was shaken, her cheek kissed, and finally Simms arrived with his entourage.

"I understand you plan to visit Charleston," he said.

"Yes—after Richmond."

"You must let me take you on a tour of my city."

"It would be an honor," she replied, flattered by the great man's invitation. "I look forward to Charleston."

Following the guests' departure, Clarissa sat before her mirror, removing cosmetics and listening to Thorndyke rave about her performance, for hyperbole was the foundation of his career. Finally, he said, "It was marvelous the way you handled William Gilmore Simms. He may be past his prime, but his taste still is influential in Charleston. If he likes you, which appears to be the case, he'll fill up the concert hall.

You're learning this business very quickly, my dear. I'm proud of you."

In Cairo, Illinois, Nathanial and Gloria booked passage on the *Queen of the West*, a paddle wheeler headed for New Orleans. Nathanial was gloomy during the voyage because it reminded him of his trip west with Clarissa, and he expected a letter from her lawyer at Fort Thorn, with notification of divorce proceedings.

Nathanial's difficulties worsened at night because he was accustomed to sleeping with his little wife. Her enthusiasm, curiosity, and experimental perversity never failed to beguile him, and he hadn't grown tired of her after three years of marriage. He paced the floor with a bottle in his hand, mumbling to himself, and Gloria pretended to sleep as she watched him go back and forth.

They arrived in New Orleans, checked into the Belleclaire Hotel, and Nathanial investigated stagecoaches headed for New Mexico Territory. He couldn't leave a nine-year-old girl alone, especially one with a proclivity to find objects before they were reported stolen, so she accompanied him, studying crowded stagecoach offices, banks, and general stores, learning the ways of the world, nothing escaping her sharp little eyes.

One day Nathanial purchased a tiny pearl-handled Colt pocket-pistol with a three-inch barrel, chambered for the .36 caliber cartridge. Outside the shop he retreated into an alley, took her doll, and inserted the Colt into the special back pocket. "You'll receive your first lesson when we're on the frontier," he told her.

He couldn't take a child to taverns, so he drank in restaurants where she consumed immense meals, her dresses becoming tighter. Hand in hand they explored the French Quarter, her mind ingesting astonishing new information, images, concepts.

One afternoon they visited New Orleans's dockside slave market, where Negroes were made to show their teeth, for healthy teeth added to the price, as with horses. They also were ordered to flex muscles or stand erect according to taps of the auctioneer's staff against the slave's body. Coffled slaves were marched to and from the market, with armed white men in attendance. A beautiful, light-skinned mulatto woman was bid for by a mass of shouting men, and Gloria detected terror in her eyes. I sure am glad I'm not a Negro, reflected Gloria.

Nathanial sat upon a crate of cargo, took a swig from his silver hip flask, and said, "This nation may well go to war over what's in front of your eyes, Gloria. Now you know what people mean when they talk about slavery."

"Why don't somebody stop it?" she replied.

"The proper word is *doesn't*, and the answer is there's too much money to be made."

She nodded solemnly, for she'd cracked a few skulls for the sake of money, but buying and selling people seemed beneath even her low standards. "The Negroes are like us," she said, shaking her head in disapproval.

"Sure, but would you give your life to free them?"

She reflected upon his question. "No."

"There's the rub, my darling. Many good people are opposed to slavery, but nobody's ready to die for Negroes, yet. In the meantime, how about some ice cream?"

She fluttered her little eyelashes and replied with a

Southern drawl, "Why, you know I love ice cream, Uncle Nathanial."

Hand in hand, they strolled away from the auction, leaving slaves in manacles and chains, the autumn wind whistling through their rags, heads hanging in defeat.

7

⟶

Jocita sat in front of her wickiup, fashioning new arrows. She had decided to return to the warrior way because the People needed every fighter they could muster for the assault on Janos. The Mimbrenos were incensed against the *Nakai-yes*, all tender feelings submerged, replaced by strategies for revenge. Soon the People would sweep into Mexico, utterly demolishing the accursed town.

Jocita knew that she could be killed on the expedition, but refused to acknowledge fear. She didn't especially love war and as a mother found killing repugnant, but that didn't mean she wouldn't punish transgressors or protect her family to the death. The People were oppressed everywhere, and old enemies like the Moquis, Yaquis, Pimas, and Papagos were teaming with the *Nakai-yes* and *Pin-dah-lickoyee*. Her anger fueled by righteous passion, she was deadly accurate with bow and arrow. At the end of Ghost Face, Jocita would kill again.

The People believed wars were won not by numbers, weapons, or tactics, but by the holiness of warriors.

And so the People prayed and purified themselves as they prepared for the destruction of Janos.

Apache boys had few chores beyond gathering firewood and were free to hunt, play, or run wild, provided they didn't disturb warriors and wives. Boys from prosperous Apache families had been given horses, and one of these was Jocita's son, Fast Rider.

He rode his brown-and-white pinto mare across the desert, a long club in his hand, searching for wayward rabbits. The creatures would add to his family's food supply, and hunting on horseback was considered perfect training for would-be warriors.

Fast Rider was alone, his bow strung diagonally across his chest, a little boy on a big horse, and both constantly scanned for danger as they hunted the elusive rabbit. Bending to the side, he poked his club into a sagebrush thicket, hoping to dislodge one of the furry fellows, but none could be found.

Impatiently, he worked hedges in the vicinity, recalling elders speaking of diminished game due to invasion by White Eyes and the Mexicanos. Although only a boy, he felt a terrible anxiety about the future, as if a cataclysm was coming, and only he could stop it. He didn't know what these premonitions signified, but they surfaced occasionally in the midst of other activity.

He rustled chaparral, provoking the strike of a rattlesnake against the club like a hard punch. The pinto mare stepped backward, afraid of the rattler, so Fast Rider steered into another direction, toward a clump of palo verde bushes, which he disturbed, hoping to scare something, anything, into the open.

A rabbit leapt forth and ran zigzaggedly across the desert floor. Fast Rider prodded his horse, who leapt forward, loving the thrill of the chase. The rabbit darted toward a hedge of marigold bushes, but Fast Rider was gaining. The son of Jocita drew back his club and swung with all his strength.

Splat.

Midway up a mountain, seated in a cave, Juh was on the lookout for enemies. The chief of the Nednai could see substantial distances, hawks floating on the updrafts, storm clouds scudding across the horizon. Juh tended to view existence as a military problem, reducible to tactics, maneuvers, and weapons, so he didn't have to think about domestic turmoil.

In moments of reverie he wondered if he should live by himself and escape the cold, unrelenting warfare of both his wives, each of whom felt he had wronged her. But he was a man who needed women and thus was forced into disgraceful compromises.

He barely spoke with Jocita at all, for her hatred was more than he could bear. Ish-keh was more pliable, for the daughter of Chief Mahlko wanted to avoid scandal, but beneath the surface he could feel her bitter resentment. And worst of all was Fast Rider, the living, breathing reminder of Jocita's unfaithfulness.

In the desert below he could see the white-and-brown markings of Fast Rider's horse as the boy hunted rabbits. Juh often wondered how the son of a White Eyes could take so readily to the holy Lifeway. *How strange that I love this child, although he is a reproach to my honor, and I further love his mother, although she has betrayed me.* Juh couldn't wait for the snow to melt, so he could relieve his frustration in battle. When we finish with evil Janos, nothing will be left except wreckage, blood, and bones.

Captain Beauregard Hargreaves and his special detachment arrived in Janos in October, 1857. The dragoons were bearded, half-frozen, smelly, and saddle sore, but no Apaches had disturbed their contemplation of the scenery. At the edge of town they were stopped by a young officer who spoke English. "I am Lieutenant Mendoza. What do you want?"

"I have been sent by General Garland of my country," replied Beau, "and I have a message for Colonel Garcia."

"You may give it to me." The lieutenant held out his white gloved hand.

"I must deliver the message in person."

The lieutenant thought a few moments, then said, "This way."

Beau and his dragoons followed Lieutenant Mendoza into Janos, a settlement of adobe huts, with a few larger homes for more prosperous residents. They arrived at the Army barracks, where they dismounted.

Lieutenant Mendoza said, "Your soldiers can rest here, and you will come with me. Your arrival was unscheduled, so do not expect the colonel to see you immediately."

"I can wait."

Beau tossed his saddlebags over his shoulder, then Lieutenant Mendoza led him inside to a small waiting room, with one wall displaying a mezzotint portrait of Benito Juarez, President of Mexico, next to the Mexican flag. Beau sat, hoping Colonel Garcia would be reasonable. If I bring this off, thought Beau, maybe I'll make major one of these years.

To pass time, he opened a saddlebag and withdrew his dog-eared copy of *Cannibals All* or *Slaves Without Masters* by George Fitzhugh.

A recently published unabashed defense of slavery, written by a middle-aged Virginia attorney, it had become widely read and quoted in the press. Beau continually searched for cogent arguments in favor of the "peculiar institution," perhaps hoping to convince himself, because he had grown up with slavery, and it hadn't appeared very efficient.

Beau read that Fitzhugh apparently agreed with his observation, because Fitzhugh admitted slavery was a far from perfect institution, but insisted that southerners could solve their problems if the abolitionists stopped stirring trouble. Fitzhugh then counterattacked by claiming that the white slave trade was far crueler than the black slave trade, because black slaves were fed, clothed, and sheltered by their masters, while poor, white Irish immigrants starved in northern cities. Fitzhugh claimed it was necessary for the strong to enslave the weak in order to protect and care for them, but Beau had graduated from West Point, seen something of the world, and guessed the weak might not agree with the proposition.

His reading was interrupted by the return of Lieutenant Mendoza. "The colonel will see you now."

Lost in America's bottomless slavery debate, Beau followed Mendoza down a hall, arrived at a broad wooden door, and entered the office of an olive-skinned officer with long, wavy black hair, with matching mustache, sitting behind a wooden desk, appearing either very tired or bored.

Beau marched to the desk like a West Point cadet, saluted smartly, then handed a document to Colonel

Garcia, who scanned the usual compliments, his eyes locating the operative line. *I request your cooperation for our mutual benefit.* But Colonel Garcia could not find any concrete plans, surmising correctly that General Garland had not intended to write anything where it could be studied. Colonel Garcia folded the paper, moved it to the corner of his desk, and said, "What's this about?"

"Apaches," replied Beau. "They raid in America, then hide in Mexico, or vice versa. General Garland believes we can diminish their range if we act in concert and thus force them to make terms with us. However, he begs to point out that if you and he request approval from your respective governments, it could take months or even years, and the Apaches will have killed many more hundreds of people, destroyed more towns, and stolen much livestock. Therefore General Garland requests that you support him without consulting your government, and don't forget that last summer Colonel Bonneville waged war successfully against the Mimbrenos, with the help of your predecessor. Now General Garland would like to repeat the campaign this summer, with you."

"But I have so few soldiers. It is limited what I can do."

"General Garland would like to offer a suggestion, with all due respect, sir. He believes that instead of remaining in Janos, responding to Apache provocations, you actually seek out the enemy, attacking wherever you find him, and denying him refuge in your country. In the meanwhile, we shall do the same, and together we will force the Apaches to make peace."

Colonel Garcia pondered the offer. The poisoning had failed, so he was open to alternative strategies. In addition, his family owned land in the area, which would become more valuable once the Apaches were eliminated, and he had political ambitions that would be aided by a defeat of Apaches. "You may convey to General Garland my willingness to cooperate," said Colonel Garcia, "and you and your men will be my guests in Janos. We will see if your methods are effective, and if not, no one will be the wiser."

And thus was an unofficial treaty concluded between the Mexican Army and the United States Army, elevating the Apache wars to a dangerous new phase.

In the cypress forests of East Texas, at the edge of a murky swamp, a log cabin served as restaurant, saloon, general store, and hotel for travelers. Parked in front was a stagecoach illuminated by the last rays of the setting sun, and some travelers sat in the restaurant, filling their bellies with beans and bacon, washed down with glasses of whiskey, while others lay in bed, resting from the arduous journey. A few roamed the surrounding country, and among these were Nathanial Barrington and his adopted niece, Gloria.

They strolled through a tenebrous jungle that once had belonged to the Caddoes, but those warriors had been vanquished long ago, and citizens could relax without fear of being scalped. Mossy cedars cast shadows over ferns shaped like violins, and tiny creatures scurried to their holes as birds flitted about, a wise old lizard watching everything, still as a board.

In a small clearing Nathanial pulled out the pearl-handled Colt pocket-pistol. "Time to learn how to use this," he said.

She stared at it, noticing the figure of a clown en-

graved on the barrel, beside words she could not read:
To my dear Gloria from Uncle Nathanial.

He kneeled in front of her and said, "If anyone ever
bothers you, just pull the hammer back like so"—he
demonstrated—"then raise it to your eyes, line up the
sights, and pull the trigger."

He fired, and the sound was so loud, she thought
her head would split down the middle. Covering her
ears with her hands and closing her eyes, she felt paralyzed.

"It wasn't *that* bad," he said chidingly. "If you're
going to be a little soldier, you can't be afraid of gunfire."

She lowered her hands. "I don't want that thing. It's
horrible."

"It might save your life someday, because there are
demented sons of bitches on the frontier, and one of
them might put his hands on you when I'm not
around. Now there are people who might say a man
shouldn't give a gun to a child, but if I were a little
girl, knowing what I do, I sure as hell would carry
one."

"Does it have to be so loud?"

"Nobody ever died from the sound of a gunshot,
and you get used to it after a while. Also, it has a tendency to kick up and to the left, so stand loose, understand? And don't be a big baby, because this thing
might save your life someday."

She accepted the gun, but required two hands to
pull back the hammer. "I'm afraid it's gonna go off,"
she said.

"It won't fire if you handle it properly, and never
aim it at a man unless you mean to kill him. You're
not afraid to kill somebody, are you?"

"Not if it's him or me," she replied.

"Aim at that tree over there, the one I just hit. Hold your arm steady, close one eye, and squeeze the trigger. It's supposed to be one smooth motion."

She raised the small, toylike weapon, aimed at Nathanial's bullet hole, and squeezed the trigger. Compressed gunpowder exploded, her hand leapt into the air, smoke roiled around her, her ears ached with the blast, and she staggered from side to side in shock.

Nathanial laughed heartily. "You're fabulous," he said, then scooped her in his arms. "I'm proud of you."

"I'm hungry," she replied, squirming to get away. "Can we eat now?"

"First let me load the chambers, in case you have to shoot somebody this very night. You never know about these things."

He thumbed in tinfoil cartridges, closed the chamber, and hid the gun in the back of her clown doll. "You must use the gun only for protection," he explained. "Not to hold up a bank. Agreed?"

It was dusk by the time they returned to the log cabin, candlelight streaming out windows, illuminating the stagecoach like a giant insect. Nathanial recalled teaching Clarissa to fire her Colt, thinking they'd be together forever, but now she was gone, probably with another man, because a pretty woman like Clarissa would not remain alone long.

A stab of jealously pierced Nathanial's heart as he opened the door for Gloria. She waltzed inside, and out of six tables, only one was vacant. She headed for it; he pulled back the chair, and she seated herself pertly, then said, "Where's the food?"

"The waiter will be here directly, and a lady does not show hunger, no matter how bad it hurts."

She glanced around. "Where's the waiter?"

It's no use, thought Nathanial. She needs to be with ladies, instead of the prostitutes she knew in Five Points.

Travelers dined noisily, whiskey in ready supply, and then the aged waiter appeared behind the big black stove; Gloria raised her hand. "Over here!" she hollered.

The waiter was bent with rheumatism, wearing old-fashioned knickers and leggings. "What can I do fer ye, miss?"

"I want supper."

Nathanial glowered at her. "Have you forgotten *please*?"

She ignored him. "And bring a lot."

"Yes, miss."

He hobbled to the kitchen, and Nathanial was about to deliver another etiquette lecture, when he heard ominous sounds in the distance. In a second he was on his feet, Colt .36 in hand, hoping it wasn't a band of outlaws.

"Easy, mister—it's only the stage from Fort Worth," said the cook, stirring a pot of beans.

Nathanial returned the Colt to its position of repose inside his belt, then sat beside Gloria and lit a cigar. The waiter brought two platters of bacon, beans, and a coarse loaf of bread. Gloria was so hungry, she wanted to eat with her hands, but would not risk the ridicule of Uncle Nathanial, to whom she listened more than he realized. So she positioned the spoon and proceeded to scoop food into her mouth.

"A lady does not eat quickly," said Nathanial. "A lady is temperate in her behavior."

"Oh, go to hell," grumbled Gloria, mouth full.

Perhaps he loved her defiance, or maybe he loved her because she was so damned adorable, or possibly because she was determined to survive and never let contrary views slow her down. Nathanial remembered the line from the Bible:

> *Except ye become as little children*
> *ye shall not enter into the kingdom of heaven*

At the next table a big-bellied salesman named McGee rose to his feet, frantically patting his clothing. "I do believe I've lost my wallet," he said.

"It's probably in the coach," suggested Stanley, the stagecoach driver, a wiry man in his twenties, sporting a wispy goatee.

Nathanial glanced at Gloria, who looked innocently at the ceiling. McGee trudged outside, then returned soon thereafter. "It ain't thar. What the hell could've happened to it?"

"Check the outhouse," suggested the cook.

"I hope it didn't fall down the hole," replied McGee as he rushed out again.

Nathanial leaned over his plate and peered into Gloria's not-so-innocent eyes. "He was sitting next to you in the stagecoach, my little darling. Where is it?"

"I dunno what you mean," the child replied haughtily.

"If you don't give it back, I'll drop *you* into the outhouse."

"Why do you blame everything on me?"

"Because you're a little bandit. I could understand

when you were poor, but now you have no reason to steal."

"Why shouldn't a lady have extra pocket money?"

"You could have asked, because you never refrain from opening that big mouth of yours when you want ice cream or a new dress, *Gertie*."

She winced at the sound of the hated name. "I'll slip it to you," she said. "Say you found it."

"Why do I have to take the blame?"

"Because you're the one who's so damned holy and all, and wouldn't you want to save a lady's reputation?"

Sometimes he felt the desire to throttle her, but instead reached down and surreptitiously took the wallet from her hand, dropping it into his coat pocket. He resumed eating, and soon thereafter McGee returned from the outhouse. "I cain't find it," he said in despair. "How the hell am I a-gonna pay fer me dinner?"

"We got lots of dirty dishes," replied the cook. "And floors to be swept."

Groaning, the victim sat heavily at his table. "I'm ruined," he declared sadly.

Nathanial planned to visit the outhouse to "find" the wallet, when the stage from Fort Worth came to a halt in front of the log cabin, followed by shouts, a commotion, and the sounds of bags being thrown to the ground. The door opened, and weary travelers appeared, bones creaking after all day in a cramped stagecoach. There were no empty tables, so they joined those already seated, but Nathanial and Gloria were in the far corner, and no one sat with them yet.

The tavern ordinarily didn't receive simultaneous stagecoaches, but an error in scheduling, plus a bad stretch of road, had caused the crowding. Meanwhile, a line formed at the outhouse, so Nathanial's effort to "find" the wallet would be delayed yet again. Amidst the consternation, the door opened to admit another traveler.

This singular gentleman appeared to be in his late forties, not especially tall nor eminently broad. He wore an Army greatcoat without insignia, and Nathanial couldn't help feeling curious about him, for he exuded dignity, yet did not put on airs as he calmly surveyed the territory. He wore a wide-brimmed vaquero hat of good quality, his beard was trimmed short and colored salt-and-pepper gray, and Nathanial figured he was a high-ranking officer headed east; he looked vaguely familiar.

Not wishing to disturb the others, the newcomer advanced along the wall, finally coming to a halt before Nathanial's table. "May I join you?"

"By all means," replied Nathanial.

The man turned to Gloria. "Do you have any objections, miss?"

"Barrington," she replied proudly. "It's okay wi' me."

"Thank you." He removed his coat, hanging it on a nail banged into one of the chinked logs that made the wall, and placed his hat on top, revealing thinning hair atop his well-shaped head. Sitting at the table, his rank could be seen on gold shoulder straps, a lieutenant colonel in the Second Cavalry, which Nathanial knew was deployed in West Texas, fighting the Comanches. As an old soldier himself, Nathanial recalled that the Second Cavalry had only one lieutenant colonel, its executive officer, one of America's foremost heroes of the Mexican War, Lieutenant Colonel Robert E. Lee.

Colonel Lee looked like a friendly terrier as he turned to Gloria. "How's the food?"

"I think you'll find it to your liking," she replied, for she was captivated by his warmth.

"I've got three daughters," he told her. "I'm on my way to see them."

"Where are they at?"

"Virginia."

"Run into any Injuns on yer way here?"

He smiled. "Not yet." Then Colonel Lee slowly turned to Nathanial. "Have we met?"

"At a distance many years ago, sir." Nathanial introduced himself, then they shook hands. "You visited West Point when I was a cadet, but I'm not in the Army anymore. Have you been transferred back east?"

Colonel Lee lowered his eyes. "No, my father-in-law has died, and I'm going home for the funeral."

"My condolences," offered Nathanial.

A melancholy expression came to the colonel's eyes. "Thank you, but we're boring the young lady." He turned toward Gloria, who was sopping her gravy with a handful of bread. "What would you like to talk about?"

"You know who you look like?" she asked. "Santa Claus."

"And I've just arrived on my sleigh."

A clever expression came over her face. "What'd you bring me for Christmas, Santa?"

"You must excuse her, sir," said Nathanial. "But sometimes she's a greedy little piglet."

"But she's completely right," replied Colonel Lee, "because a beautiful child deserves presents. I will find something appropriate in my bag later on, but I have no toys, I warn you."

Nathanial looked at Gloria disapprovingly. "It is better to give than receive, dear. What do you have for Colonel Lee?"

"A kiss."

"You're a little schemer, and you absolutely refuse to change."

Colonel Lee frowned. "You mustn't speak to her that way, Captain Barrington. She's just a child."

"If you knew what she's done within the past twenty-four hours, you'd be shaken to the marrow of your bones." Nathanial was alluding to the wallet he needed to return. "S'cuse me," he said. "Got to go outside."

He arose with great effort, then headed shakily to the door. Colonel Lee leaned toward Gloria and said, "You must take good care of him, young lady. He needs your help very badly."

"Don't you worry none about him," replied the child. "He carries a big gun and ain't . . . isn't nobody . . . anybody to fool with."

"But Army life can be quite harsh, and it's my impression that your uncle has seen a lot of war."

"Have you seen a lot of war?" she asked innocently.

Another adult might be put off by the child's challenge, but Colonel Lee detected a hungry, restless mind. "My share, I suppose."

"Then how come you ain't . . . aren't a drunk like my Uncle Nathanial?"

"Perhaps it's the grace of God, or maybe I get drunk in other ways."

"I shouldn't call him a drunk," she admitted. "He's

real good to me, I'll say that fer 'im. Today he gave me my own gun."

Colonel Lee blinked. "What for?"

"He said there are sick sons of bitches out here."

Colonel Lee reflected upon what she said, then replied. "He's right—there are. Be on your guard, and don't take any guff. But don't forget there are good men like your uncle."

Gloria narrowed her eyes. "How do you know he's a good man?"

"He's a West Pointer and certainly a gentleman."

"But there's lots of gentlemen, who really ain't . . . aren't gentlemen."

"True, but war generally burns away a man's super-ficiality, ah . . . I mean his bad habits."

"Then how come Uncle Nathanial drinks like a fish?"

"He hurts inside," said the hero of Chapultepec.

The door opened, then Nathanial stepped inside the hut, a brown cowhide wallet in his hand. "Look what I found by the outhouse!" he explained, then strode unsteadily to the table of McGee. "You won't need to wash pots and pans tonight."

With a drunken flourish Nathanial planted the wallet on the table, then reeled toward the one he occupied with Gloria and the curious Colonel Lee.

"The stars are like diamonds suspended from the neck of God," exclaimed Nathanial. He sat heavily, poured himself another drink, tossed it down, wiped his mouth with the back of his hand, and turned to his companions. "It reminds me of the summer of '51. I was in the First Dragoons, and we were camped at the Santa Rita Copper Mines in New Mexico Territory, and there was an Apache woman who was so beautiful . . . I . . . well, I suppose one shouldn't discuss such things in the presence of a child."

"But what happened?" asked Gloria, eyes a-glitter.

"Well, she returned to her people, and I returned to mine."

"Why din't'cha marry her?"

"Actually, she already was married . . . and so was I."

Colonel Lee frowned. "With all due respect, Captain Barrington, I don't think this is a suitable subject for a child."

Nathanial replied, "This child has witnessed more in her short life than you and I together, and there's nothing she can't comprehend. In fact, she's a profound thinker and something of a philosopher, I'll have you know."

Colonel Lee and Nathanial looked at the little girl, to hear whatever pearl of wisdom she might impart. "Do you think they might have ice cream?" she asked.

Meanwhile, McGee arose, holding his wallet. "There's twenny dollars missin'! Somebody stoled my money!"

Patrons glanced at each other in mutual accusation, then gradually their eyes turned to Nathanial. McGee waddled toward the drunkard who had found the wallet under suspicious circumstance and said, "You sure you didn't lift twenny dollars, afore bringin' the wallet to me?"

New Yorkers of Nathanial's class did not respond to such language, so he turned coolly from McGee and raised the whiskey to his lips.

"Hey—I'm talkin' to you!" bellowed McGee.

"Sit down, mister," replied Nathanial softly out the side of his mouth, "or I'll knock you down."

"Like hell you will."

McGee charged as Nathanial propelled his fist forward, smacking him solidly on the jaw. McGee flew over a table, then landed on a spittoon, which tipped over, flooding the area with vile liquids.

Nathanial stumbled toward the bar. "Another bottle, if you please."

The bartender replied, "Perhaps you'd best have a drink of coffee, suh."

McGee struggled to rise from the puddle of gunk produced by the upended spittoon. "He's a damned crook—'at's what he is. I want my money back!"

"I never took your damned money," replied Nathanial vehemently.

"Then who did?"

Nathanial glanced at little Gloria, who sat pale and unmoving at her table. "Could have been anybody," he said.

McGee pointed at him. "It was you, but you was afraid you'd git caught."

"I don't need your damned money," said Nathanial thickly. He reached into his pocket and pulled out a handful of coins and paper money.

It was a bad move, because McGee yelled, "Thar's my money!"

While this discussion occurred, McGee's friend Tulley was circling toward Nathanial's back, but no one paid attention to such a nondescript, stupid-looking fellow, who, as he drew closer, lifted a bottle off the bar.

"Look out!" shouted Gloria, first to spot the ploy.

Nathanial spun around in time to receive the bottle across the side of his head. It shattered, the edge cut into his scalp, and the shock combined with the whiskey he'd drunk, drove him to his knees, where McGee crowned him with a chair. Nathanial dropped onto his face, and McGee slammed him once more, to be sure of unconsciousness.

There was no sheriff, judge, jury. McGee searched Nathanial, finding the Colt .36, which he raised in the air. "He's a crook, probably a-plannin' to kill us all. I orter blow his brains out."

McGee cocked the hammer, aimed at Nathanial's head, and closed one eye.

"Just a moment," said a cultivated Southern drawl.

All eyes turned to the colonel from the Second Cavalry, who aimed his service Colt at them.

"Mind yer business," said McGee. "We ain't in the Army."

"But you're in America, and I'm placing the both of you under arrest."

"That's what you think," said a voice behind Colonel Lee, and he was Harold, another traveling companion of McGee's, wearing a lopsided cowboy hat and holding a Colt Dragoon. "Drop it."

Colonel Lee's Navy model Colt fell to the floor, then he raised his hands. McGee took aim once more at the still unconscious culprit. "It's the only way to treat a crook," he said.

"Please don't kill my uncle, sir!" implored the voice of a child.

Everyone turned to the well-dressed girl as she advanced demurely into the circle of light, clutching her clown doll. "He didn't steal your money, because my Uncle Nathanial is a rich man. Our family owns most of New York City—we're the Barringtons."

"What was he doin' with my wallet?"

"He found it—like he said." She hugged the doll

with her left arm, while her right hand fumbled at its back. "He was doing you a favor, and this is how you thank him?"

Travelers gazed accusingly at McGee and his friends, then at the innocent-appearing babe.

"Where'd the twenny dollars go?" asked McGee.

"How d'we know you didn't spend it?" asked Gloria.

McGee lost his patience. "Out of my way, you little whelp, or I'll shoot you, too."

Gertie the gutter rat set her teeth on edge as she raised the Colt pocket-pistol and fired at a range of three feet. An expression of panic came to McGee's face, the weapon fired, and the bullet struck McGee's rib cage. He was thrown backward by the force of the blow, but before he hit the floor, Colonel Lee took advantage of the confusion to deliver a solid punch to the face of Harold, while three other travelers jumped on Tulley. In moments the gang was subdued. The proprietor contributed a coil of twine, and the ruffians were bound tightly.

Colonel Lee and Gloria rolled Nathanial onto his back, while the proprietor's wife emptied a basin of cold water over his head. Nathanial opened his eyes.

"You have just demonstrated," explained Colonel Lee genially, "why an officer should not imbibe alcoholic beverages, particularly among strangers. You really must set a better example for your niece, Captain Barrington."

She smiled innocently, holding the smoking gun in the air. "You taught me good," she said, then rushed forward impulsively, kissed Uncle Nathanial's cheek, and said, "I love you."

*   *   *

By the time Clarissa reached Charleston, she knew
precisely what pleased an audience. She dared nothing new, because inspiration might produce disastrous
results before an audience of finely tuned listeners,
many of whom had seen the great Jenny Lind.

She had little time for relaxation during rehearsals,
social calls, and interviews with reporters, but managed to squeeze in the carriage tour of Charleston provided by the poet William Gilmore Simms.

As they rode down Broad Street, she noticed
Charlestonians staring at her, because everyone wondered who was the young lady accompanying the distinguished poet, and when they learned she would be
performing at the Dock Street Theater, they rushed to
buy tickets, for such are the benefits of a famous
artist's admiration.

Charleston was like New York City, a long narrow
promontory with rivers on both sides and the ocean
beyond. The South's leading Atlantic port, its wharves
were laden with stacks of cotton bales awaiting ship-
ment to European destinations.

"You will notice," said Simms, wearing a taupe-
colored stovepipe hat and white kid gloves, "that the
economy of the South has not been as affected by the
Panic as severely as the North, because the southern
economy is based on cotton, which is a real commod-
ity with a dollar value, while New York has been constructed on the shabby foundation of stocks and
bonds. There are those who believe that southern cul-
ture, which you northerners castigate with such vehe-
mence, is superior for this very reason."

Clarissa would not argue slavery south of the
Mason-Dixon line, particularly with an artist as gra-

cious as William Gilmore Simms. She'd always been attracted to older men, although youth possessed certain undeniable assets as well. Clarissa contemplated having a romance with Simms, for in the theatrical world, everybody slept with everybody else, even men with men and women with women, and she saw no reason why she should not be liberated from her narrow, puritanical upbringing.

Meanwhile, Simms regaled her with tales of old Charleston, how the celebrated Dr. David Ramsay had been shot to death on Broad Street in 1815 by a tailor named William Linnen, whom Dr. Ramsay previously had declared legally insane. Clarissa relished the company of Simms, who had a *bon mot* for every occasion.

"How did you become a poet?" she inquired.

He replied, "The poet is called as Samuel in the nighttime, by a voice whose summons he does not understand, but dares not disobey. It is the voice of his own nature—of a special endowment which tasks him wholly. It demands not only all his obedience, but all his faculties. I imagine it's similar to playing the piano."

"Sometimes I become tired of performing," she confessed, "but one cannot quit in the middle of a tour."

"At least you don't have to worry about copyrights, because in the absence of an international copyright law, foreign publishers are free to print cheap editions of my works and sell them here for less than my American publisher. Naturally, I receive not a penny."

"But you have your art, which is priceless," replied Clarissa. "What is mere wealth to a true artist?"

"Everything," replied William Gilmore Simms.

He was almost good-looking, despite his comical beard and air of mock gravity. Yet there was kindness in his eyes, congeniality in his smile.

That evening he sat in the front row during her performance, and all of Charleston's society was there. Clarissa provided a polished concert, calculated to please as she deftly fingered the keys. She'd discovered that an audience appreciated drama, so she'd give a toss of her little finger, or a delicate raising of her chin, when striking certain chords. If she decided Haydn or Mozart needed another crescendo, there existed no musical police to order her otherwise.

As usual, the audience especially enjoyed her rendition of popular minstrel songs, perhaps finding it amusing to see a blond woman singing of life as a slave. Naturally, she omitted any ditties that depicted the soul-crushing drudgery of slavery, but instead focused on more neutral numbers, such as:

> *Michael row de boat a-shore, Hallelujah*
> *Michael boat a gospel boat, Hallelujah*

She backed the song with a full piano accompaniment, giving it a grandeur and majesty different from what one ordinarily heard on plantations, not that Clarissa ever had been on a plantation. Most of what she knew about slavery had been received second- or thirdhand.

Her concert was yet another success, thanks in large part to the patronage of William Gilmore Simms, who escorted her to a gala party in her honor afterward at the home of a wealthy patron of the arts, for the poet's modest residence could not accommodate a crowd of well-wishers, and often he lacked the price of a good soup bone, never mind cases of champagne.

The party featured an orchestra and dancing, while quiet corners offered opportunities for enlightened conversation. Simms introduced Clarissa to unending streams of people; included were a few gentlemen who played the naughty eye game, as if they wanted to seduce her visually, but adulation no longer moved her, although she smiled falsely as she made her way across the parlor. It was as if she had become a symbol of everything glamorous in the eyes of her beholders, but she felt like a charlatan, and distaste with herself surprised her, for this was the fruition of her greatest childhood longing.

Jenny Lind had toured America extensively, because that was how she earned her living, but Clarissa didn't need to worry about money matters and was becoming weary of shaking hands like a trained baboon. What am I doing here? she wondered.

She said she felt tired, and naturally Simms offered to see her home. He called a carriage as she said goodbye to the faceless throngs. A Negro servant placed a cloak over her shoulders, then Simms led her to the carriage. Soon they were headed back to her hotel, passing white-columned mansions and huge magnolia trees, the moon shining over the Ashley River.

"You appear disconcerted," he said, sitting opposite her in the carriage.

"My concert tour, which began as pleasure, has become an ordeal, I'm afraid."

"But don't you realize what joy you have given tonight?"

"They applauded because you have offered the endorsement of your good taste, William. If you had not spoken for me, the theater might well have been empty."

"But I spoke because you have touched me deeply."

"My performance was inexcusably vulgar," she blurted. "I feel as if I have prostituted myself."

"Reminds me of a few lines I once wrote:

> *When thou shalt put my name upon the tomb,*
> *Write under it, 'here lies the weariest man*
> *That ever struggled with a wayward ban . . .*

She shuddered. "That's it exactly."

Simms gazed out the window at the half moon shining over the rooftops of Charleston. "But the true poet, and I include you in our sacred band, conducts us out of the present—she lifts us from the earth." The carriage came to a halt before the Charleston Hotel, where Simms kissed her hand lightly. "Good night, my dear girl," he said. "And if you're tired, rest. For you don't owe your audiences anything. Indeed, we are indebted to you." Then he bounded out and held the door for her. As she descended, he whispered, "The artist must observe closely, think earnestly, and sing boldly, with resolute purpose. That is our only obligation."

She stared at him as he returned to the carriage, waved one last time, and was drawn away by the team of horses. In a daze, Clarissa walked through the deserted lobby, climbed the stairs, and entered her suite of rooms. She felt too fatigued to turn on the gaslight, so she collapsed onto the nearest chair and in the darkness reflected on what Simms had told her.

Why can't I have the same unflagging dedication as he? wondered Clarissa. Perhaps I'm not an artist at

all, but a dilettante. Yet that great poet said I had
given him pleasure.

She felt confused, doubtful, insincere. I was happy,
but then this tour swept me away, and now I'm alone
in Charleston, my child in New York with my parents,
cared for by my maid, my marriage finished, and
somehow I must smile continually to myriads of people whom I don't know and don't especially care
about, and struggle to please them with cheap theatri-
cality, which I despise. Moreover, Thorndyke is the
most amoral man I have ever met, and an even bigger
fraud than I. My whole life has been lived under the
delusion that I'm an artist, but in truth I'm a pre-
tender, a liar, a . . .

Her mind clogged, she didn't know what she was.
It was as if the floor had opened, and she was toppling
through a dark, jagged chasm. Sorrow and self-
loathing overcoming her, she covered her eyes with
her hands and let out a sob.

"It can't be that bad," uttered a male voice on the
far side of the room.

A chill came over Clarissa, for she realized she was
not alone. Indeed, she could make out the vague out-
line of a man rising from his formerly reclining position on the sofa. She reached into her purse, her
fingers closed around the handle of her Colt .36, and
she thumbed back the hammer.

"I didn't mean to alarm you," he said, "nor intrude
into your private grief. Am I in the wrong room?"

"Yes, and you'd better leave."

He struck a match and lit a gaslight protruding like
the leg of a bird from the wall, while she took aim at
his innards. Then he turned, bathed in golden light
and sporting a black mustache, tanned regular fea-

tures, and a winsome smile that broke into fragments
when he saw the ugly snout pointed at him, an expression of determination in the eyes of its mistress.

"You're not going to kill me, are you?"

"Start walking to the door," she replied.

"This is no way to treat a harmless fool."

"How did you get into this room?"

"Perhaps my key works in your lock."

"Perhaps you're a liar."

He sighed. "I confess—I wanted to meet you, so I
bribed the cleaning lady rather handsomely. It was the
only way to speak with you, since you're surrounded
by so many admirers."

"Did it occur to you that I might not want to speak
with you?"

He appeared surprised that anyone would consider
him uninteresting or not charming, and his every gesture bespoke the ease that only wealth confers. Moreover, he appeared witty and good-looking in a swinish
detestable way, but Clarissa always had been attracted
to rogues, as well as older men, particularly when
having slept alone for so long. She lowered the gun
and said, "Don't you realize how cruel it is to invade a
woman's home and frighten her half to death when
she's in the midst of a crisis?"

He smiled warmly as he replied, "But the crisis is
over, because I am here. Name your difficulty, and I
shall solve it. If you require money, I place my fortune
at your disposal. You are an angel, and I would deem
it an honor to assist you."

As he spoke these words, he seemed so ridiculous
that she couldn't help smiling. And it was true—
somehow the crisis had passed, thanks to his magical
appearance. "The whiskey is over there," she said, in-

dicating the cabinet. "Kindly pour me a drink." Then
she sat on the sofa, thumbed forward the hammer of
her Colt, and dropped it into her purse.

He carried two glasses of whiskey, one diluted with
water, into the sitting room. He was a tall, lanky fellow, obviously an utter blackguard, but amusing.
"Permit me to introduce myself," he drawled. "I am
Tom Oglethorpe of what we call the 'back country,'
the westernmost part of South Carolina. I'm in
Charleston with a load of cotton, and someone told
me you were the principal entertainment, so I bought
a ticket, not expecting an artist so talented and even
brilliant that I have . . . well, I know it sounds common to come out and say it, but I have fallen in love
with you, although I don't know anything about you,
and you may, in fact, be the most horrid woman in the
world."

"Why is it that raving lunatics congregate around
me?" she replied. "I am a woman of modest behavior,
I try to be courteous, I have studied hard all my life—
why me?"

"Because your musical skill has moved the heart of
a man considered heartless, calculating, and something of a rake."

"I have deceived you," she replied. "What appears
as artistry is merely my studied artificiality."

He sipped whiskey, gazing at her over the lid of his
glass. "If it were merely artificial, you would not have
enchanted the entire audience. No, you carry the
magic spark, though you do not see it. Of course, I
admit you *do* have a tendency to go overboard at
times, but your talent far exceeds your silly manner-
isms. If I could play like you, I'd sit in front of the
piano all day and never get anything done."

"What is it that you do?" she asked.

"Oh, I own a small plantation."

"Do you play a musical instrument?"

"Only the harmonica."

He whipped one out of his jacket's inner pocket, dusted it against his shoulder, and blew a Negro plantation song while tapping his foot and making his eyes dance about. Technically, he wasn't a refined player, but he managed to carry the tune and appear hilarious. She couldn't help laughing, and applauded gaily at the end of his song, her resistance melting away. "I should hire you as my accompanist."

"How much would I have to pay for the honor?"

"What about your wife?"

"Actually, I'm looking for one. Would you like to marry me?" He wiggled his eyebrows.

"But you don't even know me."

"I have seen your naked soul on the stage, and now I yearn to see your naked body."

"I happen to be a married woman, and I don't want you to speak that way."

"Where's your husband?"

"Either he left me, or I threw him out. I'm not sure which."

"In other words, he's gone, and you're not married in the strict sense of the word. It's as I suspected, for you were weeping your poor heart out only minutes ago. Well, I've always believed that when a person is unhappy, he or she must start out anew. This may sound like an indecent suggestion, but why not run off with me?"

"To where?"

"Larkspur, my plantation. It's not exactly opulent, but very cozy and quite adequate, although the roof in the kitchen occasionally leaks, but we're working on it. You can be my guest, my carriage will be at your disposal, and I even have a piano, although it's out of tune."

"I carry my own tuning instruments, but what will people say when they learn you are living with an itinerant pianist?"

He leaned toward her and peered into her eyes. "My dear lady, people like us don't worry about what others say, and besides, after we're married, no one will dare criticize us."

"I would not dream of sleeping with you until after we're married."

"Of course not," he replied, a twinkle in his eyes.

The town of Mesilla existed to satisfy the needs of Fort Thorn, such as meat, vegetables, whiskey, and whores. On a Saturday night its narrow muddy streets were full of hard-drinking soldiers, vaqueros, bull-whackers, and desperadoes.

Raphael Fonseca slouched among them, hands in his pockets, sombrero on the back of his head. He wore white pants, a white shirt, no weapon, and had contempt for the Americano soldiers. They drink their money away, or give it to whores, instead of planning for their futures, he thought, spitting into the street.

He'd planned for his future, but the Apaches had stolen it, and fury sent him roaming the night. A dark, bloody cloud covered his eyes, and he estimated he should kill a dozen Apaches to even the score. How? he wondered.

He came to a square dominated by an adobe church, lights shining through its windows, a cross above the door. He wondered what God would permit children to be killed, and what religion would require a man to turn the other cheek to the most horrible outrages imaginable. Fonseca entered the church, nearly empty that time of night, but the priests had left their net open, hoping to catch the stray wayward soul, and indeed a few drunkards were passed out in the pews, resting in the bosom of God.

Raphael moved into a pew, dropped to his knees, and crossed himself. He gazed at the crudely carved and painted wooden statue of Jesus, blood dripping from his crown of thorns, and flashed on the butchered corpses of his family. No benevolent hand dropped from heaven to soothe him, and no celestial voice whispered into his ear the great comforting truth that he longed to hear. He was alone with the stench of rotting blood in his nostrils and had the urge to commit mayhem. He realized that Christianity was fine as long as no one murdered your family. How could any priest tell me to forgive the Apaches?

The Apaches had shown no mercy to his children, and Fonseca found no mercy for Apaches. Perhaps I should look not to Christ but to Joshua, who waged a war of weapons, violence, and bloodshed.

Fonseca departed the church, then cut into an alley, hoping to find a stray drunken Indian, so he could choke him with his bare hands. Instead, he saw brightness in the backyard beyond. He expected another cantina, but instead it was a barn with a lantern hanging on either side of the door, and a sign: MESILLA GUARDS MEETING TONIGHT

Curious, Fonseca drifted closer to the door, where a group of men were talking. One noticed Fonseca and beckoned for him to come closer. "Welcome. I am Roberto."

"I am Raphael Fonseca."

Roberto introduced the other men, then said, "I do not believe I have seen you before."

"I am new to Mesilla."

"We need every good man we can get."

"For what purpose?"

"We are a volunteer militia, because the U.S. Army does not give a damn about us. They have put nearly three hundred Apaches beside Fort Thorn, and the soldiers are safe in their barracks, while we are exposed to danger."

"What must I do to join the Mesilla Guards?"

"Take the oath and pay your fee."

"But I have no job."

"Senor Ortega will find one for you. He is our leader and will be here soon."

The vaquero known as Antonio snorted. "The gringos believe they can live at peace with the Apaches, but they do not realize the red devils are using them like the big fat fools that they are."

"The Americano Army," added Pedro, another of the Mesilla Guards, "is wonderful after you are dead. They will give you a fine funeral and tell your wife how sorry they are, but do nothing to punish the ones who kill you, or prevent them from killing again."

Miguel said, "The Apaches use the gringos against us, and the gringos give them free food to buy them off. If the Apaches steal your cattle, the gringos will look the other way."

Denunciations continued as a heavyset man in business suit, tie, and flowing black mustache emerged from the alley, atop a black horse with a white diamond on its forehead.

"That is Juan Ortega," confided Angel into Fonseca's ear. "He is mayor of Mesilla, owner of ranches and much property."

Ortega carried an air of confidence and indomitability as he climbed down from his horse, threw his reins over the rail, and tipped his hat to men waiting for him to speak. He proceeded into the barn, the others followed, and there were no chairs; everyone had to stand as horses looked at them bemusedly from their stalls.

Neither was there a podium, so Ortega stood in front and hitched his thumbs in his belt. He carried no paunch and appeared a vigorous leader, the typical self-made man who believes he can do anything. "Hombres, I will be brief," he began. "Ever since that reservation has been set beside Fort Thorn, we have had nothing but trouble from Apaches. They steal a horse here, massacre a family there, burn something—you know what I am talking about. Since the Americano Army has more important work to do, such as getting drunk, we must look to the safety of our loved ones. The Mesilla Guards train on Sunday afternoons, and you do not need to sign anything, just show up with your weapons. If there are any men who wish to join, please step forward."

Fonseca advanced, joining eight others in front of Ortega. As the recent widower raised his right hand, he thought, this truly is providence, but was it Joshua or the devil who answered my prayer?

On the night of November 6, 1857, the Lecompton Convention voted for a constitution with slavery, prohibited a popular vote, and forwarded the document to

Congress. The convention then dispersed in the early hours of the morning, their tricky deal completed.

Shortly thereafter, President Buchanan was advised that the states of Alabama, Mississippi, and South Carolina would secede from the Union if the Lecompton Constitution was rejected by his administration. After consulting with his southern-dominated cabinet, President Buchanan placed the full weight of his office behind the Lecompton Constitution. He decided that the nation, struggling to rise out of a depression, needed peace above all.

But the radical wing of the Democratic Party refused to abandon the principle of Popular Sovereignty as articulated by Senator Stephen Douglas of Illinois, their leader. All of Washington waited breathlessly for the collision between the President and Senator Douglas, as the press trumpeted rumors, innuendoes, and the usual lies, in their never-ending effort to sell newspapers.

The Little Giant and his comely wife returned to Washington from Chicago on December 2 and were greeted with cheers, bonfires, and a parade. After the ceremonies Stephen and Adele traveled to their mansion on Minnesota Row. "By God," declared the Little Giant in the privacy of his home, "I made Mr. James Buchanan, and by God, I will unmake him."

Next day Senator Douglas went alone to the White House to confront the President personally, and the President dared not back down. Senator Douglas was ushered into the Oval Office, and Old Buck sat behind his desk, creased and worn, like a boulder exposed to constant storms. Aides and cabinet officers left the office, and the President found himself alone with his most dangerous foe.

Old Buck feared nothing except the breakup of the Union, and after initial pleasantries, came directly to the point. "I understand you plan to oppose me on Lecompton."

"As chairman of the Senate Territories Committee, I should have been consulted before you accepted the Lecompton Constitution, Mr. President."

"I do not need to consult with you when I propose policy, Senator Douglas."

The Little Giant angrily tossed his mane of black hair. "The Lecompton Constitution is a farce, because it has not been voted upon by all citizens of Kansas."

President Buchanan felt like throwing his inkwell at Senator Douglas. "The nation is being torn apart by this issue, and the only way to heal the rift is pass the damned Lecompton Constitution. Then the crisis will pass and we can deal with the economy, which is our greatest difficulty. Every reasonable man knows that slavery never will take root in Kansas, due to terrain and climate."

"The Kansas crisis shall never pass," replied the Little Giant, "because the Lecompton Constitution is illegal, and all the power of your office, plus terrain and climate, cannot change that fact."

Old Buck narrowed his eyes. "May I remind you that no Democrat ever differed from an administration of his own party without being crushed. Beware the fate of Tallmadge and Rives."

The President referred to senators read out of the Democratic Party during the administration of President Jackson for their defiance of his campaign against the Bank of the United States.

"Mr. President," retorted Senator Douglas, "I wish you to remember that General Jackson is dead!"

They glowered at each other, and each contemplated the first fist fight in the history of the White House, but they were men of ideas, not pugilists. "The blood spilled in Kansas has been caused by your damned Kansas-Nebraska Act," accused President Buchanan.

Senator Douglas glanced from side to side, to make sure no eager reporter was lurking beneath a windowsill, notebook in hand. The Little Giant seldom lowered his voice, but lower it he did, to say, "I never realized what a coward you are, for you will not stand for the basic American principle of one man and one vote. Let me make my position clear, Mr. President. When it comes to Popular Sovereignty, I have bought my ticket and checked my baggage."

Word was leaked to the press that the President and senator had exchanged bitter words, and various versions of the encounter were supplied by both camps, but no reporter had been there, and none could say for sure. All of Washington waited anxiously for Senator Douglas's speech on the Lecompton Constitution, scheduled for December 8th, 1857.

The galleries were full on that historic day, and among the crowds sat gorgeous Adele, who had dressed and otherwise prepared her husband for his moment of glory. Yet if a foreigner had wandered into the august chamber, he might consider Senator Douglas a circus freak, with his long body and ridiculously short legs, but the Little Giant spoke in a rich baritone, understood the art and science of phrasing, and knew how to work an audience.

His posture was that of a general at the onset of battle as he began his peroration. "My fellow senators," he told them, "please permit me to say, with profound respect for the President of the United States, that on the point of the Kansas-Nebraska Act, he has made a fundamental error—an error which lies at the foundation of his whole argument!"

Senator Douglas employed the tried and true gestures of oratory, his carriage confident, perhaps even arrogant, as he described the history of the act he himself had drafted while President Buchanan had been out of the country as ambassador to England. "It was the intention of my committee, and subsequent votes of Congress, to establish the principle of Popular Sovereignty on all issues, including slavery. I have spent too much strength and breath, and health, too, to establish this principle in the popular heart, now to see it frittered away. I have been informed by men well posted in Kansas that this Lecompton Constitution would have been voted down by a majority of four to one, while others say ten to one, and twenty to one. How can we adopt this system of trickery and jugglery to defeat the fair expression of the will of the people?"

He banged his fist on the podium for emphasis, then continued, "I care not whether slavery is voted down or voted up! My only concern is that the people of Kansas have the right to express themselves by ballot! But I say to you—if this Lecompton Constitution is stuffed down our throats, in violation of the fundamental principles of free government, under a mode of submission that is a mockery and insult, I will resist it to the last!"

The galleries burst into applause, and Adele blew her husband a kiss. Sympathetic Democratic senators rose to join the jubilation, which became so loud and uncontrolled that Senator James M. Mason of Virginia, a staunch supporter of the administration, angrily moved that the galleries be cleared.

And thus did the great Democratic Party split in two, dropping the nation into the abyss.

8

The deeper Clarissa rode into South Carolina's back country, the more bizarre and almost prehistoric became her surroundings. Vine-laden trees drooped alongside a barely perceptible road overgrown with weeds and filled with holes, causing the stagecoach to rock from side to side on its leather thoroughbrace suspension. Foggy mists arose from the glens, while the sun shone brightly above the trees. It was a far cry from the airy forests of Westchester County, and she saw no prosperous family farms, only crude log shacks, wild-looking white children in raggedly clothing, and dangerous-appearing dogs.

"The land isn't fertile, apparently," suggested Clarissa to Tom Oglethorpe.

He'd removed his jacket and tie now that he was in the back country, and smoked a panatella cigar. "What makes you say that?" he asked pleasantly, one arm familiarly around her shoulders, for they had begun sharing the same bed, not out of love, but loneliness, compassion, and unwholesome desires.

She did not push him away, for they considered

themselves sophisticated individuals; they had been abroad and seen differing civilizations and felt unfettered by the standards of the mob. "The farms are so poor," she insisted.

He chuckled as he puffed his panatella. "You Yankees—you see a plot of land, you can't wait to dig it up, but we Southerners are not constantly striving, and we'd rather enjoy the Eden that God has given us than work our fingers to the bones."

"I doubt it's Eden for children who appear poorly fed."

"They play in the woods, hunt—it's not a bad life, especially when New York children live in alleyways and are fed milk from diseased cows who eat garbage, according to what I've read. We Southerners are a people who distrust the so-called benefits of industry."

They passed a fence, on the other side of which a field could be seen, covered with faded brown bushes, a rank of slaves shoveling.

"They're preparing the soil for next year," explained Tom. "And I know what you're thinking, since you're a Yankee. You look out there and see the purported inhumanity of slavery, but try to forget the abolitionist babble you've heard all your life, open your mind, and ask yourself—where would they be if they weren't slaves? Do you think Africa was paradise? Who do you think sold them to the white slave traders in the first place, but their own black brethren? Don't you know that slavery was a fine old institution in Africa long before the white man ever arrived? Don't blame everything on us Southerners, and besides, if we freed our slaves tomorrow, they'd depress the labor market, throw white men out of work, and riots would ensue. There's no simple solution to this dilemma, despite the proclamations of abolitionists. I hope you don't intend to lecture me continually on slavery. Besides, who among us is really free?"

"To be fair, you must admit we're more free than they, Tom."

"I suppose," he agreed wearily. "But the truth is more complex than either abolitionists or fire-eaters would have you believe. Please don't pass judgment before you live among us awhile. Think of this as a trip abroad, instead of trying to change us."

"All right," she agreed. "I'll look at slavery coldly and dispassionately, then make up my own mind. I have a feeling it'll be even more disgusting than I imagined, but I won't continually criticize you, and if it ever becomes unbearable, just drop me at the nearest train station."

He held out his hand. "It's a deal."

After Mangas Coloradas's strength returned fully, he scouted the terrain surrounding the Chiricahua camp, accompanied by Victorio, Juh, Barbonsito, and Chuntz. Situated on a sprawling mountaintop, surrounded by pine and fir trees, the camp was easy to defend due to steep drops in all directions; great distances could be seen from the wickiups.

Mangas Coloradas and his warriors found spacious caverns, hidden gulches, jagged ledges, and bottomless fissures. Surprise would be unlikely, although the bluecoat Army had managed to destroy well-protected winter camps of the Jicarillas and Mescaleros.

One day Mangas Coloradas and his warriors came upon Coyuntura sitting in a cave, looking at something in his lap.

"What have you there?" asked Mangas Coloradas.

Coyuntura held up the Bible. "It is a holy article of the Mexicanos. But I do not understand its power."

Mangas Coloradas accepted it, then flipped the pages. "Too bad Sunny Bear is not here, for he could tell you what it means."

"Do you think he will ever come back?" inquired Coyuntura.

Mangas Coloradas thought a few moments, then replied, "Sunny Bear shall return one day, I am certain."

The short, battle-scarred warrior known as Chuntz shook his head vehemently, for he never had liked Sunny Bear. "He will not return, because he truly was not one of us."

"You are wrong," insisted the great chief Mangas Coloradas. "Sunny Bear would have stayed forever, were it not for his family in the eastern lands. Sunny Bear may look like a White Eyes, and sometimes he is as stupid as a White Eyes, but in his heart he always will be a warrior of the People. I wish he were here right now, for he would offer valuable counsel."

There was a knock on the door, startling Dr. Steck. He cleared his throat and said, "Come in."

A tall, brawny man in a black capecoat and tan vaquero hat appeared, accompanied by an angelic-looking child. "Dr. Steck?"

"At your service," said good Dr. Steck, for he sincerely wanted to help people.

"I'm your new assistant—how do you do. Here are my orders. Name's Barrington, and this is my niece, Gloria."

Doctor Steck felt his hand being worked, then the child was presented. "Welcome," he said as he accepted the document, then read it carefully. "I never asked for an assistant, but how did you learn to speak Apache so well?"

"I lived among them for about a year."

"You must be that fellow I heard about—the officer who everyone thought had been killed—yes, of course, Captain Barrington."

"That's me, but I've resigned my commission and have devoted myself to making peace among the Americans, Apaches, and Mexicans—impossible though that may be."

Dr. Steck smiled. "I have devoted myself to the identical goal, but Washington prefers military solutions, and the military thinks I am an idiot, which I imagine was your evaluation when you were in the Army, isn't that correct?"

"We thought you didn't realize how treacherous the Apaches were," admitted Nathanial. "But after living among them, I understand their point of view. This land is not just dirt, but a holy legacy that they feel obligated to defend. You see, everything an Apache does is sacramental, even eating food and killing enemies. America represents not just an attack on their land, but upon their souls. And they don't trust you in the least."

Dr. Steck appeared hurt. "Why?"

"Because you promise what you cannot deliver."

"I have been betrayed by Washington, but we can talk more of this later, after we get you settled in." Dr. Steck turned to the child and said in the musical voice adults employ when speaking with little ones, "How do you like New Mexico, Gloria."

"The mountains are beautiful," replied the former

denizen of Five Points, "and my Uncle Nathanial will teach me to ride."

"But first," interjected Nathanial, "I must get her enrolled in school. Is there one?"

"We've got a schoolmarm, name of Gwendolyn Andrews. Smart woman."

"If she's smart, what's she doing at Fort Thorn?"

"The same thing you and I are doing here—trying to help make the world a more Christian place. She's quite interesting, because she grew up in one of the Shaker communities back east, and if I weren't married . . ." Dr. Steck let his voice trail off whimsically. "She's a tall drink of water, but don't expect a great beauty. Her allure is special, and comes from within."

"I don't need another wife," said Nathanial, "but she sounds ideal for Gloria. Where can I find this paragon of womanhood?"

"Her classroom's behind the supply room. I guess you'll have to live with me and my wife until suitable quarters can be found."

"No, we'll go to Santa Fe, where I have children whom I haven't seen for some time. When I return, perhaps you can have a nice comfortable hut waiting."

"Should be enough time, and while in Sante Fe, you can deliver a request for food for the Mescaleros to General Garland. You see, our supplies come from the Army. They are the law in New Mexico Territory, and General Garland is more or less the king. Have you ever met him?"

"Yes, but I was just a junior officer."

"How odd that you and I both prepared for other professions, yet here we are, Indian agents in New Mexico Territory. Perhaps you can help General Garland understand the Apache side better, and accom-

plish what has eluded me. You might be just what this
territory needs."

Nathanial felt nostalgic for the Army as he and
Gloria rode toward Fort Thorn's schoolhouse, their
conveyance a wagon and two workhorses. Nathanial
held the reins, and Gloria sat pertly beside him, hands
folded in her lap, like a lady. Never had Gloria been in
an Army camp, and she liked the cleanliness, orderliness, the feeling of safety that comes from knowing
an Army is available to protect a little girl.

The dragoons were in garrison—cleaning weapons,
caring for horses, and performing the janitorial work
that was so much a part of every soldier's day. Nathanial found the adobe shack behind the supply
room, looked through the window, and saw a tall, gangly woman in a floor-length dark brown dress, with
her back to a wall, lecturing fourteen students, three
of whom were Indians.

"Guess we'd better come back some other time,"
said Nathanial. "Let's go to the sutler's store until
class is out."

"Do they have ice cream?"

"Doubtful, but candy might be possible, and I can
get a drink."

He lifted her into the air, dropped her onto the seat,
and was about to board himself, when he saw a
sergeant running toward him. "Well, I'll be damned,"
said Nathanial.

The sergeant had a lumpy nose and large ears,
vaguely resembling a muscular leprechaun with red
side-whiskers. He came to a halt in front of Nathanial.
"I heer'd you was here, and yer uglier'n ever."

Nathanial held out his hand. "Sergeant Duffy, how

good to see you. And please don't salute, because I'm not in the Army anymore. I'm a damned civilian."

"You'll be back," said Sergeant Duffy. "And who is this little angel?"

"My name is Gloria." She held up the clown. "And this is Gerhardt."

"He looks like one of the men in my company." Sergeant Duffy turned to Nathanial. "Gold prospectin'?"

"You're looking at the new assistant to Dr. Steck."

"He's the biggest clown in New Mexico Territory."

Gloria replied, "I thought Dr. Steck was nice." Sergeant Duffy reminded her of Five Points.

"Everybody's nice to cute little gals," replied Sergeant Duffy, "even me, but that man wouldn't know a bull's ass from a banjo, and now you're a-gonna team up with 'im?"

"The killing must stop," said Nathanial. "I'm convinced of it."

Sergeant Duffy chortled. "All you have to do is convince the Apaches."

"And the white people, and the Mexicans."

"It's been my 'sperience that the onliest way to convince an Apache of anythin' is plant a bullet 'twixt his eyes. That's how I've stayed alive." He glanced at Gloria. "Apaches love little white girls. How'd you like to be a slave of the Apaches?"

"They'll have to kill me first," she said with determination.

Sergeant Duffy laughed. "I should have you in my company. You've got more sand than most of my 'cruits."

The schoolhouse door opened, children spilled outside, and Gloria evaluated them coldly. They don't

look any smarter than I, she tried to convince herself.
Then the schoolmarm appeared with her horsey face,
a slightly off-kilter mouth, and an upturned nose, but
she had a friendly smile and long legs; Nathanial always had been partial to long-legged women.

"New student?" she asked with a smile.

"I hope so," replied Nathanial.

The schoolmarm stood erectly, one palm over the
other, as she turned to the child. "What's your name?"

"Gloria."

"I am Miss Andrews." She glanced at Nathanial.
"And who might you be?"

"Nathanial Barrington, ma'am. I'm Dr. Steck's new
assistant, and he recommended you. And this is
Sergeant Duffy."

Gwendolyn frowned at Sergeant Duffy, who removed his hat and bowed. "Howdy, ma'am."

"Good afternoon, Sergeant Duffy. What are you
doing here?"

"I was jest talkin' with the cap'n, because he was
my commandin' officer fer a few years, an' I can
vouch fer 'im."

"A dubious endorsement," replied the schoolmarm,
then she looked at Nathanial. "There should be no
problem, provided Gloria is willing to work hard, because hard work is the foundation of all other achieve-
ments. Don't you agree?"

"Completely," replied Nathanial. "She's a good girl
and eager to get an education, aren't you, my darling?"

"Uh-huh." She didn't appear especially enthusiastic.

"She can start in the morning," said Miss Andrews.

"I'm leaving for Sante Fe," explained Nathanial,

"and I don't have anywhere to leave her, so I'll take her with me, and she can begin when we return."

"Her education is more important," chided Miss Andrews. "She can stay with me."

Nathanial smiled. "That's a wonderful idea."

"But I want to be with you," protested Gloria.

"It is more important to be educated," stated Nathanial. "I'm sorry—my mind is made up."

"You just want to get rid of me," she pouted. "So's you can get drunk and chase women."

Nathanial smiled at the schoolmarm. "The child says the damnedest things."

"I suspect she's telling the truth, but I will take care of her, fill her mind with the information she needs to know, and make you proud of her."

"You mustn't be real strict. She's not used to rules."

"She'll have to get used to them, because even grown-ups must live by rules. Where is her mother?"

"Died."

"A girl needs a woman to teach her what a man can't."

"He's taught me a lot," insisted Gloria. "He's a wonderful teacher."

"But," replied Nathanial, "you require a scientific education, which Miss Andrews has so generously agreed to provide." Nathanial turned to the schoolmarm. "I'll bring her things to the schoolhouse first thing in the morning, if that's all right."

"You can bring them this evening, unless you have a drinking engagement. In the meantime, Gloria and I can get to know each other." She turned toward her new student. "We can bake cookies."

"I love cookies," said Gloria, her mood abruptly altering.

Miss Andrews took Gloria's hand, and they headed for the door of the schoolhouse; Gloria didn't look back. Remarkable, thought Nathanial. They promise to love you forever, then leave first time a cookie comes along. "What do you know about the school-marm?" he asked Sergeant Duffy.

"She showed up one day, on her way to Californio where she planned to be a schoolmarm, but found she was needed here. She's good with the children, keeps to herself, don't gossip, real religious, used to be a Shaker they say."

"Who's sleeping with her?"

"Lieutenant Wood—the camp commander. He was with us at the Santa Rita Copper Mines, remember?"

"How can I forget the ebullient Lieutenant Wood, but I can't help wondering why you haven't pursued the schoolmarm, Sergeant Duffy. Perhaps she's yearn-ing for a grizzled old reprobate such as yourself."

"I wouldn't marry a woman taller'n me. Be too much like climbin' a tree. Who're you married to these days, Captain Barrington?"

"My present wife is divorcing me, as far as I know."

Sergeant Duffy pondered that for several moments. "Well, it ain't none of my bizness, but it seems a man should make up his mind *afore* he gits married, not af-terwards."

"If you know so much about marriage, why are you single?"

"Ain't met the right one. Besides, if'n I git married, I can't go to whorehouses no more."

"Don't you find whorehouses sordid after so many years of patronage?"

"Cap'n Barrington, if I had my way, I'd spend the rest of my life in a whorehouse."

"I've just had an idea. How'd you like to accompany me to Santa Fe? Two men riding light shouldn't
have any trouble, and you can patronize one of the
whorehouses after we arrive."

"I can't just run off like that." Sergeant Duffy
snapped his fingers.

"Leave it to me," replied Nathanial.

Nathanial performed an about-face, then marched
to the orderly room, where he didn't recognize the
sergeant behind the desk. "I'd like to speak with the
commanding officer," he said.

"He's in his office, sir."

Nathanial crossed the orderly room, banged on the
appropriate door, and a voice said, "Come in." Seated
behind the desk was a clean-shaven officer with a
friendly country face, an Ohioan a few years younger
than Nathanial. "Well I'll be damned," he said. "Captain Barrington—what're you doing here?"

Nathanial explained recent developments to Lieutenant William Henry Wood, West Point class of '49.
"In my capacity as assistant Indian agent, I've got to
go to Santa Fe. It would be customary to request an
escort, but I'll need only one man, Sergeant Duffy."

"I'll have Sergeant Branigan write the orders this
afternoon. When're you leaving?"

"Soon as I can. By the way, I left my niece with the
schoolmarm. What do you know about her?"

Wood raised his eyebrows. "Surely you don't have
designs—"

"I understand you've already staked your claim."

"I had no idea it was common knowledge, but I
hope in the fullness of time that we might be married."

"Congratulations. She's got wonderful legs."

"Aren't you married?"

"My wife is divorcing me, actually."

"In other words, no man's wife, daughter, or grand-mother is safe, because I remember you well, Barrington. I imagine you'll leap on poor Gwendolyn one of these days when I'm not around. If you do, I may feel compelled to shoot you."

"I am so disgusted with women," replied Nathanial, "I refuse to have anything to do with them. They say they love you, and the next day they're with some-body else. From now on, if I need a woman, I'll buy one at the nearest whorehouse. It's the only honest way to deal with the bitches, and I'll never trust an-other as long as I live."

Nathanial stopped for a few snorts at the sutler's store, and it was dark when he returned to the school-marm's shed, balancing Gloria's trunk on his shoul-der. Miss Andrews opened the door. "We thought the Indians had got you."

Nathanial carried the trunk into the combination parlor, dining room, and kitchen. "They wouldn't dare steal Gloria's clothes. Why—General Garland would campaign against them if they tried." He lowered the trunk to the planked floor, then turned to Gloria. "Are we getting on all right?"

Gloria nodded, apparently happy to be settled down.

"Get ready for bed," he told her. "I want to speak with Miss Andrews alone, and I'll say good-bye be-fore I leave."

Gloria looked at them knowingly, then entered the next room, leaving Nathanial and the schoolmarm near the kitchen table.

"I hope she's not giving you any trouble," he said.

"All she needs is someone to care for her and teach her what's right."

"I don't know what she told you, but she's led a harsh life. You must make allowances."

"I have always believed children prefer to be good if you give them half a chance."

They discussed fees, then Nathanial paid three months in advance. "If you need textbooks or supplies, please let me know. I'll buy whatever the school needs."

She smiled. "A benefactor has arrived at last. I have been praying for you, Captain Barrington."

"Write everything on a sheet of paper, and I'll forward it to New York. Nothing is too good for children or their teacher. I understand you were a Shaker?"

She lowered her eyes. "We called it the United Society of Believers."

"Don't be embarrassed, because I'm something of a religious fanatic myself, and we have another trait in common, because I've quit the Army, and you've left the society. I became tired of fighting Apaches—how about you?"

"I wanted to teach children who otherwise might not receive an education."

"You're a saint, Miss Andrews."

"I have many failings," she replied, a note of self-disapproval in her voice.

Nathanial wondered whether to pounce upon the unsuspecting schoolmarm, for he'd always been partial to ladies with long legs. But Gloria waited in the next room, and he might have to kill Lieutenant Wood, who appeared a decent fellow. Nathanial figured a formerly celibate ex-Shaker woman would be gunpowder in the hands of a passionate man. He found himself lusting for his daughter's schoolmarm, and just as he was reaching for her dark brown hair, the bedroom door opened.

"I'm ready to go to bed," said Gloria.

She wore her white silk robe and looked like a cherub, backlit by the candle on the dresser. They followed her into the stark but neat bedroom, she crawled into bed, and they stood on either side of her. Nathanial knew her moods and saw she was satisfied, as if she'd finally found a home, while Miss Andrews had the child she'd always wanted.

Nathanial leaned over the bed. "Be a good girl, and please don't make trouble for your teacher, all right?"

"I'll miss you," she said.

Nathanial turned to Miss Andrews. "May I be alone with my niece?"

The schoolmarm stepped back to the door, and when they were alone, Nathanial said, "I shouldn't mention this, but while I'm gone, I don't want you stealing anything or killing anybody."

"You don't trust me," she said sadly.

"Let's say my confidence was undermined when you stole that wallet in Texas."

"I've learned my lesson," replied Gloria. "F'God's sake, you nearly got shot."

"If you want to test your skills, apply them to learning, not crime. But if anybody ever threatens you, and I think you know what I'm talking about, just take your little gun and blow his brains out. Understand?"

"I wasn't afraid back in Texas, was I?"

"Never have I felt more like your proud Uncle Nathanial."

Meanwhile, in the kitchen-parlor, Miss Andrews sat on a chair near the fireplace, hands folded neatly on her lap, eyes focused on the middle distance, the pic-

ture of repose, but a troubled lady. She felt guilty
about leaving the Shaker community, doubtful about
sleeping with Lieutenant Wood (who had relieved her
of her virginity), and ashamed of lustful feelings she
experienced toward men in general.

She didn't love Lieutenant Wood, but he provided a
certain useful function. Sometimes she was tempted
to rip off her clothes and sleep with every man on the
post. A virgin until thirty-five, her frustrated desires
threatened to overwhelm her. Only Protestant theol-
ogy stood between her and total harlotry.

Desire for men had caused her to leave the Shaker
community, in addition to her need to help children.
She'd hoped to get married, but had yet to fall in love.
She found herself thinking about Nathanial Barrington, about whom Gloria had said much. The drunkard's affection for the child was touching. He's a good
man underneath, she evaluated, but he needs a good
woman to calm him down.

The bedroom door opened, then Nathanial appeared. "I'm going to miss her," he said. "Funny how
we grow attached to people."

She arose from her chair. "She loves you so . . .
why, she couldn't stop talking about you all the time
you were gone."

"What did she say?" asked Nathanial, who realized
that Miss Andrews was nearly as tall as he, and it was
rare that he met women that tall.

"She talked about how good you are."

"I have done amazingly selfish things," admitted
Nathanial.

"But God loves sinners most of all, and contrition
is the core of Christian life. You're a wonderful man,
although it probably embarrasses you to hear it."

The heat from their bodies radiated as they looked into each other's eyes from a distance of five feet. "Good night," he said. "I'll be back in about three weeks."

She followed as he groped for the doorknob. "Please be careful."

They were only inches apart. He placed his hands on her shoulders, lightly kissed her lips, and she closed her eyes, enjoying the moment. He wondered whether to press his attack, but she was a kindly religious woman, and he decided to be honorable for a change, although her long legs felt miraculous against his. Simultaneously, each took a step backward, breathing more heavily than normal. There were several awkward moments, then he said, "I look forward to seeing you again."

He opened the door and propelled himself into the cool night air. This is an excellent woman, he told himself as he climbed into the wagon. I must not treat her like a saloon tramp, and after I'm divorced, perhaps I'll marry her. The wagon rumbled toward the gate, and a smile creased Nathanial's features as he thought of sitting opposite her, gazing at her long legs.

Lost in lascivious imaginings, Nathanial didn't realize he was under observation by the post commander, Lieutenant Wood, who stood in the shadows on the far side of the parade ground, certain Nathanial had planked Miss Andrews. Lieutenant Wood pretended to be inspecting the post, a perfectly normal activity for the commander, and no one took any special note as gradually he worked his way toward the schoolhouse.

He rapped on the door, and finally it opened a

crack. "What do you want?" Miss Andrews asked
coldly.

"To see you," he replied.

"I have a child with me."

"Sure, but it's proper for *him* to come here."

"Shsshh. The child is in the next room."

He stepped into the parlor, closed the door behind
him, grabbed her chin tightly, forced her to look at
him, and said, "Did you do anything improper, my
dear?"

"You have no right to speak to me this way."

Rather than provoke himself further, Lieutenant
Wood left the schoolhouse abruptly and walked
briskly toward his adobe hut. Who the hell does Barrington think he is, coming here and interfering with
the schoolmarm's and my little romance? Next time
he wants an escort, he can whistle at the moon. And if
an Apache kills him, so much the better.

Nathanial sat on the wagon's seat as his workhorses
carried him into the night. It was another mile to
Mesilla, where he hoped to find a decent restaurant, a
thin gauze of clouds obscuring the moon and stars.

I should have married an ordinary woman like
Gwendolyn Andrews, he told himself, because ordinary women are faithful, unlike concert pianists. He
saw himself lying naked with the love-starved schoolmarm, those statuesque legs wrapped around him. It
was the first real desire he'd felt since Clarissa had
skipped, and he began to feel alive again.

In the glow of new love he did not anticipate an ambush, but fifty yards ahead, lurking behind boulders
and cactus alongside the road, were four half-starved
Mescalero warriors from the nearby reservation, armed

with knives, war clubs, and lances, but no rifles or pistols.

They observed the approaching wagon, the driver apparently asleep, and Apaches considered horses their second favorite delicacy, after mules. Moreover, articles of value doubtlessly were carried by the wagon, and the driver might have a new rifle and ammunition.

They were Lamey, Muchacho, Cebolla, and Panjaro, and they'd planned a bold act of terror as an alternative to semistarvation at Fort Thorn. As the wagon drew closer, they glanced at each other meaningfully, their eyes glowing like those of coyotes. Booty or a warrior's death was their plan, for peace had delivered no benefits.

Meanwhile, Nathanial dreamed about long legs, and the more he thought about it, Miss Andrews really wasn't *that* ugly, because who was more beautiful, she who dedicated her life to children, or she who needed the worship of the multitudes?

True, Miss Andrew's mouth was small and not well defined, like a rosebud with a bent petal, or a piece of candy that had been slightly squashed. But would the candy be less sweet, or the rose less fragrant? The more Nathanial thought about Miss Andrews, the more entangled he became in her long legs.

Nathanial came abreast of the four disgruntled Mescalero Apaches, and at a signal from Lamey, they rushed the wagon, expecting to dispatch him easily, but their quarry had lived among the Mimbreno People, and his senses remained alert regardless of lustful impulses ravaging his mind. At the first sound he drew his gun, thumbed backed the hammer, and opened fire.

His first bullet struck Lamey on the forehead, and his second dropped Muchacho. Then he turned to deal with the others and saw a war club looping toward his skull, while a lance was thrust toward his side. Nathanial threw himself backward, performed a reverse somersault on the bed of the wagon, and came up with his gun blazing. His bullet smashed into Cebolla's stomach; the warrior shrieked as he went down. Panjaro thrust his lance at Nathanial, who batted it out of the way with a sideward sweep of his left arm, then brought the barrel of the gun down on the Mescalero's head.

The force of the blow hurled Panjaro out of the wagon and onto the side of the road. Nathanial threw a dead Apache off the seat, grabbed the reins, and slapped them against the horse's haunches. "Giddyup!" he hollered.

The great equines required no encouragement, for the surprise attack had unnerved them. Straining their harnesses, they galloped down the road, the wheels of the wagon bouncing off the boulders, carrying Nathanial to Mesilla. Guess it's not as safe around here as I thought, he told himself, struggling to hold onto the reins, the cold breeze whistling past.

Panjaro's vision blurred, and he felt as if his head had cracked in two. He prodded his fingers into the wound, but his skull appeared intact.

Bodies lay nearby, making him shudder. He rolled his friends onto their backs. They were dead, but miraculously he had survived. He wanted to bury them properly, but his head continued to bleed. I will go back and get the others, he decided.

Panjaro stumbled toward the horses. It would be a disgrace to admit the war party had failed. The women will laugh at me. Finally, he climbed onto his war pony's bare back. "I cannot see well," he said. "Take me home."

Panjaro tasted the bile of defeat as he returned to the reservation. How can one White Eyes defeat four Mescaleros? he wondered. He arrived before dawn, staggered toward the tipi of Chief Zeenata, and said, "I must talk with you."

The chief crawled outside, the bandanna crooked on his head. Demoralized by too many relatives killed by bluecoat soldiers, Chief Zeenata had surrendered to the White Eyes. "What happened to you?" he asked as he gazed at Panjaro's wound.

"It is best you do not know," replied Panjaro, "but Lamey, Muchacho, and Cebolla are dead on the road to Mesilla."

Chief Zeenata scowled. "You will bring the wrath of the bluecoat Army upon us."

"The people are hungry because peace does not fill their bellies."

"A bullet should fill your belly, you renegade. Go to your tipi and stay out of sight. I will take care of the others."

Panjaro made his way among conical tipis, found the one he shared with his parents and young brothers and sisters, crawled beneath a torn U.S. Army blanket, and closed his eyes. I am tired of being hungry, he decided. When I am able, I will join Chief Gomez in the mountains.

Chief Gomez was leader of a renegade band of Mescaleros who lived in the Davis Mountains. He refused to surrender or accommodate the White Eyes in any fashion, and most of the raiding in southeastern New Mexico Territory was his work.

* * *

Next morning, Lieutenant Wood received a note from the new assistant Indian agent:

Dear Lieutenant Wood:
    Last night I was attacked by four Apaches on the road to Mesilla, and killed two or three of them, and maybe all of them. I recommend that you post a regular patrol on the road, to prevent such encounters in the future. I'm off to Sante Fe in about an hour, and will discuss these matters with you in detail when I return.
                            Nathanial Barrington
                            Assistant Indian Agent

"Too bad they failed," murmured Lieutenant Wood.

Later in the day, Juan Ortega asked to see the post commander, and Lieutenant Wood couldn't refuse an audience with the mayor of Mesilla. "What can I do for you?" asked the lieutenant curtly, as Ortega stood in front of his desk.

"I am here concerning the wanton attack on the new assistant Indian agent last night on the road to Mesilla. Why have there been no arrests?"

"The guilty parties haven't been identified."

"You know they are from the reservation, because where else would they come from?"

"The Davis Mountains, where Chief Gomez is holed up."

"Apaches are the same wherever they live, and if you do not punish them, they will be emboldened to do worse next time."

"In the United States of America, we don't punish without proof," said Lieutenant Wood.

"You will not even fight for your own people."

"A soldier must follow the law like everybody else."

"If the law does not make sense, it cannot be a good law." Ortega yanked out his gun. "This is what Apaches respect."

Lieutenant Wood looked him in the eye. "If you harm any Apaches, I will not hesitate to hang you."

Ortega grinned sardonically. "If I kill an Apache, you will hang me, but if an Apache tries to kill one of your government officials, it is perfectly fine. Do you see the inconsistency?"

"I see the law, but that may be a difficult concept for a Mexican to comprehend."

They stared at each other in undisguised hatred, for America and Mexico had fought a major war only nine years previously. Then, without another word, Ortega stomped out of the office. Lieutenant Wood leaned back in his chair and lit a cheroot, reflecting on the encounter. *I wouldn't be surprised if we had a full-scale massacre around here one of these days.*

Mesilla buzzed over the latest outrage, and for Raphael Fonseca, it carried painful memories of the night his family had been murdered. He broke into a sweat, his pulse pounded, and he had to drink cold water to settle himself down. *No one is safe,* he said to himself as he glanced around fearfully. *How much can we take?*

At the Mesilla Guards meeting on Saturday night, Juan Ortega told them, "The Americano Army will not help us, so next time the Apaches strike, *we shall strike back*! Maintain your weapons ready at all times, companeros. When the moment arrives, we must move fast."

9

Clarissa had expected a white mansion with Grecian columns, lavish rooms, and a wide veranda suitable for entertaining, but instead the so-called manor house was boxy, smallish, paint peeling, roof leaking, with slaves grouchy, tattered, and rebellious.

Not especially clean, the manor house also lacked running water and central heat, but offered comfortable old furniture. It was far more lugubrious than Fort Craig, her standard for lowdown living. She accustomed herself to the outhouse, less frequent bathing, and pork chops, while Tom spent little time managing his holdings, for that task was left to his overseer, a stout, jolly fellow named Tibbs, who carried no whip and seemed on reasonably good terms with the unenthusiastic slaves. Everyone's expectations, including Tom's, seemed modest to nonexistent. Clarissa tried to maintain an open mind, recognizing that her northern "go-ahead" opinions were foreign to old Beaulah Land.

The slave quarters consisted of a log hut, not especially crowded, with a fireplace for warmth and cooking. Most slaves weren't friendly or cooperative, but

Clarissa attributed their hostility to lack of hope for better lives.

Somehow Tom's plantation, Larkspur, endured, growing its food, refining sugar, and selling sufficient cotton to provide whatever cash was necessary. The slaves were permitted to raise their own vegetables, chickens, and pigs, a task left to the very old and very young, for everyone else had to work in the fields or the manor house.

With slaves to perform all labor, the gentry was free to indulge their favorite pastimes, which centered on hunting. Every several days the masters and their ladies would gather on someone's plantation, dogs were released, and the men rode across the countryside, shooting deer, rabbits, foxes, and anything else that had the misfortune to stumble their way, while women followed on horseback, cheering them on.

Then edible creatures were skinned, gutted, and roasted over open fires, to the accompaniment of much drinking, gambling, riding contests, and other pleasurable activities, with great bonfires blazing into the night. The men became besotted, good fellowship prevailed, and her hosts discussed a variety of subjects, from Virgil and Plato to Sir Walter Scott and Jefferson Davis, for education and knowledge of current events was considered a mark of good breeding among the planter class, and even the women were sent to special academies, where they studied the same subjects as the men, although northern propaganda portrayed belles as empty-headed, giggling children, and their men as ignorant, violent buffoons.

Clarissa's dresses grew tighter as she fell into the easy self-indulgent round of activities. Maintaining her scientific objectivity, she had to admit that planters were not nearly as anxious as northern businessmen, while the darkies whom she saw daily were no worse off than the lower tier of unemployed freemen in the North, who lived in alleyways and begged in the streets. But in her gut she still felt it was wrong for one man to own another, like a dog.

She saw herself sojourning in a strange foreign land, such as the mountains of Carpathia, with new customs and a different language, for the accents of her companions sometimes were incomprehensible. Meanwhile, they treated her as an oddity, and occasionally she was insulted obliquely, but she always smiled politely and held in her anger, like the researcher that she considered herself to be.

An important component of a planter's existence involved visiting each other's homes, most of which were as wretched as Larkspur. One afternoon, while enjoying tea and cakes with the Danforths, who lived down the road from Tom Oglethorpe, a slave spilled tea onto the lap of the mistress, who slapped the slave's face rather hard, then sent her to the fields.

The incident passed without comment, for evidently such an outrage was common, not worth discussing. Another time, riding a carriage to the Newcombe plantation, Clarissa was astonished to see in the distance a slave hanging by his hands from a tree, while a white man whipped him.

"What's that about?" asked Clarissa.

Tom shrugged. "Perhaps he tried to escape, or maybe he sassed the wrong person. Beating slaves disturbs me as it does you, and whenever I have trouble with one of them, I sell the son-of-a-bitch. You Yankees consider yourself compassionate because you merely allow children to starve in the hovels of your cities, but that slave, who is being beaten to within an inch of his life, will be fed and sheltered until he recovers. And if he does his work, he will have nothing to fear, unlike northern laborers who are fired at the whims of their bosses. Which is worse?"

Clarissa felt guilty living on the backs of others, but had no desire to make herself suffer, so she continued her southern interlude and tried not to worry about slaves, even when they looked at her with pleading or angry eyes.

In early December Clarissa and Tom traveled to North Carolina to attend a hunt given by Wade Hampton III, one of the wealthiest men in the South. Aged thirty-nine, scion of a proud old family, he owned thousands of slaves on plantations from Virginia to Mississippi, was a state senator in South Carolina, had traveled in Europe, and received his education at the College of South Carolina. If America had an aristocracy, he would have been a prince, for his grandfather, Wade Hampton I, had been a hero of the Revolutionary War.

A tall, strapping fellow with curly side whiskers attached to a brushlike mustache, Hampton welcomed Tom and Clarissa to his rustic country mansion, which reminded Clarissa of castles she'd seen in Bavaria during her honeymoon. The guests sat around a blazing fireplace, wore rough hunting clothes, and pretended to be hearty woodsmen and trappers, when actually they were exceedingly pampered individuals.

Among the women was sprightly twenty-seven-year-old Mary McDuffie, daughter of former Governor and Senator George McDuffie of South Carolina, and Hampton was betrothed to her, because his first

wife, Margaret Preston, expired during the summer of
'55.

Clarissa learned that southern men and women
were extremely charming and hospitable, yet in the
kitchen, barn, and fields, slaves worked long hours. It
would have been easier for Clarissa if her hosts were
obviously disgusting, but they were decent Americans, provided one didn't mention the occasional
whipping. Besides, no one ever suggested how to feed
slaves on the day after emancipation.

Later, while walking Clarissa to her room, Tom
couldn't help remarking on Wade Hampton. "He'll
probably end up governor of South Carolina someday,
and you may be surprised to know that he's a moder-
ate, speaking against secession, which makes him un-
popular in certain quarters, but I can tell you a story
that neatly sums up the man. Like most of us, he was
raised by a Negro nanny—she was called Mauma
Nelly. After he grew up, she became nanny for his
sons, and finally, in recognition of her faithful service,
he told her that he had decided to set her free, buy her
a farm in the North, and provide a small income. He
thought she'd be overjoyed, but instead she cried and
begged him not to send her away. 'What did I do
wrong?' she kept asking, until he withdrew his offer.
So it's true that occasionally we kill a nigra, but it's
also true that often we become quite devoted to each
other. This is a complicated land, unlike the simple
morality tales retailed by abolitionists."

Since Tom and Clarissa were unmarried, he could
not enter her bedroom, at least not openly at the estate
of Wade Hampton. They had told the lie that they intended to marry as soon as Clarissa's divorce became
final, and everyone pretended to understand. So she

and Tom kissed good night in front of her door, and she was pleased for the opportunity to sleep alone for a change.

Attired in a diaphanous pink gown, she crawled into bed. Despite rational arguments, she continued to believe that slavery was horribly wrong. While wrestling with the great issue of the age, Clarissa heard her door open. She opened her mouth to scream, when Tom appeared out of the darkness, attired in his robe. "Good evening," he whispered with a bow. "'Tis time for mice to run through the halls, searching for beautiful bits of cheese."

He removed his robe, then covered her with kisses while she lay wondering how many other mice were creeping about at that hour, and perhaps Wade Hampton was on his way to the boudoir of Miss McDuffie. There are two Souths, reflected Clarissa—the seen and the unseen.

Clarissa and Tom embraced not out of profound passion, yet the pairing brought something new and deviant out of her, which satisfied Tom greatly. I think she's in love with me, he mused as he bit her earlobe, but she was using him as he used her.

They slept briefly, and before dawn there was a knock on the door—time to get up. They heard horses in front of the main house, dogs barked, and a slave cursed beneath Clarissa's window.

Everybody enjoyed a breakfast of ham, eggs, grits, and biscuits cooked by slaves who'd been up most of the night. Then hunters and huntresses gathered in the yard and mounted their horses, whose reins were held by slaves. The seigneurial Wade Hampton wore a wide-brimmed dark brown hat with a feather in the crown and a sword in a scabbard at his waist. He

looked like a general of dragoons as he nodded to one
of the slaves.

Whining and yapping dogs were released, and they
took off like buckshot, headed for the deep woods.
Wade Hampton spurred his horse, an Arabian stallion,
who eagerly moved after the hounds, and they were
followed by the remainder of the hunting party, the
ladies riding sidesaddle, but ladies were not expected
to kill anything, only to inspire hunters.

It wasn't long before there was shooting, cheers of
victory, groans of disappointment, much joyous confusion, and the gathering of dead animals by slaves.
Even Tom managed to shoot a wild turkey that had
fled from its hiding place, chased by a dog.

In the afternoon it was reported that the dogs had
found the trail of a bear, and Hampton was going after
him, since he especially enjoyed hunting bears.
Hampton's horse galloped onward, followed by one
of his slaves, while the party followed at a cautious
distance, the men with pistols ready, no one wanting
an encounter with a four-hundred-pound monster with
five-inch claws. Horses dodged giant pines as they
raced toward a gray steep-sided cliff.

"There they are," said Tom, pointing straight ahead.

Hampton and his slave dismounted, while the bear
reared on its hind legs, back to the cliff. It snorted angrily as it looked at riders converging around, aiming
their pistols.

Clarissa thought the contest one-sided, for evidently they were going to shoot the hapless animal.
Instead, Hampton climbed down from his saddle,
drew his sword, and advanced toward the bear.
Clarissa turned to Tom, who placed his finger over his

lips, indicating she should keep her Yankee tongue silent.

Hampton raised the sword over his head, then brought it down on the bear, which raised an arm to protect itself. The blade sliced through to the bone, the animal shrieked in rage, then rushed Hampton, who backstepped quickly, cracking the bear on the skull. Dazed, blood pouring into its eye, the bear charged once more, holding its right arm for protection, but Hampton nearly chopped it off at the elbow. The desperate bear lunged suddenly, baring its teeth, and the hellish blade produced a compound fracture on its skull. The bear's vision terminated; it fell to the ground and lay still, brains steaming in the cool mountain air.

Everyone applauded politely as Hampton grinned with pleasure. Then he sheathed his sword, lifted the bear, and laid it over the saddle of a packhorse brought especially for the purpose. His head held high, Wade Hampton rode away, followed by the bear hanging head down over the saddle, blood dripping onto swishing leaves.

Clarissa felt like vomiting as she followed the others to the feast. In her mind Hampton's killing of the bear seemed to sum up, in a few frenzied moments, the truth of the South: its courage, honor, and utter cruelty. It was difficult to imagine a northern man, even her brawling husband, going out of his way to kill at close range an angry black bear.

We northerners are too civilized for serious bloodshed, she concluded, while my southern companions do not hesitate to swim in the stuff. If civil war comes, they probably will defeat us. Clarissa felt the full force of the tragedy toward which America was headed and remembered the gleam of pride on the face of Mary McDuffie as Hampton hacked the bear into submission. I might live in the South for the rest of my life, thought Clarissa, but I will never understand these people. She would dream about Wade Hampton killing the bear for the rest of her life.

After arriving in Santa Fe and having a few drinks, Sergeant Duffy headed for the whorehouse district, and Nathanial made his way to the neighborhood where his former wife had lived, where he knocked on the door of her large adobe home. A maid whom he didn't recognize appeared, looked at him coldly, and said, "What do you want?"

"Is this the Barrington residence?"

"It is."

"I'm the father of Zachary and Carmen, and I'd like to see them if you don't mind."

"They are at school, and their mother would not want you to disturb their studies."

"I'll return tonight," said Nathanial, relieved he didn't have to see Maria Dolores so soon. Then he strolled to Fort Marcy, a short distance from the Palace of Governors, and passed the familiar barracks, parade ground, and flagpole, finally arriving at the orderly room, where he found Sergeant Major Randall behind the desk. "I'm Dr. Steck's new assistant, and I'd like to see General Garland."

Sergeant Major Randall escorted him to General Garland's office, and the commander of the New Mexico Military District arose behind his desk. "I'm sorry that the service has lost you, Nathanial," he said. "How can I be of assistance?"

"I thought we should talk about Apaches, to see how best to deal with them."

"I know how to deal with them, and I can't understand why you became an Indian agent. It's an impossible job."

"Maybe, but we shouldn't starve them to death, which is happening at Fort Thorn."

"I have no extra rations, because the men don't have that much themselves."

"Without rations the Mescaleros are forced to steal."

"I understand, but there's nothing I can do."

"Except kill them."

General Garland nodded. "I'm afraid that's so, because I can't let Apaches run wild, shooting arrows into American citizens, stealing sheep, cattle, and horses. The Apaches must accommodate us, because we are not going to accommodate them. They must obey the law."

Both knew they were at an impasse, and awkwardly they parted company. Nathanial didn't look up old Army chums, because they would argue about Apaches. So he returned to downtown Santa Fe, where he intended to have a drink. *What makes me think I can bring peace between Apaches and Americans?* he thought.

He realized that the Apache problem was like the slavery issue—intractable. But someone had to fight for Christian decency. He walked west on San Francisco Street, headed toward a certain establishment in Burro Alley, when out of the passing crowd a woman's voice said, "Nathanial Barrington?"

He froze in his tracks, fearful of who it might be. A thirtyish woman with dark blond hair, wearing a sheepskin coat, approached with a smile. "Don't tell me you've forgotten me?"

"It's the former Rebecca Harding, unless I'm mistaken."

She gave him a hug. "How are you, Nathanial."

Nathanial had courted Rebecca long ago, and they'd even participated in rather exciting kissing and touching on several occasions. Now she was the wife of the man whom Nathanial considered his best friend, his former West Point roommate, Beauregard Hargreaves.

Nathanial and Rebecca separated, then examined each other. They had planned to marry, then Nathanial met Maria Dolores, who somehow had captured his fancy. "Is Beau at Fort Marcy?" he asked.

"No, he's in Mexico. What are you doing back here?"

"I'm Dr. Steck's new assistant."

"How did you deserve such a terrible fate?"

"I lived with the Apaches—"

She interrupted him. "Yes, Beau told me you nearly killed each other when you met in one of those canyons. Thank goodness you came to your senses. Otherwise, I might be a widow."

"And then perhaps I could court you again," murmured Nathanial, like the scoundrel he sometimes became in the presence of appealing females.

"I never would dream of marrying you, and thank God that He spared me your company. How many times have you been married?"

"Twice according to American laws, but my current wife is divorcing me, or I'm divorcing her—which will offer new opportunities for making women unhappy."

"When Beau returns, you must come over for supper."

"You're afraid to be alone with me, because you still have that old feeling, eh?"

"I'm a married woman, and I have two children. That's all I know."

"What if I said I couldn't be trusted alone with you."

"It wouldn't surprise me, because everyone knows what a scamp you are."

With the conversation degenerating dangerously, they decided to part. Nathanial continued to La Estrellita, a small, disreputable cantina in Burro Alley, where he stood at the bar and sipped mescal. Why didn't I marry Rebecca Harding when I had a chance? he pondered. She would have made the perfect officer's wife, but instead I wanted an exotic woman and ended with Maria Dolores.

He wondered why he'd made so many bad decisions, as a fight broke out at a card table, two men winging punches, smashing each other's noses, blackening eyes. Nathanial was in a mood to beat the hell out of somebody, but then the sheriff and his deputies arrived, arrested both of the combatants, and marched them to jail.

Nathanial wanted to drink himself into forgetfulness, but decided to stay sober for the sake of his children. So he walked to the Alameda River, sat on its banks, and looked at the sun dropping toward the Jemez Mountains in the west. As he reflected upon his past, it appeared thoroughly disreputable, as he'd hopped on one woman after another like a damned rabbit.

Gradually, the view calmed him, and he fell asleep

by the banks of the river, not awakening until sunset. After washing his face in the rippling currents, he decided the time had come to confront his first wife. He made his way to the part of Santa Fe where wealthier families resided and hoped Maria Dolores wouldn't throw a frying pan at him.

He knocked on her door, and it sounded as if a riot had erupted within. The portal was opened by a blond, tousle-headed seven-year-old boy whom Nathanial recognized as his flesh and blood. "Hello, Zachary," he said. "Remember me."

The boy hesitated, then threw his arms around his father. Nathanial hugged him, then saw five-year-old, dark-haired Carmen standing shyly in the back of the vestibule. Nathanial scooped her up and kissed her cheek. "My dearest child," he said.

"Where you been?" she asked scoldingly.

The children each took one hand and led him to the parlor, where Maria Dolores sat nervously on the sofa, every hair in place, combed to a black bun in back of her head, and she had gained many pounds since he'd seen her last, like a middle-aged fandango dancer. "Welcome," she said unconvincingly.

"Glad to be here," he lied.

"How long are you staying?" asked Zachary.

"Only a few days, because I must return to Fort Thorn, where my new job is. I'm a civilian these days."

"It is about time," said Maria Dolores, tossing in the harpoon.

Nathanial tried to think of an effective riposte, but nothing came to mind.

"Can I come with you?" asked Zachary.

"You must stay with your mother," replied Nathanial.

"I've always stayed with Mother, but why can't I stay with you?"

"You're too young."

"I'm not too young!"

"But your mother would never let you go."

"Oh, yes I would," replied Maria Dolores. "He is a bad boy, and maybe you can do something with him."

Nathanial turned to his son. "What have you done?"

"Do not ask him," interrupted Maria Dolores, "because he will lie. Some days he does not go to school, and occasionally he steals things. He also spends time with the worst boys, and I am afraid he will be arrested one day."

"If he comes with me," said Nathanial, "he'll go to school or else. And if he ever steals anything, I'll kill him."

"I'll be good if you take me with you," pleaded Zachary.

Nathanial barely knew his son, but said, "All right—but I'm going to be hard on you, and I will beat the hell out of you if you break my rules."

"It is what he needs," said Maria Dolores.

"If you had raised him, instead of having maids do your dirty work, maybe he wouldn't be such a problem."

"Where were you all those years?" asked Maria Dolores, and then she answered her own question. "Sleeping with other women, getting drunk, making a fool of yourself."

Nathanial smiled thinly. "I never realized how much I dislike you."

"You are a stupid man, and I do not know what I ever saw in you."

She arose from the sofa and walked away, swinging her wide hips, as if escaping something detestable. Little Carmen stood in the middle of the parlor, glancing back and forth at her father and mother. Then she turned and ran after her mother. "Don't leave me with him!" the child screamed.

Nathanial found himself alone with Zachary, who shrugged and said, "Women."

He understands, thought Nathanial, as a wave of familial love passed between them. The boy looked like Maria Dolores, except for his aristocratic Barrington nose. "In a few days we're off to Fort Thorn, where I shall enroll you in school. If you sass the teacher, I will stake you to an anthill and pour honey over your face."

"I always knew you'd take me someday," replied Zachary.

Maids provided two sacks, into which Nathanial and Zachary packed the boy's clothes. "Before we leave, you should say good-bye to your mother," ordered Nathanial.

"She doesn't care about me because I remind her of you."

"Yes, she does care about you, but she's too busy to show it."

"I hate her."

Nathanial dropped to one knee and gazed into his son's eyes. "You must not hate your mother. She does the best she can."

"But it's all right for you to hate her, I suppose."

"That's different, because we were married. Say good-bye to her so you can part on good terms."

Zachary would tell any lie if he could be with his father, so he stepped to his mother's office, knocked on the door, and found her sitting at the desk, her eyes red with crying, while Carmen lay on the sofa, also crying.

"I'm leaving, Mother," said Zachary.

"I cannot manage you anymore," she replied.

Zachary kissed her damp cheek, then turned to his sister, who had been his little toy. "'Bye Carmen," he said.

"You don't love me," she pouted.

"There comes a time when a man must move on."

He attempted to kiss the child, but she pushed him away. He shrugged, then returned to his father. "I'm ready," he said.

Together they departed Maria Dolores's home, headed for their new life together.

Maria Dolores's lover was known as McCabe, a broad-shouldered brute employed to break up fights and keep order at the Silver Palace Saloon, one of her many properties. He always appeared to need a shave regardless of the time of day, preferring baggy cowboy clothes for comfort. A veteran of the Mexican War, he had seen sights and committed deeds that had seared his soul.

He was considered ugly, but for some reason women always had been attracted to McCabe, and he'd slept with a good many before falling in love with Maria Dolores Barrington. But now her former husband was in town, and he feared she'd go back to him for the sake of the children, both of whom hated McCabe. No matter how sweetly McCabe behaved, the kids simply would not warm to him.

He knocked on her door, expecting his rival to open it, but instead one of the Mexican maids responded, leading McCabe to Maria Dolores's office, where she sat with little Carmen, and the eyes of both were red with crying.

"What the hell happened?" asked McCabe.

Maria Dolores was so angry, she couldn't even speak, so little Carmen explained, "Papa was mean to Mama, then left with Zachary."

McCabe hated Nathanial, whom he considered an arrogant West Point prig. They had met fleetingly after Nathanial returned from the Apaches and taken an instant dislike to each other.

"Where'd he go?" asked McCabe.

Nathanial and Zachary waited for a procession of wagons to pass, then crossed busy Washington Street and entered the Sagebrush Saloon, half empty that time of the day. There was a bar on the left, tables to the right, and a small dance floor in back, where a man played an out-of-tune piano.

Nathanial selected a table in the middle of the floor between a group of men playing poker and a gentleman reading a newspaper. Zachary sat beside his father, trying to understand what was so marvelous about a dirty, smelly hall full of derelicts and prostitutes, one of the latter approaching the table.

"Two steak dinners," said Nathanial, "and a glass of whiskey for me, with a glass of milk for my son."

"We ain't got milk," replied the waitress, a freckled wench about fifteen. "This ain't no cow barn."

"Surely, you can find some," muttered Nathanial, stuffing coins into her hand.

Her attitude changed instantly. "Yessir," she replied, then walked cheerfully away.

Nathanial believed that he'd neglected his son's education and was eager to impart his experience, knowledge, and hard-won conclusions. Meanwhile, at the bar, a cowboy fell off a stool and lay immobilized on the floor.

"That," declared Nathanial, pointing toward the inert form, "is a clear demonstration of why we should not drink excessively."

"But Mother said you're a drunk," protested Zachary.

"It's true, but I'm a drunk in moderation, and there's nothing wrong with a hand of cards, either, but don't bet the farm. And if you find yourself against a cheater, simply fold your hand and walk away. Because a gentleman does not have dealings with cheaters, he will refuse to dirty his hands on them, and you must never under any circumstances be a cheater yourself." Nathanial placed his hand on his son's shoulder and intoned, "Because honor is the most important quality a man can have, and it is better to die than dishonor yourself."

"But Mother said you were the worst person in the world."

"I sit before you in the nakedness of my sins, but if there's anything you remember—it's this: Hate is the twin of love."

Zachary feared his father, doubted his fundamental good sense, yet loved and probably hated him. "I will do as you say," he said simply.

"One of these days I'll introduce you to my Apache friends. When I lived among them, I met boys not much older than you who'd killed grown men. But this is a morbid subject. What would you like to talk about?"

"Tell me more about Apaches," said Zachary.

"Honor is the foundation of their lives. That's why they refuse to surrender to the greater military power of the white man. What're you looking at?"

Nathanial noticed his son staring toward the door, his jaw dropping open in surprise. Nathanial turned, and his blood ran cold at the sight of McCabe reconnoitering the territory. There he is, thought Nathanial—the man who's planking Maria Dolores.

Nathanial despised McCabe, because the ex-officer felt inferior to the fellow who satisfied his former wife romantically. Meanwhile, McCabe spotted Nathanial, and Zachary felt afraid, because something terrible appeared about to occur.

McCabe crossed the floor, came to a halt at the edge of the table, hooked his thumbs in his belt, and appeared ready for mortal combat. "You'd best stay away from Maria Dolores," he said, "or I'll kill you."

McCabe spoke softly, and other saloon patrons hadn't heard the threat. Cards were slapped onto a nearby table, and someone laughed at the bar. Nathanial slowly rose to his feet, his hand near his Colt .36. "Move away from the table, son," he said.

Zachary followed orders, for his father had spoken in a voice that brooked no objection. The boy looked at his father and then at his mother's lover glowering malevolently at each other with the table between them. "Get the hell away from me," replied Nathanial, also talking softly, "before I lose my temper."

But McCabe didn't move, while his face bore mute testimony to powerful emotions. "You fancy-pants son-of-a-bitch—you're real rough when it comes to women, but your temper don't impress me one bit."

Zachary stared wide-eyed as his father walked around the table and came face-to-face with McCabe. "You filthy pig," he said, staring at McCabe's eyes from a distance of twelve inches.

McCabe launched a left cross, his intention to cave in the side of Nathanial's skull, but Nathanial blocked the blow with his right arm, then delivered a solid hook to McCabe's cheek. Nathanial felt as if his knuckles had cracked, but McCabe flinched only slightly as he responded with a roundhouse right to Nathanial's liver, one of the most sensitive spots in Nathanial's body.

Nathanial felt as if someone had jammed a spear into him, but some men fight harder when hurt, and he leapt onto McCabe, reaching with both hands for McCabe's throat, but the latter stepped to the side and threw a sharp uppercut to the point of Nathanial's chin.

Nathanial saw the Milky Way and the aurora borealis as he tried to clear his head. Meanwhile, he and McCabe had caught the attention of other saloon patrons, who formed a circle and placed wagers on the outcome. Zachary had to climb on a table to see over their heads.

Matters didn't appear hopeful for his father, who was being backed up by the ferocity of McCabe's attack. Both combatants showed blood on their faces, and Zachary wondered what would happen if his father was killed. Guess I'll have to shoot McCabe, he thought in his childish mind.

Meanwhile, Nathanial realized he had lost the fine edge of speed and physical strength he'd possessed when living among the Apaches. He tried to block McCabe's punches, but unfortunately one sneaked past his guard and pulped his lips. I've got to get my offense working, determined Nathanial, as a long, looping right landed on his ear, knocking him over a table, which collapsed beneath his weight, and when Nathanial opened his eyes, he lay on the floor.

He looked up at McCabe, whose fists were balled, waiting for him to rise. Nathanial was tempted to surrender, but he thought of McCabe in bed with Maria Dolores, and the shame of being bested on the bedsheets was more than he could bear.

"You don't look so tough to me, mister Army officer," said McCabe contemptuously.

Nathanial realized how far he'd drifted from the holy Lifeway as he rose to his feet. He remembered Mangas Coloradas, Victorio, and Nana the medicine man, who had taught him the warrior way. He needed to move faster, concentrate his power, avoid McCabe's punches, and think, instead of stumble about wildly.

He went into an Apache crouch as McCabe charged, throwing punches from all angles, and again Nathanial retreated, looking for openings, blocking blows, offering lateral movement. But McCabe pressed his attack, when a sturdy jab flattened his button nose, and a hook caught him on the cheek.

McCabe didn't flinch as he resumed forward motion. But too often his punches worried only the air, while he was taking more shots to the head. When he raised his hands to protect that target, Nathanial peppered his midsection with jabs and uppercuts, finally landing a solid shot on McCabe's liver. At the moment of contact all the misery in Nathanial welled up, and he went berserk, wanting to demolish the lover of Maria Dolores.

Both men stood toe to toe, chins down, flinging punches. Nathanial felt that every solid hit would damage Maria Dolores in a remote way, and this gave him renewed strength, while McCabe's nights of drinking and carousing had taken their toll. The more Nathanial thought of Maria Dolores's treachery, the more energy he seemed to acquire. At last he was paying her back, and it felt as if a volcano erupted inside him as he methodically tore McCabe apart. The accumulation of punches, plus a straight right to the chin, finally sent McCabe reeling. He tripped over a cuspidor, then raised himself immediately, only to be thrown down again by a one-two combination to the head.

This time McCabe didn't get up, and Nathanial felt exultant, as if he'd finally defeated nagging, hurtful Maria Dolores. He grabbed a bottle of whiskey from the nearest table, took a swig, and then looked down at his adversary, who lay unconscious and helpless at his feet. Nathanial wanted to stomp him, but could not go that far. Then an odd thought occurred to Captain Nathanial Barrington, formerly of the First Dragoons: How can I make peace in this territory if I can't stop fighting myself?

High in the Davis Mountains, nestled within a ravine that White Eyes had never seen, the encampment of renegade Mescalero Chief Gomez was a scattering of conical tipis among fir trees and waxflower bushes.

Chief Gomez had decided to rest, after two weeks of roving guerrilla warfare. Thirty-two years old, he was leader of 150 Mescaleros, the only warriors of that tribe living according to the holy Lifeway, which they had sworn to defend.

They had three head of stolen cattle, enough to feed everyone for perhaps a moon, and then they'd be off again, laying waste to the countryside. Chief Gomez's warriors were young, with muscular women fighting alongside the men, and no children, elderly, or valuable possessions to slow them down. The land was filling with miners and farmers; soldiers hunted ceaselessly for Apaches, and danger was everywhere.

The women arose to prepare breakfast, while warriors remained in their beds. The fragrance of roast horse meat filled the air, then warriors crawled out from beneath fur blankets.

Chief Gomez had much worry, for bluecoat scouts might cut his trail, but guards ringed the encampment, and the renegades were ready to counterattack or flee at a moment's notice. I will stay in camp one more day, he decided, Aleeya, his wife, poked her head into the tipi. "Panjaro is waiting to see you," she said. "He wants to join us."

Chief Gomez was not surprised, because hungry Mescaleros continually fled the reservation, augmenting his force. Chief Gomez put on his deerskin shirt, tied a red bandanna around his straight black hair, and crawled out of the tipi, where Panjaro, a bloody bandage on the side of his face, sat forlornly.

Chief Gomez kneeled before Panjaro, placed his hand on his shoulder, and said with a smile, "So you finally have come to your senses."

It was Advent in the Sonoran desert, and rain pelted the canvas walls of Beau's tent, its roof leaking as he sat on his cot, smoking a cigarette and reading the Gospel according to Saint Matthew.

> *Think not that I am come to send peace on earth:*
> *I came not to send peace, but a sword.*

"Are you there?" asked a voice outside the tent.

"Welcome," replied Beau.

Lieutenant Marrero, with a bushy black beard that hid his mouth, entered the tent. "There is a problem with the men," he said. "They are tired of this scout and want to go home for Christmas."

"I'll speak with them," replied Beau.

Lieutenant Marrero shouted commands, was answered by curses, and a commotion broke out, for the soldiers didn't care to leave their tents and venture into the rain. Beau put on his gutta-percha coat and vaquero hat, then adjusted the gun in the holster on his hip, hidden beneath the coat. Meanwhile, sergeants rousted the men, pushing and insulting them, using force whenever necessary, although there were only two sergeants and twenty men. Grumbling, the men formed two ranks, dressed right, and covered down in the hissing rain.

Beau strode to a point in front of them, remained at attention, and shouted, "How many Mexican children will be kidnapped by Apaches, how many women murdered, and how many cattle stolen before you do your duty? Don't you know that the Apaches laugh at your ineptitude?"

Someone in the ranks murmured, "Listen to how the dirty gringo talks to us."

Beau continued, "You are crying like children, but to defeat Apaches, you must be tougher than they.

Don't you care about your flag? If we gringos could inflict heavy blows upon the Apaches, why can't you?"

"Just give us a chance," said another voice in the ranks. "We'll show what we can do."

"If a few drops of rain are too much for you, how can you stand up to the Apaches? Will I have to tell Colonel Garcia that you're a bunch of cowards?"

The soldiers stood straighter at the mention of that name. Beau nodded to Lieutenant Marrero, indicating he could dismiss the formation. Then Beau returned to his tent, removed his raincoat, and sat on his camp chair. Training is everything, he told himself, and after a few weeks in the field, they'll have more confidence. Give me enough time and I can make a soldier out of anybody, he thought. Next spring, when the Apaches come down from the mountains, we'll be ready for them.

Tom Oglethorpe went to town one afternoon, while Clarissa remained on the plantation, playing the piano. Toward evening, Tom hadn't returned, but Clarissa felt no jealousy, because she didn't love him in the least. After a supper of fried chicken and rice, she sat in the parlor and read John Keats:

> *I look where no one dares,*
> *And I stare where no one stares,*
> *And when the night is nigh,*
> *Lambs bleat my lullaby.*

The truth I care about is art, reflected Clarissa. But what does art require of me, and have I made a religion of art, instead of God? Christmas was coming, and she thought of her baby daughter in New York, her parents lamenting her flight to the backwaters of the South, her husband somewhere in New Mexico Territory if he still was alive. Clarissa was free to go anywhere, unlike Tom's Negroes, yet was enslaved by indecision. Should I return to Europe? she asked herself.

Her hearing was extremely acute, due to years of piano playing, and she caught traces of music from the slave quarters, then recalled the kitchen Negroes mentioning a party they intended to have. Opening a window, she heard strange cadences quite unlike Italian opera, church music, or the sentimental ballads of the day.

Roused from her torpor, she put on her coat and headed toward the slave quarters, drawn to the mysterious sounds. The air was redolent with wood smoke, lights shone through windows of the barn, and Clarissa felt enchanted by the strange music, which sounded like a man singing a weird nonchromatic tune to the accompaniment of strings, flutes, drums, and chanting. It was totally new, unlikely, impossible to conceive, not American or European, but apparently pure African.

She came to the opening of the barn, then froze at the fantastical sight of Negro men and women dancing, shaking their hips, clapping their hands, wagging their heads from side to side, as if in a trance. Clarissa didn't know what to think as she stood transfixed.

She recognized some of the slaves, but their usual sulkiness was gone as they enacted ancient tribal customs. Clarissa felt like an interloper, yet could not bring herself to leave. A fire burned in the center of the dancing circle, sending eerie shadows hopping along the wall. In a corner three girls chanted in high-pitched voices.

The repetition of musical phrases and constant beat of the drum somehow enlivened Clarissa. She watched men and women wiggling shoulders and swiveling hips, and it was amazingly erotic, yet with no suggestion of lewdness. Clarissa found herself tapping her left foot and realized she was smiling. It was happy, uplifting music, not a funeral dirge.

This is how they behaved when they were free, figured Clarissa. Then they were captured by slavers and transported in chains to South Carolina. Clarissa could see clearly that slaves were human, although perhaps not identical to her in every respect. But she felt certain they experienced the same pain and sorrow and were capable of the same happiness.

Then out of the throng walked a short old man in threadbare clothes with a long, curly gray beard and baldness atop his head. Clarissa recognized him as Ebenezer, one of the house slaves. The elder stopped before her and smiled. "Want to dance?" he asked with a semi-toothless smile.

She held out her hand, which he accepted, then led her toward the fire, where the drummer pounded and dancers writhed weirdly. The old man let go of Clarissa's hand, then worked himself into the beat, holding his hands high, whirling like a young man. Clarissa perceived that the rhythm was simple to follow, given her years of music training, and the dance steps themselves were a simple two-step with unlimited variations.

She locked into the music, moving her hips awkwardly, for she'd never danced in this manner before. Everyone examined her, not with the usual grudging

respect, but seemed to be welcoming her. Clarissa
gave herself to the dance and discovered she wasn't as
awkward as she'd thought. Indeed, the movements
felt more natural as she continued, and her many frus-
trations receded in the chanting, shuffle of feet, and
wail of the three girls.

The old man laughed. "You are a very good dancer,"
he said.

She blushed with satisfaction as she spun around,
her skirts rising in the air, and she found herself opposite a handsome young male slave with smooth ebony
cheeks, a blunt but well-formed nose, and short curly
hair. He had muscles that could crack her in two, yet
he too was a skilled and graceful dancer, and he gazed
directly into her eyes. I could give you pleasure, he
seemed to be saying.

She could not return his gaze, but continued to
dance with him, clapping her hands and rocking her
shoulders. The other dancers formed a circle around
them, chanting and stamping their feet. Drums beat
faster, Clarissa's heart raced, and perspiration covered
her body, for never had she danced with such abandon
or felt so oddly aroused. The glee on the faces of the
Negroes transported her to Africa, where she imagined herself with dusky skin, performing the marriage
ritual. So this is what it's like to be a Negro, she
thought.

The great issue of slavery somehow seemed irrele-
vant before the power of the dance. These people will
never be destroyed, realized Clarissa, as she whirled
dizzily in the light of the fire. And then, in a blinding
flash, she understood the deeper meaning of music,
that it elevated people from their humdrum lives, and
therefore was like prayer.

Just as she experienced renewed hope, suddenly the beat stopped. Everyone ceased dancing, her Negro partner shrank into the darkness, and Clarissa found herself traipsing alone. A bolt of fear shot through her as she turned to the door.

Tom and the overseer, Tibbs, had arrived, the latter carrying a shotgun. "What are you doing?" asked Tom, an angry note in his voice.

"Just dancing," she replied.

"Follow me."

She dared not disobey, for she was literally at his mercy, and if she disappeared in a nameless swamp, no one would be the wiser. She and Tom returned alone to the main house, he fixed drinks for both, then they sat in the parlor beneath the painting of an Oglethorpe patriarch.

"It does not occur to you that you have disgraced me," began Tom. "Till now, I never truly appreciated how little Yankees understand our way of life."

"But I was only dancing."

"Your partner happened to have been a nigra, and that is especially embarrassing to me, because in this country, white men do not share their women with nigras."

"But it was completely innocent," she insisted.

"Liar!" he retorted. "I saw the lustful expression on your face and your hips moving suggestively. Do you want to sleep with a nigra? Is that your sick little Yankee woman's dream?"

"Tom—you're being rude."

"Scratch a Yankee—find a nigra lover. Is that why you want to free them, so you can rut with them like the white bitch that you are?"

Clarissa found herself curiously calm, perhaps because she considered her moral position unassailable.

"Regardless of what you think of me," she replied coolly, "I have done nothing wrong. Moreover, I believe the Negroes should be freed at once, for the moral crime is far worse than the problems of feeding them next morning."

"If three million free Negroes ever descend upon New York City, I doubt you'd remain long."

"They can be educated," she replied. "Once I attended a lecture by the former Maryland slave Frederick Douglass, and he was as articulate as any white man."

"Superficially, like a parrot, perhaps."

"You are unable to see anything worthwhile in Negroes."

"That's because I've been around them all my life, and they are lazy, worthless, quarrelsome bastards."

"Yes, because they have been demoralized by your 'special institution,' and whenever one musters the courage to stand up for himself, he's either shot out of hand or beaten to within an inch of his life. Someone should enslave you, so you can learn what it's like."

He smiled, moving closer. "But I'm *your* slave, darling." He placed his hands on her hips and murmured into her ear. "Do you know how exciting you looked, shaking your ass like a nigra?"

She let him kiss her. "I would like to return to New York."

He unbuttoned the back of her dress. "I should chain you to my bed, but if you wish to leave, I shall not detain you."

"I'll bet you've been with another woman tonight, and that's why you were late."

"Women have one principal function, and it is this."

He lifted and carried her down the murky hall to his

bedroom, and she didn't struggle, for he never failed to stimulate her basest desires. Closing her eyes, she pretended he was the muscular Negro slave. She may have lied to Tom, but could not to herself.

Next morning, slaves carried luggage to the front parlor, and a carriage was summoned, time for Clarissa to leave Larkspur. As she proceeded to the door, Tom appeared with his shirt half unbuttoned, liquor on his breath, hair uncombed.

"Heard the carriage," he said nonchalantly.

"It's been lovely knowing you," she replied, extending her hand. "Thank you for your hospitality."

"It was wonderful having you," he replied, kissing her hand lightly, then sticking his tongue in the space between her fingers.

They looked at each other one last time, remembering freakish contortions and blazing mattresses, but she had tired of slavery, and he couldn't bear constant abolitionist lectures. So she turned, twirled her parasol, and walked to the carriage, where Ebenezer held the door.

"Good-bye missy," he said, a twinkle in his eye.

"Thank you for all that you have taught me."

Ebenezer appeared surprised. "What have I taught you?"

"To dance," she replied.

He beamed with pride as she climbed into the wagon. Horses pulled Clarissa away from Larkspur, and she wondered how many friendships and loves had been rent asunder by the great slavery issue. There can be no compromise on this matter, she told herself. She wanted to shout at the top of her lungs, to warn of the approaching catastrophe, but too many angry people were loose in the land, forgetting those most vulnerable. She shuddered as the carriage transported her to the train station, the first leg of her journey back to New York City.

The pawnshop sat in a rundown St. Louis neighborhood, and the graybeard behind the counter was an immigrant from Galicia, descended from a long line of Jewish peddlers. Necklaces, brooches, watches, guitars, guns, and articles of clothing passed before his scrutiny that Christmas season, each carrying its tale of woe.

The old pawnbroker tried not to judge his Christian brethren too severely, but they were a violent, hard-drinking lot, just like the Russians, and naturally they treated their humble pawnbroker as if their bad decisions and ridiculous spending habits had been his fault.

Customers visited in a steady procession, some poorly dressed, teeth chattering in the cold, while others obviously had been rich, fallen on hard times due to the Panic. In such a neighborhood many prostitutes offered the delights of their persons, but the pawn broker did not believe in monkey business.

His problem was more sellers than buyers, and often he was forced to decline an article difficult to re-sell. For this reason he was referred to as a "dirty, cheating Jew," although he tried to be a just man and live according to the laws of Moses.

One evening, the door to his ramshackle shop opened to reveal a man in his mid-thirties, of less than average height, wearing a shabby Army greatcoat and looking about embarrassedly. The old pawnbroker smiled inwardly, because many decent people preferred not to be seen in his establishment. "May I help you, sir?"

The customer's shoulders were soldierly, his back erect, and he wore a short black beard, which made him resemble the sainted Rabbi Menachem Mendle of Kotsk. He failed to look the pawnbroker in the eye as he approached the counter, then reached into his pocket and extracted a gold watch. "How much?"

The pawnbroker took out his glass and examined the merchandise carefully. The gold was high quality but worn, crystal scratched, but the mechanism ticked and was an item a prostitute might give her lover. "Vhat do you vant for it?" asked the pawnbroker in his throaty east European accent.

"Twenty-five dollars," said the man hopefully.

"If it vas in better condition, I could gif that. Vould you take fifteen?"

The man shook his head, dropped the watch into his pocket, and headed for the door.

"Vait a minute!" called the pawnbroker. "How about tventy?"

"Twenty-two," said the man. "And I'll pick it up in a month."

That's what they all say, thought the pawnbroker, for he had to evaluate his customer as well as the merchandise. This one had the look of a cashiered Army officer, perhaps a decent family man who needed to buy Christmas presents for his children, and secretly the old Jew loved the happy faces of children during the Christmas holidays, like the angels of the holy ark. "All right— twenty-two," he grumbled, pushing the ticket forward.

The man hesitated, as if he didn't want to write his name, then scratched on the dotted line as the pawnbroker counted the money.

The customer pocketed it nervously, leaving as furtively as he'd arrived. After the door closed, the old pawnbroker turned the ticket around, to read the shy stranger's name: *U.S. Grant*

It was Christmas Eve on the desert between Santa Fe and Fort Thorn, and three figures sat around a campfire, eating bacon and beans. No candles adorned fir trees, and no choruses sang Handel's *Messiah*, but Nathanial felt like a shepherd following the holy star to Bethlehem. He glanced at his son, a chubby lad in a vaquero hat, who had grown without his father, and now appeared soft, unathletic, unsure of himself on the open land.

On the other side of the fire Sergeant Duffy sat contentedly, munching his biscuit, his brain aswim with memories of the whorehouses of Santa Fe, where he'd thoroughly debauched himself.

"Do you believe in Santa Claus?" asked Nathanial of his former first sergeant.

"Where would I be right now," replied Sergeant Duffy, "if it weren't fer Santy Claus? When I seen you at Fort Thorn, and you invited me to escort you to Santa Fe, that was the work of Santy Claus."

"Do you really believe Santa Claus wanted you to go to a . . . house of ill fame?" asked Nathanial incredulously.

"It waren't no 'house of ill fame,' but a reg'lar whorehouse, and if'n I know Santy Claus, he was right thar with me."

Nathanial glanced at his son. "Perhaps we shouldn't speak this way in front of the boy."

"Hell, he's got to l'arn someways. Besides, he

prob'ly knows more'n you." Sergeant Duffy looked at Zachary. "You been with a gal yet?"

Zachary blushed. "Not yet."

"Wa'al, be careful."

Nathanial cleared his throat. "He's much too young for this, Sergeant Duffy."

"No I'm not," said Zachary, although he barely knew what they were talking about.

"But this is Christmas Eve," insisted Nathanial, "and we should direct our attention to the higher spheres. What do you think of Jesus, Zachary?"

"He died for my sins," said the boy, for his mother had sent him to church.

Sergeant Duffy snorted, "But you ain't old enough to have committed no damn sins."

Zachary considered himself wicked, because his mother said he fought too much. "I'm bad enough," he said staunchly.

Nathanial put his arm around his son's shoulder. "I'm sure it's not serious, and Christmas is the season when we forgive each other and give presents. I thought I'd give you yours now, Zachary."

Nathanial removed from his saddlebags a new Colt pocket-pistol in .36 caliber with dark walnut grips and the name *Zachary Taylor Barrington* engraved on the barrel.

"It's a beauty," commented Sergeant Duffy appreciatively.

Zachary stared at the gun lying cold and heavy in his hands. He thought it the most miraculous object, glowing deep within its depths.

"I could've bought a silver-plated model," explained Nathanial, "but it might give away your position. You don't want your enemy to see you before you see him."

Zachary held the gun in both his hands. It was heavy, difficult to aim, but incredibly wonderful.

"Your hand will grow into it," said Nathanial. "It's the best friend you'll ever have." Then Nathanial hugged his little boy, who held the Colt in his right hand like an extension of his arm. When I grow up, I want to be just like my father, Zachary told himself.

10

⟶

A letter from Rebecca was waiting when Beau returned to Janos. Eagerly, he read about Beau II
and Beth, and Rebecca also mentioned offhandedly that
she had run into Nathanial Barrington briefly in Santa
Fe, and that Nathanial's wife was divorcing him.

The envelope contained news clippings that Beau,
an avid student of national politics, ordinarily would
read next, but the part concerning Nathanial bothered
him. Now what was that about? wondered Beau as he
sat in Janos's adobe military barracks.

Unwashed, unshaven, exhausted from the scout, he
couldn't help wondering if something was occurring
between Rebecca and the scoundrel Nathanial Barrington. A man of the world, Beau suspected that
Clarissa probably had blurted the truth about her brief
session with Beau to Nathanial, who now wished to
obtain the only possible revenge, planking Rebecca.

Beau failed to perceive that a woman like Clarissa
never would admit such an act, even under threat of
the guillotine. Instead, he puffed a cigar nervously,
figuring Rebecca was bored with marriage, while Nathanial would feel duty bound to even the score.

The more Beau thought of it, the more certain he became of his wife's infidelity. He'd never mention it in a letter, but when he returned to Santa Fe, he'd confront her with his suspicions. *If I ever catch them together, I'll shoot the son-of-a-bitch on the spot,* he thought.

Nathanial was approximately two hundred miles southeast of Santa Fe, having returned to Fort Thorn with Zachary and enrolling him in Miss Andrews's school. Nathanial's duties as Indian agent resumed, and one afternoon he rode across the reservation alongside Fort Thorn, observing Mescaleros drunk, sick, arguing, or asleep in front of their tipis, with tents of whiskey traders nearby.

Nathanial fought to hold back prejudice, yet could not deny, in the cold light of that January day, that Indians had, for whatever reason, an almost insatiable thirst for whiskey, which distorted their otherwise sharp minds and transformed them into drunkards and brawlers.

Like Dr. Steck, Nathanial believed Apaches needed farm implements, seeds, education, and land where they wouldn't be molested by white men, but Washington had more important worries, such as the breakup of the Union. Finally, Nathanial arrived at the tipi of Chief Zeenata, removed his hat, and bowed. "I would like to council with you," he said in Apache language.

Chief Zeenata beckoned to the ground beside him. "You are the one who has lived with the Chiricahuas, no?"

"For one harvest," replied Nathanial. "I rode with Mangas Coloradas, Victorio, Nana, and Juh, and that is why I understand your situation. If you go raiding, the Army will hunt you down, but if you stay here, you may starve to death."

"If you know so much," replied Chief Zeenata, "what should we do?"

"Dr. Steck wants to set aside special land for the Mescaleros, where no White Eyes will trouble them, but the White Father has not granted his request."

"And he never will. I have heard the story many times, but I see nothing good for the Mescalero people."

"If a chief feels this way, the People will lose faith."

"It is better to be faithful to the truth!"

Nathanial had no rejoinder, so he sat in silence with the chief, smoking a cigarette and gazing at the sky, letting their spirits merge. Toward suppertime, Nathanial did not want to take from the tribe's meager larder, so he rode to Mesilla, where he consumed chili and beans at a cantina owned by Juan Ortega. Afterward, he made his way to the office of Ortega, who was guarded by a vaquero with a gun in his holster and a knife sticking out of his boot.

"Is he in?" asked Nathanial.

Without answering, the guard opened the door. Seated behind the desk, Ortega counted coins. "Come in, my friend." He opened a drawer in his desk and tossed Nathanial a bottle of tequila. "Help yourself."

Nathanial pulled the cork, took a swallow of the sizzling beverage, sucked wind, then settled down and said, "I've just returned from a visit to the Mescaleros, and—"

Ortega interrupted. "And you want to tell me that they never in their wildest dreams would slit a man's throat or steal his horse. You are a good man, Captain Barrington, and I respect you. You want to make peace, but at the expense of American citizens who are killed regularly, and we are supposed to be satisfied with the arrangement? You fail to understand that Apaches are a nation of murderers and have never lived at peace with anyone."

"Perhaps because no one has lived in peace with them. What did the conquistadors do with Indians? They killed them whenever they got in the way. Apaches believed themselves oppressed because they were."

"And now we are oppressors because we are peaceful farmers and ranchers? Come, Captain, and please don't tell me that this land belongs to the Indians, because land belongs to whoever can conquer it, such as when you defeated my people, the Mexicans. The only solution for the criminal Apaches is military subjection, because you cannot reason with such a people. It should not be difficult for an Army as powerful as yours, and we will help in any way we can."

Nathanial groaned. "Ever since I came to this territory, I have heard hatred from all directions, because everyone believes his opponent is an incarnation of the devil. But the only way to make peace is to stop fighting, as Christ admonished us to do."

"The Apaches do not view us as people, but as owners of valuable possessions they feel compelled to steal. This is no biblical parable." Ortega shrugged. "You have a good heart, and you feel deeply. The only problem is you do not understand Apaches."

"I lived with them for nearly a year, and from their point of view they are defending their land."

"And from my point of view *I* am defending my land."

"There is plenty of land for everybody."

"Tell that to the Apaches."

"I have, but the resolution will take time."

"In the meanwhile are we to be sources of cattle and sheep for the Apaches?"

"You have a right to defend yourself, but just make sure you don't cross the line. Otherwise, I'll bring the full weight of the law to bear against you, and if necessary, I'll clap you in jail myself."

Ortega raised an eyebrow. "You are one big hombre, but I do not think you are big enough to clap me in jail."

"Don't put me to the test," replied Captain Barrington, formerly of the First Dragoons.

It was Ghost Face among the People, the season when snow covers the land. Their wickiups scattered on a plateau high in the Chiricahua Mountains, their diet meager, they prepared for the destruction of Janos.

Many warriors had sworn to participate, and Nana, the *di-yin* medicine man, was hard at work contriving Killer of Enemies Bandoliers, the most sacred and holy items a warrior could possess.

First Nana had to kill the deer and cure the skin according to ancient rituals. Then the skin was cut into strands, measured into four parts, and each was painted either black, white, yellow, or blue, to represent the four directions.

The strands were woven into a special cord, then hung with shells, pieces of sacred green chalchihuitl, crystals, petrified wood, beads, eagle down, bear

claws, rattlesnake rattles, and circles of buckskin.
Suspended at the end was the deerskin pouch filled
with sacred pollen, bits of lightning-blasted wood,
fragments of shells, and green malachite stones.

Nana journeyed alone to the highest peak in the
Chiricahua Mountains, where he spread the bandoliers
on the rocks and prayed over them for four days and
nights, while fasting and dancing.

Chief Gomez's renegades couldn't afford prayer
and dancing during Ghost Face, because they lacked
life's necessities. Forced to continue raiding through
the snow, they operated in small bands, taking a steer
here, a mule there, a few sheep. They feared the wrath
of the U.S. Army, but figured they were safe if they
remained in motion.

Most small ranchers had abandoned the territory,
replaced by caudillos able to hire and arm private
armies of fighting vaqueros. Every wagon train was
heavily guarded, but if a vaquero fell asleep in the
saddle, he could lose his weapons, clothing, and life.

Chief Gomez and his warriors resembled wild animals more than men, with their long straight black
hair covered with dust and nettles, not an ounce of fat
on their bodies, their eyes fierce with alertness. They
rampaged across eastern New Mexico Territory during early 1858, never committing a startling outrage,
but the accumulation of minor depredations inflamed
the local populace, while the Army could not catch
fast-moving and wily adversaries.

The situation worsened daily, and it appeared to
Nathanial that a major tragedy was about to occur. No
longer did he march with his chest out, stomach in,
head level, but was bent with worry like a civilian,

hands clasped behind his back. I'll never make peace
in this territory, he admitted to himself. I'm wasting
everybody's time, especially my own. Time to resign
and move on?

Since arriving in New Mexico Territory following
the Mexican War, he'd harbored, in the deep recesses
of his mind, an ambition to become a rancher. A
growing nation needed beef, and newspapers were
full of stories about railroad bills in Congress; one
proposed a southern route through New Mexico Territory, which would more readily enable the marketing
of beef. The Apaches won't steal the cattle and horses
of old Sunny Bear, he figured. Hell, I was friends with
Mangas Coloradas, Victorio, and all the others. Maybe
it's time to start looking for land.

Miss Andrews saw him approaching as she lectured
her class on nouns and verbs. He appeared through
the distortions of the window at the same time every
day, to pick up his children, his solicitude touching
her deeply.

Zachary and Gloria sat at opposite sides of the
classroom, apparently avoiding each other, or possibly
considering the other a rival for Nathanial's atten-
tions. But they were good students; otherwise Miss
Andrews would wallop them with her ruler or the
back of her hand. Spare the rod and spoil the child
was not the philosophy of the frontier, but strict discipline produced the desired results.

She dismissed the class, then stood by the window
to see Nathanial hug his adopted daughter, then his
natural son. Often Miss Andrews dreamed of herself
as their mother, and they'd all live happily together,
but Nathanial Barrington kept his distance, and she

assumed she no longer interested him. She didn't realize that he hesitated to debauch a decent religious woman.

She looked at herself in the mirror, frowning at her plain hard features. She was surrounded by men who lusted after her, from the commander on down, but not the one who interested her most. She wondered if it was God's divine retribution as she sat behind her desk and corrected the students' papers.

That evening, Nathanial, his children, and Luiza, their maid, dined upon chili and biscuits, with milk for the children and a glass of Mexican brandy for their father. After the meal the children retired to their respective bedrooms for homework.

Luiza was aged, wrinkled, and toothless except for one brown stump on the bottom, with a big wart above her left eye. She waited until both doors were closed, then turned to Nathanial and said in her gravelly voice, "You should get married."

"It's not easy to fall in love," he replied.

"You young people—you are always talking about love, as if you know what it is. Love is making a home for children, and I can introduce you to a proper lady."

"There's no such thing," replied Nathanial caustically. "Just when they tell you they love you desperately, that's when they're planning to leave."

"That's because you treat them like your horse—you get on, and then you get off. Women need to be loved, and the way you show love is through sacrifice."

"Sure, women expect men to be slaves, and once

you do whatever they ask, they lose respect for you.
Marry again? Don't be absurd."

Clarissa stopped for a rest at the home of relatives
in Washington, D.C. and discovered there were two
main centers of social gravity in the nation's capital.
First and foremost was the White House, where the
unmarried niece of the President, Miss Harriet Lane,
held court, while the challenger was Adele Douglas,
wife of the embattled senior senator from Illinois.

Clarissa's relatives were invited to affairs at both
residences, and Clarissa accompanied them as their
guest. She had visited imposing residences and known
distinguished personages from an early age and therefore was not especially in awe of the White House.
Passing through those historic halls, surrounded by
leading statesmen and ladies, including the President,
who looked like a farmer, she couldn't help reflecting
how much warmer and congenial was Santa Fe's Silver Palace Saloon.

She met numerous eligible men during her stay in
the nation's capital, but instead was attracted to waiters, footmen, and the laborers she passed on the
streets. One evening, at a ball at the residence of Lord
Napier, the British ambassador, she examined with
more than passing interest a Negro butler carrying a
tray of drinks.

As an artist trained to plumb her soul, she could not
hide the uncomfortable truth. She was drawn to danger, excitement, fear, and melodrama, such as when
she ran off with Tom Oglethorpe, instead of a decent
gentleman such as those who flocked about her,
brought her drinks and tiny sandwiches, and promised
to escort her home.

While listening to a conversation about Cuba and
Nicaragua, which southerners wanted to annex as
slave states, she couldn't help comparing the men to
Nathanial, and had to admit that he was more interesting in his own rascally way, even unique, and as for
depravity, it was difficult to surpass the lowdown Nathanial Barrington.

She recalled the sweetness of her first meeting with
the notorious dragoon officer, the fear that he
wouldn't care for her, and the worse fear that he
would. Clarissa sat surrounded by distinguished
Americans and foreigners, beneath crystal chandeliers
and surrounded by exquisite oil paintings of British
royalty, yet felt uncomfortably abandoned. *Wasn't
Nathanial right about my performing career after all?*
she asked herself. *All it gained me was hard work,
headaches, sleepless nights, empty flattery, and the
destruction of my marriage.*

"Are you all right?" broke in a voice nearby.

It belonged to a British naval attaché named Trilling, to whom she had been introduced. She turned to
him, wiping a tear from her cheek. "Something fell
into my eye."

"Soot from one of the gaslights, I suspect. Or perhaps you're tired. Shall I see you home?"

He was tall, languid, his dark blue uniform tailored
to his slim form, with a pale complexion and sinister
half-closed eyes.

"If it's not too much trouble."

She told her uncle she wasn't feeling well, then left
with the helpful naval attaché. It wasn't long before
they were embracing in the carriage as the horses clip-
clopped over deserted streets. Clarissa's husband was
in Santa Fe, while Trilling's wife was in London, but

Clarissa didn't dare spend the night at Trilling's rooms because what would she tell her uncle? Instead, she and the officer performed a certain intimate act on the seat of the carriage, and no one would ever know, not even the driver, reins in his hands, drowsing, anxious to return home and enjoy a bowl of hot soup.

Nathanial often snored as he slept, especially after polishing off a bottle of brandy, while Luiza was half deaf. At two o'clock in the morning, when it sounded as if trees were being sawed in Nathanial's bedroom, a door opened in the darkened adobe home, then a youthful face appeared in moonlight streaming through the parlor window.

Zachary tiptoed across the floor, attired in his brown wool coat and trousers. He looked both ways, paused every few seconds to make sure the sawmill continued unabated, and finally arrived at Gloria's door, where he knocked ever so lightly. Seconds later, the door was opened by Gloria, wearing her white robe.

"Howdy," he said.

"Howdy," she replied. "Come on in."

He entered her bedroom, closing the door behind them. Then they moved closer and kissed lightly, not daring to touch hands or bodies.

"I love you," he said simply.

"I love you too," she replied, eyes downcast.

It had been this way since they'd met, although they teased and fought constantly, partially because they were normal children, and partially to throw adults off the track. She sat at her desk while he lowered himself onto the trunk at the foot of her bed. Together they gazed out the window at the full moon high over the Hueco Mountains.

"I wish we were old enough to get married," he said, although he wasn't quite sure what marriage entailed.

"Me too," she replied, for he was her first true love. "But it's taking so much time."

"I have an idea. I'll tell Father he doesn't have to meet us after school because we know the way home. I'm sure he has better things to do, and we can have fun."

They were curious puppies who wanted to explore Fort Thorn on their own, without adult supervision. They smiled as they held hands chastely and looked out the window at the moon. "Someday we'll be together forever," she said.

One of Juan Ortega's ranches was raided that winter, with cattle and horses stolen, three vaqueros killed. Ortega couldn't understand why the United States government, of which he had been forced to become a member, wouldn't stop the crimes. One day he rounded up several of his guards, among them Raphael Fonseca, then rode to Fort Thorn, where soldiers stopped them in front of the orderly room. Ortega and his men were armed, as were the soldiers, so gunplay wasn't out of the question.

"I demand to see Lieutenant Wood!" declared Ortega, on horseback in front of his men.

A door opened, then Lieutenant Wood appeared, annoyed at being disturbed. He'd been reading a newspaper article about a transatlantic cable being laid between Ireland and Newfoundland. "What is it, Ortega?"

Ortega removed his hat and made a mock bow. "Sir, the Indians are making life hell in this territory, and we request your assistance."

"There are not enough soldiers in the entire U.S. Army," replied Lieutenant Wood, "to protect all the ranches in New Mexico Territory twenty-four hours a day."

"If you get rid of those damned Apaches beside this fort, we would feel safer. Everybody knows they sneak away to commit crimes, and then return for rations. How can you let this travesty continue?"

"I suggest you take your complaint to Dr. Steck."

"Dr. Steck is worthless!" replied Ortega. "How many dead Americans does it take—fifty, a hundred—before you *do* something?"

Lieutenant Wood smiled faintly. "Sergeant of the Guard—call out the men."

Sergeant Duffy was sergeant of the guard, standing nearby with his service revolver in hand. "All of them, sir?"

"You heard me."

Sergeant Duffy walked toward the barracks, shouting at the top of his lungs. "I want a full post formation—with rifles and bayonets—*now!*"

The order was relayed across the small installation, and it wasn't long before soldiers rushed outside, carrying .58 caliber rifles with long-range sights, chambered to fire minié ball ammunition. They dressed right, covered down, and formed four long ranks at attention.

Lieutenant Wood turned to Ortega. "I am directing you to leave this fort. If you refuse, I shall place you under arrest. If you resist, I shall open fire."

"If you do not protect us, we shall be forced to protect ourselves," he said ominously.

"If you harm any Indians, I shall lock you in jail. And if you kill any, I'll put you before a firing squad."

That night, one candle provided light in the office of Juan Ortega as he sat with five members of the Mesilla Guards. "You are my principal lieutenants," he said, the air laden with tobacco smoke. "It is you who must pass the word to the others, and every man must be pledged to secrecy, because if the Army finds out what we're up to, they not only will stop us, they will put us in the calaboose. Be especially careful how you behave with Steck and Barrington, because they would be first to sound the alarm. We will assemble Saturday at midnight, then go to the reservation and take care of the Apaches once and for all. Are you with me, companeros?"

Fonseca was first to speak. "It is about time."

The others murmured their assent as Ortega placed his right fist on the middle of his desk. Fonseca laid his hand over Ortega's, then the others touched their palms onto the pile. They felt the warmth of each other's determination as all looked at Ortega.

"If all goes according to plan," he told them, "we should be able to kill them all."

"The Mesilla Guards are up to something," said Dr. Steck as he sat in Lieutenant Wood's office two days later. "I fear they plan to attack the reservation."

"I've heard the same thing," replied Lieutenant Wood. "But I have no proof."

Nathanial stirred on his chair. "What kind of proof would you require—a dead baby? We are not seers, we cannot predict the future faithfully, but it might be wise to place a military cordon around the reservation."

"You were an Army officer, Barrington. How'd it look if I stationed soldiers around the Apaches, but not around white settlers? We aren't numerous enough to take every precaution."

"If the Mesilla Guards attack that reservation," said Nathanial, "General Garland will relieve you of command."

"If I place a cordon around the reservation, I'll look like a fool."

"God forbid," replied Nathanial, "that you should look like a fool, even if it saves lives of women and children."

"But you make a possibility sound like an absolute fact, Captain Barrington. I can't claim that the Mesilla Guards are peace-loving farmers and businessmen, but neither have they committed crimes, and I can't take action that will bring a rebuke to the Army. And now, if you'll excuse me, I have work to do."

Walking back to his office, Dr. Steck said, "It's up to us, but what can we do?"

"Warn the Mescaleros," replied Nathanial.

"Do you think they don't know?"

"Why don't they leave?"

"The strong ones already have gone, in case you haven't noticed, and the remainder are dependent upon us for basic sustenance."

Nathanial shook his head in frustration. "We need a safe reservation for these Mescaleros, with farm implements and cattle, so they don't have to steal. Why in hell doesn't Washington do something?"

*   *   *

In late January, 1858, Dr. Steck's letter requesting a new Indian reservation north of the Gila arrived at the Office of Indian Affairs in Washington D.C. Charles Mix, still acting for James Denver, concurred with the position stated, so he drafted a formal letter and sent it to the Speaker of the House, the Honorable James L. Orr of South Carolina. It would be the work of Congressman Orr's committee to shepherd the proposal through the House of Representatives.

But Mix's recommendation and numerous others, including railroad bills and tariff considerations, were languishing due to continuing debate over the Lecompton Constitution. Speaker after speaker railed against the opposition, stinging insults passed across the aisles, and despite resolutions, clauses, amendments, and other tactics, the fundamental question was whether Kansas would become a slave state, thus opening the West to the "peculiar institution."

The Congress no longer possessed splendid orators like Henry Clay, Daniel Webster, or the great John C. Calhoun. Those heroes had been laid to rest, replaced by a rougher, more partisan breed, such as Representative Galusha A. Grow of Pennsylvania, chairman of the House Committee on Territories, who was to become the central player in one of the most astounding events ever to occur in the hallowed halls of Congress.

Tall, strongly constructed, thirty-four years old, Representative Grow wore a spade beard but no mustache, and the roof had become thin atop his dome. His stature was not particularly imposing, but he was considered the conscience of the Republican Party, which he had joined after defecting from the Democrats.

Despite Galusha Grow's prominence in Washington, he had come from modest beginnings, growing up fatherless in a farming settlement in the Susquehanna Valley of north-central Pennsylvania, near the village of Galewood. Hardscrabble poverty had been his lot, but with persistent effort and dedication, he had graduated from Ahmerst College and become a lawyer. He was the champion of the downtrodden ordinary American, and as far as he was concerned, the Negro was included in that category.

The critical day was February 5, 1858, when Galusha Grow arose in the well of Congress to speak against Lecompton. With all the passion of a formerly poor semi-orphaned boy, he delivered a blistering attack on President Buchanan's pernicious legislation, claiming it was "abounding in epithet and denunciations of the majority of the People of Kansas, without furnishing the facts the official record ought to show."

During the speech Grow realized that many Democrats were absent, for it was late Friday afternoon, and they'd departed for a series of free dinner parties organized by the administration, while others had repaired to their favorite taverns for liquid refreshment. Seeing his advantage, Congressman Grow terminated his speech abruptly and called for an immediate vote on Lecompton.

Congressman Alexander Stephens of Georgia, leader of the southern bloc, was caught off guard. He'd never served in the Army, but politics was warfare by other means, and he ordered a filibuster, then dispatched the sergeant-at-arms to find errant Democratic congressmen and usher them back for the vote.

Southern congressmen were enraged by what they considered the underhanded tactics of Grow, and the debate became increasingly acrimonious. It continued into the night, gaslight illuminating the ghostly scene, the galleries empty, and the voices of several clerks gave out while calling yeas and neas as the battle raged back and forth.

Some members collapsed onto chairs after speaking themselves hoarse, others reclined on sofas and slept between roll calls, and a few drank coffee and other stimulants to stay awake. Newspaper reporters had gone home for the night, never dreaming a historic encounter was about to occur.

At the height of the stormy session Grow sauntered onto the Democratic side of the aisle for a conference with John Hickman, a middle-of-the-road Democratic congressman also from Pennsylvania. "Johnny, let's put this damned thing to a vote once and for all," said Grow.

Meanwhile, John Quitman of Mississippi, a hero of the Mexican War, requested consent to submit a motion. Grow protested so vehemently from the Democratic side of the house, he woke up nearby Laurence Massilon Keitt of South Carolina.

Representative Keitt was one of the foremost fire-eaters of the South, an ardent secessionist, supporter of slavery, and hater of northern principles. A lawyer, thirty-three years old, graduate of South Carolina College, his father owned twenty-five hundred acres and more than fifty slaves. Half asleep, possibly under the influence of strong drink, and thoroughly indignant, he spotted the Republican foe in his midst. Rising to his feet, he shouted at Grow, "If you wish to object, get back on your side of the aisle!"

Grow was no effete Boston abolitionist who shrank at the first sign of physical danger. No, Grow had been a hard-working farm boy, and schoolyard brawls had been common for him. So he turned to Keitt and replied, "This is a free hall, and I have a right to go where I choose."

Keitt, seeing himself challenged, stepped toward Grow and said, "I demand to know what you mean by speaking to me in that insolent manner."

"I mean what I say," replied Grow staunchly. "What's it to you?"

"Why you black Republican son-of-a-bitch!" retorted the now thoroughly enraged Keitt.

"No Negro driver will ever crack his whip over me," declared Grow.

Both distinguished representatives of the American people rushed each other, a flurry of punches were thrown, and seconds later, northern and southern congressmen joined the fray. All the rage and passion of the slavery debate exploded, as esteemed statesmen tried to smash each other into insensibility. In the midst of it all, farm boy Grow landed a solid right on slave owner Keitt and dropped him to the floor.

Meanwhile, Congressman John Potter of Wisconsin, a compactly built, athletic man, charged into the center of the conflagration, dealing Congressman William Barksdale of Mississippi a blow to the midsection, doubling him over and sending him crashing to the floor. But Congressman Barksdale managed to arise, whereupon he was struck so hard by Congressman Cadwalader Washburne of Wisconsin, that Barksdale's wig flew off. Barksdale hastily returned the wig to his head, but he positioned it backward, sending nearby combatants into peals of laughter.

Speaker Orr seized the moment to call for order, but Owen Lovejoy of Illinois and Lucius Quintus Cincinnatus Lamar of Mississippi were heavily engaged and did not hear. Then Richard Mott, a gray-

haired Quaker from Ohio, tried to break them up, but
Reuben Davis of Mississippi aimed one last lick at
Grow, who unceremoniously knocked him cold. The
coup de grâce was delivered by Representative John
Covode of Pennsylvania, who picked up a heavy
stoneware spittoon and tossed it at the southern side,
showering his enemies with spit, cigar butts, and other
substances too reprehensible to name.

Eventually, order was restored. No weapons had
been brandished, and no one had been killed, although
many notables presented a disorderly and bloody appearance.

The debate was equally venomous in the Senate,
minus fisticuffs. One morning Senator George Badger
of North Carolina rose to present the southern view of
slavery, and he spoke almost tearfully of his dear old
Negro mammy, who had suckled him at her breast,
raised him, and taught him religion, morality, and
good table manners. He claimed that he loved her, and
she loved him, but if the Lecompton Constitution was
voted down, he couldn't take her to Kansas. Turning
to Benjamin Wade of Ohio, a champion of abolition in
the upper house, he said plaintively, "Surely, suh, you
would not seek to prevent me from taking my dear old
black mammy to Kansas, would you?"

Ben Wade was a cool, acerbic man, a longtime foe
of slavery, and a former judge. He gazed unflinch-
ingly at Senator Badger and replied dryly, "It is not
that you cannot remove your dear old black mammy to
Kansas, sir. But we do not want you to *sell* her once
you get there."

And thus did the great slavery debate continue,
overshadowing all other concerns such as the Apache
wars.

11

In the early hours of Sunday, February 8, 1858, the soldiers at Fort Thorn had no notion that a brawl had occurred in Congress on the previous Friday night. All was silent, as was the case on the Indian reservation, where Mescalero warriors lay in drunken stupors. The Indians had been plied with cheap whiskey during the evening, and even devout Mescalero women had partaken of the libations, now sprawling unconscious with their men.

However, children had not drunk alcoholic beverages, so were more alert than their irresponsible parents. One of these was eight-year-old Chino, who was stuck with his mother at the reservation, his father having been killed by Captain Richard Stoddert Ewell's dragoons during the Mescalero Wars of 1854-55. Out of the night, Chino heard the soft pad of footsteps.

In an instant he was up, but did not give the alarm because it might be Mescalero warriors returning from a raid. He poked his head outside and was horrified to see Mexicans tiptoeing closer, carrying rifles, swords, and pistols. "Wake up!" screamed Chino.

His mother grumbled sleepily, wiping an imaginary gnat off her lips. The drunken warriors barely heard him. Chino screamed again and was continuing to scream even as Juan Ortega shot him through the chest, then opened fire on the tipi, killing his mother.

The Mesilla Guards rampaged across the camp, shooting and murdering with glee. Among them was Fonseca, carrying a sword, splitting the head of a former proud Mescalero warrior too drunk to defend himself. Then he hacked the Mescalero's wife and infant child. These Indians never will kill again, he told himself exultantly, awash in blood and gore. I have avenged my family at last.

Meanwhile, at Fort Thorn, the sergeant of the guard was running to the residence of the commanding officer, Lieutenant Wood. Before the sergeant could arrive, the door swung open suddenly, and Lieutenant Wood stood there barefoot in his underpants, eyes glazed with excitement, a rifle in his hands.

"Civilians have attacked the Mescaleros, sir! It's a massacre!"

Nathanial heard shots, and his first thought was of his Colt in the holster hanging from his bedpost. Drawing it, he leapt toward the window. Shots were coming from the Mescalero camp, and he surmised what had occurred.

He dressed quickly, ran to the stable, saddled his horse, and rode hatless toward the reservation as soldiers were roused out of the barracks. The big black horse galloped through the night, and Nathanial feared that his worst suspicions had been fulfilled. It wasn't long before tipis could be seen, with figures moving about. The shooting had stopped, replaced by screams of pain and anguished pleas for help. Nathanial's horse charged among the tipis, and through the darkness the assistant Indian agent saw children lying on the bloody ground, their elders milling about dazed, some bleeding from wounds.

The Mescaleros recognized Nathanial, and a group of quickly sobered warriors advanced as he climbed down from his horse. "How could you let this happen?" asked one of them, his face wrenched by grief and agony.

"Who did it?" asked Nathanial.

Another warrior stepped forward unsteadily. "You know very well who did it—the Mexicanos from Mesilla. It is all your fault, because we trusted you!"

Nathanial felt as if he'd dropped into hell as he looked around the devastated camp. He'd expected trouble, yet was surprised that it finally had occurred. On his hands and knees, he gazed inside a tipi at a decapitated squaw and a boy with his chest split apart. The familiar odor of innards came to Nathanial's nostrils, but he did not faint or become nauseated. It was not the first time he'd seen hideous carnage, but that didn't mean he was completely cold. He struggled to hold himself under control and was tempted to ride to Mesilla and shoot Juan Ortega between the eyes.

He staggered about the scene, trying to understand, his eyes repeatedly drawn to mutilated corpses of women and babies. He could manage dead soldiers, but butchered women and children were more than he could bear. A shiver passed over him, and he wanted to shriek his outrage to the heavens, but Captain Nathanial Barrington did not snap.

The first of the soldiers finally arrived, then Dr. Steck appeared, his jaw hanging open. He too was no stranger to cadavers, having carved up a fair number during medical training, but that had been cold and antiseptic, whereas this was pure grisly horror. The good doctor found himself repeatedly looking at the sky, because the scene below was impossible to digest.

Lieutenant Wood wandered about mumbling to himself, "Sons of bitches, bastards." Finally, he turned to Sergeant Duffy and said, "Leave twenty men here, and direct the others to mount up. We're going to Mesilla."

The orange dawn glowed on the horizon as the soldiers approached Mesilla. The town was quiet, all lights out, citizens sleeping peacefully, seemingly unprotected, although Nathanial guessed he and the soldiers were under observation.

Lieutenant Wood said, "Damned civilians are more trouble than the Apaches. It's time somebody stood up to the bastards."

The column entered the village and made its way among jacales to the larger residence of Ortega. Lieutenant Wood climbed down from his horse, walked to the front door, and pounded.

A sleepy-faced maid appeared. "Senor?"

"I want to speak with Senor Ortega."

"He is asleep, sir."

"Get him up!"

"Are you arresting him?"

"Tell him that he might well hang before the night is over."

The maid widened her eyes in alarm, then retreated into the house, slamming the door in their faces.

"Threatening a civilian is against the law," reminded Nathanial, who had managed to calm himself now that murdered children were out of sight. "Perhaps you'd better let me do the talking."

"I can do my own talking!" said Lieutenant Wood in a strangled voice.

The door reopened, and Juan Ortega stood in his nightshirt, eyes half closed. "You want to see me, senors?"

Lieutenant Wood stared at him. "You son of a bitch—you're not fooling anybody!"

"But senor—I have been with my wife all night. Whatever can you be speaking about?"

A hefty madonna emerged from the darkness, and one could see she'd been a beauty once. "It is true," she said. "He was here all night."

"Liars," replied Lieutenant Wood. "You have blood on your hands."

"I?" asked Ortega, raising his pristine palms. "But I have been asleep."

"You and your Mesilla Guards are guilty of murder. You're under arrest."

"Where is your proof?"

Lieutenant Wood drew his service revolver. "Right here."

"You'll need more than that to convict me, I'm afraid."

Wood raised his gun to whack Ortega in the mouth, but Nathanial caught Wood's hand and said gently. "Let's have a talk."

He pulled Wood to the side, and they walked about twenty paces away. Wood shook with rage, not a good characteristic for a combat officer. "That scum," he said bitterly. "You know he did it, Nathanial."

"Of course he did, but you'll be the man at the southern end of the rope if you don't simmer down."

"I can't let him get away with it."

"You're not without a trick of your own." Nathanial leaned closer and mumbled a few words to Lieutenant Wood, whose eyes widened as he listened, then a smile broke onto his face. "That's a wonderful idea, Nathanial."

Nathanial bowed slightly in acceptance of the compliment, then followed the post commander back to Ortega, who continued to stand at the door with his wife, as soldiers filled his front yard and spilled into the alleys, joined by the arrival of the Mesilla Guards.

"Senor Ortega," said Lieutenant Wood stiffly, "you have convinced me that you and your friends are capable of defending yourselves, so I am recommending to General Garland that Fort Thorn be closed and the garrison withdrawn."

The half smile of superiority vanished from Ortega's face. "Now just a moment!"

"Good morning to you, sir. And when you die, I wish you the everlasting flames of hell."

Lieutenant Wood marched back to his horse as Ortega, his nightshirt flapping around his knees, ran after him. "But we are American citizens, and you are obligated to protect us from the Indians."

"You have forfeited that right, you fucking pig."

Ortega swung at Wood's head, but Wood dodged to the side, then replied with a straight right at Ortega's jaw. Ortega ducked under it and dived at the Lieutenant's waist, driving him backward. Both men fell to the ground, punching, kneeing, and elbowing each other, as soldiers struggled to pull them apart.

"I will kill you!" screamed Ortega as his men dragged him back inside his house.

"Here I stand," replied Wood, held by Sergeant Duffy and two corporals.

Nathanial sidestepped in front of Lieutenant Wood and looked at him sadly. "I hope you've got a good civilian job lined up, because I don't think you have much longer with the Army."

Lieutenant Wood's eyes popped as he struggled to break loose. "How can you be so complacent, with dead children lying a few miles away?"

"If I let go," replied Nathanial, "I'll end up in the cell beside yours. But if you evacuate Fort Thorn, I suspect Chief Gomez will do the dirty work for you." Nathanial patted the angry officer on the back. "I'll bet a messenger is on his way to Chief Gomez even as we speak."

Later that day, Lieutenant Wood led the bulk of his force on a scout, leaving behind ten soldiers to defend the fort, commanded by Sergeant Duffy. The soldiers were confident that Chief Gomez would leave them alone, because the citizens of Mesilla would be his objective.

Juan Ortega could not believe the Army would dare expose American citizens to danger. He presented a staunch front to his guards, but inwardly he feared an imminent attack on Mesilla and blamed Nathanial Barrington, whom he thought had convinced Wood to move the troops away. Barrington remained at Fort Thorn, and Ortega was tempted to blow out his brains.

Three days after the massacre, Chief Gomez and 250 angry Davis Mountain fighters were spotted heading toward Mesilla, armed with the latest stolen rifles, ready to take on the entire U.S. Army if need be, and Panjaro rode among them.

Dr. Steck and Nathanial were conferring in the former's office when news arrived of Chief Gomez's appearance. "I've got to stop him," said Dr. Steck, rising to his feet.

"I'd say that Ortega has got it coming to him," replied Nathanial.

"You're too enthralled by revenge, which is precisely the factor that keeps the wheel of hatred turning—don't you understand?"

"But there's something wonderfully satisfying about revenge," said Nathanial. "Haven't you ever got mad at anybody?"

"I'm mad at everybody, but I keep it where it does no harm." He headed unarmed for the door. "You needn't accompany me. I can manage on my own."

"If you get caught in the crossfire, perhaps I can be of assistance. Sometimes soldiers are useful, you know."

Both men rode at a canter to Mesilla, where Sergeant Duffy and the skeleton crew of soldiers already had arrived. At the edge of town Juan Ortega and the Mesilla Guards were armed and prepared to fight renegade Mescaleros.

"It's one of those beautiful New Mexico mornings," declared Nathanial cheerily.

"You sound overjoyed that Chief Gomez is coming to destroy the town," replied Dr. Steck.

"According to the holy Apache Lifeway, he has a right to execute criminals."

"Have you ever stopped to consider that your time with Apaches has made you somewhat barbaric?"

"When the American Army does it, it's for glory, honor, and the flag. When Apaches do it, they're savage beasts. Come now, Doctor. You're not being objective."

"As Christ said, we must turn the other cheek. And if the robber takes your coat, give him your pants and shirt."

"It can get awful chilly on winter nights."

"There must be a better way than killing."

Nathanial grinned as he studied the small army of Indians in the distance. "It will be enlightening to watch you convince Chief Gomez of that proposition."

The Apaches drew closer as Ortega and his men constructed hasty barricades in the streets of Mesilla. Alone and unarmed, sitting upright in his saddle, Dr. Steck urged his horse forward, and Nathanial couldn't help admiring him. "Either he's brave or does not fully understand the danger into which he rides," he said to Sergeant Duffy.

"A real dolt, you mean."

Nathanial and the dragoons followed Dr. Steck, while the Apache threat loomed out of the desert. Nathanial was pleased to note that he had no responsibility for anybody except himself, unlike Duffy.

"The happiest day of my life," said Nathanial, "was when I resigned my commission."

"Not all of us have the Barrington millions," replied Duffy. "I will defend you and Dr. Steck as best I can, but if the Apaches want to burn Mesilla to the ground, it's fine with me."

Chief Gomez and his warriors drew closer, and they were grim-faced, war-painted, bristling with weapons, in a state of controlled wrath, sitting rigidly on their war ponies. Dr. Steck headed straight for the chief, and when fifty yards from him, held up his empty right hand to demonstrate he came in peace.

Chief Gomez also raised his empty right hand, for he knew that Dr. Steck was not a warrior. Nathanial advanced to join the negotiations, while Duffy remained back with his men. Dr. Steck approached Chief Gomez, pulled back his reins, and steadied his horse. "What do you want?" he asked the bandit chief.

"We come to wipe out Mesilla," said Chief Gomez, and his warriors murmured their assent. "Please get out of the way, Steck, and tell soldiers move too, otherwise we go through you."

Dr. Steck tried to smile. "If you destroy Mesilla, the Army will send many bluecoat soldiers and wipe you out."

"Let them come," replied Chief Gomez confidently.

"But mountains and deserts will fill with soldiers. It might take two or three harvests, but they will get you. I tell you this as a brother."

"You are a White Eyes, not my brother. I cannot turn from the murderers of my people."

"We shall punish the murderers. Do not jeopardize your safety for no good reason."

"A warrior does not worry about his safety, and I do not trust you, Steck."

"Steck speaks the truth partially," said a voice in the Apache language.

All Mescalero eyes turned to the tall, blond civilian in black vaquero hat atop a black horse to the right of Dr. Steck. The Mescaleros were amazed that he spoke their language perfectly, while the doctor and the soldiers had no idea what he'd said.

"Who are you?" asked Chief Gomez.

"I have lived among the Mimbrenos, and they named me Sunny Bear."

The Mescalero warriors looked at each other significantly, for they had heard the legend of Sunny Bear, the bluecoat war chief who became a Mimbreno warrior and *di-yin* medicine man, having seen great visions and committed valorous deeds.

Chief Gomez nodded to the illustrious warrior. "What are you doing here, Sunny Bear?"

"I am working for peace, great chief. The Mesilla Guards surely deserve to die, but if you kill them, the bluecoat Army will hunt you down as Steck has said. The justice of the White Eyes is very unjust, but the survival of the People must be your first concern."

Chief Gomez pondered those words, and something told him that Sunny Bear was speaking straight. "I will take your counsel, Sunny Bear, but we have other choices which I shall not name this day."

"I hope they include the death of the Mesilla Guards," said Nathanial, holding out his hand.

Chief Gomez clasped it. "If you ever wish to enjoy the holy Lifeway, you may ride with me, Sunny Bear."

"One day I may accept your invitation, Chief Gomez."

The Mescalero chief wheeled his horse, then shouted an order to his men. An unearthly shout went up among them as they spurred their war ponies. The sound of thunder came to the cactus-strewn plain as they galloped away, leaving Nathanial with Dr. Steck and the soldiers, all mystified by the sudden turn of events.

"What did you say to them?" asked Dr. Steck.

"The truth," replied Nathanial.

* * *

Nathanial's prediction came true in the weeks to come. There was no proof that the Mesilla Guards had committed the massacre, and no charges were brought against them. They got away with murder, and in the fullness of time, the troops returned to Fort Thorn.

Meanwhile, the survivors of the massacre continued to starve, and Chief Gomez's warriors raided with renewed dedication. Matters soon returned to their normal state of mutual hostility in that beleaguered corner of New Mexico Territory.

Trains frequently broke down, and late one afternoon Clarissa found herself sitting in a snow-covered field of New Jersey, next to a row of railway cars halted due to a malfunctioning steam engine. Mechanics climbed over the black locomotive, tightening and loosening bolts, having intense conferences producing no discernable results, as jets of steam shot from apertures, sending white clouds across the snow-blanketed farmland.

The conductors had lit a bonfire and supplied food and drink, so everyone was making the best of the delay. Clarissa was restless, but gentlemen always were available, such as a fellow with dark eyes and a leer, holding a bottle. "May I fill your glass?" he asked.

She'd noticed him circling around her, attempting to introduce himself ever since Baltimore, but she saw through his game, so similar to her own. She held out her glass and he filled it with port wine. "What is your name?" he asked.

"Clarissa."

"I'm Michael. Where are you headed?"

"New York City."

"I'm on my way to Boston. Are you married?"

"My husband and I are divorcing."

He smiled, recognizing a kindred licentious soul. "I must confess that I find you enthralling. Who are you—what are you—and how can I be of assistance?"

"I am nobody, and you can't help me at all."

He turned to the side, affording an advantageous view of his finely chiseled profile, while admiring the sunset landscape. "It's so beautiful in this part of New Jersey," he declared. "Care to take a walk?"

She couldn't help smiling, because she'd never done it in the snow before. On the other hand, she was beginning to question the desirability of sleeping with a variety of men, the great exalting act becoming routine. As she raised the glass to her lips, a voice said, "Someone's coming."

All conversation stopped, because roving thieves might have noticed their dilemma, but most of the male travelers were armed, and the railroad supplied rifles for the engine crew. Clarissa placed her hand in her purse, closing her forefinger around the trigger of her Colt Navy. She remembered Nathanial, who had taught her how to shoot. *If I had married a decent man, I wouldn't be in this predicament,* she told herself.

Out of the night materialized a wagon with a man and woman sitting on the box, three children in back. The man pulled the reins and smiled. "We heered you was broke down, and thought we'd invite you to the camp meeting over yonder. It a-gonna be a grand old time." The farmer winked.

"How far?" asked Michael.

"About a half mile. You can walk it with no trouble. C'mon, we'll lead you there."

Clarissa turned to Michael. "Shall we go?"

"It's not exactly what I had in mind," he said ruefully.

Other travelers also were curious about the camp meeting. They turned to the chief engineer, who bellowed, "Go ahead, 'cause I 'spect we'll be hyar fer a while!"

Clarissa and the travelers gathered together their bottles and loaves of bread, then followed the wagon across the snowy field, hearing faint sounds of singing in the distance. Michael remained at Clarissa's side, and it wasn't long before bonfires and tents came into view.

A log platform had been erected, and upon it a preacher named Reverend Josiah Belknap exhorted throngs of believers, skeptics, and sinners who'd traveled long distances. He was a storklike preacher with a short black beard and a bald head, the gleam of the fanatic in his eye.

"You have heard it said," he hollered, wagging his bony forefinger in the air, "that the nation is suffering from the financial panic, but I say unto you that the nation is suffering from the consequences of sin! Because each one who invested in fraudulent schemes did so out of greed, passion, and concupiscence. The man and woman of pure heart has nothing to fear from the Lord God. So come forward, my friends, confess your sins and bare your hearts before the Lord. I know it isn't easy, but it just might be your last chance."

Clarissa listened without the scathing skepticism of certain other sophisticated travelers, for she'd been raised on Episcopalian Christianity, and music had convinced her that not everything can be codified and categorized scientifically. Although the preacher obviously was a crackpot, she considered his logic correct, for if each individual lived according to the commandments, America's problems would be solved.

"I invite you to bow before the Lord," called Reverend Belknap. "End your drinking, fornication, greed, and lust. *What has sin got you so far?*"

Some travelers scoffed at the raving preacher, but Clarissa pondered his words. What good have my indiscretions done me? she asked herself. In fact, they never lived up to their promise, and sometimes were quite embarrassing. And I was about to do it again when that wagon showed up.

Somehow, in her mystical artistic mind, it seemed that the breakdown of the train, appearance of the wagon, and camp meeting were acts of providence. A chorus of men and women began to sing:

> *It's me, it's me, oh Lord*
> *standin' in the need of prayer*

Clarissa felt bereft of God and realized that she'd fallen a long way. How can I ever return to that cleaner nobler time? she asked herself. Is it possible to go back, or are those days lost forever?

> *Not my father, not my mother*
> *Standin' in the need of prayer*
> *Not my sister, not my brother*
> *Standin' in the need of prayer*

Clarissa's left foot moved forward, but Michael placed his hand on her shoulder. "Where are you going?" he asked, a superior tone in his voice.

"Forward," she replied.

"Surely, you don't believe this nonsense."

At that moment she realized she was far worse than she'd imagined, for she'd been about to fornicate with a blasphemer, an atheist, one who spent his days satisfying his basest pleasures and missing the greatest satisfaction of all.

She threw his hand off her shoulder, then continued toward the platform, joining other pilgrims, hands clasped together. They were young and old, male and female, white and Negro, forming a great procession, while the chorus continued to sing:

> *It's me, it's me, oh Lord*
> *Standin' in the need of prayer*

Yes it's me, thought Clarissa as she dropped to her knees in front of the platform. Bowing her head, her eyes filled with tears when she realized that her life was in shambles, her daughter in New York, her husband in New Mexico Territory, and she removing her clothing for any knave who came along. What has it gained me? she asked herself. I have never been so unhappy in my life.

On the stage the preacher dipped his hand in the bucket of water and flicked drops onto the throng. "I baptize you in the water of the Most High," he told them. "Open your heart to God and be healed!"

As holy water struck Clarissa's face, she flashed on her husband, who had warned against the emptiness of fame, the wages of false pride, and the falsity of the mob. What did all those people mean to me? she asked herself. It was music that I loved, and Nathanial had loved it too. He didn't want me to become a performing giraffe, but I ignored him and followed instead Martin Thorndyke, who fundamentally was a liar and thief.

What have I done? asked Clarissa silently as holy water dripped down her cheeks. At least Nathanial lived the impulses of his heart, even when obstreperous and ridiculous. As for his acts of immorality when living among the Apaches, I can understand how easy it is to fall into certain habits.

She hated to admit it, but Nathanial had been right about the hollowness of public acclaim. In truth, she preferred playing at the Silver Palace Saloon, where most of the patrons barely paid attention, and if she improvised an unusually difficult passage and failed dismally, most would be too drunk to notice. She recalled rare moments of musical achievement at the Silver Palace Saloon, where she'd sung through the night, entertaining cowboys, soldiers, vaqueros, freighters, lawmen, outlaws, half-breed Indians, and everything else the great American frontier could churn up, as if out of its very sacred soil.

She became aware that others were pulling back from the platform. Opening her eyes, she was the only one still on her knees. Blinking, trying to understand what had happened to her, she raised herself from the hard-packed snow. Then Reverend Belknap dropped from the stage, landing in front of her. "Sister, your prayer was answered," he declared, flicking holy water at her face. "Go in peace to love and serve the Lord."

She returned to the travelers, where Michael waited with an expression of astonishment. "My word—I do believe you're crying," he said. "How I envy you, because apparently you've had a legitimate religious experience, but somehow, I cannot believe this foolishness."

"That's because you have become your own God," said Clarissa.

He smiled. "Were you planning to make a donation to my religion? If so, I promise a miracle."

"I'd like to see you disappear," she said.

Before he could answer, she stepped away from him, heading back to the train. She didn't need to listen to more preachers, because she wanted to think. But Michael followed her. "Did I say something wrong?"

"Please leave me alone."

"You don't know what might be lurking out here."

She drew the Colt from her purse. "I can manage for myself, thank you."

"Is that thing loaded?"

"Not only is it loaded—I have just cocked the hammer." She pointed at him. "Good day, sir."

He shrank back, holding his hands in the air. "It's been wonderful meeting you."

Snow crunched beneath Clarissa's leather boots as she made her way to the train. Wind whistled over the frigid field, but she wore three thick sweaters beneath her leather knee-length coat, and a thick wool black shawl covered her head. All she could think of was Nathanial. *I must find him and tell him the truth—that this time he happened to be right. Of course, he's not right all the time, and sometimes he's been a damned fool, but he and I certainly are in agreement on the issue of public performances.*

She recalled that they'd shared many similar tastes, and had been happy before she'd decided to win the praise of the masses. The more she thought about it, the more she realized that their love had been quite profound at times. He was even helpful around the house, nailing things together, patching their old stove at Fort Craig. No one could call him a lazy man.

A distant stand of trees whistled in the wind as she recalled the circumstances of their meeting. Somehow, they had been delivered to the same little edge of the Hudson Highlands one summer afternoon in '54, with no one about, surely a star-crossed meeting. She'd thought him appealing at the time, especially with his notorious reputation. But unlike other scoundrels, he had never tried to take advantage of her, or use his superior strength against her, and indeed, he had asked to marry her, the honorable course for a gentleman.

Maybe I didn't appreciate him, reflected Clarissa. Instead, I behaved like a spoiled child, and I'm surprised he didn't spank me. I have squandered the love of my husband for a few paltry hours of fame.

She recalled magical hours when she and Nathanial had lain in bed in their hotel off the Grand Canal in Venice, or took walks in the Luxembourg Gardens of Paris. They'd quarreled occasionally, but at least he was interesting, unlike the common cynical seducer of all-too-willing ladies.

Suddenly, in the middle of the corn field, with the pale moon overhead and a few wispy clouds in the sky, she came to a stop. I was swayed by false compliments, she realized. Thorndyke thought he could make money off me, so I embarked on the path that has destroyed my marriage, the foundation of my very life.

Clarissa trembled when she thought of little Natalie in New York City, raised by a maid. What kind of woman would desert her child? she pondered. Clarissa felt like vomiting the poison of her life—the wine, whiskey, champagne, and lost dreams.

Nathanial tried to save me, but I disdained his advice, thinking he was jealous. But Nathanial was beyond jealousy; he'd seen too much war and was unimpressed by the low tastes of the mob. He wanted peace for New Mexico Territory and needed me at his side.

Her eyes filled with tears, the strength went out of her, and alone in the middle of the field, she dropped to her knees. "I must tell him I'm sorry," she whispered to herself. "He'll probably throw me out, and I couldn't blame him, but I must admit the truth if I'm an honorable woman. Because none of us is free from sin, except Jesus."

But wait a minute, she cautioned herself silently. Do I really want to travel by stagecoach to New Mexico Territory, through land populated by warlike Indians and craven criminals, for the opportunity to throw myself at Nathanial's mud-caked boots and beg his forgiveness, even though he may well kick me out like the traitorous baggage that I am?

The answer came with stunning forcefulness. Yes!

Miss Andrews looked out her classroom window as Nathanial approached down the alley. She'd dismissed the students, and her heart fluttered with anticipation when there was a knock on the door. Then he entered, removed his hat, and the poor woman nearly swooned from thwarted desire.

"You wanted to see me?" he asked.

"I though it's time we made an appointment to go over the school's finances."

Both knew it would be improper to meet alone at night, so they scheduled a meeting for Saturday morning. After Nathanial departed, Miss Andrews made her way to the stove, where she boiled water, poured it into the wooden tub, removed her clothing, and lay in the hot, sensuous liquid.

She wondered what feminine wiles to use on him, although she hated falsity. She wished she were more scintillating, but couldn't change what she considered her fundamental plainness. What if I simply and honestly confessed my love for him? she asked herself. And if he takes advantage of my weakness and vulnerability, well . . . it will not be my fault. The former Shaker woman smiled as she closed her eyes and absentmindedly caressed herself.

At the appointed time on Saturday morning, Nathanial crossed Fort Thorn's parade ground, his wide-brimmed, tan cowboy hat slanted low over his eyes, pants tucked into his black leather boots. His Colt was jammed into a new handworked leather holster at his waist, and he was on his way to meet the schoolmarm.

Soldiers busily prepared for Saturday morning inspection, taking no special note of Nathanial. Why wouldn't he visit the schoolmarm, since his two children attended her school?

She watched him approach, hidden behind her curtain, excited and terrified. She'd run every possibility through her mind during the preceding night, from ripping off her clothes and diving upon him, to offering certain carefully worded declarations.

She clasped and unclasped her trembling hands, wishing she could control herself. Only the iron discipline of the Shakers prevented her from stuffing herself with cookies.

Finally, he knocked on her door. Her mouth dry, she took one last look in the mirror, not thrilled by what she saw, then drew a deep breath, uttered a prayer, and grasped the doorknob.

"Howdy," he said, his smile turning her knees to jelly.

Struggling to remain circumspect, she led him into the room that served as her office, bedroom, and kitchen. "Would you like a cup of coffee?"

"Don't mind if I do, but please don't fill the cup all the way."

She lifted the pot from the stove, then poured dark steaming liquid into a tin mug. He removed a silver flask from his pocket, unscrewed the lid, and added whiskey.

"Have a seat," she said.

He sat at the table, noting the bed in the corner, not that far away. She bent over the desk, gathering papers, and he noticed those long legs topped by a well-constructed rump, or that's how it appeared in his imagination, because she wore a loose black skirt. She carried papers to the table, placed them in front of him, and sat.

As she explained financial details, she was only inches away. Shuffling papers, pointing to numbers, sometimes her arm brushed his. Nathanial had been without a woman so long, he experienced prurient notions. No one could call her pretty, but she was a good woman, and her long legs mesmerized him.

The school required more desks and chairs, she told him, due to increased enrollment. She described the current state of text book publishing, latest theories of education, and the success of new steel-point pens. As she babbled nervously, he sensed her tensions, but misread them, thinking she was ill at ease with her principal contributor, not that she experienced unwholesome desires herself.

When she completed the report, he said, "How much do you need?"

She provided the figure, and he arose from the table to reach into his pocket. As she watched him, she wondered what would happen if she merely invited him to . . . she didn't know exactly what to say. He laid a stack of bills on the table. "That ought to take care of you for the time being."

"Partially," she replied softly, arising.

"But it's the amount you asked for," he protested.

"A woman has other needs," she suggested.

They stared at each other, and now he understood her agitation, for he barely could remain still himself. Then she turned away so he couldn't see her tears. How pathetic I must appear to him, she thought, then nearly jumped out of her skin as his hands came to rest upon her shoulders. He was standing behind her, close enough to feel her body.

"On the contrary," he breathed into her ear, "I find you very appealing. But I can't marry you because I'm married already, and if we were to go to that bed over there, I have a feeling we both will regret it."

"Why?" she asked.

"I'm still in love with my wife."

"What if I asked you to take advantage of me?" she replied weakly, pressing her full body against him.

"Please don't," he said through a constricted voice, trying to step backward.

Her long legs tempted him, not to mention knowledge that she was a love-starved semi-virgin. Then she faced him, and with trembling hands unfastened the top button of her dress, her small delectable breasts rising to view. Unable to forsake her ripe, pleading flesh, he leapt upon her as she let out a sigh of relief, and he carried her to the bed, where he gently lowered her, then undressed her with quick, deft movements. It didn't take long to relieve himself of his own clothing. Soon they were naked together, frantically grasping, giving full rein to frustrated longings, as soldiers stood at attention on the parade ground, and Lieutenant Wood inspected their uniforms.

During the course of the inspection the soldiers heard something that sounded like a woman's scream, but they figured it was only the call of a bird.

Three rough-looking hombres of indeterminate background watched each other's hands as they smoked and chatted, waiting to be interviewed by the commandante at Janos. The Mexican Army was looking for scouts, intending to hunt Apaches in the spring.

A Mexican sergeant opened the door and looked around warily, as if expecting to be jumped. "Moniz?" he asked.

Antonio Moniz rose to his full five feet and four inches. Half Yaqui Indian, he wore a black beard and a knife sticking out of each boot. "That's me."

"This way."

The sergeant led Moniz to an office where a Mexican officer sat behind a desk, while in the corner a bull-chested Americano officer could be seen, stroking his chin thoughtfully.

"My name is Captain Marrero," said the Mexican behind the desk. "You want to be a scout?"

"Yes."

"Have you ever been a scout?"

"No, sir."

"Can you track?"

"Yes, sir."

"How well?"

"I grew up with the Yaquis, sir."

"It will be a difficult and dangerous assignment."

"All of life is difficult and dangerous," replied Moniz.

Captain Marrero turned to Captain Beauregard Hargreaves, U.S. Army, sitting in the corner. Beau nodded his head barely perceptibly, then Marrero turned back to Moniz. "You're hired."

Chief Mangas Coloradas, accompanied by Cochise and Victorio, lay on a ledge and gazed down at Janos, city of death. Scouts had reported much military activity in the vicinity, and the war chiefs had come to see for themselves.

"It will not be as easy as we thought," said Victorio. "There are many more soldiers."

Mangas Coloradas shook his head disdainfully. "The *Nakai-yes* cannot stand up to us. At the end of Ghost Face we will strike the town head on and reduce it to rubble."

"Head on?" asked Cochise. "Such a plan will waste many warriors."

"The Mountain Spirits will not forget what the Mexicanos have done to us," replied Mangas Coloradas, who believed the religion of the old time. "We will have our Killer of Enemies Bandoliers to safe-guard us."

Victorio had been shot in the groin while wearing a Killer of Enemies Bandolier; he wasn't so sure. But he dare not challenge the great Chief Mangas Coloradas, while Cochise also held back his doubts, not yet comfortable with his new power. Moreover, Nana the medicine man had declared the portents to be favorable. "It will be as you say," replied Cochise, but he worried about thunder sticks that he'd seen, the cannon.

"Nothing can stop the People this time," declared Mangas Coloradas. "For never has our cause been more just." He made a fist and held it before them. "Janos will be destroyed!"

12

———————➤

Chief Gomez didn't wipe Mesilla off the face of the earth, but that didn't mean he had forgiven anyone for the massacre at Fort Thorn. Following the confrontation with Sunny Bear and Dr. Steck, the outraged chief and his warriors visited upon eastern New Mexico Territory a veritable hurricane of destruction, forcing the First Dragoons to take the field once more. But there weren't very many of them, and the region was vast, with impassable mountains, sudden storms, and a hidden enemy. Chief Gomez's Mescaleros slept in no permanent shelters, and when their horses became tired, the warriors exchanged them for fresh ones and kept on marauding.

Complaints reached Washington, D.C., and it wasn't long before General Garland received letters from Secretary of War John B. Floyd and General Winfield Scott, requesting action against the Apaches. As a result, soldiers continued to crash about the landscape, following tracks that invariably petered out, or scouting in vain for days on end.

The garrison at Fort Thorn filled with soldiers, while the Mesilla Guards blamed all depredations on reservation Apaches. Nathanial visited the reservation and Mesilla regularly, hearing complaints and denunciations from both sides. Apaches and whites believed in the right to avenge bloodshed, like every other nation or people in the history of the world.

I came west for my health, thought Nathanial, *but instead I have plunged into the darkest corner of the human heart, and some days even I feel like killing.* He had postponed his plans to start a ranch, due to the increased velocity of the Apache wars.

One afternoon he stood in Mesilla's small square, facing the Catholic church, a squat adobe structure with a crude cross sticking out the roof. Nathanial ambled inside, hoping to receive advice from the great beyond.

It was a small, low-roofed hall with an altar and painted wooden statues of Jesus, Mary, and the saints, illuminated faintly by candles and random light streaming through small rectangular windows. Kneeling in a pew, Nathanial heard old ladies whispering rosary prayers around him, a wagon passing outside.

A gaunt black-bearded monk in a brown robe swept the floor. Nathanial watched him send up clouds of dust as the monk hummed a Gregorian chant. When he drew close, Nathanial arose and said in Spanish, "May I talk with you, padre?"

"What is on your mind, sir?" asked the padre, who appeared approximately thirty years old.

"I am Dr. Steck's assistant, and I fear the Mesilla Guards will commit another massacre on the Mescalero reservation. I was wondering if you'd help stop it."

"How?" asked the priest.

"Talk with. Juan Ortega."

"What makes you think I haven't already? But he believes I am a befuddled religious ninny who writes homilies in the safety of my sacristy, and has no knowledge of the world."

"I feel the next massacre coming just as sure as I'm standing here," said Nathanial.

"There is nothing you can do," replied the priest. "Except pray."

Nathanial lost his temper. "Your prayers don't seem to have worked so far!"

"I pray not for special favors, but that God's will be done."

"You think it's His will to kill Mescaleros?"

"If more people prayed, we would not have such crimes."

"I need more than your ecclesiastical platitudes!"

"You and Senor Ortega have more in common than you realize, because he too is an unhappy man. You should pray for him."

"I'll never pray for that son-of-a-bitch, and please don't compare me with him. I've never committed a massacre."

"No?" The priest clucked knowingly, then continued sweeping the church.

Nathanial sat heavily in the pew, aware that Captain Barrington had killed many times in the line of duty, just as Ortega thought he was killing in the line of duty. Every murderer considers himself innocent, realized Nathanial. The worst crimes are justified by the best reasons.

Clarissa's hackney coach rumbled up noisy Broadway, passing City Hall, the Astor House, Taylor's Restaurant, and A.T. Stewart's, while newsboys shouted on streetcorners and businessmen carried brief-cases over crowded sidewalks.

The rapid pulse of the city never failed to enliven Clarissa. She stopped to buy the *Tribune*, then read about the Lecompton Constitution finally coming to its final vote in the Congress. The greatest orators in the nation, such as Jefferson Davis of Mississippi, Stephen Douglas of Illinois, William Seward of New York, and Alexander Stephens of Georgia, delivered ringing speeches, and everyone worried about war between the North and South.

While perusing the newspaper, her eyes fell on a brief article at the bottom of the next to last page.

MASSACRE IN NEW MEXICO

A report has been received concerning the massacre of Indians at a small settlement called Fort Thorn in remote southeastern New Mexico Territory. According to General John Garland, commanding officer of the 9th Department, a group of Mexicans broke into the camp on the morning of February 8 and killed eleven men, eight women, and five children, plus wounding countless others.

The page rattled in Clarissa's hand, as if God was speaking to her. She'd been thinking about her husband, and now read about the fort where he was stationed. She was certain Nathanial had been in the thick of it, and maybe he was killed.

She felt as if the Lord had hurled a lightning bolt at her. How terrible if Nathanial died before I could speak with him, she thought. I'd feel terrible for the rest of my life. Oh God, I pray he's alive. The coach turned onto Gramercy Park, headed for her father's mansion, and she observed maple and elm trees in the park where she'd played as a child. The coach stopped, Clarissa climbed up the steps, hit the rapper, and the maid answered, nearly fainting at the sight of the long-lost daughter.

Her mother arrived on the scene, her face pale, jowls hanging like curtains. "You're home," she said, holding out her arms.

They hugged, kissed, then her mother's mood shifted suddenly. She took a step backward and said, "We've heard very disturbing stories about you, young lady."

"They're probably true," replied Clarissa.

"I knew this would happen when you married the rapscallion Nathanial Barrington."

Before Clarissa could reply, servants carried her luggage into the living room. Clarissa took the opportunity to head for the nursery, her mother sputtering at her heels. "You should have listened to me!"

Clarissa found Rosita knitting on her chair, Natalie sleeping nearby. Rosita jumped to her feet and embraced Clarissa, then Clarissa tiptoed to the crib. It appeared that Natalie had grown considerably, her pale brown hair thickened. "I apologize," whispered Clarissa to her sleeping child. "I'll never desert you again."

Clarissa retreated from the room, her mother still at her heels. "When your father comes home, there'll be hell to pay."

"I shall move to the Saint Nicholas Hotel first thing in the morning. By the way, do you know if Nathanial is still alive?"

Her mother stopped short. "You can't kill somebody like Nathanial Barrington, who has a head like a block of granite, although it wouldn't be a bad idea."

"Has he divorced me?"

"Not that I know of, but that hasn't stopped you from certain shenanigans."

"Exactly what is that supposed to mean?" asked Clarissa as she entered her bedroom.

"That you have consorted with strange men."

"Come to think of it," replied Clarissa thoughtfully, "they *were* rather strange."

"They couldn't be any stranger than Nathanial Barrington. Of all the men to marry, you had to select that villain."

"Mother, you don't understand. Nathanial was a wonderful man."

Her mother reached for the dresser to steady herself. "Sounds like you're still in love with him."

Clarissa removed her bonnet. "I am, and have decided to return to him."

Her mother stared at the ceiling. "My poor daughter apparently has lost her mind. Your father always said you spent too much time alone with your piano. Please tell me you're joking."

"I'm completely serious."

"But Nathanial Barrington has behaved dishonorably to you."

"He wanted to save me from life on the stage, which turned out to be a nightmare."

"He was jealous of you, you mean."

"There's something you don't understand about Nathanial Barrington. He's not capable of jealousy, because he's too smart."

"Nathanial Barrington smart? Perhaps you sat in the sun too long when you were on that plantation in South Carolina."

They continued to squabble as mothers and daughters must, and after a while the rumble of something that sounded like a hippopotamus came from below, the arrival of Father. Wheezing, he rapidly climbed the stairs, arrived in her room out of breath, and shouted, "It's about time you returned home, young lady! I cannot begin to tell you how embarrassed I have been by you! Living in sin with a man in South Carolina, indeed!"

"I apologize," replied Clarissa, for she didn't want to argue.

"It had better not happen again!" He wagged his finger in her face, appearing on the edge of apoplexy.

"Perhaps you'd better sit down," Clarissa told her father, "because I have news."

"Don't tell me you've married a southerner?"

"I'm going back to Nathanial Barrington."

"I don't believe it!" he cried, flinging out his arms.

His wife tried to calm him. "Please sit down, Herbert."

Instead, he turned to his daughter. "There is only one possible solution. We must send her to the Bloomingdale Asylum."

Clarissa whipped out her Colt. "If anybody tries to lock me in an asylum, I'll shoot his damned lights out."

Her father stared at the gun, his daughter's finger wrapped around the trigger. "My God," he uttered. "Has it come to this?" Agitated, he found it difficult to breathe. A terrible pressure seemed to squash his chest, and his left arm went numb.

"Are you all right, Herbert?" asked his wife, and then she screamed as her husband toppled to the floor.

Clarissa sent a servant for the physician her father had dubbed Dr. Rumsoak," residing across the park.

Then Clarissa returned to her mother, who told her, "This is your fault."

Finally, Dr. Rumsoak arrived with his black bag of implements and clouds of whiskey fumes. "He's still alive," he declared after listening to the patient's chest. Then the master of the house was carried to his bedchamber, where the doctor bled him to take pressure off his heart, a common medical procedure often producing unintended results.

Clarissa's father died later that night.

Everyone blamed Clarissa for the demise of her father, and some said she had been corrupted totally by the infamous Nathanial Barrington. But Clarissa believed she had done nothing wrong, so she moved with her maid and child to the Saint Nicholas Hotel, and after the funeral the first thing she did was visit Nathanial's parents, accompanied by Rosita and Natalie.

She'd notified the Barringtons in advance, and the old folks were delighted to see their granddaughter, who reminded them so much of Nathanial. But they couldn't keep up with a babe, and finally were tired. Rosita removed Natalie from the room to continue play in the backyard, leaving Clarissa with her in-laws.

"I was wondering," she said, "if you've heard from Nathanial lately."

"Why yes," replied the colonel's wife. "We received a note the other day."

"When was it mailed?"

"Why do you ask?"

"There was a massacre in New Mexico Territory, and I wonder if he was in it."

Amalia Barrington stared, then leapt from her chair, ran up the stairs, and could be heard roaming about. Meanwhile, Colonel Barrington leaned forward, as if he wanted to say something significant.

"Yes?" asked Clarissa with a smile.

"Don't ever disappoint the Army," he said.

Amalia returned, carrying the letter. "It's dated February 12."

"The massacre was on the 8th," said Clarissa. "Apparently he's still alive, thank God. I'm so relieved."

Amalia appeared surprised. "I thought you were angry at Nathanial."

"On the contrary, I plan to go back to him, but unfortunately he doesn't know it. He's not married by any chance?"

"Not that I know of, but he mentioned a certain schoolteacher."

Clarissa nearly gagged and for a moment thought she would join her father in the grave. "I can't blame him for finding someone else," she admitted. "I plan to tell him that I have wronged him and then leave."

"Now let me get this straight," said Mrs. Barrington. "He nearly tore apart the Academy of Music when you were rehearsing, and humiliated you in front of everybody, but you wronged him?"

"He was fighting for my love, I now realize, because I had been neglecting him."

"Extraordinary," said the queen of Washington Square. "Don't you think you should warn him of your coming?"

"No, because he'll order me to stay away."

"I'd give anything to be there."

"Why don't you come?"

Amalia patted her husband's hand. "I must stay with the colonel."

Clarissa turned to Nathanial's father, who sat, a serious expression on his face, as if listening to commands being shouted on fog-shrouded old parade grounds.

13

Near the end of Ghost Face, one hundred and eighty heavily armed Chiricahua and Mimbreno warriors rode south toward Mexico, their mission to destroy Janos, city of poisoners.

Led by Chief Mangas Coloradas, Chief Cochise, and sub-chief Victorio, they numbered among their ranks such famous warriors as Elias, Esquiline, Juh, Barbonsito, Partay, and Cochise's brother, Coyuntura, carrying a Bible in his saddlebags. They were augmented by noted medicine men such as Nana the Mimbreno and Geronimo of the Bedonko clan, while in the fighting ranks rode a sprinkling of warriors on their first raid, among them two young sons of Mangas Coloradas, Cascos and Tonje.

The warriors had prepared with a dance that lasted four days, during which they'd asked the Mountain Spirits for power. Now the music had ended, they wore Killer of Enemies Bandoliers and rode in a column of twos across a desert that still showed patches of snow.

In days to come, when a bluecoat detachment was reported, the warriors headed in a different direction, fixed on the objective, Janos. But their cautious posture altered once they crossed into Mexico, where they unleased their full fury, leaving flames and death in their wake.

News of the raid spread across Sonora and Chihuahua, and substantial Mexican Army units were sent to the field, hoping to intercept the Apaches, their visit long anticipated. According to reports of newly hired scouts, the Apaches were headed toward Janos, confirming speculations of Mexican commanders and their U.S. Army liaison, Captain Beauregard Hargreaves.

Beau was in the field when the dispatch arrived from Colonel Garcia. All units were ordered to converge on Janos for the final showdown. With Captain Marrero and forty Mexican cavalrymen, Beau headed back to that ill-fated village.

Mexican Army scouts cut the Apache trail as Colonel Garcia's forces continued to deploy. On the night of February 23, the Apaches torched a ranch near Santa Cruz. Next day they hit Cuchuta eight miles farther south. Exultant with victory, riding fresh horses, the warriors sped toward Janos, where Colonel Garcia waited with one hundred and ten infantrymen plus two twelve-pounder mountain howitzers on loan from the United States Army.

As additional field units arrived, Colonel Garcia positioned them to the north and south of the city, augmenting his force to 350 soldiers, while Apaches advanced from the west. The stage was set, and every player knew his part. The collision could come at any time.

Beneath a full moon the Apaches stopped about five miles from Janos. They needed to rest horses and themselves, because at dawn the town would be assaulted.

The warriors checked weapons, conducted final rites, and all was silent, because no idle chatter was permitted in war. Nearby, the great chief Mangas Coloradas stood on an eminence and gazed down at the faint flickering lights of Janos.

The lust for revenge burned hot in his heart, for he could not forgive Mexicans who'd tried to poison the children of the People. His scouts had told him additional Mexican units were on the way to Janos, and a great battle would occur in the morning, one that would live forever in the annals of the People.

Mangas Coloradas was sixty-four years old, covered with scars, veteran of countless campaigns. He remembered when only a few *Nakai-yes* had lived in the homeland, and the People had run free as antelopes. Now pressed on all sides, the People were called to higher sacrifice. War makes us strong, thought Mangas Coloradas. We wear out Killer of Enemies Bandoliers, we have obeyed the precepts of the Mountain Spirits, and nothing shall deny us our rightful revenge.

Twenty paces away, Cochise and Victorio watched the chief silhouetted against the night sky, his nose like the beak of an eagle. They were next in command and had voiced quiet doubts to each other about the boldness of Mangas Coloradas's raid. But the People were enraged, they needed to strike a blow at Janos, and no one dared ask for moderation. So Cochise and Victorio clasped hands in friendship. "May the Mountain Spirits ride with you tomorrow, my brother," said Cochise.

"I will remain within sight of you," replied Victorio. "And you must remain within sight of me. If the battle goes against us, we cannot afford to waste warriors, as we have discussed. But you must make the decision."

"And you must watch our great chief, for he no longer is a young warrior."

"I have selected the best Mimbreno warriors for his personal bodyguard," said Victorio. "Let me speak honestly, for it is possible that I shall not return. I have always admired you, Cochise, and I consider you a fine warrior. I look forward to seeing you in the next world."

Cochise smiled. "You are a brilliant sub-chief, and you above all others shall survive, but one day everyone will reside in the next world. We shall sing victory songs unto eternity."

"And dance with the maidens," added Victorio.

"Especially the maidens," agreed Cochise. "Now that is something to look forward to."

They heard Mangas Coloradas returning. "I have bared my soul to Yusn, the Lifegiver," he said sonorously, holding his arms like a medicine man. "The time has come to avenge the suffering of the People."

Before retiring, Mangas Coloradas spoke with his two sons, who would experience large-scale battle for the first time in the morning. They sat in the shadow of a barrel cactus, and Mangas Coloradas told them, "Do not be afraid to die. For a noble death is the highest honor a warrior can achieve."

They were young men, nineteen and seventeen harvests each. "We will not shame you," said Cascos, and Tonje nodded his assent.

"When we attack, strike hard," advised Mangas Coloradas. "There can be no compassion for this enemy, no hesitation in following orders, no unworthy thoughts. Remember that you are young, your souls are spotless, and glory is your destiny." He hugged each of them. "My dear children, remember that I have always loved you." Then he ran his fingers over their Killer of Enemies Bandoliers. "May the Mountain Spirits safeguard you tomorrow on your day of days."

Less than five miles away, Beau strolled around the Mexican Army camp, making certain guards were awake. He expected the Apaches to attack outlying Mexican forces piecemeal, and could not believe they'd charge a fortified Mexican town head-on.

But Apaches craved revenge, and Beau suspected it had distorted their thinking. A terrible clash was looming however the Apaches attacked, and they obeyed no rules in close fighting. Beau wondered if he'd ever see his family again as he approached a guard snapping to attention and saluting.

Beau nodded to him, then continued his prowl. The difference between life and death was spotting the Apaches as early as possible. Besides, Beau couldn't sleep on the night before battle. An ordinary soldier's one function was to fight, but an officer worried about myriads of details, because if he erred, it would mean the loss of lives, possibly even his own.

Under normal circumstances memories of Beau's wife and family would provide comfort, but instead they caused doubt. Beau wondered if Rebecca was rolling with Nathanial Barrington on the bunk of a dirty little hotel in Santa Fe at that very moment. If I know Nathanial, he thought, he won't stop until he has thoroughly debased her.

But Beau had more important worries, such as how long fifty Mexican soldiers could hold off an Apache army until help arrived. *I wonder if these Mexicans are mad enough to fight hard, or maybe I'll be killed defending a nation of which I'm not even a citizen.*

Beau's old friend and former West Point roommate wasn't sleeping with Rebecca that night; he wasn't sleeping at all. Smoking a succession of cigars, sipping whiskey, he paced in his bedroom, wearing a black greatcoat made in New York City.

He'd awakened in the middle of the night in the grip of a frightening realization. *What if the failure of my marriage was my fault?* he mused. *Why in the hell didn't I let Clarissa have her silly musical career if that's what she wanted? Why'd I insult her, throw a tantrum, and practically spit in her eye?*

Back and forth he paced, feeling more ashamed with every round. *Why didn't I let her find the truth for herself,* he thought, *instead of constantly trying to dominate her? And if she liked to dress in pretty clothes and play the piano before audiences, so what? If I truly adored her, I would have shown it by helping instead of bullying her, just because she's a few years younger than I. Maybe I was jealous of the attention she was receiving, like the low schemer I am, instead of rejoicing at her success.*

Nathanial sat at his desk and wrote a love letter to Clarissa, apologizing for everything, begging forgiveness, and promising anything if she'd take him back. The letter was filled with words of love, and he even stole a few lines from his favorite remembered poems.

After completing the letter, he had the mad urge to

return to New York on the next stage. But she'll probably kick me in the teeth, he decided, because of my revoltingly vulgar behavior. We were destined for each other, but my conceit spoiled everything. If only I could turn back the clock and start our marriage anew.

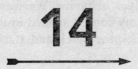

14

In the hour before dawn Mimbreno and Chiricahua warriors formed one long rank on an undulating stretch of cactus- and sagebrush-covered plain about a mile from Janos. Their bows and rifles ready to fire, faces stony, they awaited the order to attack.

Leading them, Chief Mangas Coloradas, the greatest Mimbreno who ever lived, sat solidly in his saddle, lance in hand, pistol in belt, staring ahead. His tactic was direct: He would strike the heinous town like lightning, smash it to bits, and if anyone got in their way, the warriors of righteousness would sweep right over them.

Behind the great chief, to his left and right, were his two principal lieutenants, Cochise and Victorio, and the order had been passed along that if Mangas Coloradas went down, they were to obey Cochise, and then Victorio. Behind the commanders were arrayed warriors steeled for the ultimate sacrifice.

Each knew a violent conflict lay ahead, but they'd trained for this moment virtually all their lives. Even the women warriors among them, such as Jocita of the Mimbrenos, were deadly with all weapons, especially rapidly fired arrows on horseback.

They wore their Killer of Enemies Bandoliers, which they believed would make them impervious to enemy fire. They were so angry, they felt so justified, and had been so purified, they believed the Mexican Army could not stand up to them.

Mangas Coloradas raised his lance in the air, pointed it straight ahead, prodded his horse, and the old warrior advanced, followed by Cochise and Victorio then the main force. In attack formation, the war ponies walked toward the town barely visible in the distance. The hour of vengeance had arrived.

Mangas Coloradas knew young warriors watched him, so he sat bolt upright, shoulders squared, elbows close to his waist, although he had a terrible backache and pain in his bones. I do not have many more battles left, he thought, and perhaps I will be killed this day. He looked to the sky, hoping to see the ghost of Cuchillo Negro, but the night was blank, no foreshadowing of victory or danger.

The warriors drew closer to the iniquitous village, each remembering the pain and near-death of poisoning. It was difficult for the People to imagine minds that would conceive such a crime, and only one reaction was possible. How could such dastardly miscreants hope to defeat honest warriors? The People believed that battles ultimately were decided not by numbers, but by the faith of warriors. The seeds of vengeance would be nourished by the blood of enemies.

The village came into view, all lights out, soldiers behind barricades, waiting for the onslaught. The two cannons manufactured in Harper's Ferry, Virginia, gleamed cruelly in the first glimmer of dawn, ready to fire. The great chief Mangas Coloradas took a deep breath. "My warriors!" he cried. "The time has come to avenge your sacred honor!"

He kicked the withers of his horse, and that creature had heard so much hatred toward the *Nakai-yes*, it despised them as well. Stretching its long limbs, pumping haunches and shoulders, it accelerated into a full gallop, feeling the lithe weight of the valiant chief upon his back. And from behind came the thunder of hoofbeats, as warriors sang battle songs and shouted encouragement to each other, while others like Chuntz hollered deprecations at the Mexicans. The sun peeked warily over the Sierra Madre Mountains as the warriors of the People sped across the desert, determined to transform Janos into a funeral pyre.

Mountain howitzers fired noisily, but the Apaches were spread out, and cannonballs flew through open spaces. The Mexicans then commenced musket fire, but the range was too great and the balls fell short. It looked as if the Apaches would have no difficulty penetrating the defenses of the town, but other forces were in motion as well, Mexican companies to the north and south charging toward Janos, hoping to catch the Apaches in a giant pincer.

The Mexican soldiers knew if they lost they could expect death, torture, and mutilation, while the Apaches could not shrink from their duty. The wheel of destruction spun more furiously as the warriors descended like locusts upon the barricades.

Cannons fired again, and this time grapeshot ripped the bodies of four warriors, but now the rest were at the edge of town, firing bullets and arrows. The soldiers in that sector fell backward, then Juh and Geronimo hopped the barricades, set fire to barrels of gunpowder left behind, and fled.

The powder exploded, and a huge ball of black smoke rose into the air, a breach blown into the barricades. On horseback, Mangas Coloradas led the first wave through, firing his pistol, protected by bodyguards, who laid a swathe of death around them.

Mexican soldiers retreated in orderly fashion under the command of Colonel Garcia, who prayed for his support units to arrive. Women, children, and the aged huddled in the barracks, hearing Apache screams for their blood. The Apaches set fires and gathered additional weapons from dead enemies as they forged ahead. Some warriors found a cantina and swallowed whiskey to strengthen their resolve. In the main, discipline held as the warriors unleashed a barrage of arrows and bullets, pressing ever closer to the Army compound. And in the middle of it all was Jocita the warrior woman, lobbing arrows that flew high into the air, then dropped down on retreating Mexicans. Nearby Chief Juh of the Nednai put an arrow into any Mexicano who appeared to draw a bead on his faithless first wife.

Some Apaches were on foot, others mounted, making good progress when shots erupted behind them. More Mexican soldiers had arrived on the killing ground, the moment Mangas Coloradas had been waiting for. He let out a bloodcurdling battle scream, but he'd been conspicuous leading the attack, and a well-placed ball struck his gallant steed in the throat.

The animal gushed fountains of blood as it collapsed onto the ground. Mangas Coloradas was thrown clear, helped to his feet by bodyguards, and continued on foot, rushing the barracks. The tactic of the warriors was to draw close to Mexican soldiers, attract their fire, dodge wildly, and when Mexican muskets had emptied, smash skulls and ribs with war clubs, or cut them with lances.

Mangas Coloradas's bodyguards remained close as additional Mexican companies hit the Apaches on all sides. Battle lines broke down, visibility became obscured in dust and smoke, and the fighting became hand to hand, a form at which the Apaches excelled.

Houses and barns went up in flames, while Apache hatchets, clubs, and lances were utilized at close range. But the Mexicans were armed with Colt pistols, and the Apaches discovered their Killer of Enemies Bandoliers did not convey invulnerability. Jocita sat stolidly in her saddle, bleeding from a head wound while rapid firing arrows, but many warriors went down in the volleys, including Cascos and Tonje, while Victorio bled from a shoulder wound, and Cochise had sustained a lacerated left biceps, despite wearing the bandolier given him by Miguel Narbona. The People were overwhelmed by Mexicans, but the blood of warriors was hot, and it was a good day to die.

The mood of heroic resignation transformed suddenly when the great chief Mangas Coloradas was shot through the chest. Bodyguards rushed to safeguard his inert body, then they lifted him roughly and threw him over a horse.

Command devolved to Cochise, a more modern leader, who could see no point in the cream of Apache warriors slaughtered on one day. "Enough!" he shouted. "Retreat!"

Some warriors chose to disobey the command and fight on to their majestic deaths, but even Nana the medicine man, covered with his own blood and that of

Mexicans, decided to continue another day. "Retreat!" he hollered, giving his approval to Cochise.

"Back!" cried Victorio to the Mimbrenos. "Do not fail me now!"

The combined survivors shot, lanced, hacked, and bashed their way free, but the Mexican soldiers had no terrific desire to detain them, for they had lost nearly a quarter of their complement, and it wasn't easy to reload with Apaches firing arrows at close range.

The Apaches broke loose, leaving fallen brethren behind, among them the two sons of Mangas Coloradas. It was the worst defeat in the history of the People; they fled into the great Sonoran wilderness.

Nathanial sat in the sutler's store at Fort Thorn, drinking a glass of whiskey. The futility of making peace, the demoralizing condition of Mescaleros on the reservation, and self-loathing had immobilized him. He toyed with the notion of returning to the Mimbreno Apaches, then thought of renouncing everything and becoming a Franciscan monk.

Sometimes he felt like drinking himself into unconsciousness, but needed to care for his children. Occasionally, in the dark corners of the sutler's store, tears came to his eyes. I had the most wonderful woman in the world, he thought, and all I ever did was behave like a rogue. Nathanial wanted to put his fist through the wall.

The sutler's store usually was empty during duty hours, but the door opened, and a small boy appeared. "Captain Barrington, Doctoro Steck would like to see you pronto."

Nathanial hadn't bothered to shave, his blond unruly hair hanging to his shoulders. He also exuded the fragrance of cheap whiskey, and it preceded him into the office of his employer, Dr. Michael Steck, who frowned. "Are you in your usual stupor?"

Nathanial's hand darted to his waist, and before Dr. Steck could blink a second time, a pistol was aimed at his nose. Nathanial said, "I never get that stupefied." Then he holstered the pistol, dropped onto a chair, and said, "Something important must have occurred for you to disturb my drinking."

"According to my information," replied Dr. Steck, "an army of Mimbreno Apaches attacked Janos, but the Mexicans beat the hell out of them. I wouldn't be surprised if the Apaches are ready to talk peace with us, so could you go to Mangas Coloradas and arrange a powwow?"

Nathanial stared blankly, realizing his friends had suffered a serious reversal. "Do you know the names of any dead Apaches?"

"No, but we mustn't let this opportunity pass. We can offer them land north of the Gila, where they'll be left alone."

"For how long?"

"Who can say? Washington has not yet acted on my proposal."

"You make heartfelt promises that somehow you never deliver." Nathanial raised his finger and pointed accusingly. "You more than any other man have destroyed the Mescaleros."

"Why—I've done more for them than anyone!" replied Dr. Steck indignantly.

"If you violate one of your treaties, you merely tear it up and write another, equally worthless."

"I never claimed to be perfect, but perhaps I've prevented a few drops of bloodshed along the way. It's childish to think a sudden bold gesture will bring peace, because only the slow, painstaking steps of diplomacy can do the job. Have you ever read the life of Metternich?"

"How long can peace last when it's based on lies?"

"I am *bargaining* with the Apaches, and you fail to comprehend the niceties of negotiation. But, unfortunately, you're all I've got. Will you go to Mangas Coloradas and tell him I wish to speak?"

"He might kill you for your many betrayals."

"He wouldn't dare kill me, because I'm his only chance. Who else can he talk with—General Garland?"

Nathanial thought of visiting Nana, Victorio, Mangas Coloradas, Geronimo, and all his other friends. "It'll take a while to make arrangements for my children, but sure—I'll go."

"Take all the time you need. I'd like the Apaches to stew over this defeat for a few weeks, and maybe they'll finally reach the obvious conclusion that they don't have a chance against us."

The failed warriors limped back to the Chiricahua Mountains, scouts posted to avoid another catastrophe. The People had expected the Mountain Spirits to give them Janos, but a cataclysmic setback had occurred, and Chief Mangas Coloradas appeared close to death.

He wasn't the only wounded warrior, but many had been killed, and the People could not enlist warriors from other regions. One of the women warriors had fallen, but Jocita survived, scarred on the chin and part of an ear shot off, marks she would wear proudly unto death.

She estimated that she had struck at least five Mexicans with her arrows, so the poisoning had been avenged. But the price had been too high, and she could not understand why. The pain in her heart was worse than her ear, for she suspected the Mountain Spirits had been angry at the People, perhaps because not all were as holy as they pretended, such as Jocita's episode with Sunny Bear at the Santa Rita Copper Mines.

Jocita wasn't the only warrior reflecting upon the failure of their religion. It was as if the very foundation of their lives had been shattered. Faith had held them together, but now appeared insubstantial when facing excessive odds. Expensive Killer of Enemies Bandoliers had not stopped bullets, and Nana felt especially humiliated. Once, long ago, he thought, I was a man of power, but now I have cheated not only the People, but myself. He swore to return all payments. No longer will I claim to be a medicine man, because my magic has deserted me. Why?

He could find no answer, and neither could Victorio, riding alongside Chief Mangas Coloradas, who lay head down over his saddle, arms and legs wagging with the movement of his horse. It was heart-rending to see the great chief humbled.

The full moon threw a silver sheen over the gashes and bruises on Victorio's torso, for he had been in the thick of the fight, many Mexican soldiers falling beneath his club. But he feared the responsibility that lay ahead. "Please live, Mangas Coloradas," he whispered. "I am not yet ready to lead the Mimbreno People."

Like the others, Victorio had achieved a new realization during the press of battle. Purity of spirit cannot overcome numbers and guns, and the old time has past. From now on, Victorio thought, we must follow the example of Chief Gomez of the Mescaleros. Let there be no more glorious charges, no silly notions, no vain hope. The Mountain Spirits want us to utilize our warrior skills, not fight impossible odds. And we must respect the Mexicans, for they will never run from us again.

Sergeant Major Randall knocked on General Garland's door. "Captain Hargreaves is here, sir."

"Send him in."

General Garland rose behind his desk as a dusty black-bearded, thickly built officer marched into the commander's sanctum, came to a halt, and saluted. General Garland extended his hand. "Congratulations, you have done a magnificent job."

Beau smiled, showing bright white teeth behind the beard. "I'm pleased to report that my mission was a success, sir."

"To show our appreciation . . ." said the general, tossing a black box to Beau.

He opened it, revealing the insignia of a major. A cough erupted in his throat, and his heart respiration increased, for such is the power of the bronze oak leaf insignia of a major on the mind of a captain. "I . . . I . . ."

General Garland chuckled. "I'll pin them on in an appropriate ceremony, but I just want you to know how much I appreciate your work. I won't keep you, because I'm sure you're anxious to see your family. You may take the rest of the week off, Major Hargreaves."

After leaving his horse at the stable, Beau headed home in a state of euphoria. I'm finally a major, he thought. The rank was a significant step upward from captain, and many captains never made the grade. I'm headed for a general's stars, Beau told himself. Now he could support his family on a slightly higher scale.

The mere thought of his wife caused his brow to furrow, and joy over his promotion faded like dew on a desert morning. He wondered if dear Rebecca was lying with Nathanial Barrington at that moment, and would he catch them together. Could I kill both? he wondered. Or just Nathanial? Beau strongly suspected his wife had deceived him, but if he shot her suitor, he'd never receive his major's oak leaf. I mustn't be rash, he advised himself. If they're together, I'll make no dramatic upheaval, but just turn and walk out the door, demonstrating my utter contempt for them.

Finally, he arrived at Rebecca's address, a squat adobe house slightly larger than those lived in by peasants. He knocked on the door, and presently it was opened by their Mexican maid, who appeared surprised to see him.

"Where's my wife?" he asked.

"In her bedroom, sir."

Beau's jealous mind suspected the worst as he ran down the hall, nearly tripping over his boots. He stopped at her door and knocked.

"Come in," said a soft, tired voice from within.

He yanked open the door and found his wife lying fully clothed on the bedspread, hands folded on her flat belly, alone. "Beau!" she cried happily.

He could see that she was glad to see him, but a residue of suspicion remained. He closed the door and sat beside her on the bed. They kissed.

"I've missed you so much," she told him warmly, rubbing his back.

"I was so lonely for you and the children," he replied.

"Were you a good boy?"

"How could you even suggest such a thing? By the way, is Nathanial in town?"

"No—he left shortly after the incident described in my letter. He's at Fort Thorn, where they had that massacre not long ago."

Beau had heard of the Mesilla massacre and was relieved that Nathanial had been away from his wife. "Did you invite him here?"

"Perhaps I should've had him over for a home-cooked meal, but he seemed busy. I fear he'll drink himself to death one day. He's quite broken up over his wife."

"I'm surprised he hasn't found someone else by now. He didn't make advances to you, did he?"

She stared at him. "Don't be absurd—there was not even the suggestion of it," lied Rebecca, because she didn't want to rile her husband.

Should I give her the benefit of the doubt? Beau asked himself. "I have good news. Guess who's been promoted to major."

She appeared thunderstruck, for she'd expected to be the wife of a captain forever. "At last," she sighed.

He kissed her lips. "You must have a new wardrobe, for the wife of a major will be noticed, and people will wonder if she has what it takes to become a general's wife."

She hugged him tightly. "I wouldn't have married you unless I thought you could be a general. Oh, Beau, how wonderful! Maybe they'll send us to Washington!"

She smelled clean, sweet, remarkably similar to the maid he'd married. "Are the children at school?" he inquired.

"Yes, for another hour and a half."

He unbuttoned the top of her blouse. "Then we have time."

Myra Rowland, Clarissa's mother, took ill after her husband's funeral, forcing Clarissa to remain in New York a few extra weeks. Finally, one day she walked into her mother's bedroom and said, "I'm leaving."

Myra Rowland opened her eyes. "Where do you think you're going?"

"To my husband."

"But I need you here."

"The doctor can't find anything wrong with you."

"What about Natalie?"

"She's coming with me."

"If you walk out that door, I shall disown you, ungrateful little witch."

"Not so little anymore."

Clarissa bent to kiss her mother's cheek, but her mother raised her hand as if to slap her. Clarissa caught her wrist, smiled, laid her mother's hand on the pillow, then walked to the door, on her way back to New Mexico Territory.

It was night at Fort Thorn, and Nathanial, unable to sleep, sat in the parlor of his home, reading a recent copy of the *Chicago Daily Tribune* that Dr. Steck had given him. On the front page he learned that Napoleon III and his wife, the Empress Eugenie, had survived an assassination attempt on January 14. The royal couple had been headed to the opera when an Italian revolutionary named Felice Orsini and two accomplices lobbed bombs at the imperial carriage, killing two bystanders and wounding over a hundred, the em-

peror and empress unscratched. The police had appre-
hended Orsini, who believed the emperor an obstacle
to Italian independence.

In India the British Army was fighting the Sepoy
Rebellion, considered by correspondents a particularly ugly conflict, because the Sepoys were natives
trained and armed by the British. The Sepoys had captured Meerut Cownpur and Delhi, with atrocities and
massacres perpetrated by all sides.

Nathanial shook his head in despair. Everywhere he
turned he found hatred, bloodshed, horror. He worried
about his Apache friends, slaked his thirst with whiskey,
and had nightmares about dead children. He was unable
to take steps necessary to own a ranch, because all aspi-
rations seemed pointless when measured against the
world's malevolence. Every day he sank deeper into
melancholy. When I travel to the homeland of Mangas
Coloradas, he thought, maybe I won't come back.

Sometimes, sitting on the train, Clarissa feared her
husband would dismiss her with a few carefully selected cruelties. What an empty-headed pumpkin he
must have thought I was when I thrilled to read my
name in newspapers, knowing the journalists had
been bought and paid for by Thorndyke. How disap-
pointed Nathanial must have been by my shameless
pandering to the public, she brooded.

She looked out the train window at snow melting
from bare trees in the Pocono Mountains. The train's
engine sang its staccato song, like the percussion of a
symphony orchestra. She steadied a pad of paper and
wrote notes dancing in her mind.

She often composed music out of sounds around
her, mixing in memories of plantation slave melodies,

the religious themes of camp meetings, and children's nursery rhymes. We Americans must create a new music, she told herself, as she annotated sharps and flats. Not just imitate Mozart and Beethoven. Perhaps one day I'll stitch these tunes together and write a symphony to America, but only when I am alone, so audiences cannot encourage my worse tendencies. But I'll never be free until I settle my marriage to Nathanial, one way or the other. I only hope he hasn't married that damned schoolmarm.

As the Lecompton Constitution came to a final vote, the Buchanan administration offered vacillating Democrats from $10,000 to $15,000, plus special plums such as government jobs for friends or family members, while stubborn Democrats were threatened with political ruination.

On March 23, 1858, the Senate voted 33 to 25 for the Lecompton Constitution, a tremendous victory for the administration, but on April Fools' Day the House of Representatives defeated Lecompton 120 to 112, with 22 anti-Lecompton Democrats voting with 92 Republicans and six Know-Nothings. This effectively killed the measure, a crushing blow to the President, and Kansas remained a territory.

President Buchanan felt betrayed as he fumed and stewed in his office or wandered the White House like a ghost, grinding his teeth. He had accepted party discipline throughout his career and never once defied his leaders.

One night he sat in his office, wondering how to punish traitors, when there was a knock on the door. He was startled to see his niece, Harriet Lane, wearing a pink robe. "You really must get some rest, Uncle Jim," she said.

"How can I rest when the nation is headed toward insurrection?" he asked.

"No man can suppress it alone," she replied. "Do you want to be the next James Polk or Zachary Taylor?"

James Polk had been president from '44 to '48 and died a few months after leaving office, his health broken by the slavery ordeal. Zachary Taylor, '48 to '50, had died in office for the same reason.

"I wouldn't give them the satisfaction," said Old Buck.

"No president can govern without the support of his party," she reminded him, and not many Washingtonians comprehended the hidden power of the unelected but commonsense Miss Harriet Lane. "Why not publicly limit yourself to one term and devote your energies to the needs of the nation, not the distractions and compromises of a re-election campaign? Besides, I don't think the people deserve you."

President Buchanan went to bed at his niece's behest and lay alone in his bachelor darkness, feeling as if a weight had been removed from his heart. She's right, he decided. I'll wait a decent interval, then announce my intention not to run for a second term. That will free me to do what's right for the nation, because the people don't know what they want anymore, so harangued are they by the dirty, lying press. And if Senator Douglas thinks he can do this job better than I, he's welcome to try.

Sometimes Old Buck suspected that no politician, not even himself, could solve the slavery issue, and only a massive bloodletting would bring peace to the land. I must do whatever is necessary to save the Union, regardless of how my enemies attack me, and how cowardly my decisions might be presented by the press, he decided. The reporters can whip whatever horse they like, since they never take responsibility for the consequences of their distortions. I don't want history to record James Buchanan as the last President of the United States.

At West Point relations among northern and southern students had become as icy as nearby Bear Mountain Lake. No one actually mentioned the slavery issue, for the cadets were learning to be gentlemen, treating each other with utmost courtesy, while beneath the surface fierce contempt seethed.

One afternoon Cadet Jeffrey Barrington sat alone in his room, boning mathematics for an examination, when he heard a commotion down the hall. Opening the door, he saw Cadet Frank Jesup of Maryland and Cadet Charles Paine of New Hampshire going at each other with swords.

The corridor filled with students cheering for their favorites, while Jeffrey watched silently. Jesup and Paine appeared anxious to kill each other, utilizing skills taught by the fencing master, but then the sergeant of the guard was spotted, the alarm promptly sounded, and cadets fled to their rooms, including the combatants.

Buck returned to his desk, but couldn't concentrate on mathematics. A day never passed when he didn't feel like punching an arrogant southerner in the mouth, and he knew they felt the same about him. All the tensions of the nation were gathered at West Point, where northerners and southerners lived cheek by jowl. I've just seen an opening skirmish of civil war, he realized. It is entirely possible and even likely that I will be shooting at my southern classmates one day, and they at me. I'd better learn my trade well.

15

Nathanial missed Clarissa most in the middle of the night when he tossed and rolled sleeplessly for what seemed hours on end. He recalled their honeymoon, her laughter ringing like bells. How could I have lost Clarissa? he asked himself. She loved me madly, but I neglected, mistreated, and insulted her.

A footfall reached Nathanial's Apache ears, apparently coming from the parlor. He reached for the Colt in the holster hanging from the bedpost. It might be the creak of timber on a cool spring night, he thought, but then the sound came again as someone tiptoed about.

Nathanial crawled out of bed, pulled on his pants and boots, thumbed back the hammer of the Colt, and opened his door. The parlor was empty, or so it appeared. He lit a candle, but found no thieves, Apaches, or escaped criminals. Probably a mouse, he decided.

To make sure, he thought he'd check his children before returning to bed. He crossed to Zachary's room and was startled to find the bed empty. Maybe he's gone to the outhouse.

Nathanial checked the outhouse, but no one was

there. Becoming alarmed, he rushed to Gloria's room to see if she too was missing. He opened the door and breathed a sigh of relief when he found her sleeping peacefully beneath her blankets.

Nathanial glanced around the room, but nothing was out of order. He examined the closet, but only Gloria's clothing was there. On a quirk Nathanial dropped to one knee and glanced beneath the bed. To his astonishment it appeared that someone or something was there, but it was too dark to see.

"Hello, Father," said an embarrassed voice.

Nathanial was so astonished, he became momentarily paralyzed. His son crawled forward with a nervous smile. "Guess you caught me."

"What the hell's going on here!" Nathanial boomed.

"We're getting married," said Gloria.

"Like hell you are!"

"Not right away," added Zachary quickly. "We'll wait until we're old enough, of course."

"But . . . but . . ." sputtered Nathanial.

"We're not as bad as you think," said Gloria.

Nathanial drew himself to his full height and managed to say, "I cannot have this under my roof. Zachary is going back to his mother on the next stagecoach to Santa Fe, and if I ever catch the both of you alone again, I'll get out the horsewhip."

He grabbed Zachary by the scruff of his neck and dragged him to his room, while both children begged and wailed. But Nathanial's mind was made up. "Damned little monsters," he said. "Leave 'em alone a minute, and they're up to . . ." Nathanial didn't know what to call it as he angrily pushed his son into bed.

"But it's not what you think," protested Zachary.

"I ought to beat you to within an inch of your life, or perhaps I should merely burn you at the stake, you devil."

"Don't be so mean!" hollered Gloria, who had followed Nathanial across the parlor.

"Get back to bed this instant, young lady!"

"I won't."

Nathanial tried to catch her, but the ex–gutter rat dodged out of the way, then Zachary tackled his father from behind. Nathanial fell to the floor, and as he landed, thought he heard gunshots from the vicinity of the Indian reservation. He froze as Zachary struggled to flatten his father down.

Nathanial shook off his children, his demeanor changing. "Get back to your rooms," he ordered.

"What's wrong?" asked Zachary.

"Do as I say!"

Nathanial ran to the stable, hastily saddled his horse, and rode out the door, heading for the reservation. The distant shooting had stopped, and Nathanial hoped it was a few drunken Indians firing old muskets, not another massacre. His horse galloped onward, wind streaming through Nathanial's long hair, as he tried to convince himself that the Mesilla Guards could not have struck again.

The Mescalero encampment loomed out of the night, tipis damaged, bodies lying on the ground, splatters of red. The wailing of women roasted Nathanial's soul, and a little child staggered toward him, shrieking pathetically, bleeding from a gaping stomach wound. Nathanial climbed down from his horse just as the child collapsed. Nathanial ran to her, looked at the horrific wound, then gazed at the girl's features wrenched eternally in pain.

Nathanial felt as if his heart would stop. He coughed, tears rolled down his face, and he felt wild, weird, as if he were looking down on himself from the sky above. He laid the child on the ground, closed her little eyes, and tried to pray, but was too filled with rage to ask an unfeeling God for favors.

He raised his head as an old Apache grandmother approached, bleeding from a head wound, pointing her finger. "This is your fault, Sunny Bear!" she yelled. "You speak our language, you come among us and promise peace, but this is the result!" She extended her hands to indicate the carnage surrounding her. "You are worse than Steck, because we know he is a liar, but you pretend to be one of us!"

Nathanial bowed to her judgment. It's true, he told himself. The smell of children's entrails reached his nostrils, and his passionate heart could not tolerate two massacres in a row. After twelve years of frontier service, countless battles, and skirmishes, and witness to numerous massacres—Captain Nathanial Barrington finally snapped. "By the blood of this child," he swore, "justice will be done."

In the distance the Army could be heard, spurs and harnesses jangling, sergeants shouting commands, on the way to the latest massacre. Nathanial jumped onto his horse, pulled the reins to the side, and steered toward Mesilla. "You know what we've got to do, boy," he whispered into his horse's ear.

That animal lay down its ears and extended its legs as it carried Nathanial toward his next rendezvous with destiny. Hoofbeats clattered through the night, and all Nathanial could think was *somebody's got to pay*. He hallucinated the dead child, her insides hanging out, and he couldn't help thinking about the fragility of his own little children. All his West Point training and years of military discipline could not contain the frenzy of his heart.

Lights were out in Mesilla when Nathanial arrived, and he thought it looked like Sodom, sin city of the Bible. He rode around adobe huts and outbuildings, finally arriving in front of Juan Ortega's home, where he climbed down from the saddle and knocked loudly.

No one answered, so Nathanial drew his Colt, aimed at the doorknob, and fired. The door blasted apart, and he hit it with his shoulder; it flew open. In the parlor a maid stood, an expression of terror on her face, lips trembling, unable to speak.

"Where is his room?" demanded Nathanial.

The maid couldn't respond, but a figure appeared in a doorway, wearing a white nightshirt to his knobby knees. "Who do you think you are?" Ortega asked angrily. "You have no right to barge in here!"

Nathanial was so enraged, he was tempted to shoot Ortega on the spot. But somehow that seemed too good for him. Nathanial holstered his gun, then stalked toward Ortega. "I'm going to kill you, you son-of-a-bitch," he said evenly, then dived onto the leader of the Mesilla Guards.

Ortega managed to get off a short jabbing punch to the left eye, but it didn't stop Nathanial, who was bringing one of his roundhouse rights into play. Ortega tried to dodge, but Nathanial's clenched knuckles caught him on the right temple, sending him flying toward the wall.

Nathanial followed Ortega, jabbed him in the teeth, hooked him in the kidney, took one in the mouth, but was so infuriated, he barely felt it. Filled with lust for justice, he landed heavy punch after heavy punch on

Ortega's face, spun him around, kicked him out the door, then ran after him and caught him in a headlock, twisted hard, grabbed his hair, and slammed Ortega's face into one of the posts that held the roof over the veranda.

Ortega slid to the ground, where Nathanial rolled him onto his back. Never had Nathanial felt so utterly out of control as when he pounded Ortega's face again and again. I have gone mad, he said to himself, as jagged bolts erupted in his mind. The time has come to pay for your sins, you bastard.

Then Nathanial heard footsteps, the Mesilla Guards attacking through the back alleys. "Get him!" shouted Fonseca.

Nathanial could run or open fire, but elected to charge them single-handedly, though he knew they'd kill him in the end. They crowded around, waiting to see who would take him on, when Nathanial arrived in their midst, throwing fists. He split one man's lip, cracked another's nose, blasted a third in the teeth, and kicked another in an unmentionable spot, when a club came down behind him, causing him to see wheels of fire.

They beat him to the ground, and he growled like a bear as he tried to catch one in his hands. They piled on, aiming blows all over his body, as he twisted like an Apache, snorting and grunting, delivering short chopping rights and lefts, even managing to chew off a portion of one man's ear.

But they outnumbered him, pounded him down, his face a bloody mask. He didn't hear the barrage of gunfire followed by the parade ground voice of Lieutenant Wood. "That'll be enough!"

Soldiers ripped into the mob and pulled the Mesilla

Guards off the pile, and the citizens offered no resistance, realizing they were surrounded by armed dragoons. Finally, the last two were removed, revealing Nathanial unconscious, arms akimbo. The post doctor rushed toward him, black bag in hand, examined him quickly, then said, "He's alive, but I'll need to take him to the hospital at once."

"Bring up the wagon," ordered Lieutenant Wood.

Out of the morning mist, at the edge of the crowd, a bloody apparition appeared. It was badly beaten Ortega, groggy on his feet, his bloodied nightshirt like Caesar's toga on the Ides of March, his face covered by contusions. "You are not going anywhere with that man!"

"The hell I'm not," replied Lieutenant Wood.

Ortega staggered dizzily from side to side. "I have placed him under arrest, and he is mine!"

"You have no rights that I am bound to obey!" Lieutenant Wood yanked his service revolver, pointed at Ortega's bobbing head, and said, "Consider yourself fortunate that I don't shoot you—son-of-a-bitch."

Ortega struggled to remain erect. "I am a taxpayer, and I demand the protection of the law!"

"If there was justice, you'd be hanging by your neck from the nearest tree. Please make a threatening gesture, so I can shoot you in self-defense."

Ortega perceived an agitated young lieutenant, while a detail of soldiers carried Nathanial toward the wagon. Moreover, Ortega himself had a broken nose, numerous gashes, and could not see out of his puffy left eye. "You have not heard the end of this," he said darkly.

* * *

Nathanial opened his eyes several days later, and it wasn't the first time he found himself in strange hospitallike surroundings. He tried in vain to move his head, and it felt as if ribs were broken, his nose covered with bandages. He drifted in and out of consciousness and eventually remembered he was Nathanial Barrington, assistant Indian agent at Fort Thorn, and he'd damned near beat a man to death. One morning he noticed Dr. Steck at the foot of his bed. "Are you all right?"

Nathanial whispered, "I believe so."

Dr. Steck shook his head in distaste. "You have committed an extremely rash act; therefore I have been forced to dismiss you. I assume you understand my position."

Nathanial grunted.

"However, you can still be of service. When you are well, perhaps I can hire you as special scout, and you can visit the Mimbreno Apaches. But we'll speak more when you're better."

Dr. Steck disappeared, and Nathanial fainted shortly thereafter. Next time he opened his eyes, Lieutenant Wood sat beside the bed. "Can you hear me?"

Nathanial groaned.

"Ortega wanted to press charges, so I threw him in jail. I'll probably end up court-martialed, but I'd sure like to see that bastard drawn and quartered. Don't worry about your children—the schoolmarm has moved into your house and is taking care of them. Isn't that cozy?"

Nathanial slipped into darkness, then some time later noticed the schoolmarm at the foot of the bed, beside his two children. "Everything's being taken care of," said Miss Andrews, "so you needn't worry."

Nathanial's children moved to either side of him, bent over, and kissed his cheeks.

Miss Andrews became mother to the children, in addition to their teacher. When not at school, she cleaned and refurbished Nathanial's home, to make it comfortable when he returned. She hoped he'd ask her to marry him, and one day while she was sweeping the kitchen, there was a knock. She opened the door, only to see Lieutenant Wood, her first and former lover.

She did not invite him in. "What do you want?" she asked coldly.

"You don't really think Nathanial Barrington is going to marry you, do you?"

"Perhaps.",

"But the man is not capable of love. He is a scamp, cad, and blackleg, and every soldier in New Mexico Territory knows it."

"But he is capable of redemption, like all of God's children, even you, Lieutenant Wood. Have you ever thought of praying to God?"

"As a matter of fact, I have prayed that Nathanial Barrington would die, so perhaps you'd return to me. Can't you see I'm the man who loves you most?"

She admitted that Lieutenant Wood was not that bad-looking, actually, but no Nathanial Barrington. "If anything happens to Nathanial, you certainly would be my second choice."

"Perhaps I should poison his medicine."

"I'm not marrying a murderer."

Lieutenant Wood laughed. "I don't know what I'm worried about. Nathanial Barrington can't marry you even if he wanted to. He's married already."

"But he's getting divorced."

"Or so he says." Lieutenant Wood tipped his hat as he walked away. "If you need me for anything"—he rolled his eyes—"you know where to find me."

After arriving in Nacogdoches, Texas, and ensconcing her maid and daughter in the best available hotel, Clarissa made her way to the local bank to obtain liquid assets. She carried a letter of credit drawn on the bank of New York, because it wasn't prudent to travel with bags of money on the frontier.

Nacogdoches was a booming town on the main east-west trail through Texas, and the bank stood on a street among hotels, taverns, and a variety of stores. Clarissa opened the tall, wooden bank door and joined a line in front of the teller.

She felt excited to be drawing closer to Nathanial, and in another two weeks she'd be in New Mexico Territory. She prayed he wouldn't throw her out like the snake in the grass she believed herself to be, and she continued to worry about the schoolmarm.

The other bank customers were a conglomeration of hard-bitten cowboys, businessmen, lawyers, and women of various descriptions, a far cry from the elegance of New York or even Charleston, but Clarissa felt happy on the frontier, among people whom she considered less devious than the folks in the East.

The line moved slowly; finally she reached the teller, told him her needs, presented the letter of credit, and he gave her the appropriate documents to fill out. While dating one of them, she heard a man say, "Don't nobody move."

Four of the formerly friendly cowboys had drawn guns, evidently holding up the bank! Clarissa was rocked with fear as one of them, with a brown beard, stepped toward the cage, aiming his gun at the teller's chest. "Open the door."

The teller turned the lock, then a robber in a black shirt entered the cage, opened a drawer, and removed handfuls of money, which he dropped into a burlap bag. Meanwhile, brown beard told the customers, "Line up against the wall, folks."

Are they going to shoot us? wondered Clarissa as she took her place with the others. She carried only forty-odd dollars next to the Colt .36 in her purse, but was too frightened to use the weapon, and wished she'd never brought it.

A robber in blue-and-white striped pants took off his hat. "Jest drop yer valuables in here, and let's make it quick—we ain't got all day."

He came to a stop before a man at the extreme left of the line and held out the bag. The man hesitated, so the robber hit him in the face with his revolver. The bank customer collapsed to the floor, and the robber went through his pockets, pulling out coins, a watch, and a derringer. "Now ain't that a cute li'l feller."

He moved to the next customer, a woman, who took one look at him and fainted dead away. The robber did not hesitate to tear a string of pearls from her throat, then go through her purse. Meanwhile, Clarissa wondered whether to join the other woman on the floor.

The robber continued down the line, and bank customers had become more cooperative, hastily dropping valuables into the bag. Meanwhile, black shirt emptied the drawer and was coming around with the loot. "Let's get out of here," he said.

"What's yer hurry?" asked brown beard, who

turned to the best-dressed lady in the bank and said, "Whatcha got in that there purse, ma'am?" he asked, waving the gun in Clarissa's face.

Clarissa raised her proud chin and replied. "Oh, a few odds and ends."

"Let's see what they are," said brown beard. "Open up."

Clarissa remembered a line her soldier husband had told her one night as he explained the art of war. *Surprise is the most important element of attack.* She knew that robbers occasionally massacred victims and figured she had to take the chance.

"Let's go, lady," said brown beard, brandishing his gun. "You got a pretty face, but yer life don't mean shit to me."

Clarissa took a deep breath as she opened the purse. Her hand slipped inside and closed around the handle of the Colt, but to the robber it might have been a sheaf of bills. "Here it is," she said with a smile, suddenly raising the Colt.

Brown beard's eyes widened as the first shot fired. It hit him on the collarbone, but before he dropped to the floor, Clarissa triggered again, striking the next robber in the stomach. As she drew back the hammer for the third shot, the startled robbers were jumped by other victims, a struggle ensued, someone called for help, and soon armed citizens rushed into the bank, overcoming the robbers.

Somebody brought a chair, and Clarissa lowered herself onto it, her Colt trailing smoke toward the ceiling. She stared at the two men she'd shot, one dead, the other writhing painfully, gritting his teeth. I did it, she thought, feeling proud, frightened, and disoriented.

Finally, the sheriff arrived. "What the hell happened?" he asked gruffly, dinner interrupted.

"That little lady shot these bank robbers," said the teller.

All eyes turned to the blonde in the pale lavender dress, sitting straight in the chair. She blew the remaining smoke from the end of her gun, placed it in her purse, and advanced to the window, where she calmly signed documents. "Is this bank open for business or not?" she inquired.

The season known as Little Eagles was passed in mourning among the People, and no one was sadder than Chief Mangas Coloradas, his two sons lost in the battle for Janos. He lay in his wickiup, recovering from his wound, and tragedy pervaded the camp, for the People had suffered a grievous loss. No longer could they raid with impunity in the land of the Mexicanos, while the White Eyes pressured from the east. There seemed nowhere for the People to go as they prepared for their last stand in the Chiricahua Mountains.

One day Mangas Coloradas sent word that he wished to smoke with Victorio, who made his way to the great chief's wickiup, and found him sitting inside, pale and gaunt, covered with a deerskin robe. Slowly, painfully, Mangas Coloradas filled his pipe with wild tobacco and other vegetative substances, then lit the mixture with a twig that had been thrust into the fire.

They puffed in silence, and a long time passed before Mangas Coloradas spoke in a barely audible voice. "I have committed two serious errors. The first was letting the People be poisoned, and the second

was the attack on Janos. I am no longer fit to lead the
Mimbrenos, and the time has come for you to take my
place . . . gallant Victorio."

Victorio wanted to request the mantle be passed on
to Barbonsito, or even Juh of the Nednai, but he was
an obedient warrior and bowed before his chief. "It
will be as you say," he replied. "But I have no solution to our predicament."

"Then you are truly wise . . . for there is no solution. Our enemies are strangling us, but we must fight
back as best we can."

"Why has the Lifegiver abandoned us?" asked Victorio.

"The ways of the Lifegiver are unknowable. Perhaps he has other plans for the People."

"As farmers and diggers of the yellow metal?"
asked Victorio. "I do not think so."

"Listen to me, Victorio. The White Eyes are coming, and their intrusion will be more hideous than anything we have seen heretofore. You must counsel with
Cochise and determine strategy."

"But we cannot counsel without the leadership of
Mangas Coloradas. We must have your recommenda-
tions."

"I am old, tired . . . increasingly weak-minded,"
said Mangas Coloradas. "My era of leadership is
drawing to a close. From this day forward . . . you and
Cochise shall lead the People."

Fonseca rode beside a herd of cattle, on guard duty
in the desert twenty miles south of Fort Thorn. Thanks
to his good work with the Mesilla Guards, he had
been given a vaquero job by Ortega.

Fonseca had killed so many Mescaleros, he no

longer felt pursued by demons. I have avenged my
wife and children, he thought contentedly. He recalled
how he'd shot and hacked Mescaleros during the second massacre, his special mission the killing of children. Thank you, Joshua, for delivering my enemies
into my hands.

Now he was free to remarry, sire more children,
and if he saved his money, he could own another
ranch in ten years. The Apaches will never stop me,
he thought. One day I'll be a caudillo like Senor Ortega.

Fonseca wasn't paying attention to his surroundings, for it was a peaceful night. He gave free rein to
his imagination, seeing himself with a beautiful young
wife, healthy sons, and a little house in a valley like
the one he rode through.

Something made a rushing sound to his right, but
he assumed a breeze rustled the blossoms of yellow
spiny daisies. Shortly thereafter, something smacked
his head, blotting out happy ambitions. He fell to the
ground as his horse looked at him sadly.

Five Mescalero Apaches emerged from the foliage,
and among them was Panjaro. He stuffed a gag in
Fonseca's mouth, bound his hands and feet, then other
warriors arrived with their horses. They tied Fonseca
head down over a saddle, then the Mescaleros mounted
up and set a course for Chief Gomez's secret hideout
in the Davis Mountains.

Nathanial's mood had not improved by the time he
left the hospital. Leaning on a cane, his first stop was
the sutler's store, where he bought a bottle of
whiskey, a bag of tobacco, and corn husks for the
rolling of cigarettes. Then he went home, finding it

clean but empty, Miss Andrews and the children at
school.

He sat at the kitchen table, drank, and brooded.
Then he made his way back to the sutler's store and
bought another bottle. He climbed to the hayloft in the
stable and continued to drink, but no matter how
much he tried, he could not dispel the image of the
eviscerated child.

He toyed with the notion of riding to Mesilla and
shooting Ortega in cold blood. The townspeople
would make short work of the intruder, but that was
the best part. Do I want to live in this filthy world? he
asked himself as he sank deeper into despondency.

He moved to an adobe hut in nearby Dona Ana and
sent word that he did not want to see anybody, not
even his children. He refused to talk except with the
old lady who brought him whiskey and tobacco. In
the days that followed, he continued to drink, smoke,
and become filthy, but nothing erased the image of the
torn child. Nathanial Barrington had seen one dead innocent too many, and whatever faith in God he had
possessed was gone. "If somebody killed me, it would
be a blessing," he mumbled one day as he sat with
droopy eyes at the table, flies buzzing around his
head.

16

———————————→

Fonseca knew they were going to kill him as he lay
bent over the saddle, arms and legs tightly bound.
Blood caked his hair, his body ached violently, and
he'd lost feeling in his extremities long ago. He
wished they'd shoot him and get it over with.

As a good Catholic, he couldn't help wondering
about judgment day. They killed my wife and child,
so what could I do? he asked his silent interlocutor.
He remembered a prayer his grandmother had taught
him to ward off the evil eye. *Lord Jesus Christ, have
mercy on me*. He whispered the words, feeling a small
measure of relief.

Some time later, he was aware of being pulled off
the horse. Coming to consciousness, he thought: This
must be it. He repeated the prayer. *Lord Jesus Christ,
have mercy on me*.

They unbound his hands, gave him food and drink,
and treated him roughly. Aha, he thought, as he chewed
gristly venison. They're fattening me for the kill. He
smiled as they glowered at him, and he knew such people would never forgive, because they were like him,
utterly remorseless.

After the meal, they tied him onto the horse and re-sumed their journey to the camp of Chief Gomez.

The next stop would be Fort Thorn, and Clarissa felt apprehensive as she sat in the stagecoach, her long journey coming to an end. Well, soon I'll know the truth, she said to herself, trying to stir her confidence.

She was accompanied by her daughter, maid, and a gentleman named George Bailey, a special agent sent by the Interior Department to assess the Apache situation in New Mexico Territory. Forty-nine years old, diminutive, he wore a dusty business suit and glanced repeatedly at his watch. "Shouldn't be much longer," he said.

Natalie had been lethargic most of the trip, but now looked out the window eagerly, as if aware she had returned to the land of her birth. "Da, Da," she said.

She knows her father is here, thought Clarissa, who had memorized a speech to deliver to her husband, so she wouldn't omit important points. She was afraid he'd make a scene. How pathetic I must have appeared with my need for cheap acclaim.

"There it is," said Bailey.

Clarissa looked out the window of the stagecoach and perceived a cluster of darkness amid sand and green foliage on the horizon. If he's gone, I'll follow him, she determined. I've got to admit the truth no matter how painful it might be, so I can have peace.

"I said it once," announced Bailey, "and I'll say it again. I don't think a lady should travel through this territory, especially after two massacres."

She'd heard about the second Mesilla massacre and wondered if Nathanial had been killed. Her life had been serene before meeting him, now blood and death were everywhere.

She closed her eyes and prayed silently. Oh God, I hope he's there.

As Clarissa drew closer to Fort Thorn, Nathanial awakened in his shack at Dona Ana. He'd slept with his clothes on, because he didn't like dressing and undressing. Mainly, he lay on his sofa day after day, smoking, drinking, and ruminating. The ragged old Mexican woman prepared the occasional meal that he merely picked at.

He'd lost thirty pounds, his beard was three inches long, and clothing hung loosely on his frame. He resumed drinking upon awakening, his goal to become senseless as quickly as possible. Sometimes he felt like taking a shotgun and blowing people to bits. "Oh, Generation of Vipers," he whispered, recalling a line from the Bible. "Who hath warned thee to flee from the wrath to come?"

Dr. Steck and Lieutenant Wood were on hand to greet the visiting special agent as the stagecoach pulled to a halt in front of the Fort Thorn orderly room. The first person out was a Mexican woman, an uncertain smile on her face. Next came an attractive well-dressed blonde carrying a small child, and finally Special Agent Bailey stepped down.

Dr. Steck rushed forward to shake his hand, anxious to make a good impression on a superior from Washington. "Welcome to Fort Thorn."

"I'm here," explained Bailey, "on the orders of Chief Clerk Mix. You've had two massacres, and he wants an independent assessment."

"We shall cooperate in every way," said the ever-gracious Dr. Steck.

Meanwhile, Lieutenant Wood stared fixedly at the blonde, who held her child and glanced about the post, as if wondering what next. Lieutenant Wood removed his hat and bowed slightly. "May I help you, ma'am?"

"I'm looking for Nathanial Barrington," she explained. "I'm his wife."

Dr. Steck turned about abruptly, stunned by her words. "So you're the one he used to talk about."

She didn't know what he meant, but smiled like the talented performer that she had been. "Is he here?"

"He's moved to Dona Ana," said Lieutenant Wood. "I'd be happy to arrange transportation if you like."

Clarissa cleared her throat. "Is he . . . with another woman?"

"Not that I know of."

"I've come a long way," said Clarissa, "and I'd be grateful if someone would lead me to him right away."

Lieutenant Wood ordered the nearest soldier to bring a wagon. "And make it fast!" Then he turned to Clarissa. "I'm sure Nathanial will be overjoyed by your arrival."

Dr. Steck added embarrassedly, "He's taken to drink, you know."

"It won't be the first time," replied Clarissa.

Dr. Steck escorted Bailey to his quarters, leaving Lieutenant Wood with Clarissa, the maid, and child. "Is that Nathanial's daughter?" asked the lieutenant.

Clarissa nodded.

"How delightful." Lieutenant Wood realized that his competition for the schoolmarm was about to be obliterated. Then the wagon arrived, whereupon soldiers loaded Clarissa's trunks in back. Lieutenant Wood selected Corporal Gillespie and told him to escort Mrs. Barrington to her husband's home.

The ladies climbed into the conveyance, Lieutenant Wood stepped backward, and the wooden spokes turned toward Dona Ana. My prayers have been answered, Lieutenant Wood told himself. This is indeed a joyous day. Then he ran toward the school, his dragoons watching curiously. It wasn't far; he adjusted his uniform and opened the door. All eyes turned to him, because he'd interrupted a spelling class. "Miss Andrews," he said. "May I have a word with you?"

She looked at him crossly "Not in the middle of a lesson. You should know better, Lieutenant Wood."

"It's an emergency," he replied. "Otherwise I never would have disturbed you."

"Class, study your spellers until I return."

She walked down the aisle, stepped outside, and said, "Well?" a note of irritation in her voice.

He closed the door behind her so the children couldn't hear. "Guess who just arrived at Fort Thorn?"

"How can you bother me with such nonsense?"

Lieutenant Wood grinned. "Mrs. Barrington didn't appear nonsensical in the least. It may interest you to know that she's here to claim her husband."

The schoolmarm's eyes bulged out of her head. "This is a joke in extremely bad taste."

"The joke's on you, my dear lady. Because she's on her way to him even as we speak." He laughed. "Looks like you're stuck with me."

The Shaker woman didn't know what to say, but somehow she had to admit she'd always known it would end this way. "There are worse things, I suppose," she sniffed.

"How soon can we get married, do you think?"

"We should wait a decent interval."

"I don't suppose you'd let me kiss you?"

She lowered her eyes. "Perhaps later this evening."

Sometimes Nathanial wondered what day it was as he lay in delirium on his sofa. Yesterday he'd tripped over his feet and banged his head against a door while on the way to the outhouse, leaving an ugly scab. Everything he'd believed had deserted him, the world seemed a diabolical joke, and he saw no reason to continue.

My children will get along without me, he told himself ruefully as he rose to a sitting position. In fact, they'll be better off, because I set such a poor example. It's easy for Henry David Thoreau to sit in his cabin alongside Walden Pond, writing of transcendental bliss. He doesn't have massacres to disturb his lofty meditations.

Everything seemed false when measured beside a disemboweled child. Bottles of whiskey could not drown that grotesque figure, and Nathanial felt the panic of mental imprisonment. "I can't manage this anymore," he mumbled to himself angrily, reaching for his Colt. He yanked it out of its holster, held it to his temple, and thumbed back the hammer. A feeling of relief came over him, for his personal devil dance was coming to an end.

But his mind fed new thoughts. If I'm going to die, why not take a few son-of-a-bitches with me? He saw himself riding into Mesilla, a Colt in each hand, shooting everyone he saw. They'll get me eventually, but that's the whole point. I'll go down in a blaze of glory, like a good West Point officer. But what if I kill an innocent man? Dismayed, filled with contempt for himself and the world, he collapsed onto the sofa, and for no apparent reason, recalled a poem read long ago:

> *By love directed, and in mercy meant,*
> *are trials suffered, and affliction sent,*
> *To wean from earth, and bid our spirits soar,*
> *to that blest clime, where pain shall be no more.*

He felt heavy, like an immense globule of oil melting into the cushions. Headache, nausea, and pain in the chest troubled him. He could find nothing to hang onto as he sank deeper into the bowels of the earth.

He did not hear the door open, nor the rustle of a skirt, then a gasp. Neither could he perceive the movement of feet, the sound of water being poured in the kitchen, nor the approach of those strangely familiar steps. Nathanial struggled to open his eyes, and then cold water hit him full in the face.

For an instant he thought he was drowning, then he sat upright, sputtering and cursing. He wiped his eyes with the backs of his hands and realized he had passed far into madness, because it appeared that the former Clarissa Rowland of Gramercy Park was standing in his parlor, looking at him with grave concern. "Are you all right, Nathanial?" she asked.

"What mirage is this?" he replied, terror on his face.

"It's me, standing in the need of prayer," she said gently. "Oh, Nathanial, you look terrible."

"Do I?" He glanced at his stained shirt and mucky pants, then raised his eyes to her once more. "I . . . I . . ."

He had no idea what to say, and finally decided he had lost his last shred of sanity. "Is this the asylum?" he asked, glancing about fearfully.

"It's your wife—Clarissa. I apologize for my unannounced visit, but I had to speak with you." She removed the bottle from the table and placed it out of his reach. "Can you hear me all right?"

He stared at her. "Is it really you?"

"Yes, and I've come to apologize because, although I hate to admit it, you were right about the advice you so generously offered me in New York. The life of a concert pianist soon became thoroughly wearisome and distasteful, and if I had listened to you, I could have saved myself the trouble. How superficial and silly I must have appeared. It's quite embarrassing to think about."

Nathanial struggled to clear the sludge from his mind. "Now let me get this straight. You've traveled all the way here to apologize?"

She nodded her head. "It's true."

He laughed hysterically, and she wondered if another bucket of water was required. "But I'm the guilty one!" he shouted. "If I were a real man, I would have been patient and loving, instead of breaking up your rehearsal and punching that poor stagehand."

"As a matter of fact," she agreed, "you needn't have demolished my manager's office either, but you've always been, shall we say, a demonstrative man, and perhaps that's one reason I fell in love with you. I can't ask your forgiveness, but I do want you to know I'm sorry for the pain I've caused."

"On the contrary," he replied, trying to straighten his backbone, "I should have been more kind, because I was supposedly the more mature party."

"But public performing was even more tawdry than you indicated."

Nathanial realized that it was indeed the former Clarissa Rowland of Gramercy Park, she had in fact returned to him, and the black cloud of misery evaporated like fog in the hot summer sun. He admired her pink cheeks and golden hair, her simple but fashionable clothing, that bright expression in her blue eyes, and realized he truly did have something to live for, his very own wife. He dropped to his knees, clasped his hands together, closed his eyes, and uttered, "Thank you, Jesus."

She smiled as she held out her hand. "Will you take me back?"

"I'm not a good man," he replied as he raised himself off the floor, "or even an especially pleasant one, and I am subject to disgraceful outbursts."

"Balzac said, 'A woman should always forgive the follies a man commits for her sake.' Perhaps I can teach you, as you have taught me."

He stumbled before her, his jaw hanging loose. "But I am an unmitigated swine and truly don't deserve you."

"And I'm the vainest bitch alive, but God has brought us together for some purpose, which I cannot fathom."

They were only inches apart and always had been powerfully attracted. Many events had occurred since their schism, but he saw no point in mentioning a certain schoolmarm, while she conveniently forgot an Oglethorpe, not to mention a carriage ride in Washington D.C., and certainly not the afternoon with Beau. It seemed as though they were enclosed in a golden cloud as they peered into each other's wide open eyes. Then he lifted and carried her to the bed as on their wedding night.

They embraced in the darkness, and each felt the delicious flame that had been omitted in their relations with strangers. Sinking into the mattress, they wrestled playfully, familiar with each other's curves and hollows. It wasn't long before the old oaken bed began to groan as the last nefarious effusions of the devil dance were banished from their marriage.

17

———→

Fonseca smelled campfires, heard shouts of children, and realized he had arrived in the Apache camp. He could not see well, his eyelids caked with dust, but he heard conversations nearby. He was pulled off the horse, and they cut the rope that bound his legs, but his hands still were tied behind him.

"*Arriba!*" he was ordered.

He struggled to rise on numbed feet, stumbled, dropped to his knees, and stared at Apache warriors, women, children, tipis, and dogs. Apparently he was on a high plateau, and in the distance mountains, basins, and a winding blue river could be seen. Apache warriors lifted him, and this time he managed to stand.

An important-looking Apache strode onto the scene, and Fonseca suspected he was Chief Gomez. "This is one of the *Nakai-yes* who committed the crimes at Fort Thorn," the chief declared in Apache language. "Now he is yours."

The warriors stepped backward as surviving reservation squaws advanced, knives, clubs, and rocks in their hands. Fonseca realized with a bolt of terror that

his hour had come. He tried to run, but his legs were
stiff and sore. They threw rocks at him, a few of
which bounced off his head, leaving bloody welts.

Dazed, he fell to the ground, unable to protect himself due to tied wrists. Apache women crowded
around, wielding knives, pounding him with clubs.
Strips of flesh were peeled from his body, he was
dented with blows, he shrieked hysterically, and pain
drove him to his feet once more. He forgot his prayer
and fled blindly, even as knives made deep incisions
into his muscles.

Covered with blood, he dropped again to his knees.
Opening his eyes, he saw massacred Apache children
rising from the ground around him, pointing their fingers accusingly, and one's belly had been brutally
ripped. "I couldn't help myself," he whispered to
them as he struggled to arise. Then his gaze turned to
an old Apache grandmother approaching, a bandage
on her head, wielding a lance. "Aiyeeeee!" she
screamed as she plunged it into his heart.

Some battles are fought with lances, others with
phrases. On the evening of June 16, 1858, the Republican State Convention of Illinois met in Springfield
to nominate its candidate for the U.S. Senate.

There had been no bitter contest, because the nomi-
nee had been selected by unanimous vote on the first
ballot. He was Abraham Lincoln of Sangamon County,
a former congressman, tireless worker for the party,
and well-known in Illinois due to his campaigning on
behalf of abolition, but relatively obscure in the nation
at large. His opponent in November would be the in-
cumbent Democratic Senator Stephen Douglas, the
Little Giant himself.

In the hall of the Illinois House of Representatives, the delegates rose to their feet and applauded as the tall, gangly country lawyer in loose-fitting clothes loped to the podium. Abe Lincoln had a large nose and piercing eyes, a grim mouth, and ears that looked like the wings of a bird. He laid his papers on the podium, then gazed calmly at the audience, requiring a moment to reflect upon the torturous path that had led him, a former flatboatman and lumberjack, raised in the direst poverty, to a race against one of the most famous men in the land.

It seemed impossible, yet was no miracle. He had studied and worked assiduously, often neglecting his wife and children while giving speeches in remote hamlets, sleeping in stagecoaches and on trains, and wondering what the hell made him think he could solve the problems of America.

He checked his notes one last time as accolades reverberated through the hall and men stood on chairs, shouting his name. He had been warned by advisers not to give the speech, because it raised too many alarming issues, but Abe Lincoln had decided to campaign on the truth and let the chips fall where they may.

He intended to read the speech, because politicians and reporters were present, not the usual backwoods folk with whom he joked, told stories, and performed hilarious impersonations. He would suppress his boyish sense of humor for the sake of the higher cause.

When the applause diminished, Abe Lincoln raised his eyes to the Republican throngs, took a deep breath, and said, "Mister President, and gentlemen of the convention: If we could first know where we are,

and whither we are tending, we could better judge
what to do, and how to do it.

"We are now far into the fifth year of a policy initi-
ated with the avowed object and confident promise of
putting an end to slavery agitation. Yet, under the op-
eration of that policy, the agitation has not only not
ceased, but has constantly augmented." Abe Lincoln
raised his long forefinger in the air. "In my opinion,
the agitation will not cease until a crisis shall have
been reached and passed. *A house divided against itself cannot stand.* I believe this government cannot
endure permanently half slave and half free."

They listened silently, for this was no mere exercise
in the orating arts. Abe Lincoln stood motionless,
head bowed, employing no melodramatic flourishes,
as he explained in pithy terms how Senator Stephen
Douglas's notorious Kansas-Nebraska Act had con-
vulsed the nation in sectarian strife. And what was the
great principle of Popular Sovereignty that had so inspired Senator Douglas? inquired Abe Lincoln. "That
if any one man choose to enslave another, no third
man shall be allowed to object!"

Like a skilled lawyer before a sleepy jury, Abe Lincoln broke down the facts into language anyone could
understand. His voice droned on, but his points were
sharp, even barbed. He explained how the nation had
voted against the slave-permitting Kansas legislation
in the presidential election of '56, because James
Buchanan had polled fewer votes than the combined
Republican and American Parties. Abe Lincoln urged
all enemies of slavery to unite behind his candidacy,
then warned against moderates casting support to
Stephen Douglas, just because the Little Giant had op-

posed the administration on one single issue, the Lecompton Constitution.

"Senator Douglas declares that all he wants is a fair vote for the people of Kansas!" Abe Lincoln said. "And he claims not to care whether slavery be voted down or voted up. How can anyone expect such a man to oppose the advances of slavery if he cares nothing about it? For years Senator Douglas has labored to prove it a sacred right for white men to take Negro slaves into new territories!

"But please let me say that I wish not to misrepresent Judge Douglas's positions, question his motives, or do aught that can be personally offensive to him. But clearly he is not with us now; he does not pretend to be—he does not even promise to be."

Abe Lincoln paused one last time, for he was coming to the end of his peroration. He could see all eyes on him, his wife and children in the front row, and hoped he wasn't making a public scandal of himself, for Abe Lincoln was a man of many confusions and often suffered dark moods; not even a righteous man could escape the noxious emanation of the devil dance.

"Of strange, discordant and even hostile elements we have gathered from the four winds," he roared, "and we have formed and fought the battle through, under the constant hot fire of a disciplined, proud and pampered enemy. Did we brave all then to falter now—now when that same enemy is wavering, disseevered, and belligerent? The result is not doubtful. *We shall not fail!* Wise counsels may accelerate, or mistakes delay it, but sooner or later, the victory is sure to come!"

The Little Giant was in Washington when he heard news of Lincoln's nomination, and naturally his aides and advisers clustered around to assure him it wouldn't be a demanding contest. "He's just a country bumpkin," said one of them.

"You'll whip his ass," guffawed another.

But the Little Giant was not swayed by phrases of sycophants. "You're all wrong," he told them as he puffed a cigar behind his desk. "I shall have my hands full with Abe Lincoln. He is the strong man of his party—full of wit, facts, dates—and the best stump speaker in the West, with his droll ways and dry jokes. He is as honest as he is shrewd, and if I beat him, my victory will be hard won."

Later, alone in his office, Stephen Douglas reflected upon the coming senatorial campaign. He couldn't be president if he didn't defeat Abe Lincoln, but in addition he had the Buchanan Administration sniping at him, and his health was failing.

Is this my Waterloo? he wondered dourly. Abe Lincoln was no stranger to the Little Giant, for lawyer Lincoln had appeared in Judge Stephen Douglas's court in Illinois. The Little Giant knew Abe Lincoln was easy to take lightly because he appeared awkward and countrified, but such a man would appeal to the simple people. Honest Abe definitely wasn't the buffoon he sometimes appeared to be.

There was an old saying among Illinois lawyers, and the Little Giant brought it to mind. "With a good case, your best attorney is Abe Lincoln. With a bad case, your best attorney is Stephen Douglas."

It won't be easy, but I shall defeat him, determined the popular senator. I'll impute to him the most extreme abolitionist positions, then present myself as the only viable compromise candidate who can defeat the Buchanan administration. And when it comes to stump speaking, I'm not so bad myself. I'll give that backwoods son-of-a-bitch the fight of his life.

Senator Stephen Douglas of Illinois was a skilled political operative, but something was lacking, perhaps a quality of moral sophistication, or a touch of human compassion, because not everything can be counted and codified, and many clever politicians end up outsmarting themselves.

One day that summer a procession of cowboys and vaqueros rode through Albuquerque, not an uncommon occurrence. "Where you folks headed?" asked an idler sitting in front of the barber shop, bottle in hand.

The leader, a tall, husky blond cowboy in a tan vaquero hat, pointed ahead to the open land, while beside him rode a pretty blond woman in man's clothes, also with a vaquero hat. Behind them, well-mounted, were a young boy and girl dressed like cowboys, followed by thirteen mean-looking hombres, and a wagon on whose box sat a Mexican woman with a child in her arms. The bed of the wagon was filled with supplies and something covered with canvas that resembled a piano.

The procession continued through town, and those who cared to look could see determination on the faces of the riders, because every trip to the wilderness was fraught with danger, and settlers, pilgrims, and prospectors were killed all the time.

"Good luck!" called the drunkard as he waved his bottle in the air, then collapsed onto the sidewalk.

It was another American family headed west, hoping to build a new life and new hope in a nation crumbling around their ears. They would face all the afflictions of nature, weather, and terrain, plus no

schoolhouse, no hospital, lots of hostile Indians, and
plenty of outlaws seeking to steal what outlaws were
too lazy to earn for themselves.

But the family did not appear discouraged, and
their cowboys were a rugged bunch of daredevils, not
adverse to a little gunplay now and again; some had
been soldiers. In point of fact, no one in the procession was an angel, not even the children, but still they
believed in America, they had come through the fire,
and were not afraid to fight for their own little parcel
of the world. Of such stock are great nations made.

Some nights, unable to sleep, Tobey Barrington
aimlessly roamed the streets of Manhattan, passing
taverns filled with laughter, churches closed for the
night, and derelicts sleeping in alleyways. In the darkest hours one could see every shade of human corruption, such as prostitutes fondling prospective customers,
drunkards fighting with broken bottles, or a policeman pocketing a bribe.

Tobey felt like a ghost swept along by Hudson
River breezes, for he was connected to nothing, and
everything was alien to him. Sometimes it troubled
him to know he had no love in his heart, as his brother
Nathanial had charged.

In his darkest hours often Tobey found himself near
Five Points, the notorious neighborhood from whence
he'd sprung so many years ago. Sometimes he was
tempted to return to the old alleys he'd frequented
when he'd lived by begging and the leavings of others.

Nathanial had rescued him from that pit of shame,
but not really. Sometimes Tobey felt like an interloper
in his new Columbia College setting, as if he should

be fighting for crusts of bread in Five Points. He stood in the shadows of an alley and watched denizens return to the notorious hovels within, carrying stolen goods or whatever they had scavenged. Occasionally, well-dressed gentlemen passed, heading toward the fleshpots, to be entertained by the sights and smells of poverty, not to mention the ministrations of low-cost prostitutes.

Occasionally, a soul would emerge like a specter from Five Points and head toward the bright lights of Broadway, perhaps to commit a murder, rape, or burglary. One such fellow approached, wearing a long, ragged brown coat and a stovepipe hat with the side caved in, his features smudged with soot. Tobey backed into the alley, because he didn't want to be seen, but when the citizen came abreast of him, he turned to Tobey abruptly and smiled. "Aren't you one of Nathanial Barrington's brothers?"

Tobey was so surprised, he barely knew what to say. "I . . . I . . ."

The old man took off his hat and bowed. "We've met, but I don't suppose you recognize me. I'm Fitz-Greene Halleck, a friend of Nathanial's."

Now Tobey recognized the famous author beneath his disguise, introduced himself, and said, "Don't you know it's dangerous to wander in those alleys?"

Fitz snorted. "A man was shot on Fifth Avenue a few days ago, so geography is no guarantee of safety. However, I confess that I often am drawn to low haunts to see how the common people live. How can I write about them if I don't observe their lives? Besides, danger is the most interesting subject of all. What are you doing here?"

"Oh . . . curiosity, I suppose."

"It's interesting how similar characteristics run in families, because Nathanial used to love Five Points. Have you heard from him, by the way?"

"Nobody hears from Nathanial," Tobey said curtly. "He doesn't write, and only pursues his pleasures without regard for the feelings of others."

Fitz placed an arm around Tobey's slouching shoulders. "You sound angry at your brother."

"He has been extremely selfish and irresponsible where his family is concerned."

Fitz smiled thoughtfully. "Nathanial is an unusual fellow all right, and I'm not surprised that people become weary of him. He has the temperament of an artist and is obsessed with that elusive chameleon called truth."

"But what is truth?" asked Tobey. "Is it knowable?"

"We are all mere particles of the dialogue that sometimes produces truth, but more often results in calamity. Unfortunately for Nathanial, he is an idealist in a world filled with desperate fiends. You see, your brother actually believes he can redeem the universe, but don't be angry at him, because where would we humble scribblers be without heroic jokers like Nathanial Barrington to inspire our pens? Come, my lad, let us perambulate to Pfaff's, where you shall permit me to buy you a mug of fine lager, and we shall speak of the age of heroes, of glorious damsels and gleaming embattlements, not the usual garbage of the damned slavery debate. Why, I'd rather spend an hour alone with Nathanial Barrington, listening to him ramble on about Indians, than with the greatest politicians in the land."

Following two months in New Mexico Territory, Special Agent George Bailey wrote a preliminary

draft of his much-anticipated evaluation of the
Apache wars. His information was based on extensive
interviews with soldiers, settlers, cowboys, bull-
whackers, and all who'd speak with him, but no one
expected an official of the U.S. government to travel
into dangerous mountains and actually speak with
free-roving Apaches.

> *The testimony of all who have any knowledge
> of the Apaches concurs in pronouncing him the
> most rascally Indian on the continent. Treacher-
> ous, bloodthirsty, brutal, with an irresistible
> propensity to steal, he has been for years the
> scourge of Mexico.*
>
> *The amount of property stolen by these Indi-
> ans over the years is incalculable. According to
> the returns of United States marshals, there were
> taken in New Mexico Territory alone, between
> 1st August and 1st October 1857, 12,887 mules,
> 7,050 horses, 31,581 horned cattle and 453,293
> head of sheep.*
>
> *Grave doubts are expressed whether any
> process short of extermination will suffice to
> quiet the Apaches.*

During the season known among the People as
Thick With Fruit, they traveled to the higher eleva-
tions of the Chiricahua Mountains to harvest chokecherries. Warriors patrolled the area, to warn of
snakes, bears, and other predators, such as the bluecoat Army, while squaws advanced among heavily
laden bushes, dropping handfuls of plump red cherries
into baskets.

One of these women was Jocita of the Nednai clan,

first wife of Chief Juh, herself a foremost fighter. Despite her widely acknowledged prowess in battle, she especially enjoyed being with her sisters, performing their time-honored task of picking chokecherries, and speaking of children, men, and the future of the People. She believed women had a special understanding that men did not know: The earth would abide.

It was sunny, peaceful, and cool, reminding her of when she'd been a girl, romping in the wilderness with her friends. Yet even then there had been danger, which had increased throughout her life, but she tried to be hopeful and see the happy side. It will be many harvests before the White Eyes find this remote place, she consoled herself as she placed a chokecherry into her mouth. At least we can live according to the Lifeway a while longer, and when the ultimate struggle comes, we shall be thankful for this happy time.

She gazed at children wrestling playfully in a clearing not far away, her son, Fast Rider, among them. He was becoming taller, his hair turning darker, and he was as wily a fighter as any of them. One day he will ride with the warriors, she told herself, and smiled a secret smile as she returned to the cherry patch.

She remembered the boy's father, the bluecoat war chief called Sunny Bear, and imagined that occasionally Sunny Bear thought of her as well. Something powerful and strange had passed between them one night long ago, burning a brand on their quivering souls. The Mountain Spirits gave us one special time of pure pleasure, she realized. Perhaps we were not strong enough to endure such ecstasy, or maybe the Mountain Spirits did not want us to spoil their perfection.

Yet I know that Sunny Bear shall return one day, she thought, because no matter how many women he marries, and how many children he sires with them, he will never forget me. And I will not forget him either, in this world or the next. For such a love can never die.